EVER Dark

Solis Lake Academy
Book One

K.D. SMALLS

Ever Dark: Solis Lake Academy Book Two

First Edition published 2024

Copyright © 2024 by K.D. Smalls

Edited by C. Eileen Editing & Kyla Kuhns
Cover Design by Maree Rose

This novel is entirely a work of fiction. The names, characters and incidents portrayed in it are the work of the author's imagination. Any resemblance to actual persons, living or dead, events or localities is entirely coincidental.

This is a work of fiction that includes sexually explicit language and situations. All characters portrayed in sexual situations are 18 or older.

K.D. Smalls asserts the moral right to be identified as the author of this work.

SOLIS LAKE ACADEMY

Dedication

For those damaged by the darkness...
keep fighting.
Your light will prevail...
and will burn a bitch to ashes.

Note from the Author

If you, or someone you know, has been a victim of sexual assault, please reach out for help. You can call the National Sexual Assault Hotline through RAINN at 1-800-656-4673. You can also chat online with a trained staff member who can provide you with confidential crisis support at online.RAINN.org.

Trigger & Content Warnings

Sexually Explicit Content
Adult Language
Physical and Sexual Assault (on page)
Arranged/Forced Relationship
Toxic Relationship
Manipulation/Blackmail
Coercion
Kidnapping
Murder (off page)

Please reach out to K.D. Smalls with any
questions or comments at kdsmallsauthor@gmail.com

one Everly

A tidal wave of emotions crashed through me.

Disbelief.

Fear.

Anger.

I was frozen, my body unwilling to respond as my brain screamed at me to move, to fight, to do any-fucking-thing. But instead I sat in the oversized office chair, my mind still trying to process Alaric Thorpe's catastrophic words.

"The cost for your father's failure," he explained, his grin becoming almost predatory, *"is his life."*

His. Life.

"Daddy," I whispered, the word getting stuck in my throat.

"I'm so sorry, sweetheart." My father hung his head in shame, defeat etched across his face. His shoulders were hunched, his eyes fixed to a spot on the floor, not looking an inch in my direction.

"Daddy, no, please," I pleaded, my hands gripping his forearm, willing him to meet my eyes. He shot me a quick glance, tears threatening to spill over. Rage raced through me, my father's resignation adding fuel to the inferno consuming my body. I turned my eyes, and anger, on the person responsible for all of this bullshit. Alaric. Fucking. Thorpe.

"You bastard!" I spit the words in his direction, wishing they were venom that would eat through his skin like acid. He simply smirked, his gaze roaming over my body like he owned it. I would be cold and buried before that ever fucking happened.

"Pet, the deal is done. You're mine now," Austin chirped happily from his spot next to me. I spun in my chair, my eyes shooting daggers into his stupid fucking face. He looked at me with the same smirk his disgusting father wore, and it made the urge to drive my fist into it grow by the second.

So that's exactly what I did.

Remembering everything Griff taught me, and making sure my thumb wasn't tucked into my fist, I reared my elbow back, launching my arm at his face. My knuckles connected with bone in a sickening crunch.

Austin howled in pain, and blood immediately spurted from his nose. Even though I'd used the proper technique, my hand ached from the impact. I shook it out as Austin gripped his face, his pathetic cries muffled by his hands.

Adrenaline flowed through my veins, the satisfaction of my punch bringing an oddly timed smile to my face. I went to pull my arm back again, ready to go for round two when a hand wrapped tightly around my bicep. Turning to my right, I saw that Thorpe Senior had moved around the table and was now holding me back from beating the ever-loving fuck out of his son.

"Get your fucking hands off of me," I growled, my voice sounding feral. I was not about to become a fucking pawn in this sick game. His fingers loosened their grip, but he kept his hand where it was. I glared at him through narrowed eyes.

"Now darling, there's no need to be rude." He spoke in a patronizing tone, as if I were a child caught playing in my mother's makeup. He turned to look at his son, sighing deeply in disappointment. Pulling a handkerchief from his jacket, he thrust it into Austin's hand before speaking again.

"Austin, there's no need to antagonize our beautiful Everly." Austin huffed in response, glaring at his father for apparently taking my side.

I knew better, though.

Where Austin was emotional, reactive, slithering his way under my skin like a goddamn serpent, Alaric Thorpe was the polar opposite.

Cold, calculating, and always in control.

He released my arm—finally—and I yanked it away, rubbing the spot roughly as if I could erase his touch.

My mind was a swirling mess. The contract my dad had signed. The fact that his life was on the line if I refused to go with Austin. My guys. Fuck. What was I going to do? How was I going to explain this to them? I couldn't sacrifice my dad, not even for my own happiness. But could I really give them up? Could I really be Austin's *pet*? The thought alone made bile rise in my throat.

Mr. Thorpe took his seat again at the head of the table, his hands clasped together on the mahogany top. He looked as if he was preparing to start a board meeting, not describing in detail his sick plan to seek revenge on my family for an imaginary slight. I peeked over at my dad, but he was still frozen in his seat, fucking catatonic.

Christ, it was just like after mom's funeral all over again.

"Everly, darling," Alaric began. I swore to Christ, if the man called me darling one more fucking time I was going to take off my heels and beat him to death with them. "I know this is probably a bit of a shock to you. But please understand, this is not a negotiation. You *will* be with my son. Now, contrary to what you may believe, I am not a cruel man."

I barked out a harsh laugh in disbelief. Did this man actually believe the bullshit that came out of his mouth? He narrowed his eyes at me, an obvious warning to keep my mouth shut, before continuing.

"As I was saying, I understand that there will be an adjustment period. We will give you some time to sort out your, ahem, personal affairs. Let's say by the end of the year?" he asked, as if he was scheduling his car for a fucking oil change. "That way we can have you home by Christmas."

Home? As if I was just going to move into their house? What in the actual ever loving fuck?

"Over my dead fucking body am I going anywhere with either of you," I bit out forcefully.

Mr. Thorpe closed his eyes for a moment, taking a deep breath through his nose. When he opened them again, he leveled me with a cold stare that turned the blood in my veins to ice.

"Well, my dear, it will either be your dead body, or your father's."

My heart galloped against my ribs, his words piercing straight through my chest. Jesus, fuck! How was I going to get out of this? I needed my guys. I needed Griff's logical, level headedness. Chase's flirty, easy-going attitude. Knox's protective possessiveness.

I needed them.

I stood up, the urge to flee overwhelming. I had to get out of this room, now. I snatched my clutch from the table. Once the small bag was in my hand,

I could feel it vibrating nearly nonstop. I had been gone too long, and the guys were probably frantic. How was I going to explain all this?

Oh, sorry guys. I snuck away to meet my brother, but it was a trick, and now I apparently belong to the Thorpes because my dad signed my life away in some fucking death contract.

Yeah, that'd go over real well.

As I walked by Austin, a bloody hand shot out, grabbing my wrist harshly. I could feel the sticky liquid press into my skin as he tightened his grasp, the bones grinding together painfully. I tried to yank away, but he held fast, his fingers digging into my flesh.

"Don't forget who you belong to, *pet,*" he said, his voice low, pure malice laced through his words. His nose had stopped bleeding and was starting to swell, two matching black eyes beginning to form on his fucked up face. "And just know, unlike your little boyfriends, I don't fucking share."

With that he let go and shoved me back, a bloody handprint now on my forearm, the spot throbbing from his tight grip. I briefly considered using my caster ability to send his ass flying across the room, but decided getting away from him was the better choice.

I scrambled around the table, finally reaching the door. Looking back at my dad, I found him still sitting there, fucking shell shocked and silent. Anger surged through me again.

In the entirety of this whole fucked up situation, he hadn't once tried to save me. Hadn't told Thorpe to go fuck himself. Hadn't come to my defense at all. Hurt clawed at my heart, my father's betrayal splintering it into a million fractals. Guilt and confusion warred in my head.

I refused to become Austin Thorpe's *pet*, but I also couldn't let my father die.

I didn't know what the fuck to do.

I quickly grabbed the handle, but paused when I heard Mr. Thorpe speak, his words an ominous warning wrapped in pleasant phrasing.

"We'll see you soon, darling."

I could feel my body vibrating with rage as he used that fucking name again, and while I wanted nothing more than to drive my stiletto heel into his face, I wanted out of this room more.

Ripping the door open, I thrust myself into the hallway, sucking in a large lungful of air. I hadn't realized how suffocating the conference room was, although I shouldn't have been surprised. Between Austin and his dad, their egos were enough to fill Madison Square Garden.

I kicked off my shoes, reaching down to scoop them up before I took off down the hall at a dead sprint, needing to be as far from them as possible.

Once I finally reached the lobby, my eyes scanned the space for my guys. Several party goers cast glances my way, no doubt taking in my disheveled appearance and the blood on my arm. Not seeing my men, I pulled my phone from my clutch.

Forty-seven missed calls.

Twenty-six text messages.

Fifteen voicemails.

Fuck.

I quickly hit Griff's contact, my brain telling me he would most likely be the calmest of the three. The line rang once before his deep voice answered.

"Everly, where the fuck are you?" I could hear his worry through the line, tears springing to my eyes. My knees suddenly felt like they would give out, and I made my way to a tufted bench that was tucked into a small alcove. I sank onto the seat, my body crashing from all the adrenaline.

"Griff." His name came out on a sob, a lump forming in my throat.

"Baby, where are you? Are you okay?" His voice was frantic. I could hear Chase and Knox in the background, demanding information that Griff didn't have.

"I'm-I'm in the lobby. Please come."

"We're on our way, but baby, don't hang up. Are you alright?"

"No," I whispered. I could hear their heavy breathing through the phone as they worked their way through the crowd to get to me.

A few seconds later, I saw Chase burst through the ballroom doors. He swung his head around, his eyes frantically scanning the lobby. Spotting me, he sprinted across the marble floor, landing on his knees as he reached the alcove.

He reached up, cupping my face, tipping it this way and that while assessing me for injuries. I was sure my face was a wreck, mascara streaked down my cheeks from my tears. I was shaking, my body trembling from the night's heinous revelations.

Knox and Griff were right behind him, each taking a spot beside me on the bench. When Knox noticed the blood on my arm, he let out a deep, animalistic growl, reminding me of his snow leopard.

"It's-it's not-not mine," I stammered out. I was suddenly exhausted, my body sagging forward into Chase's gentle hands. He propped me up against Knox, who quickly wrapped an arm around my back, the other reaching across and holding my thigh, essentially cinching my body to his.

Chase stood, pulling his cell out of his pocket. He stabbed the screen a few times before lifting it to his ear. After a moment, he started speaking to someone on the other line.

"Hey, we've gotta go...Yeah, no.... Something happened with Everly...I don't know, Dad. I'll call you later. Mmhmm. Bye." He hung up, tucking the phone back into his jacket.

I shivered from my place next to Knox, the adrenaline crash leaving me chilled in the cool air of the lobby. Griff stood up, taking off his suit coat. Knox released me long enough for Griff to tuck the jacket around my shoulders, pulling it tight over my chest. He brushed his lips over my forehead softly before sitting back down.

I looked up to see Chase striding back toward us. I hadn't seen him leave, but then again, I didn't think my brain was firing on all cylinders since escaping the board meeting from hell.

"They're bringing the car around now. Let's head out front."

All three men had a hand on me as I rose. I pushed my arms through the sleeves of Griff's jacket, sinking into the warmth his body had left behind.

Knox kept an arm around me while Griff took my hand in his. Chase walked directly behind me, his hand finding the nape of my neck. The feel of their hands on my body was like an anchor, keeping me from drifting off into the nightmare of this evening.

We walked to the waiting limo, Chase climbing in first. I scooted onto the seat beside him, laying my head on his thigh. I curled up next to him, my legs tucked under my dress. Maybe if I made myself small enough, the Thorpes wouldn't be able to find me.

But then what would happen to Dad?

I shuddered, my brain lingering on the idea.

My father's life was essentially in my hands. If I refused to give Austin what he wanted, refused to play into his father's sick game of revenge, I was effectively signing my dad's death certificate. But I couldn't fathom *belonging* to Austin, becoming his pet, his plaything.

I'd rather die.

I closed my eyes as Chase softly stroked my hair, the tender action such a sharp contrast to Austin's cruel, painful one earlier. The limo was silent as we

8

pulled away from the hotel, my eyes growing heavy with each passing mile. Unable to fight any longer, I slowly drifted toward the darkness.

Two

Chase

We waited until we knew Everly was asleep, watching until her chest began to rise and fall in a slow, steady rhythm, before any of us dared to speak.

I looked across the limo to where my best friends sat; Knox was nearly vibrating with rage. Griff was trying to put up a calm, collected front, but I could see his anger and frustration just under the surface.

The moment of sheer panic when we realized Everly was missing was something I never wanted to experience again. I couldn't breathe, like all the air had been sucked out of that giant fucking ballroom. I probably looked like a mad man, pushing and shoving my way through the crowd, yelling my

Larkspur's name. And when I hadn't been able to put eyes on Austin either, the sense of dread that crept up my spine was nearly crippling.

I knew in my gut that motherfucker was involved somehow; I just fucking knew it.

Griff had immediately started calling her phone while Knox ran to the ladies' restroom. I'm sure he scared the shit out of some high-society women, but I didn't give a fuck if he caught some trophy wife with her panties down. We checked every nook and cranny in those damn bathrooms and the ballroom. We were just getting ready to split up and search the whole fucking hotel, floor by floor, when she finally called.

The second I heard the word 'lobby' come through the line, I took off, nearly knocking over several of my dad's business associates.

But I didn't give two shits.

I needed to get to my girl.

When I spotted her sitting on that bench, her tear-stained, face pale and frightened, it took everything in me not to kill every motherfucker in the vicinity.

Someone had hurt my Larkspur and heads would fucking roll.

"Chase," Griff's whispered voice cut through my thoughts. I glanced up, my eyes leaving Everly's body for the first time since getting in the limo.

I met my best friend's gaze, his face full of fear for our girl. But beneath the fear, I could see the same anger that raged through my veins.

"What do you think happened?" he asked, his eyes continuously flicking to Everly's face.

"I don't know, man. But I'd bet my last fucking dollar that it has everything to do with Austin fucking Thorpe." His name tasted bitter on my tongue, and I was silently cataloging all the ways I could kill him with my bare hands.

Knox growled from his spot next to Griff. I knew he was angry with himself for letting her go alone to use the bathroom, but to be honest, so was I. I couldn't fathom what he'd been thinking, letting her go off by herself. I knew raging at him wouldn't help, wouldn't change whatever had happened to our girl, but goddamnit, I was pissed.

"Why the fuck did you let her go by herself, man? After everything that has happened, why?" I didn't mean to sound like an asshole, or maybe I did. But I knew the second the words left my mouth that I had just placed the blame squarely on Knox's shoulders, even if he didn't deserve it.

"Fuck you, Chase!" The words were a whispered hiss, fury lacing each syllable. "She said she was using the bathroom. Gave me a whole speech about how she was an adult and could go on her own." His voice quieted, regret and guilt taking the place of his rage.

His eyes softened as he looked at the girl who had become his entire world. "I didn't want... I wanted to, I don't know, let her feel like she had some control. Some power. That asshole stole so much from her..." His voice trailed off, and I immediately felt like a dick.

"I know, I'm sorry, man," I apologized. Griff spoke up next, ever our level-headed peacekeeper.

"Look, let's not sling around blame until we know what actually happened. We'll just let her sleep, and when she wakes up, if she's up to it, we can get the full story. Yeah?"

"Yeah, okay," I agreed, looking over at Knox, hoping he could see that my anger wasn't truly directed at him but at the fucker who hurt our girl. "We good, Knoxy?"

In typical Knox fashion, he huffed out a response, giving me a quick nod before locking his eyes back onto Everly's sleeping form.

The blue interior lights inside the limo cast ethereal shadows across her beautiful face. She would have looked peaceful, if not for the way her delicate eyebrows scrunched together on her forehead.

Even asleep, she was worried, upset.

I trailed a finger lightly over her cheek, following the line her mascara had made when it mixed with her tears. The guys and I settled into our seats, each of us lost in our own thoughts while the limo took us back to school.

I carried my Larkspur upstairs to our suite, the guys and I opting for the elevator in a bid to let her sleep a little longer. By the time we'd reached the door, however, she began to stir, her beautiful blue eyes fluttering open while she was curled in my arms.

"Hey, Larkspur. We're home," I told her softly, not sure where her head might be. She looked up at my face, a small smile tipping her lips up ever so slightly.

"Hi," she whispered. Griff pushed the door open, then stepped back so I could enter first with our girl. An image of me carrying Everly through an open doorway flashed through my mind, except instead of the blue evening gown she currently wore, she had on a white wedding dress.

Filing that thought away to the back of my brain, I walked us over to the sofa while the guys moved around the apartment. I settled Everly next to me

13

on the cushions, helping her take off Griff's suit jacket. I took a second to shed my own coat and tie, loosening the top few buttons of my dress shirt as well.

Moments later, both guys joined us. Griff was carrying a pair of sweats, a sweatshirt, and a damp cloth. Knox walked over from the kitchen, a bottle of water in one hand, vodka in the other. I lifted an eyebrow, earning myself a shoulder raise from my quiet friend.

"Wasn't sure which one she'd want," he reasoned, looking at Everly. "Little Monet, do you need a drink?"

She silently leaned forward, snagging the bottle of vodka. Twisting off the cap, she threw back a small mouthful, gasping at the burn. She returned the bottle to the table as Griff moved to her side.

Without saying a word, he pulled her up to stand, spinning her small frame so her back was to his front. He gently pulled down the zipper of her stunning gown, exposing the expanse of her perfect skin. The dress dropped to the floor around her bare feet, coming to rest in a pile of satin on the small area rug. She stood before us in nothing but a lacy, navy blue strapless bra and matching thong.

My dick stirred to life at the sight of her tanned, toned body. I tried to will away my growing erection as I watched Griff wipe her arm clean of the blood before dressing her in his sweats. I might think with my dick a lot of the time, but even I knew that now was not the time to engage in a foursome.

Once Everly was dressed again, she wiped her face with the cloth Griff had provided. When she was finished, Knox scooped her up, tucking her next to him at the other end of the sofa. I couldn't begrudge his need to hold her. When we'd arrived, it had been a struggle to release her and not keep her wrapped in my arms forever, safe and protected from the evils of the world.

Griff parked his ass on the coffee table in front of us. He reached out, planting a hand on her knee, looking at her with soft, adoring eyes. She moved her sapphire gaze between the three of us before looking down at her lap. Her voice came out on a whisper when she finally spoke.

"I'm sorry," she said softly, fresh tears falling from her red-rimmed eyes.

My heart broke at her words.

In that moment, I wanted nothing more than to erase every bad thing that had ever happened to my sweet Larkspur. She consumed my very soul and the idea that something—or someone—had hurt her was killing me inside. I would raze Solis Lake, Emporia, and the whole damn world if it meant I could take away her pain.

Knox squeezed her tighter, pressing a kiss to the side of her head before leaning his own against it.

"Baby," he said, his voice strained. I knew he was relieved she was safe, but he was fighting back anger as well. "Everly, what happened?"

She sucked in a ragged breath, a shudder working its way through her body. I reached behind her, snagging a blanket we kept on the back of the sofa for when we were too drunk or tired to drag ourselves to our rooms, wrapping it around her shoulders.

Griff swiped his thumb along her cheek, wiping away her tears.

"Blue, just tell us what happened, baby. We can't help if we don't know what's going on." I envied his rational, logical approach when all I wanted to do was find Austin Thorpe and pull his limbs from his body in slow, torturous ways. She looked down at her lap again, her tiny hands pulling absently at the edge of the blanket.

"I'm sorry, Knox," she said softly. "I-I lied. I didn't go to-to the bathroom. I'm sorry."

Knox's entire body tensed, and I braced myself for an explosion. He closed his eyes, and I could see him physically holding all of the anger inside his body. The last thing he wanted was to lose it in front of Everly, but it was obvious he was walking a tightrope with his emotions. I could see his jaw grinding in frustration before he spoke.

"Where did you go, Everly?" His words were quiet, and I knew he was struggling to keep himself under control. He'd been furious with himself for letting her go, but now to find out she lied... I had the distinct feeling some of that anger was currently being redirected toward our girl. I couldn't picture my friend losing it on her, but who the fuck knew. I'd beat the shit out of him if he even so much as raised his voice to her.

As if sensing his anger, Everly curled in on herself, reminding me of how she looked in the days after Austin's attack. I glared at him over her head, silently ordering him to get himself in check.

He swallowed roughly, closing his eyes again. Angling his body toward hers, he gripped both sides of her face with his hands before he turned her to him.

"Little Monet," he spoke, his voice wavering with emotion. "Baby, we can figure that out later, okay? Right now, we need to know where you went and what happened."

I could see her body relax a fraction in relief. I wrapped my hand around her thigh, squeezing the soft flesh in encouragement.

"Come on, little Larkspur," I coaxed. "I bet once you tell us, it won't seem so bad, yeah?"

I knew the words were a lie.

Deep in my bones, I was certain that whatever happened was fucking terrible. But I needed her to start talking, and if I had to put on a brave face and say some pretty words to get the job done, I would.

She was silent again, and just when I didn't think she'd tell us anything, her voice came out in a broken whisper.

"He-he sold me to them," she stuttered. "My dad signed a contract giving me to the Thorpes."

three
Everly

I could feel the tension in the room rise as rage rolled off my three men. I couldn't bring myself to meet their eyes, a maelstrom of emotions swirling in my gut. My chest was tight with fear at the words I needed to say.

"Blue, what do you mean your dad *sold* you?" Griff questioned, his voice rising.

I knew out of the three, he would take this exceptionally hard, given that his mother had done essentially the same thing when he was a child. The difference was, he escaped. There was nowhere for me to run, only an impossible decision to make.

Swallowing down the bile rising in my throat, I shook my head. I needed to start from the beginning if they were going to understand the fucked up scenario I was currently in. I turned, trying to look at Knox, but unable to meet his eyes, guilt eating at my insides.

"While Knox was at the bar getting us a drink, Morgan came to the table." I heard a growl rumble from Knox's throat. Reaching out a hand, I tentatively laid my palm on his muscular thigh, unsure how he would react to the contact. Instead of pulling away like I'd feared, Knox placed his hand over mine, squeezing it gently. I knew he was still hurt by my deception, but it seemed his anger was slowly dissipating. "She said that my brother wanted to talk, but he was scared you guys would try to kick his ass if you came with me, so he wanted me to come alone. I told her I would." Griff let out a *'fuck'* under his breath.

I pulled my knees up to my chest and sat back against the sofa, pulling away from them. They all let me go, eyes narrowing in suspicion at my movement.

"When Knox came back, I lied," I confessed. "I told him I needed to go to the bathroom. That I didn't need an escort. That I'd be safe. I'm so sorry." My voice cracked on the last word, and I risked a glance at my quiet artist. As his eyes flashed with anger and hurt at my words, another piece of my fractured heart broke.

"I convinced him to let me go, and once I was out of sight, I went down a hallway to the conference rooms. That's where Morgan said Evan would be. But when I got inside, it wasn't Evan waiting for me."

I felt Chase stiffen at my side before he spoke.

"It was fucking Thorpe wasn't it? They fucking lied to you, tricked you, didn't they?" The words stung as they came out of his mouth, reminding me of each terrible thing that happened tonight.

"Yes," I answered softly. I looked up at Griff to see him staring intently at me. While I knew he was mad, I also knew he was processing each detail, filing them away to analyze later. His eyes softened when they met mine, giving me the strength to continue.

"Austin was there. I argued with him for a minute before…" The words were stuck in my throat, emotion at my father's betrayal keeping them from breaking loose.

"Before what, Blue? You're doing great, just keep going," Griff encouraged, his big hand landing on the top of my knee. I heaved out a sigh, my body drained from the night even though I'd slept the entire way home.

"Before my dad and Mr. Thorpe showed up. Mr. Thorpe went on this tirade about how my dad stole my mom from him and how he loved her first when they were in college. But my parents have never mentioned him before, ever! My mom loved my dad!" The words were pouring from my mouth now, needing to be done telling this twisted story. "And when my dad signed his contract, Thorpe tricked him. He wrote in the contract that my dad owes him a favor, and if he reneges, then he-he—" I couldn't get the last word out.

If I told them, if I said the words out loud, it made them real.

I felt Chase's hand on my bicep, squeezing gently in the same place Alaric Thorpe's fingers had gripped me so roughly just an hour or so ago. But where Thorpe's touch left me feeling weak and scared, Chase's had the opposite effect. As if he had somehow infused me with his caster strength, I felt a surge of power, giving me just enough to push the last words past my lips.

"He dies."

Knox shot up from the sofa, the dam holding his emotions back finally breaking.

"Motherfucker!"

He picked up the bottle of vodka from the coffee table and chucked it across the room. Shattering on impact, liquor sprayed across the wall, glass fragments littering the floor.

I gasped, flinching at his outburst. I knew Knox had a temper, and I'd seen him lose his cool on more than one occasion. To be the cause of that anger was a devastating feeling, but I knew I deserved every ounce of his rage.

I'd broken his trust, all their trust, and now I had to face the consequences.

"Knox!" Griff shouted, standing from his spot, throwing a hard look in Knox's direction.

Knox's chest heaved, his rage palpable in the small space. He ran a hand through his dark, wavy hair, mussing the strands. Coupled with the wildness in his eyes, he looked utterly unhinged, feral.

Griff barked at him again.

"Sit your ass down. You flying off the goddamn handle isn't going to help anything."

The two men glared at each other for nearly a minute before Knox finally relented, taking his spot back on the sofa. He planted his elbows on his knees, his head resting in his hands. Griff slowly lowered himself back to the coffee table, his eyes moving back to me.

"Blue," he spoke softly, like I was some sort of wild animal that might run off at any moment. "You said if he breaks the contract, he dies? Is that correct?"

"Yes." The single word tumbled from my mouth on a quiet sob.

I still couldn't wrap my head around the entire thing. Did Thorpe mean he'd *murder* my dad? What kind of sick asshole was he? Over a woman he never even had in the first place? My mind began to spiral, unable to turn off the horrific images of Alaric Thorpe ending my dad's life.

Fingers snapped in front of my unseeing eyes, bringing me back to reality. I sucked in a lungful of air, not realizing I had been close to hyperventilating. Griff cupped my cheek with one hand, using the other to place my palm against his chest.

21

"Breath with me, Blue," he softly commanded. I took several deep breaths that matched his. When my breathing had calmed, I uncurled my legs, and Griff placed my hands in my lap.

I turned to look at Chase, hoping he could provide me with any information on Thorpe.

"Chase, you've known them longer than any of us. Would Alaric Thorpe really kill my father?" I gripped his forearm tightly, panic and desperation fueling the frantic thoughts coursing through my mind. But before Chase could answer, Griff spoke again.

"I don't think Mr. Thorpe would outright kill your dad, Everly. He's a widely known businessman. Now, with that being said, I think there are other factors at play here." I could always count on Griff to be logical, looking at all the facts.

"What other factors?" Chase questioned, removing my hand from his arm and twining our fingers together. He brought my knuckles to his mouth, leaving a soft kiss on each one while we listened to Griff explain.

"I think he tricked your dad into signing a soul-bound contract."

"Well, what the fuck is that?" Knox asked from my other side. I knew he was still teetering on the edge of another explosion, so I threaded my fingers through his, linking me to two of my three men.

"I read a book last year in my Caster Origins class. There was a unit we studied about dark magic. Soul-bound contracts were used by dark casters. They bind the soul of the signer to the person who wrote the contract. If they break the contract, their life is forfeited. Their abilities, both caster and elemental, are transferred to the other party." Griff recited the information as if he had the book in front of him. Given his photographic memory, he might as well have.

Knox remained silent while Chase processed Griff's words.

"How do we break it? 'Cause Griff, I can't–I can't let Austin have me, I'd rather die. But I–I can't lo–lose my dad." A sob wracked my chest at the thought of either scenario happening. I broke down in another round of tears.

Griff dropped to his knees in front of me, his hands coming up to each side of my neck. He tilted my face slightly, angling me, so I was looking directly at him. Greens and golds danced in his hazel eyes, a sunburst of color exploding from around each pupil. Fierce determination shown back at me.

"I don't know, Blue," he said. "But I promise you, we will find a way to break this."

"Larkspur"—Chase swallowed roughly before speaking—"Did Thorpe mention how long you have? I mean, before they—" He couldn't finish the sentence, the thought of me going with Austin making the hand not holding mine clench into a fist.

I sifted through my memory of my meeting with the fucking Thorpes, trying to remember everything he had said.

"He told me I have until the end of the year to sort out my 'personal affairs'. I'm guessing he meant you guys." I looked at each of my men in turn, unable to fathom how I could give them up. The end of the year. It was already the middle of October. That only gave me a little over two months to find a way out of this stupid fucking contract.

"Blue, did your dad say anything? Anything that might help us?" Griff asked.

I shook my head. My dad had been like a statue when I'd left. I don't even know if he realized I was gone. "No, he barely said two words after Thorpe told us about the contract."

We all sat in silence for a few moments, processing the night's events, when suddenly a giggle bubbled up through my chest. A few seconds later, it was a full on belly laugh. I had to tug my hands free from Knox and Chase to wipe the tears from my eyes.

"Griff, man, is she okay? Like, is she having a breakdown or something?" I heard Chase ask from next to me. His question caused me to laugh harder, earning me concerned looks across the board.

After another thirty seconds or so, I was able to stifle my giggles enough to speak.

"Sorry," I said, clearing my throat and wiping away the last few tears from the corners of my eyes. "I was just running through what happened earlier, and I realized I forgot to tell you something."

"Jesus, there's more?" Knox asked, his voice full of exhaustion.

Another tiny giggle escaped before I answered.

"When Austin made a comment about me being his," I explained, "I saw red. I-I punched him in the face. Pretty sure I broke his nose."

A beat of silence passed between the four of us before Chase barked out a loud laugh.

"That's my girl! Fuck yeah!" He scooped me into his lap, planting a kiss straight onto my mouth. I kissed him back, laughing into his lips when I heard Knox behind me.

"Hell yes, our girl's a badass. Guess that explains the blood, then." He leaned across the sofa to press a firm kiss against the side of my neck.

From his spot on the floor, Griff asked, "Did you remember not to tuck in your thumb?"

I twisted around in Chase's lap, so I could see his handsome face. His eyes scanned down to my hands, clearly looking for any injury. I lifted both into the air, flexing my fingers to show him I was okay.

"Yes, Daddy Griff, I remembered," I teased.

Griff's eyes flashed with heat before he shook his head at me.

"Come on, let's get you to bed before I have to put you over my knee."

four

Everly

C hase refused to put me down, carrying me all the way to his bedroom. Griff and Knox had disappeared into their own rooms to change out of their suits before joining us. When they came through the doorway, though, I was not expecting to see a king-size mattress being carried between the two of them.

"What the hell are you guys doing?" I asked as they flopped the mattress on the floor.

Coming to stand in front of me, Knox gently gripped my chin with his thumb and index finger. "Little Monet, did you really think any of us were going to let you out of our sight after everything that's happened?"

My face flushed at his words while Chase and Griff pulled Chase's mattress off its frame. Griff quickly teleported the frame out of the room, leaving us with two king-size mattresses in the middle of the floor. Looking around, I realized we didn't have nearly enough blankets or pillows for everyone.

"Griff, can you teleport me to my room? I want to grab my duvet and some extra pillows."

"Sure, Blue, come on." He reached out, grasping my hand.

In the blink of an eye, we were standing in my bedroom. A soft yellow glow shined through my window, the lamp post outside giving me just enough light to find my desk lamp. As I flicked it on, I caught movement out of the corner of my eye. Knowing who my visitor was had a small smile tugging at my lips.

I strode over, pushing the window up. I had started leaving treats on the ledge for my furry little friend a few weeks prior. Some days I would open my window while I painted, and he would sit just inside the frame and watch while I worked. I wasn't sure why he had chosen my window as his hang out spot, but I liked him just the same.

I leaned out the window a tad, sitting on the wood while reaching for his fluffy head. Stroking his fur with my index finger, he nuzzled into my touch.

I felt Griff come up beside me, watching as I pet my visitor. He had hopped from the branch onto my window sill, fully enjoying his head scratches.

"Who's your friend?" Griff asked, a smile on his face.

"Just a little black squirrel that lives in the tree. He comes to visit me most days."

"What's his name?" Griff reached out a hand, stroking a long finger down the squirrel's spine. It let out a soft chitter, before jumping into my lap.

"Oh! Well, hello there!" I squeaked out, surprised by the little guy's actions. This was the first time he'd actually come into my room.

Remembering Griff's question, I responded. "I hadn't given him a name... what about Onyx? Since he's black."

Griff wrapped an arm around my shoulders, pressing a kiss to the top of my head.

"I think Onyx is perfect."

Once I left Onyx some food in a small dish—strawberries seemed to be one of his favorites—we grabbed a bunch of blankets and pillows to take back to the guys' suite.

Before we left, I stared sadly at my closed bedroom door, wondering if my brother had even noticed I'd left the ball. I tried to tell myself there was no way he could have known what would happen tonight, but his betrayal with Morgan stung like salt on an open wound.

Griff teleported us and our blankets back to Chase's room. We made up both beds before settling in for the night, all three guys teasing me about the number of blankets and pillows I'd brought back. I mean honestly though, could you *really* ever have enough?

Griff lost the coin toss when it came to who slept next to me, so he was sprawled on the far side next to Chase. Knox had refused to sleep next to anyone but me, shooting daggers at his best friends before taking up the left side of the bed. He curled around my back, an arm cinched around my waist, while Chase lay facing my front.

The guys had asked if I wanted to watch a movie, but I could see the exhaustion written on their faces, so I declined the offer, and we turned off the light.

As I lay in the darkness, my brain cycled through any and all possibilities that could save my dad, and myself, from the shit situation we'd had thrust on us. Frustration quickly set in as I realized there wasn't a single one.

At least, none that didn't end with me on a leash or my dad in a grave.

I stared into the dark room, letting my eyes adjust until I could make out the shape of Chase's body in front of mine. He'd gone under first, his chest rising and falling in a deep rhythm. I could hear Griff's soft snores from across the bed, telling me he'd finally fallen asleep as well. Knox was wrapped around me like a cocoon, one strong arm over my side, his hand splayed across my stomach.

I released a sigh, my fingers playing with the edge of the blanket. I knew there was no way I was going to be able to sleep, not with all the thoughts racing through my head.

What if I ran?

But could I really leave my guys behind?

I couldn't ask them to give up their lives here at Solis Lake to follow me.

"Little Monet, I can practically hear the gears turning in your head. What's on your mind?" Knox's breath brushed across my shoulder, goosebumps rising on my skin.

I'd changed into a soft camisole before bed, and his words warmed my cool flesh. He pulled me tighter to his body, his hardening dick nestled between my ass cheeks. I pushed back against him, earning myself a low groan.

"Mmm, Everly, do you need me to take your mind off things?" His whispered words traveled straight to my clit, my core clenching with desire.

I desperately needed his touch to help me forget, if only for a little while.

29

"Please, Knox."

His hand slipped down the front of my borrowed sweatpants, straight into my panties to find my already slick folds.

I don't think these men had any idea just how many pairs of my panties they'd ruined with their dirty talk. He dipped a finger inside my wet pussy, dragging the arousal up to my clit. Using his thumb, he began to rub small circles, causing a slow burn to build in my lower belly.

Knox thrust a finger inside my entrance, pumping it in and out slowly, hooking it to hit that sensitive spot deep inside before adding a second. He continued to torture my clit with the pad of his thumb, sending me closer and closer to the edge. Just when I thought I was going to fall, he pulled his hand out of my sweats.

"Hey!" I hissed out quietly, my body feeling empty at the loss.

Before I could utter anymore protests, Knox pushed both my sweats and panties down my legs. Realizing the direction we were headed, I quickly shucked them off my feet, leaving me bare from the waist down.

Knox wasted no time, pushing his boxer briefs low enough to free his pierced cock. I felt it bounce off my ass cheeks before Knox hitched my leg up over his thigh, opening me to him.

"You'll have to be quiet, little Monet, we don't want to wake the others," Knox whispered before thrusting into me, seating himself to the hilt in one go.

"Aahh!" I covered my mouth with my hand, muffling my cry. Knox began to rock inside me, his piercings rubbing my inner walls in the most delicious way. I angled my hips to take him deeper as he slowly stroked in and out of my body.

I could feel Knox's mouth at my ear, his breath coming out in shallow pants as he picked up his pace, careful not to jostle my body too much.

"That's it, Everly, you're taking my cock so well." His words of praise had me grinding against him. I closed my eyes, reveling in the feel of him inside me, a low moan escaping my lips. Knox's fingers dug into my thigh in warning.

"Careful, little Monet, we don't want to wake Chase."

"Too late." The sound of Chase's gravelly voice had my lids popping open, and I was met with dark, lust-filled green eyes, moonlight slicing over his handsome face.

"Larkspur, did you need some help falling asleep?" he teased, his husky voice washing over me, as Knox continued fucking my pussy.

"Yes, Chase," I whispered into the darkness. I felt him slide closer, his fingertips finding my soaked pussy. He flicked my clit, making my body jolt with need. I clenched around Knox, squeezing his dick until he cursed.

"Fuck, Chase, she likes whatever you're doing. She's damn near strangling my cock."

A devilish grin crept along Chase's face, the moon granting just enough light for me to see. His thumb began to rub against my sensitive bundle of nerves while his fingers played with my pussy where it stretched around Knox.

"Knoxy, mind if I join you?" Chase asked before sliding a finger into my soaking cunt alongside Knox's cock. My body tightened, and the stretch from Chase's thick digit coupled with Knox inside me had me nearly seeing stars.

"Fuuuckkk, Chase," Knox groaned. He buried his face into the back of my neck, his thrusts coming harder, faster.

Chase worked my clit like a man on a mission, sending me closer and closer to the edge. My vision blackened around the edges as my orgasm barreled through my body. Knox's fingers dug harder into my hip with each punishing thrust. My pussy tightened around him, his piercings rubbing in just the right way to send me headlong into another orgasm.

"Knoxy, you better fill our girl up fast, otherwise you're going to be wearing my cum along with her," Chase ground out, pulling his fingers from my pussy as I slowly came down from my high. I watched with hungry eyes as he shoved his sweats down low enough to release his hard cock, stroking it in rough twists.

Needing no further instructions, Knox gave one final thrust before finding his own release. "Jesus Christ, Everly," he breathed heavily.

"Better move, Knoxy," Chase warned again, his breaths coming in heavy pants. I squeaked as Knox pulled out quickly, the motion stinging slightly.

Knox grabbed my inner thigh, opening me wider for Chase. He jerked himself a few more times before hot streams of his cum coated my flesh, mixing with mine and Knox's releases. Chase leaned forward slightly after emptying himself, two fingers pushing their combined cum back inside me.

"Just putting it back where it belongs, little Larkspur," he said with a wicked grin.

He kissed my nose before shimmying out of the bed and making his way to the bathroom. I could hear the sink running, and he returned a moment later, crawling back in next to me.

"What, no washcloth?" I teased.

Knox's voice growled into my ear. "Not tonight, Everly. You'll wear our cum inside that pretty little cunt until tomorrow morning. And even then, I may just fill you up again."

five

Griffin

Morning light streamed through Chase's bedroom window, hitting me square in the face. I rolled away from the offending sunshine, not ready to be awake. Last night's shit show at the ball had exhausted me, and I'd fallen straight to sleep once my head hit my pillow. Now, however, the sun's rays were determined to make me rise and shine.

I rolled off the bed, stretching out my muscles as I stood from the floor. Thank god Chase had ordered us all high-end mattresses at the beginning of the semester, otherwise sleeping with no box spring could have proven quite uncomfortable.

I glanced at my girl and best friends snuggled into the mountain of blankets Everly had insisted we needed. She was nestled into Chase's side, her head resting on his shoulder, her arm sprawled across his bare chest. Knox had wrapped himself around her back, one hand cupping her breast.

I chuckled, covering my mouth to muffle the sound.

Even asleep, the need to touch her was overwhelming. I couldn't blame them though; I'm sure my hands would be all over her too if I'd been next to her all night.

I quietly padded into the bathroom, emptying my bladder before splashing some cold water on my face and quickly brushing my teeth. Tiptoeing out of the bedroom, I made my way to the coffee maker in the kitchen. I filled a filter with Everly's favorite crème brûlée flavored roast and set the machine to brew.

Rummaging around in the fridge, I began pulling out the ingredients for scrambled eggs and set to work chopping peppers, onions, and tomatoes. Once everything was prepped, I whisked some eggs in a mixing bowl, folding in my veggies before pouring it all into a hot pan.

As my eggs cooked, I grabbed four mugs from the cupboard, filling one for myself. I was just getting ready to throw some bread in the toaster when Knox stumbled into the room, his dark hair sticking up in a multitude of directions.

"Morning, Sunshine," I grinned as I tossed the bread in to toast. He glared at me in response. "Coffee?"

Knox grunted an answer, accepting the mug I pushed in his direction. He sipped it carefully for a few minutes, letting the caffeine work its magic. Once I knew he was semi-functional, I tried engaging him again.

"You sleep okay? I know we were all pretty tapped out by the time we went to bed."

"Yeah, I slept alright. Had to help Everly fall asleep, though." A sly grin played at his lips, his dark eyes dancing with mischief. Before I could ask what he meant, Chase and Everly made their way into the kitchen, no doubt following the smell of the coffee and eggs.

I snagged her hand, pulling her to my body, planting a soft kiss on her lips. Even with the dark circles sitting below her eyes, she was the most beautiful woman I'd ever seen. My sweatpants sat low on her hips, and I noted that she must have rolled them about eight times to get them to stay up. Her nipples poked through the fabric of her top, the thin cotton not leaving much to the imagination. I planted another kiss on her nose before releasing her.

"Coffee, Blue?" I poured her a mug and placed it gently in her hands. She smiled up at me, her red-rimmed blue eyes crinkling at the corners.

"Thanks," she replied before taking a small sip. Her eyes closed, a pleased moan coming from her throat.

I glanced at Knox and Chase, their eyes fixed on her sinful body as she enjoyed the hot drink. Before I could get too lost in her sexy sounds, I remembered my eggs just in time, turning off the stovetop, so they wouldn't burn. Finishing up the toast, I plated the food, pushing the dishes across the counter toward everyone.

We ate in silence, but I could see the wheels turning in Everly's pretty head, most likely replaying last night's events. She looked exhausted, her usually vibrant eyes a more muted shade of blue. I finished chewing my last bite of toast before placing my plate in the sink. Taking a deep breath, I spoke, knowing I was about to ruin everyone's morning.

"So, we need to talk about last night."

Chase let out a loud sigh while Knox pinched the bridge of his nose. "Can't we just have five more minutes of blissful ignorance? Please, Daddy Griff?" Chase whined, a teasing tone to his voice. I could feel my cheeks heat at the nickname, Everly and Knox chuckling at my reaction.

"No, Chase," I admonished, "we need to figure out exactly what we're dealing with and what we can do to break the contract Mr. Blackwell signed." I grabbed the coffee pot, refilling Everly's mug before topping mine off.

"Where's mine?" Knox asked, a shit-eating grin on his face. His scruff was dark against his skin as he scratched it absently. I shot a glare in his direction. Seemed that getting laid last night had vastly improved his mood.

"You can have more when you contribute something useful to the conversation, asshole." I pointedly put the pot back in its spot on the coffee machine, Knox huffing in response. I sipped on my coffee before addressing them again.

"I'm going to head over to the library today to do some research. I can get access to the texts on dark magic since I'm an academy tutor. There *has* to be something there."

I'd been wracking my brain since last night, trying to remember everything I knew about soul-bound contracts, which admittedly wasn't much. Hopefully the library would yield better results; it hadn't failed me yet.

"I'll come with you," Everly responded, before softly adding, "but I need to go home and talk to Evan first." Her blue eyes welled with tears, the thought of facing her brother clearly overwhelming her already frayed emotions. Chase reached out, tugging her into his chest as he wrapped her in a fierce hug. The gesture spoke of his complete and total devotion to our girl, his attention focused solely on her.

"You want some back up, little Larkspur?" He spoke the words against her hair, planting a kiss to the top of her head. "I can come with, if you want?"

She snuggled into his chest, closing her eyes.

"No, I need to do this alone." Her voice held such a sad tone of defeat that it nearly broke my heart. I couldn't stand to see my Blue so beaten down. We needed to find a solution to this contract and fast.

"I'll walk you, just give me ten minutes to shower and get dressed. Sound good?" I crossed the short distance between us, pulling her from Chase's arms. He reluctantly released her, mumbling about me being a thief. I winked at him over her head as I cupped her jaw. She leaned into my touch, her features softening as I caressed her delicate skin.

"Sure, Griff." She turned away, padding across the room to our sofa. She curled up in the corner, pulling a blanket off the back and wrapping herself in it. "Let me know when you're ready." She looked so small and sad, huddled into the cushions.

Nope.

That wouldn't do at all.

"Change of plans, my Blue girl." I strode with purpose to her spot on the couch, hoisting her in my arms before she had a chance to protest, the blanket falling away. I marched us down the hall and into my room, not stopping until my feet met the cool tile floor of my bathroom.

"Griff, what are you doing?" Everly's voice squeaked as I carried her. I could feel my friends at my back, but this was going to be a private party for two. Before they could get into the bathroom, I kicked the door shut, using my hip to pop the lock. Everly cocked an eyebrow at me as Knox cursed through the closed door.

"You fucker!" His voice was muffled by the thick wood, and I chuckled at his response.

"You assholes had her last night. Now, it's my turn." I spoke to Chase and Knox, but my heated gaze never left Everly's blue eyes. I watched her pupils dilate, her cheeks flushing at the implication in my words. I sat her down slowly, her body sliding down mine until her feet met the floor, brushing along my rapidly hardening dick as she went.

"Let me take care of you, Blue." I tucked a stray hair that had escaped her bun behind her ear. Her eyes closed, and I could see the tension in her shoulders relax some from my touch. "Why don't you get out of these, and I'll get the shower started." I tugged on the waistband of her sweats before moving to the large, white tiled shower tucked into the corner of my bathroom.

Having Chase Stone as a roommate certainly had its perks. His parents had paid to have our bathrooms completely remodeled before we'd returned to campus this fall, giving us all enormous walk-in showers, stunning marble countertops, and beautiful tile floors.

I grabbed a couple towels from the small cupboard next to the vanity, then reached in to turn on the shower. Water cascaded from the expensive showerhead Chase had insisted we all needed while more shot out from the jets mounted on the wall. I cranked up the hot water, steam quickly billowing up and fogging the clear glass.

I gripped the back of my t-shirt, tugging it over my head with one arm before I tossed it in the hamper. As it cleared my head, I heard a soft gasp from across the room, and I grinned. Apparently, my girl liked what she saw. Slowly turning around so she could get her fill, my breathing stopped when my eyes found her body.

Her very *naked* body.

It wasn't like I had never seen Everly naked before. In the last three months it had become a pretty regular occurrence, something I was incredibly grateful for. But my god, she looked perfect, her tanned body a sharp contrast to the white tile that filled the bathroom. It was as though every fantasy I'd ever had was brought to life, right in front of my eyes.

She'd taken her hair down from its messy bun, her chocolate locks cascading over her shoulders and tickling the tops of her breasts. I watched her nipples hardening into small peaks as she drank in my bare chest. Her delicate fingers trailed over her toned stomach, teasing the skin ever so slightly until goosebumps formed in their wake. My eyes roamed over her, stopping when they hit the apex of her thighs.

"Everly," I breathed out, unable to say anything else. I would never get enough of her flawless body, never get enough of the perfect way she tasted.

I was on her in two steps, my mouth crashing down on hers with a savagery that surprised me. I needed her, needed to possess her, dominate her. Reaching down, I gripped the backs of her thighs, my fingers digging into her flesh. She groaned against my mouth in response.

"Up," I commanded. With zero hesitation, she leapt as I lifted and wrapped her petite legs around my waist. I carried her to my vanity, a gasp breaking free as I sat her perfect little ass on the cold marble.

Pulling away from her lips, I kissed along her jaw, then down her neck, nipping and licking along the way. I continued moving down her body, groping her breast with one hand while my other trailed along the inside of her thigh. Her chest heaved with desire as I gently pushed her back against the mirror, her elbows and forearms bearing her weight.

Dropping to my knees, I lifted her legs and dangled them over my arms, opening her to me. Her pussy shined in the bright bathroom light, her arousal coating the perfectly pink skin. I licked my lips as I prepared to worship at her altar.

"I want to hear you scream my name, Everly," I growled as I leaned in, giving her a long, slow lick from entrance to clit.

Fucking delicious.

six

Everly

M y body shuddered as Griff ate me like a man starved. His tongue lapped at my skin, the tip flicking my clit over and over until I was buzzing with need. My head tilted back, meeting the mirror as I moaned in pleasure.

"Jesus, Griff." I was having difficulty forming words as his tongue speared the entrance to my pussy in rapid movements. He moved it back to my clit, slowly entering me with two long fingers. The stretch was immaculate, my arousal allowing them to slide right in. He began pumping them in rhythm with his tongue as it assaulted my sensitive nub, my body climbing higher toward release.

"That's right, Everly. Such a good girl. Now give me what I want and cover my face with your cum." His dirty words sent me hurtling headfirst into a vicious orgasm, my legs shaking from the pleasure his tongue was pulling from my body.

I was a panting mess, my hair sticking to my forehead as a light sheen of sweat coated my skin. I swallowed roughly, willing my heart rate to return to normal. Opening my eyes, I was met with a blaze of greens and golds as Griff grinned from between my legs.

With a predator's grace, he slowly stood, his hard dick lining up perfectly with my pussy. Before I could take another breath, he was pushing inside, filling me to the brim.

"Fuck, Everly. This pussy was made for me." He stared at the place where our bodies met, slowly pulling out only to thrust back in fully. It was a deliciously torturous motion that had my toes curling.

"Griff..." His name came out as more of a moan than an actual word as he built me back up, his thrusts picking up speed as he rutted into me. His eyes held a feral look, and he gripped my hips with such force, I'd be surprised if I didn't end up with bruises. His chest rose with each breath, and I could tell by the tight set of his jaw that he was close. He slipped one hand between us, his fingertips finding my clit with practiced ease.

"You'll come again, Everly, one more time. You'll give me one more." Griff's demanding words shot straight to my core, my body clenching around his thick cock. He groaned before glaring at me. "You will come *before* me, Everly. So don't even fucking try it." And with that he doubled down, rubbing my clit in tight circles until my back arched, and I was screaming out my release.

"GRIFF!"

Unable to see anything but the explosion of colors happening behind my eyelids, I sank into the pleasure racing through me. Blood roared in my ears, and I was pretty certain my soul left my body. As I tried to regain some brain function, I felt one of Griff's strong arms band around my middle, pulling me close. He thrust several more times, each movement erratic and full of his wild need to claim me. With one final plunge into my body, he stilled, filling me with his seed.

He took a shuddering breath, leaning forward until his forehead was pressed to mine. We stayed like that for several minutes, the steam from the shower filling the air around us. Once our breathing calmed, Griff stood, pulling free of my body. He watched as his cum leaked from my swollen core, a wolfish grin on his face at the sight.

"Alright, dirty girl, let's get you cleaned up."

Thirty minutes and another orgasm later, we finally emerged from the bathroom to find a very irritated Knox waiting in the living room. I glanced back at Chase's bedroom only to see the door open and the room empty. My eyebrows drew together in confusion as I looked at Knox. His eyes darted between me and Chase's doorframe, an odd look on his handsome face.

"He had to run out." Okay, vague.

"Where did he go?" I asked. Why was Knox being so weird about this?

"Umm..." Now we had moved from vague and into suspicious. I planted my hands on my hips, staring my boyfriend down.

"Knox. Where. Did. He. Go?" My attempt at dominance must have failed because instead of giving me the information I demanded, heat flared in Knox's eyes, his gaze skimming the length of my body. I'd thrown on the sweats and cami from earlier, planning to change once I got back to my own room, and I knew my nipples were poking through the thin fabric, giving him quite the eyeful.

"Knox!" I snapped my fingers at him, breaking him out of his trance.

He winced at my uncharacteristically harsh tone before answering. "He had to go deal with a project for one of his classes."

A project for one of his classes? I looked at him, still not understanding what project he meant.

"Knox, what are you talking about? What project?" I filtered through my brain, trying to remember what assignments Chase had coming up. Nothing for his math class. He was working on a paper for his Caster Botany course, but it wasn't due for another few weeks. Magical Defenses didn't have any homework. That only left...

"Did he go meet Heather?" The words came out in a calm tone that belied the anger slowly seeping into my body.

Knox rose from the couch, quickly making his way across the room to me. His hands landed on my upper arms, his thumbs caressing the exposed skin. Out of the corner of my eye, I could see Griff moving into the kitchen.

"What's going on?" he asked, taking in my tense posture.

Knox ignored his question, his eyes focused on my face. "Little Monet, he didn't have a choice. She called him, said she fucked up their potion for class. Apparently, she let it simmer overnight and burnt it to a crisp." He cupped my jaw as he continued, "Chase didn't want to leave, baby, he really didn't.

But if he didn't go try to salvage what was left, he said they'd end up failing. I think he was going to try to get some more herbs from his professor then meet up with Heather to restart the potion."

I softened a bit in Knox's hold, still annoyed that Chase had left to meet Heather. I knew how important our potions class was for his environmental conservation major, so I tried to suck it up.

A hand stroked down my shoulder, Griff's voice coming from behind me. "He wouldn't just leave without a good reason, Blue. I'm sure he didn't want to go. Especially to go meet *her*."

They were right. Sighing heavily, I planted a soft kiss to the corner of Knox's mouth before stepping away from them both. I needed to trust Chase, trust that he meant it when he said he loved me. He'd given me no reason to doubt him thus far, so I pushed my jealousy aside for the time being. I had much bigger issues to deal with at the moment.

"I need to go see if my brother is home." Exhaustion swept through me, the thought of having to confront Evan making me feel bone-tired. I knew I was potentially walking into a powder keg, unsure how my brother would react when I told him what Morgan had done. Would he care? Would he take her side? I hated that I had no idea what the hell was going on in my twin's head.

"Come on," Griff said, taking my hand. His touch always held such a sense of reassurance, a feeling that everything would be alright. It gave me a small bit of comfort as I contemplated the task at hand. "Let's get you home. I'm going to head to the library to get started on some research."

"I was gonna go to my studio, but I can stay with you if you want little Monet." Knox was throwing on a sweatshirt, paint smears staining the front. I couldn't help the small smile that tugged at my lips as I wondered if he owned any clothing that was paint-free.

"No, it's okay, Knox. I need to talk to him alone." They both nodded silently, knowing this was something I needed to do by myself. And as much as I wanted their support, I honestly didn't trust Knox not to break my brother's face. I'd seen him fly off the handle before, and I knew he was already pissed at Evan.

The guys grabbed their backpacks while I gathered up my clothes from the night before. I shivered, thoughts from that fucking boardroom flooding my brain. I needed answers from my brother, and I needed them now.

We all shuffled into the hall and quickly made our way to my suite. Needing to rip the Band-Aid off and get this over with, I gave them each a kiss goodbye before unlocking my door. But both guys pushed by me and stepped inside, doing a quick sweep of the living room and my bedroom, as if they expected Austin to jump out and kidnap me at any moment. Although, with how crazy we knew he was, it didn't seem out of the realm of possibility.

Once they were satisfied I was alone, Knox wrapped me in his ink covered arms, holding me tightly as he kissed me breathless. My head was spinning by the time we broke apart, but Griff didn't give me a moment to come back down before his lips were pressed against mine with just as much passion. Finally releasing me, they both walked to the door. Griff shot me one final look as his hand turned the knob.

"Come by the library when you're finished. I'll be in my study room." The statement didn't hold his typical dom tone, but it was still commanding nonetheless. I nodded my head, letting him know I'd see him later.

"And little Monet," Knox growled, "you call one of us if you need *anything*. I mean it." I could tell by the tight set of his jaw that he was struggling to leave me alone. I plastered on a smile, trying my best to exude a confidence I didn't feel.

"I'll be alright. I'm just going to get changed and wait for Evan." I gestured toward my bedroom. "I'll be fine." It was a lie, and while we all knew it, neither man called me on my bullshit. "I love you."

I finally shoved them out the door, pressing my back to the hardwood once they left. I took a deep breath, then moved to my room. Closing myself inside, I quickly hung my gown in the back of my closet. I couldn't look at it without being reminded of everything that happened the night before, but I also couldn't part with it. Not when I'd felt so beautiful, so wanted by my men the moment they'd seen me wearing it. So for now, it would live tucked away behind my other dresses. Once I deposited my shoes on a shelf, I grabbed some clean panties, a bra, and some leggings, pairing them with a thin camisole and a rowing sweatshirt I'd stolen from Chase and cut so it hung loosely off my shoulder.

I snagged my sketchpad, charcoals, and colored pencils from my night-stand, figuring I'd draw while I waited for my brother. Making my way back to the living room, I tugged one of the arm chairs over to our tall windows, so I could see the morning sun streaming through the fall leaves. I began working, getting lost in the way the rays illuminated the autumn colors.

Just as I was getting ready to add Onyx to my drawing, I heard movement from Evan's bedroom. Startling me from my work, I set my sketchpad on the coffee table. I listened intently to the muffled voices coming from Evan's room, but the thick door made it nearly impossible to make out what they were saying. *Goddamn thick-ass wood.* Was he on the phone? Or was there someone inside with him?

My heart leapt into my throat at the thought, but I couldn't focus on it for long when I saw his doorknob begin to turn.

I was pretty sure it took eighty-four years for the fucking thing to open, revealing my brother, shirtless with a pair of SLA sweats hanging off his lean frame. All my anger at him from the night before melted away, and I rose, ready to run to my twin.

I'd made it to my feet when I spotted a flash of bleach blonde hair step around him, his old Staunton Prep shirt hanging around her thighs.

"Morning, Everly." Fury licked through my veins, the sight of her smug smile making me consider homicide.

Motherfucker.

seven
Everly

My fist balled up, even as I tried to talk myself out of laying Morgan flat on her ass. Her talon-like nails raked down my brother's chest as she leaned up to give him a kiss, bile rising in my throat at the sight. Choking down the vomit, I cleared my throat, finally getting Evan's attention.

"Hey," he said, his cheeks burning red when he realized I was witnessing Morgan and her attempt at finding his tonsils. He stepped away from her, and the move made me feel a tiny bit better.

Morgan, however, wasn't deterred by my presence in the least. She nuzzled into his side, arms wrapping around his lean waist. I glared at her, considering if I could get away with moving her away from him using my caster powers. Wanting to avoid a fight with my brother, I reluctantly let the idea go.

Out of the corner of my eye, I spotted her shitty little handbag, the one she'd had with her the night before. A second later I sent it flying, and the satisfying thud as it hit her in the gut had a victorious smile spreading across my face.

Oops.

"Everly!" my brother scolded me, his eyes narrowed before he checked over his cunt of a girlfriend. I ignored his angry tone, continuing to glare at the twatwaffle before me.

"*She*"—I gestured at Morgan, my voice holding an air of disgust—"needs to leave."

"Excu—" the bitch attempted to interrupt me, but I continued speaking right over her.

"You and I"—I pointed between my twin and myself—"need to talk. Now." I crossed my arms, my tone leaving no room for argument.

I could see panic flare in Morgan's beady little eyes when she realized I was going to throw her under the bus and back up over her for what she'd done at the ball. She opened her mouth to speak again, but luckily my brother kept my ears from being assaulted by her shrill voice.

Evan scrubbed his hands down his face, sighing deeply. "Morgan, I'll meet up with you later, k?"

I staved off the urge to roll my eyes, not wanting to piss my brother off before I'd had a chance to talk with him privately. Flicking my fingers, I pushed her purse closer to her feet, since it had fallen to the floor after *accidentally* hitting her.

She stared at him, her plain brown eyes fixed on my twin's green ones for a long moment before she let out a little huff of frustration. "Ugh, fine. Text me when you're ready for round three... or would it be four?" She smirked at me, and it took all my willpower not to fling her right through our living room windows.

I was a fairly strong telekinetic. It would be oh so easy to just....

"Yeah babe, I'll call you later." He ushered her to the door where they spoke in hushed voices for another minute. The sounds of their kissing made me nauseous, and I didn't think I'd ever been so grateful for a door in my entire life once ours closed behind her skank ass.

My brother meandered back to the kitchen, pulling out some coffee and a filter from the cupboard before filling the pot. Once he'd set the machine to brew, he turned toward me, his back leaning against the stone counter.

"So, you ready to apologize for how you acted last night?" Evan's lips were drawn into a tight line, his frustration evident.

My anger surged, getting the better of me before I could stop it.

"I'm sorry, what?" I huffed out. "You want *me* to apologize? How about your bitch of a girlfriend apologizes for setting me up last night, Evan? How about that? Or did she forget to tell you that part while you were fucking her?" I was gesturing wildly with every word, my rage boiling over.

"Maybe she should apologize for lying to me. For telling me you wanted to talk, but instead delivering me to Alaric fucking Thorpe and his creep-tastic son. Maybe she should apologize for *that,* Evan!" I was shouting now, my chest heaving as fury raced through my body.

To his credit, my brother looked shocked. His green eyes had gone round, but it could have been from me nearly screaming at him. Evan and I didn't fight often, and when we did, it was over stupid shit like him leaving the seat up or me tossing his leftovers in the trash. We were best friends... or at least we had been.

Until fucking Morgan came along. God, I hated that girl.

"What are you talking about?" he asked, spinning away from me to pull two coffee mugs from the cabinet. He quickly poured us each a cup, sliding mine across the counter before grabbing my crème brûlée creamer from the fridge. I picked it up wordlessly, pouring in a small amount, just enough to turn the black liquid to a shade of dark brown. I took a sip before answering, the hot drink sliding down my throat and warming my chest. Closing my eyes, I let out a deep sigh.

"Exactly what I said before, Evan." I fixed my blue eyes on his green ones, my heart stuttering for a moment at how much they reminded me of our mom.

Mom. The woman at the center of this whole fucking mess.

"Morgan found me last night. She said you wanted to talk, alone, and told me to go to one of the conference rooms to meet you. Only when I went to the room, it wasn't you. It was Alaric and Austin Thorpe." A sob crept up my throat as I forced the next words out. "And Dad."

His eyebrows scrunched together in confusion, and he pulled his cell phone from his pocket. He began swiping at the screen as though it had personally offended him before turning it to me.

"Dad texted me halfway through the night, said he'd gotten sick and couldn't make it. So try again, Everly." Angry disbelief was laced through his words, each one slicing at my heart. What in the actual fuck was going on? I snapped my fingers, the phone lifting from his hand before gliding over to me. I looked at the text message on the screen.

> Dad: Hey bud, not feeling well. Not gonna make it tonight. Have a great time!

"What the fuck? No, Evan, I *saw* him last night! He was there! He was in that conference room with the Thorpes! They—" I was frantic now, willing my brother to listen as I tried to explain.

"Save it, Everly. I did ask Morgan to find you, tell you I wanted to talk. She told me you said no, that your guys would kick my ass if I tried to talk to you. So stop lying," Evan spat the words at me, more angry than I'd ever seen him in my life. He glared at me, clearly having made up his mind already. Tears welled in my eyes, spilling over and running down my cheeks.

"Evan, no, that's not—" But before I could get another word out, he was gone. He'd sped off using his caster ability, his door slamming shut, the sound of the lock clicking into place like a goddamn shotgun blast in the quiet that followed his departure. I let out a soft gasp, coming to the realization that my brother, my twin, my first best friend, thought I betrayed him.

"Evan," I whispered his name into the empty space. I walked to his door, leaning my forehead against the smooth wood grain. I could sense him there and a deep part of my brain told me my twin was just on the other side, mirroring my stance and my pain.

I placed my palm to the mahogany, my fingers splayed out, wishing he would open the door. I stood there for what seemed like forever, willing him to come out, but it never happened.

I could have easily disengaged the lock with a simple snap of my fingers. But I couldn't face his anger. And I couldn't face the fact that he didn't believe me.

I eventually dragged myself from his door and back to my bedroom. Flicking my wrist, I shut myself in, stripping off my leggings and sweatshirt before crawling into the few pillows and blankets I'd left behind last night. With one final snap, I turned on my Bluetooth speaker, needing something to drown out the silence currently taking me under. I closed my eyes, tears still leaking down my face.

I was just about to fall asleep when I heard a soft scratching at my bedroom window. Cracking one eye open, I saw Onyx sitting on the ledge, his fluffy black tail blowing in the wind. I snapped my fingers, the window opening just enough for him to scurry inside. He hopped onto the sill before loping across the floor and onto my bed. The cold October air rushed inside behind him, and I snapped my fingers again quickly, locking the window and drawing the curtains closed, leaving my room with only a hint of light.

Onyx crawled tentatively up to my pillow where I was snuggled on my side.

"Come on, little guy." I patted the pillow next to me, and he quickly climbed up. I scratched the top of his head, right between his ears. Onyx snuggled into the cotton pillowcase, his fluffy tail wrapping around him like a blanket. I sighed, sadness filling my chest.

"At least you're not mad at me."

I contemplated calling one of the guys, but I knew they were all busy with their own stuff. I'd told Griff I would meet him at the library, but I needed just a few minutes to wallow in my grief. I closed my eyes, trying to shut out the world, just for a little while.

eight

Knox

After leaving Everly at her suite, I walked quietly with Griff across campus. We were both silent, lost in our thoughts. He gave me a fist bump before climbing the steps to the library, while I continued down the stone walkway toward Vox and my studio. Using my key fob, I unlocked the side door that led to the art studios in the basement, quickly making my way through the maze-like hallways with ease.

Setting my bag off to the side, I meandered around my large work table. It had a scaled down replica of my future architecture firm, the main piece of my senior project. While utilizing traditional architectural forms, it specifically focused on using enchanted water elements to add not only aesthetically pleasing pieces, but also ways to break up large spaces within the building.

The water features would require periodic maintenance spells, but overall it was a solid project that I was confident would earn me an A.

I sat my ass on one of my stools, going over every square inch of the model, making sure each piece was perfectly in place. Tiny chairs and desks were spread out methodically across the miniature replica, each spot painstakingly thought out. I had even created a small water cooler and tiny coffee mugs that sat on top of a resin and wood boardroom table. I'd created that specific piece after meeting Everly, the blue resin running through the middle of the table matching her eyes.

To the outside world, I probably seemed like a messy, hot-headed artist. My painting areas were always splashed with acrylics, and the vast majority of my clothes held paint stains that wouldn't come out. I worked out my emotions through my art when I couldn't deal with them any other way. But underneath it all, I was actually an OCD, hyper-focused asshole who fixated on the most minute details within my projects.

I think that was what caused me to lose my cool when it came to Everly. Or, well, when it came to Everly being hurt. It was shit that was out of my control, and I *hated* that. And lately it felt like each time she'd been hurt, it'd been on my watch.

Realizing I'd moved the same miniature chair at least six times, I sighed deeply, rubbing my hands down my face. My scruff was coming in thick, but I resisted shaving since I knew my little Monet loved it. I couldn't concentrate, knowing we'd left her alone at her suite.

Pulling out my phone, I called Griff. The line rang a few times before his voice came through.

"Yo, what's up?"

"Did Everly make it to you yet?"

"No, I was actually just going to call you to go check on her. I've got half a dozen books pulled out, so I'm gonna be here a while." I could hear the stress in his voice, and it filled me with worry. Griff was our resident problem solver. If he was having a hard time finding a solution to our Thorpe dilemma... well, let's just say it didn't leave me feeling very confident.

"Yeah," I answered him. "I'll head back to her place and see if she's okay." Not waiting for a response, I hung up. Snagging my bag from the ground, I made short work of closing down my studio, unease growing in my gut with each passing minute. I pulled my phone out again, this time calling Everly.

One ring. Two. Three.

"Hi, you've reached Everly. I can't take your call right now but if—"

Fuck.

I dialed again. One ring. Two. Three.

"Hi, you've reached Ev—"

Panic started to seize my chest. Rationally, I knew she was probably home, most likely with her music blaring as she painted. Or maybe she was talking with Evan. But it still wasn't like her to not answer.

I could readily admit I was terrified the night before when she was missing. The guilt that I was the one who had let her go off on her own ate at me.

I was also still pissed at her for lying to me. And now that she wasn't answering her phone again, well, that same fear from before was slithering up my spine, mixing with the anger and making for a volatile combination. I jogged across campus, my feet flying up the stairs of our dorm. This was one of those times I wished I could teleport like Griff. I made it up to the fourth floor in record time, knocking on Everly's door the moment I reached it.

Silence followed, and I bounced in place nervously. I knocked again, harder this time, small shocks of pain lancing my knuckles as they connected with the hardwood. More fucking silence. I raised my hand, banging on the door with my palms, the loud sound echoing down the otherwise quiet hallway.

A slow roll of anger was building inside me, and I was ready to pound through the goddamn door if necessary. Where the fuck was Chase and his super strength when I needed him?

Just as I was getting ready to start banging with both fists, the door opened, revealing an irritated Evan staring back at me.

"What the fuck do you want, Knox? I was just leaving." He glared at me, a look I met with one of my own, noting the overstuffed duffle bag slung over his shoulder. But I didn't have time to argue with him, no matter how much I wanted to break his fucking face for how he'd spoken to Everly the night before.

"Where's your sister?" I growled, that feral, animalistic side of me bubbling just under the surface. I could feel my snow leopard scratching at the back of my mind, demanding retribution for Evan's previous infractions against my girl.

He narrowed his eyes further before jutting his chin toward her bedroom. I turned, noticing it was shut tightly. "She's probably in there, pouting since I called her out on her bullshit lies from last night," he bit out. I swung around toward him, pissed-off, shock at his words rippling through me.

"Evan, what the fu—"

He stopped me with a raised hand. "I'll tell you the same thing I told her. Save it. Morgan told me what you guys said about kicking my ass." He stood a bit straighter, puffing his chest as if preparing himself for a fight. "I care about her, so you all can fuck off with your opinions, because I'm *not* breaking up with her." Evan shoved by and through the doorway before I could respond.

"If my sister decides she wants to apologize, I'll be at Morgan's." And with those words, he took off down the hall in a blur toward the stairs.

What the fuck was he talking about? Why would Everly need to apologize?

Shaking my head at his words, I brushed them aside. I needed to lay eyes on Everly.

Now.

Making sure the door was shut behind me, I quickly moved to her closed bedroom door. I could hear her Bad Omens playlist muffled by the thick wood.

"Little Monet?" I called through the mahogany, rapping my knuckles on the wood.

No answer.

"Everly?" My voice was louder this time, anger from my brief conversation with Evan creeping in.

Still no fucking answer.

Now, I was getting pissed.

Why couldn't anyone open a fucking door on the first knock in this place?

"Fuck it." I nearly ripped my shirt as I tore it over my head, toeing off my shoes as the fabric brushed my hair. My pants and boxer briefs hit the floor, and a moment later, I was down on four tiny paws, surrounded by piles of denim and cotton. My soft mouse whiskers brushed the fabric as I crawled over it, making a beeline for the gap at the bottom of the door.

Flattening my body as much as physically possible, I wiggled through the small space, my furry belly brushing along the floor. I popped through quickly, my tail bobbing behind me as I scurried across the dark hardwood.

When I met the plush cream carpet in the middle of the room, I shifted back, my toes pushing through the soft fibers. Everly had insisted we help her put it under her solid wood-framed queen-size bed. Chase, of course, had used the opportunity to show off his caster strength, easily holding the bed up while Griff and I unrolled the carpet.

I stretched to my full height, my eyes adjusting to the dim room. I could see a lump in the middle of the bed, the blankets rising and falling in a steady rhythm. Tiptoeing across the quiet space, I knelt next to the bed so I could see Everly's face poking out of the blankets she was cocooned inside of.

Just as I was about to wake her, movement at the top of her pillow caught my eye. A small furry head popped up, the black squirrel's eyes nearly glowing in the soft light as it stared at me.

"Hi buddy," I spoke softly, tentatively reaching out so he could sniff me. "I just came to check on our girl. You keeping her company?" His whiskers tickled my fingertips as he inspected me for any danger. Deciding I was safe, he slowly stretched out, before rearranging himself on her pillow and snuggling in once more.

I sat on the edge of Everly's bed, pushing stray hairs away from her perfect face. Her brows were drawn together, and although I knew she was sleeping, I also knew she wasn't resting. I trailed the knuckles of my left hand down her cheek, her skin damp.

She must have locked herself in after arguing with her brother. I didn't know what he was talking about earlier, saying we were going to kick his ass, but if he had made my girl cry, well, he might not be far off base.

Seeing the stress marring the perfect canvas of her face, I kissed her forehead before whispering her name.

"Everly."

Her eyelids fluttered, and she slowly opened them, the cerulean orbs finally focusing on me after a few seconds.

"Knox?" She sat up, the blankets falling away to reveal she was still in her clothes from earlier. The movement disrupted her furry visitor once more, and he chittered his displeasure before climbing to sit directly in her lap.

"What are you doing here?" she asked as she absentmindedly pet the little black squirrel.

Cupping her jaw, I tried to ignore the anger that was still simmering in my veins. "I was worried, baby. You never showed up to the library to meet with Griff." I grew more irritated with each word that fell from my mouth. "Why didn't you call or text one of us?"

Her eyes welled with tears, and I immediately felt like an asshole. *Fuck.* I pulled her quickly toward me, squishing Onyx between us until he managed to squirm his way out. I felt her body trembling as she cried.

Way to go, Knox. No wonder Griff and Chase always call you an asshole.

"Little Monet," I whispered into her hair, stroking her back with my fingertips. "I'm sorry, baby, I didn't mean—I was just worried, and when I couldn't reach you, I freaked out a bit." Her tiny arms wrapped around my naked torso, and I could feel her tears against my chest.

After a few minutes, she sat up, wiping at her eyes with her fingers, the bright blue rimmed in red. I was so tired of seeing her cry. All I wanted was for my girl to be happy again. She sniffled, looking down as the squirrel cautiously crept back into her lap. She began stroking his jet black fur before she spoke, her words a near whisper.

"I'm sorry Knox. I know I keep letting you down."

Jesus, I was such a dick.

I moved quickly, scooping her and Onyx up and into my lap before she could say another word. I felt her silky legs against my bare skin, and my dick began to thicken at the contact. I tried to will away my growing hard on, but I was struggling as she wiggled around.

"Everly." My voice was a bit more gruff than I meant, so I started again. "Baby"—the words softer this time—"you're not letting me down." Using my index finger and thumb, I tipped her chin, so I could see her beautiful face more clearly. "I'm angry, but not with you, I promise. I'm angry at the fact that I can't keep you safe. That I feel like *I'm* letting *you* down."

"Promise you're not mad?" Her eyes glistened with unshed tears as she looked at me. This sweet, perfect creature owned every inch of my heart and it broke at the doubt in her words.

"I promise, my little Monet," I whispered, leaning slightly forward to catch her lips with mine. I kept the kiss as innocent as I could, given my dick was currently poking into the back of her thigh. Pulling away, I lifted her gently, placing her back into the blankets, Onyx still sitting in her lap.

"Now, let's go meet Griff at the library, before I change my mind and strip you down." I waggled my eyebrows at her, only half joking about getting her naked. Resisting Everly when she was fully clothed was hard enough, but when she was only in underwear and a nearly see through tank top?

Forget it.

Deciding to be the chivalrous southern man my mother had raised, I spun, snatching up an oversized SLA sweatshirt off the floor and throwing it in her direction. "Here, put this on so I can focus," I teased. Just as I went to unlock the bedroom door, I noticed Everly's eyes drinking in my tattooed body. I chuckled, a smug smile tugging at my lips.

"You gonna get dressed, little Monet? Or do you see something else you'd like to try on?" I prowled a few steps closer before she launched a small pillow into my chest, laughing. I grinned at her, happy I could at least make her smile.

"I was just wondering why you're naked, that's all. Not that I'm complaining. It's quite the view." She bit her bottom lip, and my quickly hardening dick twitched against my thigh.

I pushed my fingers through my hair, barking out a laugh. I probably looked like some sort of psycho, showing up in her bedroom completely naked.

"I knocked," I explained, "but you didn't answer. I panicked, shifted into a mouse and crawled under your door."

Jesus, when I said it out loud, I really *did* look like a psycho.

"I'm sorry I worried you," she replied, her voice going soft. "I guess I passed out, and with my music on, I just didn't hear you. I'm sorry."

"Hey now, no more apologizing." I tossed the pillow back at her playfully. "Get dressed so we can go meet your brainiac boyfriend."

Everly climbed out of bed, my eyes glued to her as if she were a rare painting. Her toned legs flexed with each movement, her ass cheeks peeking out from the bottom of her panties, giving me just a tease of the gloriousness I knew to be hiding underneath. I could feel myself getting hard again, but I didn't give a fuck at this point. Let her see what she did to me.

Once we were both dressed, Everly peeled and sliced up a banana for the squirrel who seemed quite at home here in her bedroom. "Who's your friend?" I asked teasingly, nodding my head at the little black fluff ball.

"His name is Onyx," she explained, giving it a scratch before meeting me at the door. I took her hand and led her out of the suite. We walked silently down the stairs, our fingers laced together. Just as we reached the landing, she tugged on me gently.

"Thank you, Knox," she whispered, "for always saving me."

I gently cupped her cheek, leaning in close. Other students milled around us, but I barely noticed. They didn't exist when I had my girl in my arms.

I pressed a gentle kiss to her forehead. "Little Monet, I will always come for you. As long as you are mine, I will *always* save you."

nine

Chase

It was Friday evening, and holy shit did coming back to classes after the break suck. Add in the shitstorm that Everly's dad created by signing that contract, and it double sucked.

Scratch that.

Quadruple sucked.

Thank Christ rowing was nearly over, our last regatta coming up tomorrow morning. I was looking forward to spending the day kicking ass in our final race and the night wrapped up in my girl's arms.

Unfortunately, the succubus also known as Heather had been taking up far too much of my time during the week with her idiotic questions about potions. I put her off as much as possible, but I couldn't completely ignore her without tanking my grade. I'd even offered to do all the work, just so I wouldn't have to see her outside of class but no dice.

The damn girl was constantly texting me to come explain some easy, mundane thing from our notes that any first year caster could answer. I couldn't decide if she was incredibly smart, taking advantage of the fact that I was her partner, or incredibly stupid...

My money was on incredibly stupid, particularly if she thought I'd ever leave Everly for her.

I was also waiting impatiently on information from one of my dad's private investigators. I'd called him the day after the ball, looking for any information we could use against Austin in hopes of gaining some sort of leverage, something to turn the situation in our favor.

"Chase, why would you need a private investigator?" my mom's sweet voice came over the line. I was surprised when she'd initially answered, especially since I'd called the office, but she explained that she was only there to have lunch with Dad. I silently sent up a prayer to whomever was listening, hoping that would be me and Everly one day.

"I need to look into Austin Thorpe, Mom."

"Alaric's son? What for?" she asked before I heard her scolding my father's lunch choice. "Carrick, no, you can't have the fries, not with your cholesterol." I chuckled to myself, an image of her swatting the deep fried goodness out of his hand running through my mind.

"Chase, what exactly are you looking for?" Dad asked, chewing loudly in my ear. I'd bet the twenty in my wallet that he was scarfing down the food before mom snatched it away.

Figuring it was best to just lay all my cards on the table, I explained what went down at the Autumn Ball between Everly and the Thorpes. I heard my mom draw in an audible gasp when I told them about Austin's attacks on Everly.

"Oh, that poor girl. Your dad said she was absolutely lovely. I can't wait to meet her." I grinned, despite the reason I was calling.

"I know, Mom, she really is amazing. She's such a talented artist, and she's smart and sweet. God, she's so beautiful..." I could have gone on forever, but my mom's laughter cut me off.

"Chase Thomas Stone, if I didn't know any better, I'd say that you loved this girl," she teased. I could hear the smile in her voice, and it had a big goofy one spreading across my face.

"Oh Mom, you have no idea. I'd do anything for Everly."

And it was true. I'd move heaven and earth if it meant I could fix this fucked up situation we'd found ourselves in and save my girl.

Dad had given me the number for the private investigator he'd hired, a man by the name of Lou Martinez. I gave him a call as soon as I hung up with my parents, and he'd agreed to look into Austin and get me any information he could find. During our conversation, it dawned on me that, despite having known Austin for nearly fifteen years, I really knew nothing about him. I didn't even know what his caster ability was.

Lou said it would be a week or so before I would hear from him; we were currently at six days, and my patience was wearing thin. I was crossing my fingers that he'd deliver some major dirt, something we could use to make Austin stand down, but I had my doubts.

Dad had his PIs and a forensic accountant combing through every scrap of paper over at Thorpe & Stone, looking for evidence of Alaric's embezzlement, and they'd turned up squat so far.

Something had to fucking pan out.

I was sitting on the stone ledge of the academy's fountain, my zip-up hoodie hanging open while I cooled down from my run. With the rowing season coming to an end, I was trying to maintain my current level of workouts, and adding in an evening run around the lake was a simple way to keep up my cardio.

Everly had a late art class, so I told the guys I'd pick her up when I was finished. We were still making sure she had an escort around campus, not wanting to take any chances. No one had seen Austin since the night of the ball, but I didn't trust the weasely little fucker not to try some shit. Rumor around campus was that his dad had pulled him out of school for 'personal reasons'. Personal my ass; he was up to something, I just didn't know what.

The doors of Vox swung open, my attention immediately on the mass of bodies flooding through the wood frame.

And then she appeared.

My Larkspur.

My breath caught in my lungs as I stared at her. Her head swiveled as she searched the quad for me, and I took the moment to admire her beauty.

She was dressed in a pair of dark blue jeans, a faded Falling in Reverse band tee over top a white long-sleeve shirt and her hot pink Converse sneakers. She'd piled her hair on top of her head, tendrils falling down into her face. I watched as she pushed them out of her eyes, those blue sapphire orbs seeking me out like hot stars in the night sky. Even in the simplest of outfits she was stunning. She was so goddamn beautiful it nearly hurt.

I could tell the moment she spotted me, a wide smile gracing her perfect face.

I hoped to God she'd always look at me that way.

Standing from the fountain, I jogged across the quad. It was as though there was an invisible thread, drawing me to her, tethering us together. When

I reached my girl, I quickly snatched her around the waist, spinning her in the air. Her answering laughter made my heart soar.

"Chase!" She flung her arms around my neck, squeezing tightly.

"Hi, baby," I whispered in her ear. We stayed like that, wrapped around one another for who knows how long, two souls bound together, existing only for the other.

Sometimes, when I was alone, I thought about how quickly I'd fallen in love with Everly. My feelings for her had come on like a tornado, sudden and without warning, completely obliterating everything I thought I knew.

Girls had always come easily; I wasn't a relationship kind of guy, but making sure I got laid every weekend was a simple task. Cocky as it sounds, most of the time women typically threw themselves at me.

But it was different with my Larkspur. There was an immediate connection with her unlike anything I'd ever felt before. It probably seemed ridiculous to some, the instant love we all shared with her. But I knew in my bones, in the deepest parts of my soul, what I felt was real. There was no denying how deeply my love for Everly ran.

Seeing her for the first time, it was like the planets aligned, and the universe said *"Here she is Chase, this is the one."* I couldn't stay away, even if I'd tried.

I put her down slowly, letting her tiny body slide down the length of my torso, the feel of her breasts against my shirt making my dick stir to life. *Not now, dude!* I was under strict orders from Daddy Griff to return Everly to our place for a night of relaxation and... *group* activities.

Her heated blue eyes gazed up at me through thick black lashes, deep cerulean pools that could easily have me doing anything her heart desired. She bit her bottom lip, the pink flesh trapped between her straight, white teeth. Using my thumb, I pulled it free.

"Keep that up, Larkspur, and we won't make it back to the suite to play with Griff and Knox. I'll bend you over right here for the world to see." She gasped softly at my crass words, and I could see a flush creep on her face in the last remaining bit of dusky sunlight.

Flashing her a grin, I stole her backpack and grabbed her hand, tugging her along at my side. She giggled, her tiny legs struggling to keep pace as we quickly moved across campus.

Just as we reached the bottom steps of Bliss Hall I felt Everly's body stop, standing stock still at the base of the stairs. Her face was filled with a mixture of what I can only describe as absolute sadness and murderous rage all rolled into one.

Following her line of sight, my eyes landed on her brother and Morgan going up the steps to one of the other dorms. Morgan's arm was looped around Evan's waist, and his was secured around her shoulders, tucking her into his side, completely unaware his twin was only yards away.

"Evan," Everly whispered, his name nearly lost in the breeze that flowed through the quiet area. The anguish in her voice tore at me. I wanted to march over and beat the shit out of Evan for hurting my girl, his sister, this way; her tiny hand in mine was the only thing stopping me.

She'd filled us in on their fight the day after the ball, and to say I was pissed was the understatement of the century. I still couldn't believe Knox hadn't just knocked him out that night, but apparently my friend had a modicum of restraint.

Knox wouldn't be so kind the next time he saw Evan alone.

Tears filled my Larkspur's eyes, and she swallowed roughly, choking down a sob at the sight of her brother with that bitch. Squeezing her hand, I drew her attention back to me.

"Come on, baby, let's head up before Knox and Griff think I kidnapped you. We'll help take your mind off things." Tugging her closer, I placed a gentle kiss to the top of her head. Pulling her into my side, I shot one more look over my shoulder to see if Evan and Morgan were gone.

Still wrapped around each other at the door of Morgan's building, I rolled my eyes, but not before catching sight of a purple bracelet on Morgan's wrist. The plum colored stones almost seemed to glow in the waning light. Probably just a reflection from the lamp posts beginning to turn on.

Not giving it another thought, I skimmed my fingers along Everly's side, just where her t-shirt and jeans met, leaving a tiny sliver of her delicious skin exposed.

Everly sniffled as we made our way inside. She was quiet as we climbed the stairs, wiping her eyes every few seconds. Unsure of what to say, of how to comfort her, I stayed silent, making sure to let her know I was there by holding her tightly to me.

With every step, I could feel her breast brush the side of my chest, her ass swaying just below my hand. Blood began to descend to my groin, my dick growing harder as we neared the fourth floor. By the time we'd reached my suite, my cock was tenting my athletic shorts, obvious in all its glory.

Unable to control myself any longer, I shoved her against the wall next to our large wooden door. She gasped, her blue eyes going wide in surprise. I watched as her pupils dilated, shock morphing quickly into desire.

Crowding her, I pressed my hard on into her belly, letting her see just how much I wanted her, needed her. I leaned in close to her ear, letting my fingers creep under her t-shirt along the silky skin of her taut stomach. I kissed the sensitive skin where her jaw and neck met, sending shivers through her body.

"Better get inside, little Larkspur," I growled. "It's time to play."

Ten

Knox

A loud thump sounded on the wall outside our suite, drawing my attention from the architecture book I was studying. Popping out an earbud, I waited to see if I'd actually heard something or if I'd just been studying too long. This book was fucking dry as hell, and I'd nearly fallen asleep twice already.

Suddenly, our door burst open to reveal a red faced Chase, Everly slung over his shoulder in a fireman's carry. I could see her flushed cheeks as he strode by, and I quickly slammed my book shut, tossing it on the coffee table.

"My room. Now." Chase ground out, and I noticed the large tent in the front of his shorts. Fuck, Everly must have gotten him all worked up on their

70

way back from class. My evening had just gone from dull and boring to hot as hell.

"Griff!" I hollered, not caring in the least if anyone in the neighboring suites heard me.

Griff appeared in his open doorway, rolling backward in his desk chair. His glasses were on top of his head, an open book lay in his lap. He leaned into the hallway just in time to see Chase come marching through with our girl.

"My room. Now." Chase repeated the command to Griff, striding straight to his own bedroom. Griff scrambled from the chair, tossing the book across the room where it landed on his bed. I watched as he quickly shed his t-shirt, leaving him barefoot in just a pair of blue jeans.

Following suit, I nearly tore off my faded black Hinder tee, leaving it on the hardwood floor. As I walked toward Chase's bedroom, I began loosening the drawstring on my sweats when I heard a loud moan.

"Ahh, Chase," my sweet Monet cried out. Apparently they'd started without us.

Guess I'd have to play catch up.

I froze as I reached the doorframe, reveling in the sight before me.

Chase had her on her back, her tanned legs hooked over the crook of each arm, fucking wildly into her. His hips snapped with each thrust, the sound of skin slapping making my dick hard in an instant.

I reached into my sweats, palming my thick length, my fingers running over the metal on the underside. I'd started the piercings shortly after I turned eighteen, adding one or two a year until I had seven total. The extra sensitivity they brought was completely worth the pain and months without sex during the healing process.

I stroked myself as I watched Chase, his back muscles flexing with each deep thrust. He was panting as Everly moved with him, her tits bouncing in tandem with their erotic dance.

Releasing one of her legs, he reached a hand between their bodies, and from the look of pure ecstasy on her face, I knew he was playing with her clit.

She was a fucking vision when she came. Her lips formed a perfect 'O' shape as her eyes rolled back in her head. There were times I enjoyed watching the guys make her come almost as much as I enjoyed being the one to wring an orgasm from her tight little cunt.

"Fuck!" My little Monet finished with a yell, her back arching from the mattress.

Chase followed her, pumping into her a few more times before his hips finally came to rest flush against hers. He dropped her other leg, leaning down to gently kiss her soft lips.

I slowed my hand, my cock still rock hard in my sweats. Remembering Griff, I glanced next to me to see his pants unzipped, his dick in his hand mirroring my own.

"Looks like it's our turn, Knoxy," Griff chuckled. I rolled my eyes at the nickname. Once Everly used it, I knew there was no escaping. Resigned to the fact, I followed him as he made his way to our girl.

Griff strode across the room, his dick bobbing with each step until he was at the foot of the bed. Chase was climbing off, leaving Everly open wide on the mattress below him.

I watched in rapt fascination as his cum slowly leaked out of her swollen pussy. The sight made me impossibly harder, and I knew I needed to get my dick inside her before I came in my pants like a fucking fifteen-year-old.

Griff's deep voice broke through my lust filled thoughts as he told our girl exactly what was about to happen.

"Everly, are you going to be good and use that pretty mouth while Chase gets your ass ready for me? I'm going to fill your tight little hole while Knox fucks that sweet pussy. Are you going to be a good girl for us?"

I watched as she wordlessly nodded in agreement, her pupils blown so wide, the beautiful blue I loved was nearly non-existent. She was leaning back on her elbows, her bare chest rising in rapid movements as she panted. My mouth watered at the sight of her spread out for us, her dusky pink nipples standing in peaks atop her breasts.

I found myself turned on by Griff's dominating presence, and even more so by Everly's willingness to comply. Listening to him issue orders, his voice rough with desire, I realized how much I enjoyed watching my friends fuck my girl. Seeing her experience unbridled passion at their fingertips was a kink I never knew I had.

Chase was back by the bed, having disappeared to my room to get Everly's plug and some lube. He drizzled some of the cool liquid on the metal toy, the blue jewel shimmering in the soft light of his desk lamp.

Griff began removing his pants, and I quickly followed suit, climbing next to Everly on the opposite side. He quickly flipped her, so she was on all fours, her perfect peach ass high in the air.

Realizing I hadn't uttered a single word since they arrived, I leaned in close, kissing and nipping at the skin where her shoulder met the long column of her neck.

"Hi, baby," I said softly, my breath ghosting against her skin. I smirked as I saw goosebumps raise along her arm. "You ready for some fun?"

"Mmmm..." was the only response I got, Chase apparently having fucked away her ability to speak. It was short lived, though, when she let out a sharp yelp as Griff swatted her ass. She hung her head, her entire body quaking at the pleasure the smack brought.

"Knox asked you a question, Everly," he warned, his stern voice echoing through the sexually charged room. He rubbed his hand over the quickly reddening spot on her tanned skin.

"I'm sorry, sir," she panted, her pussy dripping with arousal at Griff's rough touch. She lifted her head to look at me. "Yes, Knox, I'm ready for some fun. Please fuck me."

"Why don't you show Griff and I just how much you want to get fucked, my little Monet? Get this dick nice and wet with that beautiful mouth." I brought my length up to her face, kneeling on the mattress next to Griff. He was stroking himself, watching as Everly parted her lips.

She licked at my head, the feel of her tongue like velvet on my throbbing cock. I shuddered at the sensation, already fucking close to blowing my load, and she'd barely touched me.

Goddamn, this girl would be my undoing.

As Everly took me deeper into her mouth, her cheeks hollowing with each inch, she reached out and began stroking Griff in tandem. After a minute she switched, her delicate fingers encircling my swollen cock as she deep throated Griff.

I knew the moment Chase breached her ass, her body tensing under his touch. I reached my hand to the back of her head, guiding her up and down Griff's dick.

"That's it, Everly, suck on Griff while Chase makes you feel good." She hummed her approval, earning a low groan from deep in Griff's chest.

"Jesus, Blue girl, you suck my dick so good. Why don't you use your tongue to count Knox's piercings before I blow down your throat?" His voice was strained with the effort of holding back.

Everly released his dick with a loud pop, quickly swapping again, so my cock was buried in her throat. I watched it disappear into her mouth, the feel of her tongue running along the metal making my balls draw up.

I looked to where Chase was working the plug in and out of her ass, his fingers plunging into her soaked pussy at the same time. Once he finally had it fully seated, he dropped down behind her, shoving his face in and licking her drenched core. She trembled, her grip on Griff's dick loosening as she climbed closer to her release.

I pulled her off my length, wanting to see the pleasure on her face as she came.

And Jesus fucking Christ, she was perfect.

Like a goddamn goddess, her flawless body shook as Chase sent her careening over the edge with his tongue.

I watched as her blue eyes slowly rolled back in her head, her arms giving out until her chest was flush against the mattress, her ass still in the air, held up by Chase's strong grip.

Griff chuckled beside me, his hand working his dick with slow, measured strokes.

"Oh, sweet girl, you don't think you're done, do you?" He threaded his fingers through her long, dark tresses, pulling her up, so she rested on her forearms. Her breaths came in ragged gasps, her blue eyes glassy as they stared at Griff.

Everly's next words nearly made me come on the spot.

"Will you fuck me now, sir?" she panted, before turning those gemstone orbs to me. "Both of you?"

A growl erupted deep from within my chest, and I nearly threw Chase out of the way as I flipped her over. Griff had already taken a spot on the bed, his upper body leaned back against Chase's tufted headboard.

I picked Everly up and placed her on top of Griff, her back to his front, as I knelt between her spread legs. He reached around, cupping both of her breasts as he pulled her flush to his hard chest. His dick was tucked between their bodies, giving me a clear view of her wet-as-fuck pussy and the blue jewel adorning her ass.

"I'm gonna take this out, so Griff can fill that perfect ass, baby," I said and groaned, gently pulling the plug free. I tossed it to the foot of the bed, my need to be inside her overriding every other thought.

Chase rejoined us, kneeling at her side, a large hand fondling her breast as Griff massaged the other. He was nipping and sucking at her neck, drawing out small gasps and moans as he worked her over.

I saw Chase holding the open bottle of lube, and I reached for it before a depraved, feral thought crossed my mind. Letting the saliva pool in my mouth for a moment, I spit directly onto her tight hole, the liquid glistening as it mixed with her own arousal.

"Fuck," I whispered, staring where I marked her with my spit. She was mine. The animalistic side of my brain was screaming the word.

Mine. Mine. Mine.

"Griff, lift her," I ground out. Placing his hands on her hips, he guided them up, his dick popping free before lowering her back down. Without a second thought, I quickly snatched the bottle of lube from Chase, dumping it all over Griff's shaft. In the next instant, I raised Everly up again, just enough to line his dick up with her ass, seating him just inside.

Everly gasped at the intrusion, the sound quickly turning into a low moan of pleasure as Griff swiftly worked his way inside. I watched his dick fuck into her, the image seared into my brain.

Fisting my own length, I surged forward, filling her in one go. It was a tight fit with Griff in her other hole. He gave a shout as I entered her, my piercings rubbing along his dick through the thin membrane separating us. I palmed the backs of Everly's thighs, holding her open for us.

I was close, and knowing I wouldn't last long, I looked at Griff, seeing the same thing in his eyes. We needed her to come one more time.

As if reading my mind, he ordered Chase through gritted teeth, "Chase, make her come again, rub that perfect little clit until she's begging us to stop."

Goddamn did he know how to turn that dom thing on and off. Motherfucker was gonna make me come if he kept that shit up.

Chase reached down, rubbing two fingers across her swollen nub. She cried out at the contact, her body a writhing mess between us.

I pummeled my body into hers, watching as Griff and I alternated our dicks in and out of her body. I felt every rub of my metal along her walls, each downstroke sliding through her scorching heat.

The tingle at the base of my spine warned me this was going to end far sooner than I'd like, but there was no stopping the effect Everly had on my body. Moving my eyes up her curvy frame, her tits bouncing with each thrust, I watched the moment she imploded.

Her body arched, clamping down around Griff and I so tightly I could barely move. Griff groaned, the hard set of his jaw giving away how close he was to following her.

"That's right, Larkspur, come all over their cocks. Such a good girl," Chase praised as he continued to rub her through her orgasm. Once I could move again, I began thrusting harder, my grip on her thighs tightening to the point I knew she'd have bruises later.

But I didn't give a fuck. This would let the world know she was mine while my cum leaked from her body.

Griff fucked into her from below, our rhythm faltering as we both neared the edge.

A moment later he bottomed out, yelling his release.

"Fuck, Everly! Fuck!"

I quickly followed, thrusting as deeply as I could, wanting to paint her womb with my seed, a deep primal part of my brain urging me to mark her in the most basic way. Hot jets of cum erupted inside her as I brought my forehead to hers. I stared into her eyes as I filled her, neither of us needing words, just simply existing together in the moment.

For a long minute, the only sounds in the room were our heavy breathing, each of us struggling to stay on this plane of existence after that earth-shattering performance.

Once my breathing had slowed some, I gently pulled out, watching as my cum slid from her core. Griff lifted her slowly until he was free from her ass, rolling to his side to make room on the bed. Chase scooped our girl up, laying her in the middle next to Griff.

I flopped down on the mattress beside her, my eyes growing heavy with each passing second. I could make out the sound of running water, and a few minutes later, Chase picked up my sleepy Monet again, this time carrying her off to the bathroom.

I chuckled as I heard him softly say, "Good girls earn bubble baths."

eleven

Everly

"Blue?" Griff said, his nose still stuck in the book he was studying.

"Yeah?" I giggled. He always looked so hot when he was in tutor mode. I gazed at his casual attire as he sat at his desk, his blue and gold flannel pajama pants sitting low on his waist. Thank God he'd thrown on a white t-shirt, otherwise I don't think I would have gotten any studying done at all.

It was Sunday afternoon. Griff and I were trying to get in a little more study time since all day yesterday and last night had been spent celebrating Chase's final regatta win. He'd had a team get together, one final practice to end the season, while Knox had holed himself up in his room to paint. He'd seemed a bit on edge, so I'd left him to work through whatever was on his mind.

Griff and I had been at it for hours, me cramming for my water elementals class while he continued to devour every text he could on dark caster magic and caster history. I was sprawled across his bed in my pink sleep shorts and oversized sweatshirt, my hair piled on top of my head and held in place with a paintbrush.

"I think I found something," he murmured. I sat straight up, hopping off the bed and zipping across the room. I didn't realize I had moved so fast until I was nearly on top of Griff. I bumped into his chair, moving him slightly and startling him from the book.

"Jesus, Blue, how did you do that?" He gawked up at me. He was wearing his reading glasses, something he didn't do very often, but goddamn if they didn't give off a Clark Kent vibe. He took them off, tossing them on his desk before standing. I moved back, giving him some room, his large frame towering over me.

I shrugged at his question. The speed was something I had noticed a few days ago, but I'd brushed it off as just a weird, one time thing. "I don't know. It happened the other day, too, when a gust of wind came through my room and knocked one of my paintings off an easel. I was able to grab it before it hit the floor."

"Where were you when it happened? Like where in your room?" He was staring at me intently, like I was a new chapter he was trying to memorize.

Hesitantly, I answered, "I was standing in my bathroom doorway."

"Holy shit," he whispered, the words barely audible.

"What? Why did you say 'holy shit' like that? What's going on, Griff? Did you find something that would help my dad?" I was beginning to panic a bit since he still hadn't told me what he'd found while reading. I was praying it was the answer to getting us out of this fucking soul-bound contract.

"Sorry, Blue girl. I didn't mean to worry you." His cheeks tinged pink. "No, I haven't found anything for your dad. But I did come across some information that I think may help you, maybe. I—I think Onyx is your familiar."

"My what?" I looked at him dumbfounded. What the hell was he talking about? "Griff, what's a familiar? And why do you think I have one? Oh Jesus, is it something bad? Is it something the Thorpes gave me? Christ, is it like a disease or something?" I was rambling like an idiot, but I needed answers.

"It's nothing bad, Blue girl, calm down." He chuckled, taking my hand and leading me back to his bed where my books and note cards were scattered across the comforter. "Sit." His tone grew stern, and I automatically parked my ass on the mattress. This man could literally ask me for anything with that voice, and I'd say yes.

He knelt in front of me, his large hands on my knees. "I think Onyx is your familiar," he repeated. Before I could question him again, he continued. "There have only ever been about one hundred reported cases in caster history, but basically a familiar is a creature that is connected to a caster on a deep magical level. They can sense when you're near, if you're hurt, or in danger, and they can enhance your caster magic. Some people have even been known to develop new abilities. They're extremely rare."

I tried to process his words, but I was still having a hard time understanding how he'd jumped to this conclusion. I mean, Onyx was just a little black squirrel. Right?

"Griff, how do you know he's my familiar? I mean, he doesn't look any different from any other squirrel." I gestured to where Onyx had taken up residence on Griff's windowsill. He certainly didn't *look* magical, snoozing away in the warm morning rays, the sunlight glistening off his midnight black fur.

"Everly, let me ask you this: does Onyx always seem to be around? He's either in your room, or he finds his way into whoever's room you're staying in. I watched him crawl out of your bag last night when you got here." *So that's how he got in, little sneak.*

I shook my head, standing from the bed, knocking Griff over with how quickly I moved. He landed on his ass with a loud thud that rattled his overflowing bookshelf.

"Fuck, I'm sorry, Griff," I apologized, bending down to help him up. He hoisted himself from the floor, laughing as he adjusted his sleep pants.

"Everly, you have super speed. The same as your brother. Onyx has brought on a new ability. It makes sense that it would be the same as your twin's, if you think about it." His matter of fact tone made it obvious that he completely believed what he was saying.

I was still skeptical.

"Okay, but why would I have a familiar, Griff? There are millions of casters in the world. Why would the universe pick me?" I crossed my arms over my chest, ready to argue any point he made.

His eyes softened as he tugged my arms free, pulling me closer and forcing me to wrap them around his waist. Not that being this close to Griffin was ever a hardship. I laid my cheek on his chest, listening to his heart beat. If I closed my eyes, I could almost imagine that it was beating in rhythm with mine.

"According to the book I was reading," he explained gently, "some historians and magical philosophers believe familiars appear when a caster will experience a significant hardship, like a battle, and will need the added support. A few go on to further hypothesize that the universe sends familiars to certain casters after they experience a great loss." He squeezed me tighter, already anticipating my reaction.

I sucked in a gasp, his words like a sucker punch to my chest.

A battle.

A great loss.

Mom.

My eyes stung as they filled with tears. I buried my face in Griff's chest, blinking them away furiously. I couldn't break down right now, not when something so potentially life changing was happening. I pulled back, shaking away the grief filled thoughts of my mom and focusing on how this could help us find a solution to the Thorpe issue.

"So, what does this mean? Can Onyx help us beat Austin and his dad?" I looked hopefully at Griff, needing to hear some good news for once. He gave me a tight-lipped smile that did nothing to reassure me. Letting out a deep sigh, my shoulders drooped as the air whooshed out.

"I honestly don't know, Blue. I hope so. But only time will tell."

I left him by the foot of the bed and walked across the room to the windows. Onyx was curled up, fast asleep, his fluffy tail curled around his small body like a blanket. I scooped him up, instantly waking him. He chittered at me for a moment before climbing my arm, perching himself on my shoulder. Once settled where he could see the room, he calmed down and began nuzzling into my neck. His soft whiskers tickled the sensitive skin, and I giggled.

"It's like he was made for you," Griff mumbled, slowly approaching me and my furry companion. He tentatively reached out, gently stroking along Onyx's spine with his index finger. He stopped his ticklish torment on my neck, turning to look at Griff. His little head cocked to the side as he studied my boyfriend, his nose twitching with each pass of Griff's finger. Then, just as quickly as he'd stopped, he started to snuggle back into the collar of my sweatshirt, eventually making his way into the hood where he sunk into the fabric.

Griff chuckled to himself as he padded across the room to his bed. He began picking up all my shit, piling it on his nightstand before lying on top of the comforter, his head resting on the pillows.

"Come here, Blue girl," he ordered. "Let's take a break. It would seem your little friend has decided it's nap time." I quickly followed his instructions, crawling gently up the bed until I was seated next to him. He carefully lifted a sleeping Onyx out of my hood and waited until I was comfortable before placing him on the pillow just above my head.

"Thank you," I whispered, not wanting to wake Onyx again. I snuggled into Griff's side as he wrapped his muscular arm around me. I closed my eyes, breathing in Griff's sandalwood scent that always held a hint of old books.

"Anything for you, Everly. Now hush and go to sleep."

I giggled sleepily at his order.

"I love you, Griffin."

"I love you, Everly, so much. Now sleep, my Blue girl."

And as I drifted off, he kissed my hair, and I swore I heard him whisper, "Someday, I'll fill a library with all the ways I love you. But even then, it still wouldn't be enough."

twelve

Griffin

The semester was winding down, but that only meant everyone on campus was busy getting ready for the home stretch before final exams. We still had two weeks to go before Thanksgiving break, and I was swamped. Between tutoring, researching possible solutions for Everly, and my own classes, I was lucky if I found time to sleep each night.

Realizing I was going to be late for my Advanced Magical Philosophies class if I didn't hurry my ass up, I grabbed my bag and snapped my fingers, landing myself in the back corner of Professor Schoepke's classroom. I hurried to my seat with five minutes to spare before class began.

As I made my way down the row of desks, a hand shot out, skinny fingers tipped with red nails wrapping around my wrist. I stopped, looking down to see that it was Morgan, and I sighed, yanking my hand away.

"Hi Griff," she purred. I glared in her direction, not offering a response as I continued on to my seat.

Before I could sit down, however, I noticed a stark white envelope on my desk, my name written across the front in bold, block lettering.

Looking around, confused, I sank into my seat, dropping my bag on the ground. My gut churned with apprehension as I stared at the mysterious envelope. Something about it had me on edge, my own name taking on a menacing look in the black ink.

Checking my watch, I saw I still had a few minutes. I tentatively reached for the thick white package, my fingers tearing along the seam. I pulled out a folded piece of crisp parchment, neat black handwriting filling one side. I unfolded it and began to read.

Griffin,

I'm sure by now, my lovely pet has informed you of her father's agreement with my own. I am very much looking forward to bringing her home, where I can rid her of the bad habits you and your friends have allowed her to develop. I will need to teach her to behave properly. Although, part of me hopes she puts up a fight like she did in the woods.

I will need for you and your friends to end your... relationship, as you call it, with my pet. Immediately. I simply can not have her carousing around campus with you three when we all know she now belongs to me. And trust me, Griff, I know exactly what happens at SLA, even when you think I'm not there.

You and your friends have until Thanksgiving recess to break things off with my pet. If you don't, not only will you lose her (and you will), I will also ensure that you lose your scholarship and your place at the academy. I may even decide to ruin your reputation by releasing the details of your childhood. I'm sure the world would love to know all about your mother's drug habit and her willingness to sell you off.

It would truly be a shame if any future employers heard about your troubled upbringing. I mean, given your past, it wouldn't be far-fetched to believe you might follow in your mother's footsteps.

Or if Knox's project, the one he's spent countless, painstaking hours on, somehow caught fire, ruining his chances of opening an architecture firm.

Or if Chase and his family were found stealing from their company.

And please, before you rush off to tattle to my pet about this letter, remember that she is bound to me, both legally and magically thanks to her father. I would hate for anything to happen to him or her brother... or even my dear pet herself. My father is a well connected man, and tragic accidents happen all the time. Car accidents. Fires. Muggings after work.

My preparations for her arrival are almost complete, so I will need you to make sure you follow through on my instructions quickly. I don't care how it's done, Griffin, but you will end whatever it is you have with her.

I'll be seeing her soon.

Austin

My hands shook as I read the letter again, each threat nearly jumping off the page. I didn't even care so much about the ones made against me. But he'd threatened my family, the ones I held closest.

Fuck! I threw the letter on my desk, unable to think clearly. How was I going to fix this? I couldn't let Austin hurt Everly or the guys. Even as pissed as I was at her dad and brother, I wouldn't let Austin near them either.

Panic gripped me, my breaths coming in shorter and shorter bursts until it felt like I wasn't breathing at all. My chest was tight, as if an elephant were sitting on me. My vision tunneled until all I could see was that fucking letter, mocking me from the desktop. The racing of my heartbeat thundered in my ears, drowning out the beginning of Professor Schoepke's lecture.

Fuck, I was having a panic attack in the middle of class. As quickly as I could, I shoved the letter and envelope into my bag, standing swiftly from my seat and moving toward the door.

"Mr. Cardarette, class isn't over." I stopped just short of the doorframe, taking in as deep of a breath as possible before turning to face my professor.

"Sorry, Professor. I'm not feeling well." The look on my face must have been believable because he shooed me away.

"If you're feeling better, I need you to stop by to see me during office hours later today to discuss a new tutoring student," he called after me as I exited the room.

"Sure thing, Professor," I threw over my shoulder, hauling ass into the hall before he could reply, the door closing loudly behind me.

I leaned against the wall, focusing on my breathing.

In.

Hold.

Out.

In.

Hold.

Out.

I repeated the process for several long minutes until I could feel my heart rate begin to slow, my breathing evening out. I pulled the letter out of my bag, reading over it once more. I think I was hoping maybe I'd had a stroke or an aneurysm, that maybe I'd hallucinated Austin's threatening words. But there they were, screaming at me from the sterile, white paper.

I needed to get out of here, before anyone saw me looking like a goddamn lunatic. Tucking the letter away in my pocket, I shouldered my bag and snapped my fingers, teleporting back to my suite.

I landed in my room, exactly where I'd been standing before I left for class only ten minutes earlier. God, had it really only been ten minutes? It might as well have been a lifetime with the anxiety roiling in my gut.

Tossing my bag on my bed, I pulled the letter from my pocket and set it on my desk. I narrowed my eyes at it, as if it would spontaneously attack me from its place on the hardwood top. I thought over its sinister contents, the dark words playing on repeat in my mind.

I'll be seeing her soon.

That fucking asshole.

I didn't know what to do. If I told Everly and the guys, it would only make them worry. The last thing I wanted was to upset my Blue girl even more than she already was. No, I would keep the letter to myself and hope to God I could find a way to keep her safe.

I lingered in my room for about an hour, attempting to study but failing miserably. My thoughts were scattered, jumping from one idea to the next of how we could break that stupid fucking contract. Deciding enough time had passed that no one would know I'd been in my room instead of class, I peeked out my door to see if the coast was clear.

I stepped out, padding silently to the kitchen. I could see Everly's head bobbing up and down to a beat I couldn't hear, her earbuds tucked into her ears. Grabbing a beer from the fridge, I popped the top before quietly creeping up behind her, glancing down at the sketchbook in her lap.

My breath caught in my lungs when I saw it was a portrait of me. The golds and greens she'd used for my eyes had them nearly jumping off the page, and a relaxed smile was spread across my face. It was almost jarring to see, the drawing such a stark contrast to how I was currently feeling. In my shock, the bottle slid from my hand, crashing loudly to the floor, beer spraying everywhere.

Everly screamed, spinning around, her sketchbook flying from her lap as she took a defensive position. Her actions gave me a sense of pride as I watched her crouch, her fists raised, ready for an attack, remembering everything I'd taught her during our self defense lessons.

I barked out a laugh despite the fact my feet were covered in IPA, and there was a huge puddle forming on the floor.

"Relax, Blue girl, it's just me. Sorry, I didn't mean to scare you." I raised my hands, showing her I was unarmed, and I chuckled when it registered on her face that I wasn't a threat.

"Christ, Griff, you about gave me a heart attack!" she yelled playfully, retrieving her sketchbook and colored pencils from the floor. A few had rolled under the sofa, and I watched as she bent to find them, her round ass sticking up in the air.

"You gonna clean up the beer you spilled? Or help me find my pencils? Anything useful?" she teased, wiggling her ass at me.

"I'm enjoying the view from here, thanks," I said and laughed, moving to grab a roll of paper towels to mop up my mess. I made quick work of soaking up the IPA, disposing of the empty bottle in the trash, before moving around the sofa to help Everly collect the rest of her pencils.

"Oh, now he helps," she sassed, sticking her tongue out at me.

"Somebody's feeling bratty this afternoon," I said, deepening my voice to draw her attention. Her blue eyes darkened with lust as they raked over my body. I pounced without warning, grabbing her around the waist, tugging her down to the sofa, so she was below me.

Her toned legs instinctively spread to accommodate my frame, and I loomed over her, taking in each freckle that decorated her perfect face. She was so beautiful.

I couldn't let her go, no matter what Austin threatened.

But I had to find a way to keep her safe.

Something on my face must have belied my thoughts because she scrunched her eyebrows together, giving me a serious look.

"What's going on in the big old brain of yours, Griffin Cardarette?" She stroked a hand down my stubbly cheek, her fingers teasing lightly over my skin. Her blue eyes softened as she stared into my own, and I watched as my entire future flashed in them.

I could see her, chasing around a little boy with hazel eyes while she held tightly to our daughter, a beautiful baby girl with blonde curls and her mother's eyes. My Blue's belly swollen with another miracle ready to pop. A house we would share together with Chase and Knox. It was all there in her sapphire eyes, everything I never knew I wanted but now realized I couldn't live without.

I rolled us so she was lying on my chest, my arms wrapped securely around her tiny frame. I planted a kiss to the top of her head as she snuggled into my body; I loved the way she fit so perfectly against me.

We lay like that for a long time, wrapped around one another, until I felt her breathing deepen, telling me she'd fallen asleep. I stroked my fingers along the bare skin of her arm, the tank top she was wearing leaving her tanned skin exposed. Chase was constantly trying to put his sweatshirts on her when she was here, but Knox and I knew she preferred to paint and draw in tanks, saying she could move more freely that way.

I closed my eyes, knowing I needed to get up soon to meet Professor Schoepke for his office hours. From what he'd said, he planned to add another student to my tutoring roster, most likely someone from our Philosophy class.

I gently pulled my phone from my pocket, shooting off a quick email to my professor that I'd be on my way soon, but I would probably be a bit late. I just needed a little more time with my Blue, where I could pretend the world wasn't crashing down around me, where I wasn't keeping Austin's threats against my family a secret.

I just needed a little more time.

thirteen

Everly

Walking across campus to the library, I admired the rich autumn colors spread out among the trees. Tugging Chase's rowing hoodie around myself, I took in the deep reds, burnt oranges, and rich yellows that hung from the branches, the leaves that had fallen covering the ground like a blanket. The temperatures had finally gotten the memo that autumn had arrived, and the chilly air had me shivering. Probably should have grabbed a heavier coat, but it was too late now.

Solis Lake truly was a beautiful place in the fall. I'd snuck away a few nights back, telling the guys I was headed to the studio to work, when I'd really gone to the pier to watch the sunset down by the lake. It wasn't *really* a lie; I'd taken a sketchpad and some colored charcoal sticks with me, capturing the last of the sun's rays over the water, the stunning autumn colors creating the perfect backdrop. I just needed a minute to breathe, a minute to myself to simply revel in the beauty around me and not the horror show my life had become in recent weeks.

I listened to two girls walking just ahead of me, their conversation about the academy's upcoming Fall Festival catching my interest. Chase and the rowing team were hosting some carnival games, so he insisted we go. He said it would be an opportunity to finally have a little fun and forget about our worries for one night. Knox immediately disagreed, saying we needed to lie low until we could sort out a plan to free my dad and I from Alaric Thorpe's twisted plan. Griff's opinion had fallen in the middle; one night to cut loose while we continued searching for a solution.

"It's so fun," the brunette in front of me said, her high ponytail swishing from side to side. I was pretty certain she was in my Magical Defense class, but I couldn't remember her name. Her companion, a girl with a short black bob, answered.

"The flyer said they're going to have the dunk tank again this year. Hopefully they get some cute guys for it."

The brunette leaned in as if sharing a secret. "I overheard Morgan say Griffin Cardarette was signed up. He's definitely a hottie. Him and his two roommates." My attention was instantly piqued at the mention of my guys.

"You know she's trying to get him back since he dumped her for that new girl."

"I heard she's dating all three of them. But Morgan said she and Griff are just on a break, so I'm not sure." My blood boiled at Morgan's outright lies. She had some fucking nerve going around telling people she and Griff were 'on a break'. I'd give her a break; I'd break her fucking face. I fucking knew she was just toying with my brother.

And what was this about Griff signing up for the dunk tank? He hadn't mentioned shit to me, but apparently fucking Morgan knew? Anger seared through me, and before I could stop myself, I barreled between the two girls, nearly knocking the brunette off the sidewalk.

"What the fuck!" she yelled at my back.

"Hey, wasn't that—" I barely heard her friend's words as I marched down the path toward the beautiful brick building that housed the campus library. I didn't stop to apologize for my rude behavior. I knew I was acting crazy, but the rage I was feeling had my feet carrying me away before better judgment could win out.

I stomped up the wide stone steps, leaves crunching under my Converse. I hauled the heavy wooden door open, heat blasting me in the face from the vents in the entryway. Once inside, I made a beeline for the stairs that led to the third-floor study rooms.

Griff and I were planning to meet at four to go over our lab notes for Potions. I was a bit early, but I was hoping he'd already be in his favorite study room so we could talk about the bullshit I'd just heard.

Marching through the stacks, I made a sharp turn down the hall that led to the study rooms. Griff's favorite was the last on the right, tucked into a corner with two windows that overlooked the courtyard. He'd explained that having the natural light and ability to open the windows for fresh air always helped his tutoring clients stay focused.

The door was slightly ajar, and I could hear muffled voices coming from inside. I slowed my pace, checking my watch. I knew Griff had a tutoring session from three to three-thirty, and I didn't want to interrupt if they were still working, but as I drew closer, I was able to recognize a voice that had my blood pressure shooting through the roof.

"Griff, come on, you promised." God. Fucking. Damnit.

"Yeah, Morgan, that was when we were still dating. And you signed me up without telling me, remember?" he answered her with an exasperated sigh. I stopped just outside, leaning against the wall and angling my head toward the opening.

"Griff, come on," she purred at him. I balled my hands into fists, imagining smashing her in the face as I listened. "It's all for a good cause. And besides, you'll look so good in the water if someone manages to dunk you this year." I peeked through the crack in the door, blood rushing in my ears as I watched her stroke a finger down Griff's bicep, his muscles straining the sleeves of his black henley.

"Morgan, don't do this," he said gently. Too fucking gently for my taste. "You know I'm with Everly now. *You're* the one who fucked around on *me*, remember? You can't just decide you want me back now that I'm moving on." Why was he being so nice to her? This was a very different Griff from the one who was murderous when he'd found out the part she'd played the night of the ball.

"I told you before, Caleb was a mistake. I want to make things right with us. You can't tell me you don't want me anymore, Griff." I should have stopped her there, should have burst into the room and told her to remove her slutty, cheating fingers from my boyfriend. But something held me back. I needed to see how Griff would handle this, and I prayed he'd make the right decision.

Still peeking through the opening of the door, I watched as Morgan cupped Griff's jaw, his eyes closing. My heart was in my throat. I knew Griff was a kind soul, never wanting to hurt anyone, but I had at least expected him to move from her touch. A bracelet of purple crystals adorning her wrist glinted in the afternoon sun, the stones almost appearing to glow as she spoke.

I couldn't focus on it, though, my eyes still glued to the hand she had on Griff. Why hadn't he pushed her away already?

"Morgan," he finally spoke, his eyes opening as he looked up at her from his spot at the table. She was standing at his side, her leg pressed against his thigh. "Even if I did want to get back together—and that's not what I'm saying— but even if I did, I'm with Everly. I love her." The breath whooshed out of my lungs at his admission, and I clasped a hand over my mouth to muffle the noise. He had rejected her advance, but the hint of hesitation in his voice had alarm bells ringing in my head.

"Look," he continued, *finally* moving out of her grasp to stand, "you should probably go. Everly doesn't know that I've been tutoring you, and she'll be upset if she shows up and you're still here."

What. The. Actual. Fuck.

Tears welled in my eyes at Griff's betrayal. He'd been tutoring her?

"You didn't tell her?" I could hear the fucking smirk in her voice, the self-righteous tone making her think he secretly wanted her back. But did he? He'd been lying about tutoring her for who knows how long? He'd never once mentioned it to me. Wasn't that the type of shit we should be telling each other? Being honest with each other about?

His duplicity broke my heart, especially as I thought about Morgan's lies and the way she'd sent me to the Thorpes the night of the ball. He'd been ready to teleport her ass to the moon for sending me into the lion's den like that. So, what changed?

My mind skidded to a stop. Did he decide I wasn't worth the trouble? He'd been up late each night, pouring over any text he could find, searching for any information on how to break the contract. Had it just become too much? Had *I* become too much?

My spiraling thoughts were interrupted as Morgan packed up her books, Griff finally answering her question.

"You know I didn't, Morgan. She'd be fucking pissed. Plus, I'd never hear the end of it from Chase and Knox. I'm only doing this because Professor Schoepke asked me to, and tutoring is a requirement of my scholarship. Please don't read more into it."

Hearing that calmed my racing heart, but only a fraction. He was still lying to me about seeing her. My trust in him was splintering with each passing second. Realizing I didn't want to get caught eavesdropping, I quickly stepped into an open study room, quietly slipping into the dark space. I listened to them step out into the hall as I hid in the darkness.

"I'll keep your secret." I watched from the shadows as she quickly stepped into him. Lifting on her tiptoes, she planted a quick kiss to his lips before dropping back down. "See you later, Griff."

His cheeks turned a shade of pink that I usually loved; the same shade as when he was ordering me around in the bedroom. But now that pink just reminded me of his deception. Bile rose in my throat, and I swallowed roughly to keep from vomiting all over my sneakers.

Morgan sauntered down the hall, Griff watching until she disappeared through the door to the stairwell. He blew out a deep breath, running a hand over his short brown hair before he checked his watch. Mimicking his actions, I looked at my own wrist. 3:58. Nearly time for our study session.

Griff scrubbed his hands down his face, a frustrated sigh leaving his lips. He turned, walking back toward the room he'd been tutoring Morgan in for God only knows how long.

Should I confront him? Call him out on his lies and bullshit? Tell him I knew he was meeting up with his cheating ex?

I thought about it briefly. Storming into the room, laying out everything I'd heard. Would he confess? Come clean about his lies? Honestly, how could I trust anything that came out of his mouth now? Deciding I'd give him one last chance to tell me the truth, I wiped the tears from my eyes and made my way to him.

Taking a deep breath, I pushed the door open, a fake as hell smile plastered on my face.

He looked up from his textbook as I entered.

"Hey Blue girl!" He stood, meeting me at the door. He leaned in to give me a kiss, but I turned my head at the last second, giving him my cheek instead. I just couldn't stomach the idea of touching his lips with mine. Not after *her*.

"Hey back," I responded, setting my bag on the table. I started rummaging through it, pulling out my Potions book and notes. My heart was thundering in my chest as I tried to remain calm. "So, how was your session?" I quickly glanced up to gauge his reaction.

"Oh, it was fine," he answered, his eyes darting between me and his open notebook. He swallowed, his Adam's apple bobbing in his throat. Wanting to press him, I questioned him further.

"Who was your student?"

He froze, his body going rigid. It was only a split second, and if I hadn't seen him with Morgan earlier, I may not have even noticed. His shoulders relaxed as the next lie fell from his lips.

"Oh, umm, just some guy that needed help with Magical Philosophies. Pretty easy." He opened his Potions text to the next project we had due, as if he hadn't just obliterated the last remaining shred of trust between the two of us.

"Just some guy. Right," I murmured as I sat down. I stared at my notes, the letters swimming together on the page. Griff, my chivalrous, kind, sweet

Griff, just lied straight to my face. My chest ached as my heart broke with his words.

I needed to get out of here.

Snapping my notebook shut, I shoved it in my bag, startling Griff.

"What are you doing? You okay?" A frown wrinkled his forehead as his eyebrows scrunched together. "I thought we were going to study?" He reached for me, but I moved out of his grasp.

"I can't. I—" The air caught in my lungs. I couldn't do this with him. I couldn't listen to him feed me more lies and try to rationalize why he was with her. I couldn't.

So, I lied instead.

"I don't feel well. Sorry, my head just started to hurt. Raincheck?" Slinging my bag over my shoulder, I moved quickly toward the door, not even waiting for an answer. Crossing the threshold, I glanced back.

Confusion clouded his handsome face, and I could see the concern in his hazel eyes. I hesitated for a second before the hurt from his deception came roaring back. He began to climb out of his seat to follow, already tossing his materials in his backpack.

"You stay," I said, turning back toward the hall slowly. "Maybe you can squeeze in another tutoring session with your student from earlier. I'm sure *she'd* love the extra time."

I heard the sudden intake of air as he processed my words, but I couldn't bear to look at him for another moment. I quickly exited the room, wondering when exactly everything had gotten so fucked up.

fourteen

Everly

Racing through the library, I tugged my backpack up on my shoulder, trying to escape the large brick building without drawing attention to myself. The stacks of books blurred as I rushed by. I'd made it to the main doors, shoving through them and hauling ass down the stone steps I just climbed not too long ago.

Wiping the tears from my eyes, I found myself falling as I suddenly collided with someone, my body bouncing backward. I watched as my books spilled from my backpack all over the sidewalk, my limbs tangled with the tall girl who'd landed on top of me. A bright swath of pink hair fell into my face as I tried to get my bearings.

"Oh my God!" the girl squeaked out, her voice light and airy, reminding me of how a fairy might sound. "I'm sooo sorry! I was checking my phone and didn't see you! Are you okay?" We separated ourselves, each of us standing and brushing off our clothes. I looked up at her, the bright pink hair catching my attention once more.

She was pretty, like a punk pixie princess, her pink hair long on the left side of her head while shaved close to her scalp on the right. Her dark blue eyes were lined in black, and her ears were adorned in a multitude of piercings. Her Ramones sweatshirt was cut along the neck, making it hang off her shoulder, and I could see the lines of a tattoo peeking out on the top of her shoulder. Black, acid washed jeans and a pair of Docs completed her ensemble.

"Yeah, no, I'm okay," I assured her, kneeling down to retrieve all my stuff that was now decorating the sidewalk. I started throwing items in my bag, trying to stem the embarrassment I was feeling at having nearly been taken out while fleeing from my lying boyfriend.

I picked up the last book, my Potions text—what I should be studying right now with Griff, not running from the lies he fed me—and tears sprung to my eyes. I dropped the book, unable to stop them from running down my cheeks.

"Hey," the girl said softly from behind me, her hand lightly gripping my shoulder. I felt my cheeks flame, completely embarrassed at how badly I was losing it in front of this complete stranger.

"Sorry," I apologized. "I'm fine, really." I shoved the last book in my bag, although it took a few tries as it kept hitting all of my other shit.

"Goddamn it, just fucking go in!" I shouted at the book, finally getting the stupid thing into my bag.

"That's what she said," I heard the punk girl giggle beside me, and God help me, it was the funniest thing I'd heard all day. I sat back on my ass, a laugh bubbling up from my chest. The next thing I knew, I was laughing hysterically, my stupid bag and my stupid book nearly forgotten. Nearly. Then, the memories of why all my stuff had ended up all over the sidewalk came rushing back, and I abruptly stopped laughing.

"So, what'd that book ever do to you?" Punk Girl asked. "I mean, I took Potions last year, I didn't think it was that bad." I turned so I could see her better. She gave me a warm smile, her eyes crinkling at the corners. There was something about her that just seemed... nice. Friendly. And God, did I need a friend right now.

"It's not the class," I explained, wiping at my eyes once more. "It's my partner. Who also happens to be my boyfriend. Or well, I don't really know what he is now. I just found out he's been lying to me."

"Shit," Punk Girl whispered, "that sucks. I'm really sorry." We both stood again, facing each other this time. She extended her hand toward me. "I'm Stella. Stella Bancroft."

I shook her hand, pushing my hair from my face. "I'm Everly."

"Well, Everly, how about I buy you a cup of coffee? Penance for nearly taking you out?" Stella gave me a wide grin, and I couldn't help but smile back.

"That sounds great."

Half an hour later, I found myself sitting across from Stella in the student lounge inside of Vox, laughing as she cast a tiny glowing rabbit that hopped across the floor before disappearing in a puff of blue smoke. She smiled, pulling the small flute from her lips. I sipped my caramel macchiato as I giggled.

"So, you're a Bard? That's pretty fucking cool," I said, swallowing down the warm coffee. "I've only ever read about you guys."

"Yeah, there aren't too many of us. It is pretty fucking cool, though." Tucking the instrument into her bag, she finished off the last of her chai latte, setting the empty cup on the table. Wanting to show off my own powers a little bit, I snapped my fingers, the cup lifting off the table and gliding through the air to the garbage can across the room. I plopped it inside, grinning at my new friend.

"You're a telekinetic? See, now that's cool. If I want to move shit, I have to cast something with my flute. I wish I could snap my fingers and move shit around." Stella crossed one long leg over her knee. She had to be at least five-foot-ten, towering over my measly five-foot-two frame. She had a lithe figure, willowy, with long slender arms and legs. I partly wondered if a strong gust of wind would blow her over.

"Yeah, it's okay." I nodded at her nonchalantly. Ever since we'd come to the conclusion that Onyx was my familiar, I had noticed that my telekinesis had grown stronger. I was able to move larger objects over greater distances with ease. I'd never been a weak telekinetic, but I also had never been able to levitate myself across the suite until just the other day. Moving smaller, inanimate objects had been more my speed. Anything larger than a suitcase was usually more difficult and drained me much faster.

Not anymore.

Onyx had been sitting with me and Chase, and I was complaining about the chips being *all* the way in the kitchen—fifteen feet is a long way when you're hungry from a marathon sex session—when Chase suggested I just float myself over there.

"Come on, Larkspur, I bet you can do it," he coaxed, trailing a finger along my bare thigh. He was lounging on my sofa in nothing but his gray sweats, my legs dangling over his lap. Onyx was perched on the back of one of the armchairs, his fluffy tail curled around his jet black body as he napped peacefully.

"Chase, I can't. It's too far. I'm lucky if I can levitate myself two inches off the ground," I whined, desperately wanting the barbecue chips I knew were sitting in the cupboard. I felt goosebumps raise on my skin where Chase's fingers were teasing me. "You better stop that," I warned. "I don't think I have another round in me."

He chuckled darkly. "A bet then. If you can move yourself to the kitchen using only your telekinesis, I get to take you back to bed. If you can't, then you're free for the rest of the night. Deal?"

"Fine." I laughed. "But, you're gonna be awfully lonely when I only move a few inches off the couch." I stood up, pushing the loose hair from my face. Closing my eyes, I concentrated on lifting my body off the ground. A moment later, I could feel the cool air of my suite brush the bottoms of my feet, telling me I had indeed levitated. Focusing deeper, I imagined myself moving across the room.

I heard Chase gasp, breaking my concentration, my feet landing on cold tile. My eyes sprung open to reveal I was in the middle of my kitchen. I spun around, completely shocked that I'd been able to levitate myself so far. Chase was grinning at me from the sofa.

"Better get those chips, Larkspur," he said smugly. "You're gonna need the energy for what I have planned."

"So," Stella broached cautiously, "what had you hauling out of the library like your ass was on fire? You mentioned something about a lying boyfriend?"

I swallowed roughly, memories of Griff's betrayal running through my mind yet again. I looked at Stella's friendly eyes and found a kinship in them that I'd only ever had with Celeste. I smiled at her sadly.

"Yeah, I just found out he lied to me about something pretty big." I took another sip of my drink, sadness sitting in my chest like a lead balloon.

"What did he lie about?" she asked before quickly adding, "Shit, sorry! I mean, you don't have to tell me. In fact, you can tell me to fuck off. I just thought maybe you'd want someone to talk to about it. But seriously, just tell me to fuck off, and I'll leave." Stella rambled the words, grabbing her bag from the floor next to her overstuffed chair.

The student lounge was filled with an eclectic mix of furniture; from modern chairs with hairpin legs to large tufted armchairs. Shelves with books about the history of the academy filled the walls along with student art. I'd spotted a piece by Knox as soon as we'd walked in, a beautiful sunset over Solis Lake done in his trademark acrylics.

Flicking my fingers, I pulled Stella's bag from her hands, gently placing it back on the floor. "It's okay," I told her, chuckling at her frantic energy. She was a lively one, her blue eyes sparking with energy. "Actually, it would be nice to talk to someone besides my boyfriends for once. My best friend lives back home, so I don't get to see her much."

She gawked at me for a moment before speaking again. "I'm sorry, did you just say *boyfriends*? As in plural, more than one?"

"Uh, yeah," I answered, now feeling mildly uncomfortable. Maybe confiding in her wasn't such a gre—.

"Can I be you when I grow up?" The serious look on her face had me laughing. She giggled along with me for a minute before I finally answered.

"I don't know if you'd want to be me, my life is pretty fucked up at the moment."

"Well, as your newly appointed best friend at SLA, I want to hear all about it." She tucked the long part of her bright pink hair behind her ear, settling back into the chair expectantly.

"Where do I begin?" I sighed. So much had happened in the last four months, I didn't even know where to start.

"I find the beginning is usually the best place," she said with a smile.

And that was how I made my first real friend at Solis Lake.

fifteen

Knox

Throwing on a paint stained hoodie, I made my way into the living room. We were supposed to pick Everly up in a little while for this fucking carnival, and to say I was less than thrilled was an understatement.

It wasn't that I didn't want to spend time with Everly. I did. I just wanted to spend time with her in the safety of our suite, where I didn't need to worry about that fucker Thorpe making a surprise appearance. No one had seen him since the night of the ball, slithering away like the fucking snake he was. I couldn't wait to get my hands on the bastard. The bruise he'd left on Everly's arm lasted a week before finally fading away. I planned to leave bruises all over his body. Preferably with a baseball bat.

Chase was bouncing around the living room like a damn puppy while Griff read yet another caster text, most likely about dark magic. He'd been killing himself, pouring over any and every book he could find, hoping for a solution to the fucking contract Mr. Blackwell signed, forfeiting Everly's life in the process. I knew things weren't good between Griff and my little Monet. They'd barely spoken the last two days, Everly making excuses about why she couldn't be at the suite when he was around.

There was a sadness in her beautiful blue eyes that I was 99% sure Griff was responsible for. I loved my best friend, but the fact our girl was hurting because of him made me want to beat the shit out of him. He'd been tight lipped about what happened, pissing me off even more. My patience was wearing thin with the whole situation. Griff needed to figure his shit out. Fast.

I scanned over my two best friends. Griff was wearing his trademark outfit: an SLA hoodie and jeans. I was somewhat convinced that he single handedly kept the bookstore in business with all the SLA apparel he owned. Chase was clad in an SLA rowing shirt, his last name emblazoned across his broad shoulders along with navy blue joggers that I was sure were strictly for Everly's benefit. Looking down at my own gray sweats, I grinned.

"About time!" Chase bounded over, attempting to wrap me in a bear hug that I easily side stepped. "Get back here!" he shouted, twisting around. He wrapped his arms around my waist before hoisting my ass into the air. *Goddamn caster strength.*

"Chase, put me the fuck down!" I thrashed wildly, trying in vain to escape his grasp. My body shook as the vibrations from his laughter rumbled through his chest and into my back. He had my arms pinned at my sides, most likely for his own safety. Motherfucker was going to have a broken nose if he didn't let me go soon.

As if reading my thoughts, he released me a moment later, chuckling as I dropped to the floor. Spinning quickly, I launched a punch straight to his gut, a loud "Oooph" coming from his mouth as he doubled over, my fist making contact with his hard abdominal muscles. He recovered quickly, tackling me to the floor in a lightning fast move. We rolled around, throwing playful punches into each other's sides until my shoulder bumped Griff's shoe.

"You two about done?" he huffed as he stood, tossing the book he'd been reading on the coffee table. A sour look crossed his face, his annoyance with our antics obvious. Well, too fucking bad. It wasn't our fault he'd fucked up with Everly and was suffering the consequences.

"What crawled up your ass?" If he wanted to be an asshole, I could be one right back.

"Nothing, let's just go," he mumbled, moving toward the door. Just as his hand hit the knob he paused. "On second thought, why don't you guys go pick up Everly? I'll meet you at the carnival." He started to open the door, his back still to us.

Before I could respond, Chase answered. "Man, you need to work this out with her. I don't know what happened, since you won't fucking talk to us, but fucking fix it. Fix. It. I'm tired of seeing you mope around, and I'm really fucking tired of seeing her sad all the time. So, fucking. Fix. It."

Griff hung his head, shoulders slumped forward in defeat. "I know, man. I'm trying, but I don't know if she'll forgive me." Before we could question him more, he slipped out the door.

Everly looked fucking edible in her painted on black skinny jeans, holes ripped across the thighs. My favorite was the one right below her left ass cheek, giving just a tiny peek of tanned flesh every time she walked. It was slightly warmer tonight, so she'd matched it with a gray cropped hoodie and a pair of red Converse, her hair pulled back from her face in twin french braids. She was always beautiful, but she looked exceptionally gorgeous when her hair was up, giving a clear view of her perfect face.

As much as I'd bitched about going to this fucking carnival, the carefree smile spread across Everly's plump lips was completely worth the stress I'd felt all day leading up to our arrival. We'd left Chase at the duck pond game, he and one of his rowing teammates manning it for the first hour the carnival was open.

My little Monet and I wandered for a while, until she spotted a game booth with large stuffed unicorns for prizes. She turned, giving me her best puppy-dog eyes.

"Pleeease Knox?" she'd begged, pulling on my arm. I couldn't tell this girl no, of course.

But I could make her work for it.

"What do I get out of it, little Monet?" I gave her a wolfish grin. The carnival lights shone all around us, giving everything a soft, almost otherworldly glow. The Fall Festival committee had taken over the grassy area between the main buildings on campus, setting up small booths with games and carnival food. They'd even hired a local band to play, their music drifting through the quad.

The aroma of fried dough and candied apples permeated the air, while the sounds of laughter rang through the open space. I'd already purchased Everly and I both spiced hot apple ciders, and she was currently eating handfuls of popcorn from a red and white striped box.

Everly smiled at me, her blue eyes dancing mischievously in the glimmering lights. "What do you want, Knoxy?" She bit her bottom lip in that sexy way I loved, sending all the blood rushing straight to my dick.

I stroked my chin, weighing my options as I stared at her. My God, she was beautiful. It drove me crazy just how deeply I loved her. It made me damn near feral to think of anyone hurting her. I'd burn the whole damn campus—the whole damn world—to the ground to keep her safe.

Some days, when I thought about the Thorpes and their fucked up plan to take Everly, I became so enraged I could barely contain it. I'd broken more than one canvas when the anger had boiled over. Seeing her now, smiling, looking around at all the students milling about, it was hard to believe we were in such deep shit with everything else.

"If I win you a prize, we go find one of your other boyfriends and sneak off to my studio for a little while. How's that sound?" My eyes trailed down her body, taking in every delectable inch.

"I mean, that sounds like a win-win for me, so yeah," she agreed, looking away before adding quietly, "but can it be Chase?" I could see the flash of hurt on her face, her non-mention of Griff hanging heavily in the air between us.

"Yeah, baby, whatever you want." I cupped her face with my hands, stroking her cheeks with my thumbs. "You gonna tell me what's going on with you two?" It was the first time I'd point blank asked her about it, and I was hoping she'd give me a straight answer.

Shaking her head, her blue eyes glistened as tears welled in them. Not wanting to ruin her evening, I decided to let the issue lie. I could ask her about it again later, once we were home and I had her naked, wrapped in my arms.

"Okay, baby," I whispered, leaning in to kiss her forehead. "Come on, let's win you a big ass unicorn." I laced our fingers together, pulling her toward the game booth, one of those games where you had to knock over the milk bottles using a softball.

Piece of cake.

I paid the kid running the booth—some underclassman who was on Chase's rowing team—and grabbed two of the three softballs he set on the counter. Wanting to make Everly sweat a little, I lobbed the first ball, missing the milk bottles completely.

"Oops," I said, fighting the grin that was threatening the corners of my lips. I glanced quickly at her, worry creasing her forehead. "Let's see if the second one is better."

I aimed for the top milk bottle, hitting it dead on and sending it careening to the floor. Everly let out a cheer, and I laughed as she attempted to clap with the popcorn box still in her hands.

Keeping up the ruse, I pretended to give myself a pep talk. "Okay, last one, better make it count." Glancing over at my girl, I met her eye and threw her a wink before launching the ball straight into the two remaining bottles. They crashed off the pedestal, landing loudly on the ground below.

"Knox!" Everly whooped, the popcorn box flying from her hands as she threw her arms around my neck. I caught her, spinning us around as she laughed at my victory. I gently placed her back on her feet, giving her a quick peck on the lips.

She surprised me when her tiny hand connected with my chest, the swat light and playful.

"You totally played me!" she accused, still laughing.

"I don't know what you're talking about," I replied, running my hand through my dark hair nonchalantly. "It was just a lucky throw, that's all."

Smirking, I winked at her before accepting the obnoxiously pink unicorn from the booth attendant.

"My lady, your prize." I bowed dramatically, holding out the stuffed animal in offering. I wasn't typically the type for public displays of affection and goofiness, but for my girl, I'd do anything. Even if it involved a glittery pink unicorn.

She laughed again, accepting the prize and hugging it tightly to her chest. "Thank you, good sir."

Grabbing her hand, I tugged her into my side. Shooting a glance at my watch, I steered us off in the direction of Chase's game booth.

"Chase's shift should be just about over," I leaned down, whispering in her ear. "And since I won you that ridiculous unicorn, you've got your end of our deal to hold up." She looked up at me with fire in her eyes, the blue shimmering in the carnival lights hanging overhead.

"Well, far be it from me to not fulfill my part of the bargain," she replied, a sassy grin on her face. "Lead the way."

With my arm wrapped firmly around her shoulders, I guided us through the dense crowd. As we walked, I continuously scanned the area, looking for any signs that Austin may be nearby. I was always on edge that he'd suddenly turn up on campus and hurt my girl, but I tried to keep my worries to myself. I knew Everly was stressed enough, no need to add more to her plate.

I could hear Chase's loud laughter before we'd even reached the duck pond game. As we rounded the corner, I saw him handing out a blow up hammer to one of his teachers, Professor Moore, I think was her name. She laughed along with him, taking the hammer before walking to the next game.

"Chase!" Everly called out, getting his attention. As if she were a lighthouse in the dark, he immediately found her in the crowd. I could tell by the look on his face that she was the only one he could see. I knew, because it was the same way I looked at her.

"Larkspur!" He quickly jumped over the wooden frame holding the booth together, bounding over to us in a few quick strides. He scooped her out of my grasp, the unicorn nearly hitting the ground as he swung her around. I was able to grab it at the last second, snagging it by the tail before it landed in the dirt.

"Damn it, Chase, I worked hard for that!" I bitched at him, only half serious.

Everly laughed, still wrapped up in Chase's big arms. "Oh yeah, so hard," she teased. She turned to look at Chase. "Knox made a bet with me, but he totally played me! Made me think he couldn't knock over the milk bottles in one of the games."

Chase sat her down, pushing a few stray hairs from her face. "Well, it looks like you got a prize, so it seems to have worked out in your favor." He gestured to the plush animal in my hand, and I realized how ridiculous I must look holding on to it. I quickly tossed it at Everly, bopping her in the chest.

"Oh, it definitely worked out in *all* our favor," I replied, my voice growing deep as I thought about our bet. "I told our girl that if I won her a prize she had to sneak off with us for a little alone time over at my studio. You in?"

A wolfish smile spread across Chase's face, his gaze roaming over Everly's body. "Little Larkspur, that doesn't sound like much of a bet."

She shrugged, a smirk pulling at her lips.

Stepping up beside her, I swatted her ass, making her let out a surprised yelp.

"Best get moving, little Monet; it's time to pay up."

sixteen Everly

I looked at Knox and Chase, greedily taking in the sight before me. It really wasn't fair that they both looked like goddamn Greek gods, all muscled bodies and chiseled features. I could already feel the dampness between my legs, and a wicked thought crossed my mind.

"Knoxy, do we have to go to the studio?" I purred, leaning into his chest.

"I mean, we don't have to. Do you just wanna go back to our place instead?" I could tell he thought I was rethinking our plan. But that wasn't the case... I was just considering a change of venue.

"No," I said softly, walking slowly backward away from them both toward the lake. "I was just thinking... It's a beautiful night. It'd be a shame to spend it indoors, that's all." I grinned as I watched the wheels in their heads spin. "Besides, the lake is beautiful this time of night."

I saw the moment it clicked in Chase's brain. His eyes lit up with a mischievous glint, and he stalked toward me. Before I could utter another word, he tossed me over his shoulder, walking swiftly from the crowded area, my prize dangling from my hand. It would seem this was his preferred way of getting me from point A to point B these days.

"Knoxy! Let's go! Our girl wants to see the lake!" Chase called out over his shoulder. I heard footsteps rapidly approach from my place against Chase's back, and I laughed as Knox's sneakers came into view. When he was close enough, I lobbed the unicorn at him, laughing when I saw him dive for it.

They both looked sexy as hell tonight, each in a pair of sweats that left nothing to the imagination. I could be mad, knowing other girls on campus were getting treated to the same view, but I knew my guys only had eyes for me. Well, at least I was sure that was true for two of the three. Thoughts of Griff and Morgan filtered through my head, their exchange in the library quickly filling my mind. I slammed my eyes shut at the images.

Nope.

I would not let them ruin tonight.

I swatted Chase's ass in an attempt to shake off my sour mood, his answering gasp making me giggle.

"Madam! Manners!" His playful scolding was followed by a swift crack to my jean-covered ass, and I cried out.

Before I knew it, the noise of the carnival had faded and was replaced with the soft sound of waves lapping at the sandy shore. I could hear crickets in the distance, their nighttime symphony adding to the serenity of our location.

I was startled from the tranquility when strong hands gripped my waist, flipping me rightside up. The blood rushed in my head, making me dizzy for a moment, and I swayed on my feet. Another set of hands steadied my shoulders, and I suddenly found myself trapped like a rabbit between two wolves.

Stars twinkled overhead, a full moon peeking between the clouds that littered the night sky, casting enough light for me to make out the hungry look on Knox's face. He gripped my hips, his long fingers digging into the denim. He pulled me closer, the bulge in his sweats pressing into my belly.

Chase stepped closer, and I could feel his hardness against my back. I shivered when he brushed his lips against my neck, goosebumps raising all over my body. Knox leaned in on the other side, and they both began teasing my sensitive skin, nipping and licking the flesh until I was panting.

I felt Knox's right hand slide under the bottom of my cropped sweatshirt, his deft fingers trailing along my abdomen, then higher and higher until he reached my breasts. He squeezed one, then the other, before pushing down the cups of my bra, releasing them completely.

Chase had worked his way up to my ear, biting the lobe with enough force that I gasped.

"Mmm, does my Larkspur like a bit of pain with her pleasure?" he whispered. I drew in a ragged breath, unable to form words. I couldn't, not with their hands roaming every inch of my body.

Chase's arms snaked around my middle, his fingers quickly finding the button of my black jeans. He expertly popped it open before lowering the zipper, the sound of the metal teeth coming apart barely audible over my heavy breaths.

His hand descended into the denim at a painstakingly slow pace, but I grinned when he stopped and groaned.

"Seriously, Everly? Again?" Chase's growl vibrated against my back. Knox was still kissing along my neck and jaw but paused when he heard Chase speak. He raised his head to look at me, his brow cocked in an unspoken question.

"Again, what?" Knox asked, his brown eyes nearly black in the dark.

"Tell him Larkspur. Tell him what you did. Or rather, didn't do," Chase murmured, his fingers resuming their descent toward my core. He brushed them over my clit, and I inhaled sharply. He whispered in my ear again, his voice nearly inaudible.

"You'd better tell him Everly. Or I'll stop." I felt his index finger tap the bundle of nerves in warning, and I whimpered, not breaking eye contact with Knox.

"I may have forgotten panties when I got dressed earlier," I explained, shrugging my shoulder in a barely there attempt at indifference.

Heat flashed in Knox's eyes, and he groaned loudly before grabbing my face with both hands and crashing his lips into mine. His kiss was all consuming; like it was me he needed to survive, not air, food, or water. Just me and this moment. He quickly parted my lips with his tongue, swirling it against mine in a wicked dance.

Chase went back to kissing my neck while his fingers played in my slickness. I pushed my hips back against him, an unspoken plea that I needed more. Understanding, he slid one finger into my core, then two, my arousal making for an easy entry. Using the pad of his thumb, he began rubbing circles against my clit, causing my body to tremble between them.

Grinding his hard cock into my back, Chase continued to work me over, sending me closer and closer to my release. Knox's mouth moved against mine while his hands alternated between massaging my breasts and pinching my sensitive nipples.

As if they had timed it, Knox gave one final tug just as Chase thrust inside me, adding a third finger and sending me careening over the edge into an orgasm. I cried out, Knox swallowing down my shout as pleasure shot through my body. My legs turned to jelly, and I sagged in their arms as I came down from the high of my release.

Knox planted a soft kiss to my lips as he pulled away. Chase slowly withdrew his hand from my jeans, and I glanced over my shoulder just in time to see him pop his fingers into his mouth. He closed his eyes, sucking my arousal from them, and I flushed at the deep moan that rumbled from his chest. I licked my lips hungrily, my eyes swinging between the two of them.

"Your turn," I purred, dropping to my knees in the soft sand, bringing me level with their dicks. Without hesitation, I quickly tugged down Chase's, then Knox's sweats just low enough that their impressive lengths bobbed in front of my face. My mouth watered at the sight.

I reached up, taking each one in hand and began stroking them in sync, the action earning me two sexy groans of pleasure that had me smirking in the dark. I leaned forward, ready to take Chase in my mouth first when I heard my brother's shout from behind me.

"Jesus fucking Christ, Everly!" Anger and disgust filled his tone. Knox and Chase tucked themselves away in the blink of an eye, and I straightened my bra before spinning quickly to stand. "Are you really out here in the open, fucking around with two guys? Christ, have some goddamn self-respect!"

He marched over, until he was only a few feet away, his long arms crossed over his chest. The scowl on his face told me just how angry he was at finding me here.

But, you know what?

Fuck him.

"Oh fuck off, Evan," I yelled back. "I'm out here with Chase and Knox! It's not like I'm out here hooking up with two random guys! They're my boyfriends!"

"Do you even hear how ridiculous that sounds?!" he roared at me. "You're fucking three different guys!" He threw his arms in the air, gesturing wildly with each word. My heart broke as I thought about how rapidly things between my twin and I had deteriorated. I looked at Evan, wondering when we'd gone from best friends, literally one half of the other, to this screaming, angry mess that I didn't even recognize.

I could feel Chase and Knox at my back, their tension palpable in the cool night air. Hell, I could feel Knox vibrating with anger from his place behind me.

Then, as if this situation couldn't get any worse, I spotted Morgan a few feet behind my brother. She gave me an evil smirk as she strode over, stopping at his side. She gripped his arm, and the same purple bracelet she'd been wearing that day in the library caught the moonlight, momentarily drawing my attention. He quickly placed his arm around her shoulders, and I caught sight of a similar bracelet on his wrist.

"Evan, you can't beat yourself up over your sister's bad decisions," she purred at him, that sickening saccharine smile she used plastered across her face. This bitch had a lot of nerve saying my decisions were bad. "If she wants to get around and give herself a bad reputation, that's on her."

"You bitch!" I shouted. "You're the one who has slept with half the campus!" Rage flooded me, the words pouring out like hot lava. "Have you told my brother about your library rendezvous? Hmm? How you've been trying to weasel your way back into Griff's life and bed?"

I could hear Chase behind me, asking what I was talking about, but I was too fired up to respond. A flash of panic crossed Morgan's face before she leaned into my brother.

"Everly, I don't know what you're talking about. The tutoring center assigned Griff to help me with my Magical Philosophies class. I can't help that they paired us together." The lies rolled off her tongue so easily, my brother eating them up as he looked at her adoringly. I nearly screamed in frustration.

"Evan, what the hell is wrong with you!? Can't you see she's using you?" Desperation for my twin to see the truth had the words coming out on a sob.

His lip curled in disgust before he spoke again.

"Mom would be so disappointed in you."

I inhaled sharply, stumbling backward, his words piercing my heart like a dagger. Chase caught me, wrapping me in his strong arms, as though he could shield me from my brother's cruelty.

"Evan, that's enou—" he began, but was cut off when Knox marched silently toward Evan. Before anyone could utter another word, he landed a solid punch to my brother's face, the crunch of bone breaking loud in the quiet that surrounded us. I gasped as blood immediately began to flow down Evan's face, and he wasted no time launching himself forward, the two landing on the moonlit sand.

They wrestled, trading punches back and forth, sand flying everywhere until Knox finally got the upperhand. He pinned Evan down, straddling his thin waist before raining fist after fist down on my brother.

I screamed at him, Chase still holding me tightly to his chest.

"Knox stop! Stop it! You're going to hurt him! Knox!!"

Finally breaking free from Chase, I ran over to where they'd landed, grabbing hold of Knox's arm before he struck again. My brother's face was a bloody mess, one of his eyes already swelling shut. Knox tried to shake me off, but I held fast. As pissed as I was with Evan, I couldn't let Knox beat the fuck out of him.

"Fucking let go, Everly," he growled.

He turned to look at me, his eyes full of rage, and for the first time since we'd met, I was actually afraid of Knox. His temper was something I'd never worried about, but seeing the unhinged look on his face, I could admit I was scared.

"Knox, please," I begged. "He's my brother. You're going to kill him if you don't stop."

He stood quickly, knocking me backward onto the sand. I landed hard, the air whooshing from my lungs in a loud gasp at the impact. Chase rushed over, helping me stand while yelling at Knox.

"What the fuck man! You could have hurt her! What the fuck is wrong with you?!" I held onto his arm, partially to steady myself, but mostly to keep him from tearing Knox apart.

"What the fuck is wrong with me?" he snarled at Chase. He was pacing like a caged animal along the beach, his hands gripping the long hair on top of his head. He'd been planning to cut it right before Thanksgiving break, so his mom wouldn't complain when he came home, the chocolate strands beginning to curl from the length.

"I'm sick of feeling like every time she's with me, something bad happens! I'm tired of feeling like I can't protect her!" he shouted the words, each one like a shard of glass cutting my skin. "And now, the one time I CAN protect her, she wants me to stop! Make up your fucking mind, Everly!"

I drew in a ragged sob. This wasn't my Knox. Before I could even think to respond, Chase answered, his voice low and menacing.

"Knox, man, I don't know what's going on with you, but you better back the fuck off and get out of here before I fucking do something we're all gonna regret, you feel me?"

He stopped pacing, turning to look at me. I could see the moment he realized just how badly he'd fucked up, regret and remorse flashing in his eyes.

But I was too hurt to care.

He stared at me for a moment longer before he shifted, the claws of his snow leopard shredding his clothes as it sprang forward. He turned, glancing once more over his shoulder, our eyes locking, before he took off into the darkness.

Once Knox was out of sight, I tried to pull free from Chase's grip, but he held me tightly.

"Morgan, take Evan home," he instructed gruffly, glaring at her, his own anger bubbling just under the surface. "You fucking tell any anyone what happened here, and I will fucking end you. Understand?"

"Sure Chase, whatever you say," she answered with a scowl on her face. I spun in Chase's arms, looking up at him.

"I need to make sure Evan's okay." I looked at him with pleading eyes, begging him to let me go. His jewel toned eyes stared into mine for a moment before he released me.

I ran to where Morgan had my brother leaning against her. His face was littered with cuts and bruises, his once straight nose crooked and swelling more with each passing second. As I got closer, he held up a hand, halting my approach.

"Back off Everly, haven't you done enough?" He licked his bottom lip, wincing when he met the spot where Knox's fist busted it open. His arm was around Morgan's shoulder again as he leaned against her.

They turned, heading back toward the path that led to the main campus, my brother shuffling slowly away. My chest ached and my body was trembling, adrenaline still coursing through my veins from the fight. I still couldn't believe Knox had said the things he did, and my heart hurt when I replayed them in my mind.

Just as the tears began to fall, Morgan glanced over her shoulder, a positively gleeful smile on her face.

"Oh, Everly," she called out, "Austin says hi."

seventeen

Chase

I dragged my feet into the Potions lab, dreading the next hour where I'd be stuck having to watch Griff's attempts at working with Everly. Things were tense between them, and I had to assume it was because of Morgan after what Everly said at the beach nearly a week ago.

She'd been noticeably absent from our suite, and the only times I'd really been able to see her had been at the dining hall, in the few classes we shared, or at her place. Even then, she was quieter than normal. I'd initially thought it was because of the bullshit with her dad and brother, but after Griff had blown us off at the festival, I knew something else was going on.

Everly and Knox were on the outs as well after his blow up the night of the festival. What had started out as such a great evening ended miserably as

I'd held my Larkspur through the night, her soft sobs like little knives in my heart. It felt like our perfect little foursome was falling apart at the seams.

Coming back to the present, I caught Heather staring at me, her tits nearly falling out of her low-cut shirt. The girl really couldn't take a hint, parading herself in front of me like a goddamn show pony at every opportunity. I had told her, repeatedly and with lots of small words so her brain could understand, that things were over between us, that I was happy with Everly. Yet this fucking girl just would not let it go.

I knew my Larkspur was pissed. We'd had our first big fight two days prior, when I canceled our plans, so I could meet Heather at the library to study for our upcoming lab. I couldn't trust her to not overcook the ingredients again like she had with the last assignment. Luckily, I'd been able to sweet talk Professor Moore into giving me some extra Blueglow Moss and Cardamom, so I was able to salvage the healing elixir that Heather had so royally fucked up. But it cost me a night with Everly, and I wasn't sure she was over it.

"I'm sorry, little Larkspur," I apologized again, but the hurt on her face told me it was a lost cause.

"Yes, Chase, I heard you the first time," she snapped, rolling her eyes. She crossed her arms over her chest, pushing her breasts up. I had to make a conscious effort not to stare, knowing that would only escalate our argument if she caught me gawking at her chest. I moved in front of her, rubbing my hands along the smooth skin of her upper arms.

"Baby, you know I'd rather spend the evening with you. I promise I'll make it up to you. I just can't risk her fucking up another assignment." I was trying to reason with her, but I wasn't making much headway.

Everly had been angry when I'd let it slip that Heather had cornered me in the stairwell before class the other day, trying to charm me back into her bed. Not that it was going to work. Everly was my everything. She was livid though, threatening to storm Heather's dorm room and use her telekinesis to toss her ass into the middle of the lake. Eventually she went back to her room, alone, to paint, leaving me feeling guilty as fuck.

Trying to focus on my notes, I kept throwing glances over my shoulder, checking to see if she was looking my way. Between our fight and the fact that we still didn't know how to save Everly's dad, I'd never seen my Larkspur so wound up. It had been nearly three weeks since all the bullshit that went down at my dad's gala, and we were still no closer to finding a solution. And we were running out of time.

The only saving grace was that Austin had mysteriously disappeared from campus. I'd heard from some of the guys on the row team that he'd left for 'personal reasons'. Fucking coward.

"Chase," Heather whined next to me. I rubbed my temples, her nasally voice like an ice pick to my brain.

"What, Heather?" I answered her through gritted teeth, mentally counting down the days until this semester was over. We were closing in on Thanksgiving break, fourteen blissful days where I would be free of Heather's bullshit. I had talked with the guys, and we planned to surprise Everly with a trip to my family's cabin a few hours away before coming back to spend the holiday with my parents at our home outside of Emporia. She hadn't talked with her dad since the ball, and I knew for a fact she wasn't speaking to Evan, so we knew the time away would do her good.

"Can we meet tonight? I'm still having trouble understanding the right mixture for the sleeping potion." She batted her lashes, her attempt at sexy nearly comical. I rolled my eyes and heaved out a sigh.

"No, Heather, for the umpteenth fucking time. I have plans tonight. I already canceled on Everly, so I could save our asses from the last lab that you fucked up. I can't cancel again. If Potions is so hard for you, get a fucking tutor."

She leaned in close before I could step back, placing her hand on my bicep, her breasts brushing my chest. Panic at her brazen actions lanced through me, and I shot a look in Everly's direction only to see her glaring at Heather's hand. A half second later Heather's stool shot out, sending her straight onto the tile floor. She shrieked as she landed with a hard thud, her ridiculously short skirt flipping up to expose an obscenely bright pink thong. I quickly averted my eyes, not wanting to see any part of her body.

Several students around us gasped as Morgan came rushing over from her table to help Heather. The she-bitch shot Everly a death glare before a sinister grin crept onto her face.

"What's the matter, *Emberly*? Scared you're not enough for Chase? He never was a one woman man."

Fucking bitch.

"Morgan, shut your—" I tried to cut her off, but she continued.

"Or maybe Griff would be interested in reliving some old memories. I'm sure I could convince your brother to share."

I knew her cutting words hit their mark as I watched Everly's face fall, grief filling her beautiful blue eyes.

"Get the fuck out of here, Morgan," I growled, taking a menacing step in her direction. "No one wants to hear any of your bullshit."

Heather's backpack flew off the table, landing on the floor, the items inside scattering at her feet.

That's my girl. I covered my mouth, trying to cover the small smile that tugged at my lips.

Looking behind me, I could see Griff trying to hold Everly, but she was pushing him off, clearly not wanting him to touch her. His tortured hazel eyes met mine, and I could see his pain, the utter devastation he was feeling at the rejection.

"And take Heather with you. You two fucking deserve each other," I snarled at the girls as they scurried back to Morgan's spot, finally leaving me alone. I shot a quick look to the front of the room, making sure Professor Moore was still busy going over lab reports with a couple of students, before I quickly made my way to Griff and Everly.

"Larkspur, I'm sorry—" I started to apologize but the words died on my tongue as Everly began packing up her belongings. I looked at Griff in confusion, his face mirroring my own.

"Blue, what are you doing, baby? Class isn't over." He reached out a gentle hand, attempting to stop her movements. She tugged her arm away, and continued throwing her textbooks into her bag at an alarming rate.

"I'm done. I can't be here. I can't watch Heather try to fuck Chase in the middle of class. And I can't watch Morgan take all of your attention while she brags about stealing my brother from me. It's bad enough you've been seeing her behind my back. I'm done." The words tumbled from her mouth, each one slicing me open, soaked in her anger.

"Everly, please," I pleaded with her. I knew she'd been upset about Heather, but the things she'd said about Griff surprised the fuck out of me. I looked at my best friend, his face twisted in pain. I reached out, attempting to pull her toward me, but she jerked away, her face contorted in anger.

"Just stop, Chase!"

I stepped back, the sharp sting of her words like a slap to my face. She may as well have hit me with how deeply her words cut. I watched her, taking in the way her dark hair laid in contrast to the bright blue of her shirt. Her jeans hugged her ass in a way that had my dick twitching in my joggers, and I had to mentally tell him to stand down.

Now was definitely *not* the time.

I lowered my hand, watching her zip up the gray SLA rowing sweatshirt I'd given her when the weather turned cold. I loved how she swam in the oversized fabric, and knowing she was wearing something of mine gave me a sense of pride. At that moment, however, all I felt was shame.

Everly slung her backpack over her shoulder, her eyes finally landing on me and Griff. I'd spent so many hours lost in those beautiful blue orbs, her body wrapped tightly around mine as she told me she loved me. All that filled them now, however, was hurt and pain. Guilt tore through me like a rip tide, shredding my heart even further as I saw the tears threatening to spill down her perfect face.

"Larkspur." Her name came out broken, my heart shattering as I tried to process what was happening. "Everly, please, little Larkspur," I pleaded one last time. I took a risk, taking a step closer and placing my hands on her waist. Her body tensed at my touch, the action like a bullet straight to my heart. She didn't even want me to touch her. I quickly pulled my hands away, not wanting to upset her further.

She didn't want me.

Everly skirted around the lab table and quickly made her way to the door, disappearing into the hall. I stared after her in shock, wondering what the hell had just happened. I looked to Griff, only to see the same expression on his face. He sat his ass down heavily on his stool, running a hand over his short brown hair.

Feeling defeated, I silently shuffled back to my seat. My chest felt hollow, like a piece of my soul was missing. I zoned out for the rest of class, my notebook remaining closed on the tabletop.

Did she really think I was still interested in Heather? I thought I had made it clear; Everly was it for me. Shit, I was already considering how I was going to keep her in my life after graduation. Knox and Griff, too. Pricing apartments in Emporia that would accommodate the four of us. I was all in. Did she not see that?

Sadness began to give way to anger. I was willing to give my Larkspur *everything*. I shared her with my best fucking friends, and she couldn't accept my word as proof that I only wanted her? What more did she fucking want from me?

My thoughts continued to spiral until a sharp pain shot through my hand. *Fuck*! Looking down, I realized I'd snapped a pencil in two, one of the jagged ends stabbing into my palm.

"Goddamn it," I mumbled, pulling the piece of pencil from my skin. Blood began running down my forearm as I applied pressure to the wound. A hand on my shoulder had me spinning quickly on my barstool, my patience nearly at zero for anyone touching me. I was met with a concerned looking Griff who stared down at my bloodied hand. He quickly grabbed a roll of paper towels from a nearby supply shelf, ripping off several sheets and pressing them to my palm.

"What the fuck, Chase?" Griff whispered as he attempted to stem the blood flow. I looked at him in a haze, my thoughts muddled as the anger dissipated from my body. Had I really just been so angry with Everly that I stabbed myself with a goddamn broken pencil? What the fuck was wrong with me? I loved Everly. This wasn't her fault.

A wave of anger and rage washed over me, the need to hurt someone flooding my veins. I spun in my seat to see Morgan's gaze fixed on me.

Fucking bitch.

I stood quickly, yanking my hand from Griff's grip. I stalked toward Morgan, ready to shove my pencil in her fucking eye. I half heard Griff behind me as he attempted to defuse the situation.

Fuck. That.

"You fucking bitch," I hissed as I reached her table. "Don't you ever fucking push at me, you goddamn psycho! Is that what you've been doing? Fucking with everybody's emotions? That how you're keeping Evan around?" My voice continued to rise until I was nearly shouting at her in the middle of the classroom.

"Mr. Stone!"

Professor Moore's voice cut through my rage fueled thoughts, her words like a bucket of ice water dumped over me. I hung my head before turning toward her, guilt and shame sitting heavy in my stomach.

"Mr. Stone," she repeated. "That is quite enough. You are excused from the rest of class. I expect that you will be in better control of yourself when we reconvene later this week, yes?" I could tell by the pissed off look on her face that it wasn't a request. I nodded, giving her a half-hearted, "Yes, ma'am," as I quickly grabbed my belongings off my desk, shoving everything into my bag as best I could with my uninjured hand.

Griff's fingers gripped my forearm, my eyes meeting his.

"Your hand, man. Let's get it taken care of before you go." He spoke softly, pulling me to a table at the back of the room.

"Mr. Stone...." Professor Moore's tone held a warning that if I didn't move my ass I'd be in even deeper shit.

"Just one second, Professor. Chase just needs to get his hand healed." He turned to her, flashing her his biggest boy next door smile. "Thirty seconds, I promise."

"Thirty seconds, Mr. Carderette." Her tone gave no room for argument. Griff hauled me to a table tucked into the corner where a nerdy looking boy sat, his eyes going wide as we invaded his space.

"Preston, right? Preston Lawrence?" Griff sidled up to the lanky guy. He pushed his glasses up his nose in typical geek fashion as I took in his buttoned up appearance. A collared shirt poked out the top of his oversized SLA sweatshirt while pressed khakis covered his skinny legs. His auburn hair was sticking up every which way, as if he'd just woken up and rolled out of bed right before class. I ran my gaze over him while he answered.

"Yeah, I'm Preston." His voice quaked, and I was growing more impatient by the second.

"Griff, what—" I started to ask my friend, but he cut me off.

"Preston, you're a healer, right? I remember you saying that was your caster power during our Intro to Casters class freshman year." Fucking Griff and his photographic memory. "Can you help my buddy out? He cut his hand pretty badly."

Preston pushed at his glasses once again, and I had the overwhelming urge to rip them off his face. I didn't feel Morgan pushing at me anymore, so this was my own assholishness taking over. I balled my uninjured hand into a fist, so I didn't act on the impulse. He studied me for a moment before standing, his brown eyes making me feel incredibly vulnerable. Even stretched to his full height, he didn't come close to Griff or me, the top of his head barely making it to my shoulder. I took a deep breath, reminding myself that he was doing me a favor.

"I'd really appreciate it, man." I held out my hand for him to see. Luckily the bleeding had slowed some, but the wound was still open, and it was beginning to hurt like hell.

He took my outstretched hand in his own, turning it palm up, his own hands trembling slightly.

"You okay, dude? Can you do this?" Jesus, what if he melded my bones together or some shit. Fuck. That's all I needed on top of Everly fucking rejecting me and Morgan screwing with my emotions. I was just getting ready to pull my hand away when his quiet voice broke through.

"Yeah, yeah, I can help you. Sorry. I just never thought I'd be asked to help Chase Stone." He looked at me with adoration, fucking hearts in his eyes. Jesus Christ, could I just catch a break today? What the fuck? Before I could respond, Griff spoke again.

"Thanks Preston, I know Chase really appreciates it, don't you Chase?" Griff elbowed me in the ribs, shooting me a look before nodding his head toward Preston. "In fact, you should join us for dinner later. How does that sound?" He tipped his head toward Preston again, clearly waiting for me to follow along.

"Uh, yeah, sure. Meet us at the dining hall later. Six sound okay?" I looked at Griff in confusion. All I wanted was to get my hand fixed, grab my stuff, and sort out all the bullshit that had happened between me and Everly. Why was Griff trying to set me up on a dinner date with Preston fucking Lawrence?

Preston's face broke out in a huge grin. "Okay! Six is great!" He took my hand in his more firmly, inspecting the damage I'd done. As he prodded my wound, I thought over Everly's words. Fuck. I knew things hadn't been great between us, but her visceral reaction to my touch had fear growing in the back of my mind. A warmth filled my hand, and a soft blue light pulsed from Preston's fingertips, but I barely even registered it as the gash in my hand knitted itself back together with his power. One singular thought kept running through my mind.

I couldn't lose her.

eighteen Everly

I slowly made my way up the five flights of stairs until I reached the end of the hall near the Potions lab run by Professor Moore. I pushed open the door next to the lab, giving me access to yet another damn flight of stairs that led to the rooftop greenhouse where I'd find the ingredients Griff and I needed for our sleeping potion. Once I was at the top, I stepped out into the chilly, night air.

I'd texted Griff a brief message saying I'd get our supplies from the green-house, still not ready to be around him. Was it stupid and dangerous for me to be out alone? Yes, and I knew the guys would be pissed when they found out. But honestly, I didn't give a shit. Did that make me a bitch? Probably, but I needed some time away from them and all the drama that seemed to find us.

Things had been incredibly tense since Knox's explosion at the carnival, and Griff still hadn't confessed to his meetings with Morgan. I felt like I was slowly losing all of my guys. I didn't even know where the fuck Chase was right now. I hadn't seen him since I'd run out of Potions earlier that day.

Glancing down at my list, I double checked the items once again. *Lavender, jasmine, marigold, and peppermint.* We would be boiling the ingredients together before letting them simmer and mix for at least a week. It was a tricky potion; not mixing it long enough would yield a weak potion, while simmering too long would turn the ingredients bitter and unusable. Luckily it was Friday, so I had the weekend to get it right.

As I approached the greenhouse, I couldn't help but admire its beautiful structure. Standing at least sixty feet long, it spanned a good portion of the rooftop with its rectangular shape. Large paneled glass windows made up the walls while slanted panes sat on the roof, ready to absorb the sun's warm rays during the daytime.

I could feel the warmth of the building as I walked closer, soft lights guiding my way to the door. I pulled it open, stepping into the lush greenery that filled the space. The air was thick with humidity, and sweat immediately beaded on my hairline. With all the moisture in the air, I'd be a big, frizzy mess by the time I got out of here, and I internally groaned at the thought.

Shelves made up u-shaped bays with more plants than I'd ever seen in my life. Each bay had a sign at the end, listing all the plants in that specific area. Looking around, I noted there were at least ten bays per side, with a long planter type table running down the main walkway. A wide variety of plants were stacked high, making it nearly impossible to see from one bay into the next. Vines wrapped around the metal irrigation pipes that hung from the ceiling, a plethora of brightly colored flowers growing between the leaves.

The large ventilation system outside hummed loudly. I imagined it would be difficult to hear if we ever came up here for class. Continuing on with my shopping list, I snagged a small basket near the door to carry my items before moving further into the greenery. I stopped every so often to sniff the different florals, some smelling better than others. Deep in one of the first few bays, I found a section of larkspur flowers, and a sad smile spread on my face.

My mind took me back to the picnic in the woods with Chase earlier in the semester, our first official date, the first time we'd slept together. Looking back, I think I knew then that I loved him. He'd been so sweet, putting so much thought into that outing, from the location to the food. Even the care he'd taken when using his earth magic to hide us from any prying eyes was tender and thoughtful.

A pang of guilt hit me at the way I'd been treating Chase lately. I knew it wasn't his fault that Heather was still after him, just like it wasn't his fault she was his lab partner. I knew I needed to rein in my jealousy over the time he spent with her, but goddamn, I couldn't help the resentment I felt each time he left to meet with her. Seeing them work together during class was enough to make me daydream about using my telekinesis to 'accidentally' fling her out a window.

Images flooded my mind of them together, their bodies tangled up in passion. I felt sick to my stomach at the thought. Trying to shove it out of my mind, I pushed on through the greenhouse, approaching the last few bays. I had gathered nearly all my ingredients, peppermint being the last one I needed.

As I read the sign at the opening of the second to last bay, I heard what sounded like a soft moan. Standing up straight, I strained to hear over the loud ventilation. Suddenly the system kicked off, leaving a deafening silence in its wake. In the next moment, I heard a voice I instantly recognized.

"Oooh, yes, Heather. Fuck baby, just like that..." His deep voice echoed through the humidity, crushing my heart as it bounced off the dew covered windows.

No. He wouldn't.

"Fuck, that's so good. Goddamn, that mouth. Best I've ever had."

There was a loud pop, the sound of a wet release before her nasally voice entered the quiet of the greenhouse.

"Better than hers?"

No.

"Fuck yes, baby, so much better. Get back on there and let me fuck that pretty little mouth." I heard her gag in the next moment, the sound telling me he was indeed fucking her face.

My heart thundered against my ribs, strong enough that I thought it may beat straight out of my chest. It may as well be on the floor at this point, mangled into a bloody heap from Chase's betrayal. The room swam around me in a blur of green, my knees nearly giving out. I braced a hand against a wooden shelf, the leaves of the damn peppermint plant I was looking for brushing my skin.

I leaned forward, peering between the stems and vines, hoping I wasn't about to see one of the men I loved with another woman. But there he stood, facing me, gray sweatpants pulled down around his thighs, Heather on her knees before him.

His fingers gripped her brunette hair tightly as he thrust roughly into her mouth. I could hear her sloppy sucking as she took him deep in her throat, her hands gripping his toned legs. I stood frozen, unable to move, unable to fucking breath, yet unable to look away.

All the nights he said he was going to work on their projects for class.

Every time he told me it was over between them.

That she didn't matter.

That he loved me.

A sharp pain bored into my chest, like a knife straight to my heart. Tears blurred my vision, but I couldn't look away. It was like watching my entire world collapse on itself in slow motion. With each deep thrust, Chase fractured another piece of my soul until I was sure there was nothing left but dust.

His motions became erratic, and I knew from experience that meant he was close. He plunged in one final time, nearly choking her as he came, his head thrown back between his shoulders.

"Fuuuuck." His loud groan filled the space, pulling me out of my stupor. I dropped the basket I'd been holding, my hands trembling from the riot of emotions running through my body. The sound didn't go unnoticed.

Chase lifted his head, his emerald green eyes finding mine in an instant. He stared at me, his face a mask of indifference. Not a hint of remorse or regret. Heather stood, wiping his cum from her lips and brushing her hair from her face. She hadn't noticed me lurking behind the plants, privy to their illicit greenhouse rendezvous. My brain wondered how many times they'd met here. Or did they have another spot where they could meet up to fuck and fuck me over?

A quiet sob broke free from my chest as I tried to suck in a breath, my body going into shock at Chase's deception. He continued to stare at me as Heather doted on him, kissing his neck and whispering into his ear. He hadn't even bothered to pull up his pants, his fucking dick still hanging out and half hard. He gripped her ass with both hands, giving it a firm squeeze before kissing her, his green eyes never leaving mine.

I could barely hear Heather's moans of pleasure as my boyfriend fucked her mouth with his tongue, the blood rushing through my body, roaring in my ears.

I have to get out of here. I need to get out of here.

A panic swept through me, my mind racing with the need to escape the nightmare I was witnessing. I stumbled backward, crashing into the shelves behind me before running from the bay and down the main walkway. It felt like I was running through tar, unable to move fast enough away from the devastating scene I'd just witnessed.

I slammed through the greenhouse door, flinging it open with such force that it bounced back, nearly hitting me. But I didn't stop. I needed to keep moving, to get as far away from Chase and Heather as possible.

My brain was a mess of anger and sadness, while my heart lay shredded in pieces, the wreckage tossed around like one of Chase's row boats during a hurricane. My feet barely touched the steps as I rushed down the dark stairwell, moonlight casting shadows on the concrete walls. I had just entered the main hall when I finally stopped to catch my breath.

Silence surrounded me, but my heart was beating so loudly that anyone in the room would have been able to hear it. I sucked in air as I leaned back against the wall. I was dizzy from running so hard, and the cold wood panel helped to cool my overheated body. My head was still spinning, my brain trying to rationalize the events in the greenhouse, but there was no explaining away what I saw.

Chase.

My Chase.

With Heather.

A shudder wracked through my body as the tears broke free, streaming down my face in rivulets. I honestly thought he loved me, with his sweet words and gentle touches. But it had all been a lie. A way to get into my pants, another name to add to his long list of conquests. I should have known he wouldn't change.

Every interaction I'd witnessed between the two of them ran through my brain like a film reel. Each time her fingers traced down his strong arms, her nasally giggle when he'd say something funny. How he would continuously look in my direction with what I thought was guilt over her flirtations. I knew the truth now, though.

It wasn't guilt at all. He just didn't want to get caught.

I pulled my phone from my pocket, hitting Celeste's number. I needed my best friend. The line rang twice before her voice filled my ear.

"Eves! What's u—"

I cut her off before she could get another word out, a sob tearing out of my throat through the line.

"C," I cried. I clutched the phone to my ear.

"Babe, what's wrong? What's going on?" I could hear the panic in her voice and the sound of her moving, but I couldn't get the words out. I couldn't bring myself to say it out loud. *"Everly Margaret, answer me, damn it! You're scaring me!"*

"C, he—he cheated—cheated on me." I finally stammered out the words.

"Who cheated on you? Not one of your guys? No way," Celeste questioned, disbelief evident in her tone. Shit, I wouldn't believe it either, if I hadn't just witnessed my heart being ripped from my chest at seeing Heather down on her knees for Chase.

My Chase.

Another sob tore through me. I could hear Celeste trying to talk me down, so I took a deep breath in an attempt to calm myself enough to speak.

"I saw him, C. Chase was with her. Heather. She was blowing him in the greenhouse." I rubbed my forehead with my free hand, a sharp laugh suddenly breaking free. "Jesus, it's just like with that jerk from Staunton. What is it about me that makes my boyfriends cheat?"

"And you're sure it was Chase? Like you're absolutely positive it was him?"

"Yes, C, I'm absolutely positive. He looked right at me when I caught them," I explained. "Didn't even stop when he saw me, just kept right on going." I closed my eyes, wishing I could wake up, and this would all be some terrible nightmare.

"Eves, I'm so sorry. Let me pack a bag, and I'll be there in less than an hour." I could hear her dresser drawers being pulled open, the sound of her shoving clothes into a duffle coming over the phone.

"I thought he loved me, C," I whispered. "I thought they all did." How did I go from being head over heels for three seemingly perfect men to my entire world falling apart in a matter of days?

"I know, Eves. I'll be there soon. Just hang tight until I get there. I love you."

"Love you, too." I ended the call, staring at the background on my phone. It was a selfie Chase had taken of the four of us. We were piled onto the sofa in the guys' suite.

Knox was shoving at Chase's face while kissing the top of my head.

Asshole.

Griff was giving me a sweet kiss on the cheek.

Liar.

Chase was laughing as he tried to kiss Knox.

Cheater.

I was hanging on by a thread, my brain and body headed for a complete breakdown any minute. I started walking across the main corridor when a shape moved from the shadows. I gave out a frightened shriek, stumbling over my feet before landing on the hard marble floor. Scrambling away, the dark figure advanced on me, trapping me between it and the wall.

I opened my mouth to scream, but before I could get a sound out, something was blown into my face. I sputtered, inhaling the fine particles before I could think. I felt the magic's effects almost instantly. My body began to freeze and stiffen, indescribable panic gripping me. Fear clawed at my mind as I tried unsuccessfully to crawl away. It was as if my body were made of stone, my limbs unwilling to move an inch.

I tried again to make a sound, but even my vocal cords were frozen, my eyes and lungs the only things remaining unaffected. My wide, terror filled stare was focused on the shadowed figure that now stood directly in front of me. A glint in the moonlight caught my eye a half second before I felt the pinch of the needle breaking my skin.

No, no, no, no!

Every self defense lesson from Griff flew straight out the window, my body unable to follow even the most basic of commands. Not that they really would have helped, given I was frozen like a fucking statue.

A statue. Fuck!

The living statue powder, that must be what this asshole had blown in my face. Whatever had been in the needle quickly worked its way through my bloodstream, and suddenly my eyelids grew heavy. My attacker knelt down, their face obscured by a black ski mask, watching as I struggled to stay awake.

The last thing I heard before my eyes closed was a whisper.

"I told you he was mine."

nineteen

Griffin

Chase and I met Preston later that evening for dinner as promised. It was almost comical to see the healer fawn over my best friend. I was certain Preston had asked Chase nearly every question conceivable and could probably give a full dissertation on all things Chase Stone.

After we said good night, with the promise of another dinner in the near future, I texted Knox to meet us at the suite. We needed to sit down and have a serious conversation about what the fuck was going on between us and Everly.

I hadn't been able to bring myself to have a conversation with my Blue girl about that day in the library. She'd caught me in a lie I shouldn't have told in the first place, and I deserved every ounce of her anger.

I didn't know why I hadn't just told her the truth about tutoring Morgan in the first place. I could try to fool myself into thinking it was because I didn't want to hurt her, but in all reality, I didn't have an explanation. At least not a good one.

The letter from Austin was still hidden in my top drawer as well. I hadn't even mentioned it to the guys. I was sinking deeper and deeper with all the lies, my head barely above water.

When Professor Schoepke asked me to come by his office, Morgan was the last person I expected to be there. His request that I tutor her through the rest of the semester for Magical Philosophies wasn't something I could exactly turn down, given the stipulations of my scholarship, but goddamn if I wasn't kicking myself for not being honest with Everly from the beginning.

I'd only just started tutoring her a few days before Everly's discovery, and that was over a week ago. An entire week of my Blue girl not speaking to me, avoiding me at every turn.

I was dying inside, and it was no one's fault but my own.

Chase and I made our way up to the fourth floor, silence between the two of us. I knew he was hurting just as badly as I was, given the way Everly blew up during Potions. My friend was doing everything he could to try and ease any doubt she had, but damn did Heather and Morgan just keep stirring the pot.

I texted her while we were at dinner, hoping maybe I could meet up with her, talk things out, but she'd shut me out yet again.

Griff: Hey Blue girl. Do you wanna go to the greenhouse together? Get our ingredients for the next lab? Thought maybe we could talk too.

Everly: No. I'm already on my way to get everything I need.

Griff: Oh... well, can I come over when you get back? So we can talk?

Everly: I don't think so. Besides, I'm sure you're probably all booked up, what with all your new tutoring clients.

Fuck.

Griff: Please Blue, let me try to explain. Come over when you're finished at the greenhouse. Please. I miss you.

Everly:....

Those dots gave my heart a moment of hope until they disappeared, no message to follow. I pulled out my phone, rereading the messages before scrolling further up the text thread to stare at the pictures she'd sent me of her and the guys while I was taking an exam. I'd nearly choked when a shot of Chase's dick between her breasts had popped up on my screen. My notification settings got changed pretty fast after that one.

We made it inside, Chase immediately heading to the fridge and grabbing out a six pack of beer. He sat down with a loud sigh, popping the top and downing half the bottle in one go. Great. So it was gonna be *that* type of night. He quickly polished off the rest before opening a second, guzzling it down just as quickly as the first.

"So, you're just gonna get drunk, then?" I'd seen Chase do this one other time. He'd bombed a huge exam in one of his business classes during second year, and it had completely tanked his grade. He had to repeat the entire course the next semester.

But this wasn't the time to drown our sorrows in alcohol. I needed him if I had any hope of fixing things with Everly and saving her from Austin and his dad. Knox had been MIA since the fight at the carnival. Chase filled me in late that night once he'd finally gotten Everly calmed down enough to sleep.

"Griff, it was crazy, man. Like, I've never seen him so angry," Chase commented once he'd finished recounting the night's events. I was beyond pissed at Knox and how he'd treated our girl. I understood being angry with Evan, but Knox had taken it too far.

"You know he's got a temper, Chase. And when it comes to her"—I nodded my head toward his closed bedroom door—"it comes out ten fold."

"Yeah, dude, but this... something wasn't right, Griff. I'm telling you. That wasn't our Knoxy on the beach tonight."

As if I didn't have enough on my plate already, now I had Knox and his fucking temper to contend with as well. From what I could tell, he'd been sleeping at his studio most nights since the fight, only coming home to shower and grab clothes. I knew his absence was hurting my Blue, adding on to the stress she was carrying thanks to me and the Thorpes. I flopped down next to Chase, snagging the last beer from the pack.

"Hey! Those are mine!" he cried, giving a half-hearted attempt at stealing it back. I took a long pull, letting the cool liquid slide down my throat. The hops danced across my tongue, and I could tell by the taste it was one of the stronger beers that Chase liked to keep around. Fuck, that meant he was gonna be shit faced soon, having put away five of the six in the pack.

We sat in silence for a while, each of us lost in our thoughts. I knew mine were centered on our girl, and I'd bet my last twenty Chase's were too. His eyes were closed as he leaned back on the sofa, his head hanging over the back cushions. I'd actually thought he'd fallen asleep until I heard him softly speak.

"What'd you do man? Why is she so mad at you?"

I sucked in a breath, his question catching me off guard. It wasn't the first time he'd asked, but I always deflected, changing the subject or saying I had to run to class.

But I was done lying.

That's what had gotten me in this whole mess in the first place.

"I lied to her," I answered, my own voice soft in the quiet of our suite. "I lied about Morgan."

He sat up, his glassy green eyes locking on mine. He was definitely well on his way to drunk, but he stared at me with the intensity of a stone-cold sober man.

"What do you mean, you lied to her about Morgan? What about Morgan, Griff?" He was confused, his brows furrowing as he thought over my initial response. I readied myself for him to knock me the fuck out as I gave him the truth.

"A couple weeks ago, Professor Schoepke asked me to tutor Morgan for our Advanced Magical Philosophies class. I couldn't say no, since tutoring is a requirement of my scholarship," I explained, watching as my words worked their way through the haze of alcohol. "I didn't tell Everly. But she found out. She caught me with Morgan at the library."

I sighed, realizing just how bad it all sounded when I said it out loud.

I couldn't blame Everly for thinking I cheated. I'd lied, snuck around with my ex... all because I thought I was protecting my girl, and look how far that got me. Everly wouldn't even look at me, let alone talk to me long enough to explain what had happened. I looked over at Chase, surprised he hadn't decked me yet.

My best friend sat quietly, contemplating my words for several long moments before he spoke.

"Did you cheat on her?" His voice was low, and I could hear the edge he was teetering on, his struggle not to put me through the wall.

"No, Chase, I promise you, I would never, *ever* cheat on Everly." I downed the rest of my beer before continuing. "It fucked me up every time Morgan would cheat on me. I would never do that to Everly, man. I love her."

"Then why not tell her what you were doing, Griff? That seems pretty fucking shady if you didn't have anything to hide." He narrowed his eyes at me, most likely still trying to assess if I was lying or not. It also could have been the booze working its way through his bloodstream.

Tipping my head back, I stared at the ceiling, trying to figure out how to explain my shitty logic for lying to Everly. For lying to my best friends. I still hadn't told Chase or Knox about the letter.

"I lied to you, too," I said softly, needing to give him the truth. "The day Professor Schoepke asked me to tutor Morgan, I found a letter on my desk before class started." I paused, the threats from Austin flashing through my mind. But Chase needed to know.

"It was from Austin. He threatened us, all of us, if we don't end things with Everly by Thanksgiving. He's fucking crazy man. He threatened to get me kicked out of school and fuck up any chances of a job. He threatened you and your parents, said he could make it look like you guys were stealing money from your dad's company." The words poured out of me as I rambled, unsure of how much Chase was really comprehending since I basically threw a grenade of information in his lap. I took a deep breath, giving him a minute to sift through my word vomit.

"Why didn't you tell us? Tell me? I'm your best friend, man." Chase's voice was quiet, and I could hear the hurt as he spoke. Glancing over, I saw him leaning forward, his elbows resting on his knees as he steepled his fingers under his chin.

"I panicked, Chase." I scrubbed my hands down my face, sighing deeply as I rubbed the two day old stubble. Before I could explain my shitty reasoning further, a loud knock came from our door.

Chase shrugged. "Knox probably forgot his key again." His drunk ass made no attempt to get up, so I hauled myself off the sofa and toward the door. I twisted the knob and pulled it open.

"Knox, how many ti—" I began to lecture him about how many times he'd forgotten his key, but I stopped short when I realized the hall was empty. I stuck my head out, looking up and down the corridor, but there was no one there. Stepping back, I felt something brush my arm, almost as if someone were walking by.

Weird.

I closed the door, shuffling back to the living room to continue my conversation with Chase. Even in his inebriated state, I could tell my lies had hurt him. Just as I rounded the arm of the sofa, I watched as the front of his shirt was yanked forward, drawing him into a half standing position. Chase let out a loud yell.

"What the fu—" He was cut off when his head snapped back, blood erupting from his nose. He yelped, holding his face with one hand while swinging wildly with the other. I heard a loud hiss and watched, frozen in place, as the empty beer bottles on the table crashed to the floor seemingly on their own.

What in the fuck was going on?

Chase was still yelling, blood pouring from what I assumed was a broken nose.

"Who's there?! You motherfucker, show yourself!" Chase roared into the room.

Suddenly on the floor a few feet away, the small body of a girl spontaneously appeared, long blonde hair pulled back in a ponytail giving me a clear view of her face.

"Celeste?"

"Surprise," she spat, turning angry brown eyes to Chase. "Now where's my best friend, you cheating son of a bitch."

twenty *Everly*

"Everly."

Who's trying to wake me?

I burrowed deeper into the softness of the mattress, not ready for consciousness yet.

"Everly."

Gentle fingers stroked across my cheek, no doubt pushing my hair out of my face. I nuzzled into the touch, trying to move closer to its source. I couldn't figure out which of my guys was brave enough to try to rouse me. The hand continued to caress my skin as I tried to roll, but my right leg felt stuck, something keeping me from moving it.

Then without warning, those gentle touches turned harsh, the fingers digging into my face as they squeezed roughly, and I whimpered in pain.

"It's time to wake up, *Pet*."

No.

My eyes flew open, terror gripping me at the sound of his voice.

No, please God, no.

I recoiled, my body slamming in the wall behind me. I tried to jump from the bed, but quickly realized why it'd been so difficult to move earlier.

I was fucking chained to a goddamn bed frame.

The metal chain was connected to a thick shackle secured around my ankle, rendering me unable to move from the shitty bed I was currently on. I pulled on the chain with all my strength but it was useless, the motherfucker wasn't moving.

My eyes darted around the room, quickly landing on the living embodiment of all my nightmares.

Austin fucking Thorpe.

I snapped my fingers, trying to use my telekinesis to throw him from the bed, but nothing happened. I snapped several more times, but still nothing. What the fuck! I nearly screamed in frustration. Why wasn't my magic working?

Austin leered at me, his eyes raking over my small frame as I quickly moved to the foot of the bed putting as much distance between us as possible. With my movement, the chain went slack enough for me to curl my knees into my chest, and I wrapped my arms around them protectively, as if that would keep me safe from this fucking psycho.

"Oh now, Pet, don't be like that." He had the audacity to actually look like my actions hurt him, a frown on his face when I scrambled away.

"What the fuck, Austin! Unlock me now!" I screamed at him, rattling the chain in my hand.

"No, Pet. You're mine." He grinned, the smile showing too many teeth and sending shivers down my spine. "I arranged for us to spend some time here together, alone, since you belong to me now."

"The fuck I belong to you!" I spat, rage running through my veins like wildfire. My chest heaved, fear settling deep in my stomach, panic seizing my insides. I was trapped, alone in a room with Austin. I thought back on all the times at the gym with Griff, working on my self defense. While I knew I couldn't fight my way out of this situation, his number one rule was to always remain calm.

Sucking in a deep breath, I scanned the room in an attempt to get my bearings. I was in what appeared to be a small bedroom, a simple twin bed, one wooden nightstand with a ceramic lamp on top, and a tall armoire tucked into the corner.

The walls were painted a bland shade of gray, four solid walls without a window in sight, and a large wooden door sat opposite my spot on the bed. I needed to be smart here and keep my cool. Maybe I could use his sick obsession with me to my advantage.

"Austin, please," I pleaded, softening my voice. If I could convince him I wouldn't run, maybe he'd unlock the chain. "It's hurting my ankle. Can you unlock it, please? I promise I won't run. Please."

He rose from his spot, crawling toward me at the foot of the bed. It took every ounce of strength I possessed not to cringe as he drew near, reminding myself that I needed to play the long game here if I wanted to survive.

"Pet," he said, stroking a finger down my cheek. Bile rose in my throat at his touch, burning as I swallowed it down. "It's adorable that you think that will work. Do you really think I'm stupid enough to let you go? I'm keeping you shackled until you can admit that you're mine." He spoke in such a sweet way, that had I not heard his actual words, I might have thought he was a decent human being.

But he wasn't.

He was a delusional psychopath.

And I was trapped with him.

I balled my fist, ready to strike, but he anticipated my action, catching my wrist tightly in his hand. He squeezed so hard I cried out, the bones grinding together painfully. I tried to hit him with my free hand, but he was able to subdue me completely as I swung in a blind frenzy.

"Pet, that's not very nice," he taunted, holding my wrists with one hand as he gripped my chin with the other. He dug his fingers into my cheeks, pain erupting from his harsh touch. "Looks like we need to work on your manners, Everly."

"Austin," I choked out. "Griff and Chase and Knox will all be looking for me. My brother will be looking for me." I was in full blown panic mode now, completely unable to predict what he might do next. The pressure on my wrists continued to increase, and I worried he might break my arms.

Then, just as suddenly as he'd attacked, he released me.

He rose from the bed, his nonchalant, cocksure attitude about *fucking kidnapping me* fueling his swagger as he made his way to the door. I decided I wasn't above begging at this point, so I continued.

"They'll wonder where I am, Austin, even Evan. They'll notice when I don't come back and they'll look for me." My voice cracked as a sob broke from my chest. "Please, let me go. Please."

He turned back to face me just as he reached the door, his long arms crossing over his chest. I stared at him, my vision going blurry as tears welled in my eyes.

He was dressed casually in a pair of jeans and a three-quarter zip pullover with the SLA crest, his dull brown hair pushed back from his face. His mud-colored eyes roved over my body, making me feel naked even though I was still fully clothed.

Thank God for small favors.

"Oh Pet," he sneered, a gleeful shimmer filling his eyes. "Who do you think let me bring you here?" Without another word, he made his way through the door, closing it behind him. I could hear the sound of several locks engaging as he left, trapping me inside.

I sat in stunned silence long after he was gone.

There was no way.

No fucking way.

But my mind continued to play on repeat all the different ways I'd been hurt by them recently, making me question everything I thought I knew. I swallowed roughly, emotion clogging my throat as more tears continued to fall.

Griff lying about Morgan.

Knox blowing up at me.

Chase with his fucking dick down Heather's throat.

A loud sob broke free, and I trembled as the possibility they betrayed me started to seem more and more likely. Had it all been a lie? Did they get bored? Was I just not worth the trouble?

I wiped the tears from my cheeks using the backs of my hands, bending forward until I could grab the lone pillow that rested against the headboard.

Curling myself into a ball, I tucked the pillow under my head before pulling the blanket loose to wrap around myself. My body felt cold, numb. I burrowed under the covers, wishing any of my guys were here with me.

But were they even my guys anymore?

As the adrenaline from my confrontation with Austin wore off, my eyelids grew heavy, the effects of the sleeping potion still flowing through my veins. I let my eyes flutter closed, praying that when I woke this would all be a terrible, terrible dream.

I woke with a start, quickly remembering where I was when I saw the shackle linked around my ankle, trapping me in this godforsaken room. Looking around, I found myself alone, the room dim, the only light coming from the small lamp on the nightstand. I didn't remember turning it on, or the overhead light off, and a shudder ran through my body.

That meant Austin was in here while I was asleep.

Again.

Fighting back the bile rising in my throat, I patted myself down quickly, making sure my clothes were all still in place before releasing a deep sigh. Deciding I would take advantage of my captor's absence, I pulled on the chain to see how much slack I was working with.

Much to my dismay, it wasn't much. I could stand from the foot of the bed, but just barely. And forget about walking around the small room. Huffing in frustration, I sat back on the bed, trying to figure out how in the hell I was going to get myself out of here.

Surely the guys would come for me... Right? Someone had to have noticed I was gone by now. If not one of the guys, then maybe...

Celeste!

I was supposed to meet her at my suite! She would realize I was missing! Hope bloomed in my chest, knowing my best friend would go straight to my men when she figured out something wasn't right.

But the question remained, would they help her find me?

As I ran through scenarios in my mind of them rescuing me, I almost didn't hear the door as it creaked open. I scurried back until I was flush against the wall, tugging the blanket tightly around myself as an extra barrier. A dark figure loomed just outside, the shadowed body too filled out to be Austin.

Who the fuck...

They stepped closer, the light revealing their body inch by inch until I could finally make out a face. A handsome face, full of a week's worth of scruff and the darkest chocolate brown eyes I'd ever seen.

"Knox!" I sobbed, throwing the blanket off as I tried to climb off the bed, nearly face planting in the process. "Knox! Help me get this chain off before he comes back." I began pulling on the chain again, rattling it loudly as it clanged against the metal frame.

Knox stayed in the doorway, his muscular arms crossed over his broad chest. His eyes were narrowed as he took in the scene before him, rubbing a tattooed hand over his scruffy beard.

Unease swirled in my gut the longer he remained in the doorway. Why wasn't he trying to break the chain? What was he waiting for? And where were Griff and Chase?

Something was wrong.

"Knox, please. We have to get out of here before Austin comes back! You have to help me break the chain!" I frantically shouted at him, tears springing to my eyes as the unease turned to despair.

He stared at me for a few more moments before finally speaking, his dark brown eyes glaring at me in the dim light.

"Now, Everly, why would I do that?"

twenty one

Chase

Well a sucker punch to the face is one fucking way to sober up. I leaned my head on the back of the sofa, placing the bag of frozen veggies across the bridge of my now-crooked and broken nose, sighing as Griffin tried to reason with Celeste.

"I know what she said, Cardarette! She told me that she caught *that* motherfucker"—she stabbed a finger in my direction, spitting the words like an angry kitten—"getting his dick sucked by that slut Heather in the greenhouse earlier." Her blonde ponytail whirled around as she spoke, like the propeller of an airplane. It took everything I had not to giggle as the image of Celeste's head on the front of an airplane ran through my mind.

Okay, maybe I was still a little drunk.

161

"What?" Griffin questioned her in disbelief. "When did she say this happened, Celeste?" Griff ran a hand through his short brown hair, tugging on the ends in frustration as he tried to remain calm.

"Does it matter?" She glared at him, her tiny hands resting on her hips in what I'm sure was meant to be an intimidating stance. When Griffin didn't answer, she let out an exasperated breath. "She called me a little over an hour ago, sobbing. She could barely fucking talk she was so upset." She shot me a look that spoke of more violence if she got her hands on me.

Jumping in before Griff could respond, I answered her.

"I was at dinner with Griff and Preston until about an hour ago. Then we came back here, where I was planning to have a nice evening getting drunk and wallowing in self pity. That is, until *someone* decided to break my fucking nose." I shot her a glare, taking the ice pack off my face. Maybe I could give Preston a call, see if he could fix it for me...

"Look, pretty boy, all I know is my best friend in the entire world called me, hysterical, because she said she caught *you* cheating. What the hell else was I supposed to do?!" She threw her hands in the air, clearly not believing my story. "I drove here as fast as I could and snuck in behind some students when they came into the building."

Griff held up a hand, interrupting her. "Wait, so have you actually seen Everly?" He narrowed his eyes, and I could practically see the gears in his brain spinning as he tried to piece everything together.

"Once I got inside," Celeste continued, rolling her eyes while pointedly ignoring him. "I went straight to her suite, but no one answered when I knocked. I must have stayed outside the door for a good ten minutes before I finally came here." She tugged her cell phone from her back pocket, quickly swiping at the screen.

"I called her at least a dozen times. It rang the first few, but then started going straight to voicemail. It's not like her to not answer, especially when she was so upset. I texted her a bunch, too, but nothing."

Not answering Celeste, I looked at Griff. "Can you teleport us into her room? Maybe she's painting with her earbuds in? Didn't hear the door?" Griffin nodded as he moved toward me on the sofa, but Celeste cut him off, putting her tiny body between us.

"Oh no, asshole, you're not going near her. Griff can take me." Fury shone in her eyes and even as fucked as everything was right now, I was grateful my Larkspur had such a fiercely loyal friend. "You sit your ass there and think about all the ways you're going to try to make this right with my girl because I will fucking gut you if even a word of what she said is true."

Grumbling 'fine' under my breath, I watched as Griff quickly took her hand and they disappeared. No sooner had they left than my phone chimed from the coffee table, the sound indicating a new message. I leaned forward quickly, the throbbing in my nose making me see double for a moment. Goddamn that girl packed a hell of a punch. Closing my eyes, I blew out a deep breath before trying again, this time moving slower as I grabbed the phone.

Swiping at the screen, I saw it was an email from Lou Martinez, the PI my father recommended. I quickly opened it, my eyes scanning the words.

Mr. Stone,

I was able to acquire the following information on Austin Thorpe. His father has been able to make many records from his youth disappear, so it's been a bit more difficult to get the information that I initially anticipated. I found records from a psychiatric facility, but they are sealed so it may take me some time to crack them. I will continue to dig and update you as more becomes available.

Parents: *Alaric Thorpe, Melody Thorpe (deceased when Austin was ten, cause of death inconclusive, case still open, foul play suspected but not proven)*

Schools: *Emporia Magical Arts Prep (expelled for possible assault of female teacher- inconclusive investigation), Solis Lake Prep (graduated), Solis Lake Academy (currently attending)*

Elemental Power: *Fire (has been investigated numerous times for fire related crimes, never charged; see notes below)*

Caster Ability: *Mimic*

Additional Notes: *The teacher he was accused of assaulting at EMAP was found two years after he was expelled, burned alive. He was investigated as a suspect, but was cleared when his father provided an alibi.*

I will hopefully have an update for you soon. Reach out if you have any questions.

Lou

I read over the email again, my beer-soaked brain trying to make sense of the words. I knew Austin's mom had died when we were kids, but I thought she had a heart attack or something. My parents had never mentioned that there might be foul play. Thinking back, I realized that was around the time my parents started distancing themselves from the Thorpes, Austin not coming to our house anymore unless it was a business function.

And what the fuck was this shit about his teacher? Did he hurt her? Fuck. Anxiety began to eat away at my drunken state. His elemental power was fire, and she'd been fucking *burned alive*. I knew Austin was psychotic, but Jesus, was he a goddamn *murderer?*

I scanned the words a third time, my gaze lingering on Austin's caster ability.

Mimic.

I wracked my brain trying to think if I'd ever even heard of that before, but nothing came to mind. Maybe I should have paid more attention in my Intro to Caster Abilities class during first year...

I focused on the email, making mental notes of each detail. Anything to distract myself from Celeste's accusations. Nothing about what she'd said made any sense. What the fuck could my Larkspur be talking about, saying she saw me getting a blowjob from Heather? Something else was going on here, that was the only explanation.

Suddenly Griff and Celeste appeared before me, Celeste ripping her hand from Griff's the moment they materialized. She stomped away from him, her posture tense, like a snake coiled, ready to strike.

"Well, was she there? Where is she? Why didn't you bring her back?" The questions tumbled from my mouth, my head swiveling to look between the two of them. I could see the worry and concern in Griff's hazel eyes, and the last of the alcohol cleared from my brain.

What in the fuck was going on?

And where the fuck was my Larkspur?

"She wasn't there." Griff's voice was strained, anxiety clearly written across his face. "No one was. Her backpack was still there, but if she went to the greenhouse like she told Celeste, she may not have taken it with her. Her phone was missing."

He sat on the sofa next to me while Celeste continued to pace the room, her cell in her hands, no doubt texting our girl. Every few steps she'd glance in our direction, glaring at us both before going back to her phone.

I was still in shock over her accusations. No, not her's. *Everly's.* My Larkspur believed I cheated on her. A lump formed in my throat, and I swallowed roughly. How could she think I would ever hurt her so deeply, that I could ever want another woman? She was my world.

Griff scrubbed his hands down his face, pressing the heels of his hands into his eyes for a moment before speaking.

"Something's not right. Even if she was this pissed at us, there's no reason why she wouldn't respond to Celeste. Something's wrong." He stared at the floor, his hands folded between his legs as he leaned forward on his elbows.

I watched Celeste pace for a few more moments before speaking to Griff in a low tone. "She seems even more pissed than when she got here. What happened while you were gone?"

Griff let out a deep sigh as he leaned back on the sofa, his eyes closing briefly as he softly spoke. "She asked me how Everly had been doing. Said she felt like she was distant lately, like she was hiding something. I thought she'd told her about the ball, but when I brought it up, she flipped shit. Apparently our girl failed to tell her BFF about the contract and everything else."

Yikes. Well, that explained Celeste's worsening mood since coming back.

As if sensing we were talking about her, she stopped pacing, her arms at her sides as she leveled us both with an icy glare.

"Where is this Thorpe fucker? I think he and I need to have a little chat about him keeping his hands to himself." I could see her tiny hands flexing, her fists balling up in anger. Having been on the receiving end of one of those little suckers, I'd love to see her land a punch on Austin's smug fucking face.

"We don't know," Griff answered her as I daydreamed about Celeste kicking the shit out of Austin. It really was a fun thing to think about.

"What do you mean you don't know? He fucking assaulted her and now he's after her and you DON'T KNOW WHERE THE FUCK HE IS?" She was shouting by the time she finished, and I winced as her words hit their mark. We should have been doing more to keep Everly safe. Fuck! I leaned forward, my head in my hands as guilt washed over me like a tsunami.

Celeste went back to her phone, mumbling under her breath. Pretty sure I heard the words 'incompetent morons' and 'kick all their asses' before Griff got my attention.

"Did you hear back from the PI yet?" He was still staring at the floor, shame from Celeste's words cutting him deeply. "This all reeks of Austin."

"Actually, yeah, he emailed me while you were gone." I picked up my phone, opening the email before handing it over to Griff. He scanned it quickly, that photographic memory of his storing away all the details. I watched as his brows scrunched together before his eyes widened.

"Holy fuck," he said, his voice so low I could barely hear it. He stared at my phone like it held government secrets, his eyes boring holes through the screen. I waited for him to give me more of a response but after several long seconds, I realized he was still transfixed on the message.

"Griff, speak man, what's up?"

"He's a goddamn mimic, Chase. Do you know what that means?" His jaw tensed as he spoke, and I could see him grinding his teeth together in frustration.

"No, Griff, I fucking don't, so why don't you explain it to me." Now I was fucking irritated. Everly thought I'd cheated on her, and now she was potentially missing, and we were no closer to finding her. And my nose still hurt like a motherfucker.

He narrowed his eyes at me for a moment before drawing in a deep breath. He closed them momentarily, and when they opened he seemed calmer, but by only a fraction.

"Mimics are an exceptionally rare type of caster. They have the ability to take on the form of other people. While they can't mimic another caster's abilities, they look and sound *exactly* like them. It's a huge drain on their magic, so they can only do it for short amounts of time without the use of dark magic." He rattled off the information so fast I barely had time to register it.

"Wait, hold up," I held up a hand before he could continue. "You're telling me Austin can pretend to be other people?" What in the actual fuckery? Then the light bulb suddenly flicked on, and rage swept through my body like a tidal wave.

"That motherfucker!" I raged, swiping my hand across the coffee table, sending the remaining bottles crashing to the floor.

I heard Celeste yelp at my outburst, but I was too goddamn pissed to give a fuck. That piece of fucking shit had pretended to be me, I fucking knew it.

Now the question was, did he have Everly?

twenty-two · Everly

I stared at Knox, unable to comprehend his words.

"Knox, we need to go, now!" I repeated, tears now streaming down my face in wet rivulets. I pulled on the chain, the rough metal scraping at my palms as I tugged with all my might. Goddamn it, why did I have to get fucking super speed as a secondary power and not strength like Chase!

I cried out in frustration when I felt a jagged spot dig into my hand, breaking the skin. Blood quickly coated my palm, but I was too confused by what was happening to register the severity of the wound.

Knox moved further into the room, staying near the wall opposite me. He looked at my injured hand, a mask of indifference on his handsome face. He was dressed in a pair of spotless jeans and a clean, navy blue SLA hoodie. It was a bit jarring to see him in something not splattered in paint, but I pushed the juxtaposition away, the confusion over Knox's odd behavior at the forefront of my mind.

"Please, Knoxy." The quiet plea came out as a whisper as I hugged my hand to my chest.

"Everly," he said my name with an exasperated sigh, like I was inconveniencing him by being fucking kidnapped and locked up. "I don't *want* to free you."

You know that moment in a movie where the record needle scratches the vinyl and everyone freezes?

Yeah, that's what happened inside my brain when those words came out of Knox's mouth. A mouth that had explored my own more times than I could count. A mouth that whispered sweet words to me as I fell asleep in his strong arms. Before I knew what was happening, I was howling with laughter.

Because this had to be a joke.

Right?

I gasped, trying to suck in air as my laughter morphed into something more akin to hysterics. Knox continued to stare at me with the same impassive look as I descended into a blubbering mess atop the cheap comforter, blood now dripping down my arm and staining the blue fabric.

Rolling his eyes at my reaction, Knox finally strode toward the bed, his long legs eating up the short distance in just two steps. Studying my tear stained face for a moment, his dark brown eyes bored into mine, but there was something different about them. The passion and fire that typically filled Knox's chestnut gaze was absent. Instead all I saw was a coldness I'd never witnessed from my tortured artist.

His hand shot out, gripping my chin roughly between his thumb and fingers. He tipped my head back, so I was staring up at him, the angle hurting my neck. I tried to wrench free, but he held fast, looking at me with so much disgust it nearly made my heart stop beating.

"Everly, listen very carefully to my words," he ground out, the low timbre of his voice full of hate. "I don't want you anymore. You're more trouble than you're fucking worth at this point."

I inhaled sharply, tears welling in my eyes once more, his words like a slap to my face. My mind was screaming at me, begging me to say something, anything, but my voice was frozen, the air stuck in my lungs.

"I love you, Knox," I finally squeaked out.

With his free hand, he reached out, harshly palming my pussy through my jeans. I gasped, trying to pull away, but he had me trapped between his body and the wall.

"Did you honestly believe that I loved you? Your tight little cunt was fun for a while," he taunted, stroking a finger along the seam of my pants before squeezing me painfully through the fabric. I cried out, but he refused to let go. "But I'm tired of sharing it with two other guys."

My brain decided at that moment to wake the fuck up, and I thrashed in his arms, bucking wildly in an effort to wrench myself from his hold. His hands suddenly left my body, and for a fleeting moment I thought I'd gotten free, only to feel a sharp sting as he backhanded me across the face.

I whimpered at the impact, a coppery taste filling my mouth. I wiped my lip, the back of my hand coming away bloody from where he'd split it open.

Without another word, he stepped away from the bed and moved across the room toward the armoire.

I pulled the blankets around me, trying to shield myself from the man I once thought loved me. A man who said he'd fill a thousand canvases with his passion for me. A man I thought I had a future with. Now he was like a stranger, someone cold and vicious, who took pleasure in hurting me. My chest ached, grief lancing through me like a spear straight to my heart.

He opened the large wooden doors of the antique piece, revealing a small flat screen inside. Picking up the remote, he flicked on the TV, the screen coming to life.

I gingerly touched my cheek where he'd struck me, wincing as my fingers brushed the quickly swelling skin. When did Knox, my Knoxy, become this... stranger? I never in my wildest dreams could have predicted I'd ever be on the receiving end of Knox's fists, yet here I was, with the bruises to prove it.

Knox's voice cut through my thoughts, drawing me back to the horrific now that was my life.

"If you don't believe me"—he nodded at the TV—"take a look. None of us want you anymore. You were fun for a while, I'll give you that. But honestly, did you really think you'd be able to keep all three of us on a leash? Especially Chase?" He laughed cruelly, obviously taking great delight in my current situation. "Honestly, three men, Everly? It's no wonder your brother called you a whore. Maybe Austin can break all those bad habits."

All I could do was gape at him. Who was this nightmare of a man?

Once he'd finished laughing, he hit another button on the remote, the screen filling with a grainy security recording. There was no sound, but I could easily make out the two people on the screen.

Chase.

And Heather.

This time however, they weren't in the greenhouse, but instead an empty stairwell. I watched in horror as Chase pinned her to the wall, kissing her savagely while reaching a hand under her skirt. She threw her head back, ecstasy clear on her face, even with the poor quality of the recording. He continued to finger fuck her for several minutes, her body writhing against his as she found her release.

I sat silently, my eyes fixed on the screen. I sucked in a gasp when he finally pulled his hand from her body, thanking God it was finally over.

But the universe decided to fuck with me some more.

I watched as he pushed his athletic shorts down around his thighs, his hard cock springing free. Then, as if she weighed nothing, he hoisted Heather into his arms, slipping into her with ease. He kissed her passionately as he began fucking her against the wall.

I squeezed my eyes shut, but the image was seared into my brain forever.

"Please, turn it off," I whispered, bile rising in my throat. I swallowed it down roughly, the burn bringing me back to a reality I didn't want to face. "Knox, turn it off."

He stared at me, a smirk playing on his full lips as he twirled the remote in his hand, Chase still fucking Heather on the screen to his right.

"Turn if the fuck off!" I shrieked, sobbing as I buried my face in my hands, pulling my knees into my chest.

He chuckled darkly; the only other sound filling the space was my ragged breathing. I was broken, irreparably, my heart splintered into a thousand tiny pieces. A small voice in the back of my mind continuously screamed this was wrong, that something wasn't right. But the proof was there, plain as day on the screen before me.

I drew in a shuddering breath. "How long?"

Knox snickered, setting the remote on the shelf next to the TV. "Since before the ball," he explained with so much nonchalance I wanted to punch him. "Not too long after they were paired up in Potions. Guess you just weren't enough for him."

I swallowed against the tennis ball sized lump of emotion in my throat. "Did you know? Did Griff know?"

This time he tipped his head back as he barked out a laugh, but it was hollow and cold. I recoiled at the harshness of the unfamiliar sound. "Of course we knew. All those times he disappeared to 'help her with homework'"—he used his fingers to make air quotes as he spoke—"he was off fucking her. That video is from the day he told you she tried to kiss him in the stairwell. Although from the looks of it, I'd say maybe he wasn't telling the full truth. What do you think?" He was taunting me, an evil glint I'd never seen before lighting up his dark chocolate eyes.

"Fuck you, Knox," I spit at him. But even as I spoke, my soul felt like it was dying, the reality that I was losing my guys, that maybe I'd never really had them to begin with, crushing the last bit of hope I had of him rescuing me.

Lightning fast, he pounced. He pinned me against the bed, using the weight of his body to hold me to the mattress. His strong thighs bracketed my own while he gripped my wrists with a bruising force.

"That can be arranged, Everly." His hot breath fanned across my face, and I shook as he loomed over me. Terror slithered up my spine as tears leaked from the corners of my eyes. He leaned in close, using the tip of his tongue to lick the salty liquid from my cheek.

"Your fear always tastes so good."

I whimpered in absolute horror. I stared at him through blurry eyes, my mind a muddled mess. All the lies, the cruel words, the devastating deception were too much. I closed my eyes, unable to look at him anymore. He could take what he wanted from my body. It didn't matter anymore, not with how wholly he had crushed my heart.

Without warning, he smashed his lips to mine, the brutality pushing my already split lip into my teeth, fresh blood flowing from the reopened wound.

My eyes popped open to find his searing into me. For a brief moment they almost looked three shades lighter, the deep chestnut more of a muddy dull brown, but just as quickly he shuttered them, his tongue lashing against my sore lip, lapping at the blood leaking out.

Just as quickly as he'd started, he yanked himself away, moving quickly toward the door. He turned to face me, his lips coated in deep crimson. An unnatural smile played on his face, sending shivers through my body. I was frozen, still in shock from his vicious assault, and too scared to move a muscle.

"You should really watch the rest of the video, Everly. It's got all kinds of fun stuff on there. Chase and Heather. Morgan with Griff. Makes for some really good viewing." He winked at me as the contents of my stomach roiled violently. I said nothing, unable to speak around the emotions clogging my throat.

He pulled the door open, stepping across the threshold before looking back.

"Good-bye, Everly." He closed the door tightly behind him, the sound of the locks clicking into place barely audible over blood rushing in my ears.

I stared blankly at the scene on the TV, Chase still inside Heather, frozen in pleasure, imprinted forever in my mind.

The pain in my lip faded as a cold numbness blanketed my body. Pulling off my sweatshirt, I used my teeth to rip off a strip of fabric, looping it around my injured hand before lying on my side. I turned my back to the room, huddled in a ball on the lumpy mattress.

Knox's voice rang through my head. *Chase and Heather. Griff with Morgan.*

I closed my eyes, the deep chasm in my heart throbbing at his cruel, callous words.

I don't want you anymore.

twenty-three Knox

It had been days since I'd laid eyes on my little Monet, and I was dying inside. I wanted to kick my own ass for the way I'd spoken to her that night at the beach. How could I have been so fucking stupid?

She was hurting, and instead of making it better, I'd freaked the fuck out, making everything one hundred times worse. The absolute devastation on her face when I'd accidently pushed her was something I would never forget. Honestly, I was surprised Chase hadn't murdered me when I'd knocked her over.

I could only hope she'd give me a second chance to make it right.

But that meant I needed to nut up and stop being a pussy. I'd been hiding out at my studio for the last week, sneaking into our suite at odd hours to shower and grab clothes before going back into hiding. I avoided our place at all costs, so I wouldn't have to see my betrayal in her eyes everytime she looked at me. I'd even skipped our Water Element class this entire week, knowing she would be there.

That night on the beach, the rage had been uncontrollable. When Evan insulted Everly, I saw red, and the overwhelming need to hurt someone took over. Looking down, I noticed my knuckles were still bruised in spots, the skin scabbed over where it split from the force of my strikes.

Evan landed a few good blows, my ribs still sore from his punches while the bruising on my left cheek had finally faded. It would have been easy to go to the health clinic or even ask any of the healers on campus to help me, but I needed to live with the pain. It was a reminder of how much I'd hurt my little Monet.

I pulled out my phone as I eyed the canvas currently occupying my easel. It was an acrylic piece I'd been working on since that night at the beach. In the center was a man's chest, hands tearing the flesh open. Instead of a heart inside, however, there was the outline of a woman, a beautiful woman with long, dark hair piled high on her head, curled in on herself in sadness.

My own heart was in tatters, ripped to shreds by my own goddamn hands when I'd hurt my girl.

I opened my texts, pulling up the thread I had with Everly. Neither of us had so much as sent a carrier pigeon after my brawl with her brother. I'd written and deleted at least a hundred different messages, none adequately conveying the guilt currently coating my insides like tar. I had a slew of unread messages from the guys as well, most of them angry texts about how I'd so epically fucked everything up.

I'd never in my life put my hands on a woman; my mother might be a stuck up southern debutante, but she made sure I was raised with good manners and core values. And while I knew I didn't actually hit Everly, the idea that I caused her any type of physical pain just wasn't something I could live with.

I would rake myself over hot coals if it meant I could earn even a sliver of her forgiveness.

I sat on my stool, staring at my phone for another minute, my leg bouncing up and down before I stood, shoving it in the pocket of my hoodie. It was one of Everly's favorites; she'd snagged it one day, using a fine bristled brush to delicately paint her name on the inside of the right sleeve. I'd made sure it had adequate time to dry before washing it, ensuring her swirly manuscript stayed intact.

I wasn't ashamed at the tears brimming in my eyes as I looked at her beautiful handwriting. I needed to make things right with my girl. And that started with me, on my knees, groveling at her cute little feet.

I locked up my studio, making my way swiftly through the maze of hallways before shoving through the side door of Vox, the cold night air whipping me in the face. I pulled up the hood of my sweatshirt and started walking toward the dorms, my head tucked low to avoid the wind whistling around me.

I played through apology after apology in my head, hoping I would land on the right words to say to Everly. And as much as it pissed me off, I knew I'd eventually have to apologize to her asshole brother, too, although I still firmly believed he deserved to have the shit kicked out of him.

Lost in my thoughts, I didn't see the person walking toward me until it was too late, colliding in a tangle of limbs, both of us crashing backward. My hood slipped off as I struggled to steady myself.

"Sorry, man, I didn—" I began to apologize, but the words died on my tongue when I saw Evan straightening himself in front of me. Rage immediately flooded my veins, and all I wanted was to pummel him where he stood. Judging by the look on his face, he felt the same way.

"Watch it, Montgomery," he snarled, bending to pick up his backpack from the sidewalk. He scooped up the textbook that must have fallen out, shoving it in the bag before shoulder checking me as he shoved by.

I heaved out an exasperated sigh, rolling my eyes upward. I guess this would be my first step in earning Everly's forgiveness. I turned, so I could see his back as he walked away.

"I'm sorry."

His footsteps halted, his body stopping as my words rang through the empty quad.

He turned slightly, his profile visible over his shoulder.

"What did you say?" His voice was clipped, and his shoulders were bunched around his ears, taut with tension.

Rolling my eyes, I repeated myself. "I said, 'I'm sorry'." I shoved my hands into the pocket of my hoodie, the cold night air chilling them. He finally turned all the way around, stalking back in my direction.

Once he was just a few feet away, he stopped, glaring at me with green eyes a shade or two lighter than Chase's. I remembered Everly saying they were the same color as her mom's, and I wondered if the reminder tore at his heart when he looked in the mirror, like I knew it did to my girl each time she looked into her brother's eyes.

"You're fucking *sorry*? You broke my damn nose, Knox!" His fists were balled at his sides, but if it was another fight he was looking for, he wouldn't find it with me. I knew brawling with her brother again definitely wouldn't get me back in Everly's good graces, and that was what I needed to focus on. Step number one? Apologizing to Evan.

I took a deep breath through my nose, exhaling the air slowly before I spoke. "I'm sorry, man. I shouldn't have hit you," I agreed. But he wasn't getting off the hook that easily either. "But you shouldn't have spoken to your sister the way you did. You broke her fucking heart, man." I gritted my teeth, fighting back the urge to launch my fist into his face again as I remembered the hurt in her eyes when he'd brought up their mom.

He closed his eyes, running his hands over his face before letting out a deep breath. When he opened them, I could see the guilt shining back at me, matching my own.

"I know, Knox." He hung his head in defeat, the fact that he'd hurt Everly so deeply finally sinking in. "I didn't mean what I said. But something came over me on the beach, and I was just..." He paused for a moment before continuing. "I was so pissed at her, and I don't really know why. It's never really bothered me that she was with you guys. I don't know what the fuck happened." He shook his head, obviously just as confused as I was by his reaction that night.

A thought popped into my head, and I knew I needed to tread carefully. I took a cautious step forward.

"Evan, can I ask you a question without you getting pissed?"

He looked at me warily, his eyes narrowed. "Depends on the question."

I took a deep breath, preparing myself to get punched once the words were loose. "Do you only feel that way when you're around Morgan?"

He cocked his head at me in confusion.

"What do you mean?"

Rubbing at my week-old scruff—although, by this point I guess it could just be considered a beard—I tried to find a way to ask the question that was bugging me without provoking another fight. Deciding there was no good way, I just blurted it out.

"I think Morgan is manipulating your emotions about Everly."

His whole body went rigid, the weight of my words hitting their mark as I watched him filter through the possibility that just maybe I was right.

Before he could respond, his cell started ringing from his pocket. He pulled it out, his brows pulling together in confusion before he answered.

"Celly?" I could hear the high pitched shrieking of Everly's best friend over the line, and he winced as she railed at him. I struggled to hide a smirk, knowing she was laying into him about his sister.

A vibration from the pocket of my hoodie interrupted my eavesdropping, and I pulled it out to see Griff calling. Swiping the screen, I answered. "Hey, man, I was just on my way home. Is Everly there? I need to—"

"She's missing, Knox. Something's wrong." His words hit me like a twenty pound sledgehammer straight to the chest. For a moment it was like I forgot how to breathe, the world spinning out of focus around me. I looked over at Evan, his face a pale white, terror-filled eyes looking back at me.

"Knox!" Griff shouted, bringing my attention back to the phone. I shook away the stupor. I needed to focus on what the fuck was happening with my girl.

"Griff, what do you mean, she's missing? Where the fuck is she?" I growled, panic and anger fusing together in my blood, a dangerous combination for anyone who may have hurt my little Monet. I could hear Evan's voice raising, asking the same questions, his tone growing frantic.

"She's missing. No one's seen her. She made a call to Celeste, but when she got here, Everly was nowhere to be found. We don't know where the fuck she is, man." Griff was typically the calm, cool one of our group, so the fear I heard plainly in his voice had me scared fucking shitless.

"What should I do? Should I start searching campus?" A deep seated dread started coursing through my body now, any number of terrible scenarios running through my brain. Griff's stern voice pulled me back from my mind's downward spiral.

"No, come home," he ordered. Silence followed, and I had to check the screen to make sure the call didn't disconnect. Before I could ask, he spoke again. "Chase's PI sent over what he could find about Austin. It's bad Griff. She's in serious fucking danger."

The air whooshed out of my lungs, the information like a sucker punch to my gut.

Fuck!

But the shock quickly turned to rage, washing over my body until I was nearly vibrating. I would kill that motherfucker if he so much as laid a goddamn finger on her.

"I'm on my way; I'll bring Evan with me." Not waiting for an answer, I hung up, shoving the phone back in my pocket.

Spinning to find Evan, I strode quickly to where he was standing, his face ashen, and his phone still in his hand, staring blankly at the ground. I grabbed his upper arms and gave him a firm shake, his head snapping up to meet my gaze. Tears swam in his green eyes, and I could see the terror behind them.

"She's missing, Knox. Celeste said that they don't know where she is. Where's my sister?" His voice trembled, breaking on the last word. "I can't lose her, Knox." He swiped away a tear. "We have to find her."

"I know, Evan." I forced more bravado into my voice than I felt but, apparently, I was going to have to be strong for the both of us. He looked so broken.

In a completely uncharacteristic move, I pulled him in, wrapping my arms around him, and holding him tight to me. A sob erupted from his chest, his body shuddering as the reality of the situation set in.

I held him like that for a few moments before releasing him. Holding him at arm's length, I dipped my head slightly, forcing him to meet my gaze.

"Evan, we have to go meet with the guys. We have to figure out where she is. Can you do that? I need you to answer me."

He shook his head, wiping furiously at his tears, determination filling his eyes. "Yeah, man, let's go. Celeste is there, too." He shoved his phone in his pocket before shouldering his bag.

He easily kept pace with me as we hightailed it across campus, making it back to the dorms in record time. Part of me wondered why Evan didn't just use his caster power and speed ahead, but I think deep down he didn't want to be alone with his guilt over his last interaction with his sister.

Same, buddy.

Taking the steps two at a time, we finally made it to the suite. Using my key fob, I unlocked the door to find Griffin, Celeste, and a busted up Chase pacing around the living room.

Throwing my bag on the sofa, I turned to Chase, taking in the two black eyes and swollen nose on his usually pretty boy face. "What the fuck happened to you?"

He hiked a thumb over his shoulder at Celeste. "Tinkerbell over there punched me."

Despite the circumstances, I barked out a laugh. "What'd you do? I mean, I'm sure you deserved it, but call me curious."

It was Griff who answered for him from his place at the kitchen counter. He was staring at his laptop, scanning over something on the screen. "Celeste thinks he cheated on Everly."

My head swiveled to Chase. He held his hands up, his mouth opening to defend himself when suddenly a blur flew by me. In the next instant, I watched as Evan drew back his arm, his fist connecting with Chase's face in a loud crack.

"The fuck, man!" Chase bellowed, holding his quickly swelling jaw. Spinning, Evan sped to Celeste, sweeping her into his arms. He cupped her cheek, scanning her face for any injuries.

"Are you okay?" he asked her softly and goddamn.

Evan was fucking in love with Celeste.

She looked up at him, hearts in her eyes, before answering.

"I'm alright." Her cheeks flushed, and it was obvious to anyone in the room that these two were head-over-fucking-heels for each other. Morgan would blow a fucking gasket.

I smiled at the thought.

Chase was sitting on the sofa, nursing his wounds, a bag of frozen veggies pressed against his jaw. "She's the one who fucking attacked me, asshole," he grumbled.

Remembering what Griff said, I glared at my friend, hoping I'd heard wrong. "Chase, why does Celeste think you cheated on Everly? Because if you did, man..." My muscles tensed, prepared to go to fucking war for my girl.

"I didn't fucking cheat on her!" Chase yelled, his words slightly garbled by the swelling in his jaw. Bloodstains dotted the front of his SLA rowing shirt, and I had to wonder just how hard Celeste hit him. Part of me wanted to give her a high five. "She thought it was me, but it wasn't! It was Austin!"

Evan let out a low growl. "What do you mean it was Austin? What does Thorpe have to do with any of this?" He continued to hold Celeste, his arms wrapped protectively around her small frame. She was dressed in a lime green hoodie and black leggings, fuzzy princess slippers on her tiny feet while her hair was tucked up in a messy bun.

Tinkerbell... got it.

Griff strode over, taking a seat in one of the arm chairs, placing his laptop on the coffee table. "He has everything to do with it. And right now, we think he has your sister."

twenty four · Everly

The sound of the door unlocking roused me from my restless sleep. Even unconscious, my brain tormented me with images of Chase fucking Heather, Knox holding me down while taking what he wanted, Griff standing by and letting it all happen as Morgan laughed at his side.

I didn't move from my spot on the bed, instead choosing to stare at the gray wall, my eyes focused on the tiny bubbles and imperfections in the paint. I felt the bed sink behind me, and without even seeing him, I knew it was Austin. The tiny hairs on the back of my neck stood on end, his proximity putting my body on high alert.

"Pet," he crooned, stroking a finger down my bare arm. "You hurt yourself. I can't have you injuring yourself, that simply won't do." I glanced at him over my shoulder, watching as he pulled a small vial from his pocket. I quickly scooted away, not wanting him to drug me again.

"Oh, don't worry, my Pet, this will fix your hand."

With a gentleness that belied his usually brutal ways, Austin tugged on my shoulder, forcing me to roll toward him. He unwrapped my hand, blood still seeping slowly from the angry wound. He stretched my fingers, flattening my palm before sprinkling the contents of the vial over it. I watched as the light blue powder coated the gash, my skin knitting itself together. There was a burning sensation, the skin pinching as it healed, but it was over before I had a chance to register the discomfort.

I pulled my hand away, holding it close to my chest. "Thank you," I mumbled quietly, my voice hoarse from crying. I sat up slowly, tucking my knees under my chin before wrapping my arms around them. I stared blankly ahead, my mind a hail storm, images of my men's betrayal raining down until it was all I could do not to break completely.

Austin sat beside me in silence, his head tilted slightly as he studied me. He was wearing different clothes from earlier, but if I had to guess, I didn't think I'd been here more than a day. Although, with no clock and no way to see outside, it was impossible for me to be sure.

Just enough time to completely destroy my entire world.

A sob broke free before I could stop it, tears spilling freely down my cheeks as I broke. I covered my face, weeping for the men that betrayed me, for the love I thought we shared. My body shook as grief took hold.

"Oh now, Pet, as much as I love your tears, we have more pressing matters to attend to." Austin's voice startled me from my misery. He was standing in front of me, his hand outstretched. "Well, let's go. It's time for our first date."

What in the ever loving fuck?

"Austin, I'm not going on a date with you. You fucking kidnapped me!" I gaped at him, shocked at his complete lack of understanding. Although, I guessed I shouldn't be that surprised, given that he did orchestrate this entire fucked up situation.

"Pet, I did not *kidnap* you." He rolled his eyes, irritation creeping into his tone. "I'm simply collecting what is mine based on your father's contract. And I thought after speaking with Montgomery, you would understand *they* no longer want you. You're mine now. Completely."

How was it possible to be this delusional? Judging by the confident look on his face, Austin firmly believed the bullshit spewing from his mouth. Just as I opened my mouth to argue, my stomach decided this was the best time to let out an obnoxiously loud growl.

"See? You're hungry. Perfect timing. I have dinner all prepared." Leaning across the bed, he picked up a set of metal handcuffs, and before I could respond, he grabbed both of my wrists in a tight hold, securing the restraints with practiced ease, my stomach nauseous at the idea.

With my hands restrained, he pulled a key from his pocket, popping it into the shackle around my ankle. It clanged open loudly, and I reached down awkwardly to rub the chafed skin.

Holding the chain between the cuffs, he tugged me from the bed, my legs wobbling a bit as I stood. My bladder took that moment to wake up, screaming its need for release.

"Austin, I need to use the restroom." I darted a look at him. This sweet, caring act he was giving had me on edge. I was waiting for the other shoe to drop, for him to spiral out of control and attack me as he'd done before.

"Of course, Pet. This way." He placed his palm at the small of my back, my body tensing at his touch. He either didn't notice or didn't care as he guided me to the open door.

Stepping through, I realized we were in some sort of cabin, giant logs making up the walls surrounding us. Two mocha colored leather sofas sat facing each other in the center of what I assumed was the living space, a large, stone fireplace the focal point of the room. To the right was an open kitchen with wooden cabinets and natural stone countertops, commercial grade appliances scattered throughout.

I spotted take out bags on the island, and my mouth watered when I smelled the burgers I knew were inside. But before I could eat, I needed to relieve the pressure in my bladder. Austin walked us forward, his hand still pressed firmly just above my ass. He brought me to a door just off the living room, flipping a switch inside.

"Here you go, pet. I'll wait for you here." I awkwardly shuffled by him into the small half bath, the room containing only a toilet, small vanity, and a floating shelf that held miscellaneous bathroom supplies.

I quickly shut the door, pressing my back against it. I let out a shuddering breath, grateful to be away from Austin for the moment. His personality switch was unnerving, setting me on edge.

I needed to get the fuck out of here. My eyes zeroed in on the small window next to the toilet.

Bingo.

I quickly used the toilet, taking care of business as fast as possible. When I was finished, I tried to push the window up, but it was stuck in the track. Fuck. I knew I didn't have much longer before he'd come in to check on me. Using every last ounce of strength I had, I shoved the window open as far as it would go, praying I would fit through.

Bracing my cuffed hands on the windowsill, I climbed onto the closed toilet, pushing my upper body part way through the window. As I attempted to hoist myself the rest of the way through, my goddamn ass bumped the shelf hanging over the toilet, a canister of cotton balls crashing to the tiled floor. Glass shattered loudly, and I froze for a moment.

"Pet?" Austin called through the door, the knob jiggling violently. "Pet, I hope you're behaving."

Frantic and out of time, my feet slipped on the lid, leaving me hanging out the window. I began kicking blindly, trying to find anything to push off of and propel myself forward. I could hear Austin yelling from the other side of the door, his fists pounding on the wood, promising punishment when he caught me.

I gasped at the sound of splintering wood, and not half a second later a scream tore from my throat as rough hands grabbed my waist, yanking me back inside the tiny bathroom. I thrashed wildly in his grip, throwing my head back and connecting with his face. The impact made my vision go dark for a moment as my head swam.

"Fuck!" Austin howled, but his grip only grew tighter, squeezing until my ribs were screaming in agony. My skull throbbed from where I'd headbutted him, and my ears were ringing loudly.

He pulled me from the bathroom, throwing me to the floor in the living room. I landed with a loud thud, pain shooting through my hip as it connected with the hardwood. I cried out, coming down awkwardly on my left wrist, a distinct cracking sound filling the room. Trying to ignore the shooting pain, I scrambled backward in an effort to escape.

He stalked toward me, like a scene from a horror movie, blood dripping from his nose and mouth. He grinned, his teeth coated in red. His eyes found mine, and I could see the violence waiting for me in their depths.

"Pet," he spoke calmly, an unsettling contrast to the way he looked. "That wasn't very nice. That's twice now that you've broken my nose." He swiped the back of his hand under his nose, smearing the blood across his cheek. "I think it's time you learn some manners, don't you?"

"Get the fuck away from me!" I screeched, my legs kicking at him as he quickly approached. "Help! Someone, help! Hel—" The air caught in my lungs as his foot connected harshly with my ribs. Indescribable pain raced through my side, and I struggled to take in a breath. Another swift kick had me crying out. By the third all I could do was whimper.

I curled myself into a ball, my still cuffed hands covering my head, as if they would keep me safe. I drew in raspy breaths, each one brutal as my lungs struggled to expand against the agony in my side. There was no way he hadn't broken at least one of my ribs.

Suddenly my hands were yanked from my face, fingers tangling in my knotted hair. My scalp screamed as he used my hair to pull me upright, angling my face, so I had no choice but to look at him.

He was breathing heavily, rage burning in his eyes. He looked every bit the monster I knew him to be.

He brought his face close to mine, so close that his breath ghosted over my lips. I gagged at the proximity before sobbing, the movement making my injured ribs throb.

"You will learn to obey, Pet," he ground out, his jaw so tense it was a wonder he could speak at all. His grip on my hair tightened, and I winced at the pain. "One way or another, I will break you." He released my hair, pushing my head back slightly as he leaned away.

I went to roll, but before I could, the back of his hand smacked against my cheek so hard I saw stars. I fell back, my head connecting solidly with the wood floor and darkness swept over me.

A throbbing in my skull woke me, my eyes slowly opening, allowing me to see I was back in the fucking bedroom. I tried to move, but my body screamed in pain, black spots dancing in my vision, a harsh reminder of Austin's 'lesson'. Curling in on myself, I took shallow breaths in an effort to ease the pressure on my broken ribs.

Once I was able to see straight again, I sat up slowly, each movement carefully calculated and drawn out to minimize hurting myself further. After what seemed like an eternity, I was finally upright. Well, sort of. I was still hunched over, the searing pain in my ribs not allowing me to stretch fully.

I looked down at my swollen wrist, the skin mottled with deep blues and purples. At least he'd had the decency to take off the cuffs before locking me back in this fucking prison. I wasn't chained to the bed anymore, either. Austin must have assumed all the damage he'd done would leave me unable to escape.

Or he didn't plan to let me out again.

A sob wrenched from my chest, despair carving out a deep hole where my heart had once been. A heart that belonged to three men I thought would be by my side forever. A heart that was now dead, ripped to pieces by the evil and cruelty they'd shown. And yet, I couldn't help missing them so deeply that the pain in my soul far outweighed all the injuries to my body.

I pushed my hair from my face, my fingers brushing my swollen cheek where Austin hit me. My head was still throbbing and, if I had to guess, I probably had a concussion from when I'd hit the floor.

I gently lay back down, absentmindedly noticing the bloodstains that now littered the blue comforter. Lying on my back, I stared at the ceiling, not really seeing it as I drifted into the deep recesses of my mind.

The places where I kept memories of my mom, of Celeste and Evan, of my guys before they betrayed me. I sank into those memories until sleep pulled me under once more.

twenty-
five
Griffin

W e worked well into the night, pouring over any scrap of information
we could find about mimics. It was close to six AM, and my eyes were
burning. Taking off my glasses, I flung them on the coffee table, slamming my
laptop shut. We were still no fucking closer to finding Everly.

Celeste stirred from her spot on the sofa. She was snuggled into Evan's
side, his arm wrapped around her possessively. I studied them, watching Evan
as he scrolled through his phone, checking out any possible locations where
Austin might be holding Everly, his head nodding to the side every so often
as he fought sleep.

Honestly, we couldn't even prove she'd been kidnapped, and that lack
of evidence was my reasoning for not involving the authorities. Evan im-

mediately demanded we go to the campus police after we explained what transpired over the last few months between Everly and Austin.

He'd been enraged, hearing how Austin assaulted his sister, the deal their father had made, and the way Morgan manipulated the entire situation to her benefit. Catching a glimpse of several long, colorfully worded texts he'd sent to my ex, it was clear he was done with her bullshit.

I'd pulled him into the kitchen in an attempt to calm him after he nearly stormed out, hell bent on ripping Austin's head from his body.

"I'll fucking kill him Griff. If he touches her, I swear to god, I'll burn his ass to ash." His fist erupted in flames as he banged it on the counter. Celeste's head whipped around at the loud thump, and she eyed him cautiously before turning back around to look over some topographic maps of the campus Chase had been able to pull up online.

Looking for a way to distract him before he burned down the whole damn building, I tossed a dishcloth on his fiery hand to smother the flames before grabbing two beers from the fridge. My brain needed a break from the multitude of articles I had pulled up on my laptop about mimics. Popping the tops, I slid one into his waiting hand.

I took a long pull, watching Evan as he watched Celeste with Chase, the muscles in his jaw ticking each time she laughed at my best friend.

"You don't have anything to worry about there," I said quietly, gesturing to the living room.

Evan took a drink of his beer before answering. "Don't know what you're talking about." His weak attempt at denial had me biting back a smile.

I chuckled, shaking my head. Everly had confided in us just how in love Celeste was with Evan. And judging by the way he'd held her earlier, I could see the feelings were mutual.

"Chase is all about Everly," I continued. *"Tinkerbell there is cute and all, but no offense, she's got nothing on your sister."*

Evan scoffed, putting the bottle of beer to his lips, speaking so softly I almost didn't hear his next words.

"You're fucking crazy, man. She's perfect."

Now they were curled up together, Celeste catching a few hours of sleep while the rest of us continued our search for any clues that could lead us to Everly. My stomach growled, earning me a smirk from Chase, although, with how bruised up his face was, it looked more like a grimace.

He stood from his spot in one of our arm chairs, stretching out his long body after hours spent huddled over maps and blueprints he and Knox had gathered from inside the administration building.

Being a tour guide with master keys came in handy every now and then.

Rummaging through the cupboards, Chase found a few bags of chips, tossing them on the coffee table for me to pick at. Low rock music filtered through Knox's heavy door, the distinct sound of Breaking Benjamin meeting my ears. He'd disappeared around four in the morning to paint, needing a break from the high tension filling our suite.

We were all struggling, feeling helpless in our mission to find Everly. Knox's music suddenly cut off, and a moment later there was a loud crash from his room. Rushing to my feet, I raced down the hall toward his room. Flinging open the door, I was met with a sight I was not prepared for.

Onyx was hanging from Knox's hoodie, his fluffy black tail flicking wildly as he chittered. Knox was trying to pull him off and yelped when Onyx nipped his hand, drawing blood with his sharp little teeth. The squirrel leapt off my friend, landing on the floor soundlessly, before scurrying away.

"What the fuck did you do to Onyx?" I strode over to where Everly's familiar was huddled under Knox's desk, still loudly chittering. I bent down, trying to coax him out, but he just glared at me.

Could squirrels even glare? Fuck if I knew, but it looked like this one could.

"I didn't do shit to him!" Knox threw his paint covered hands in the air. "I saw him scratching at the window, so I let him in, and he fucking attacked me!" He sucked the side of his finger, stopping the blood before grabbing a Band-Aid from the drawer of his desk. He'd learned a long time ago to keep some on hand when he went through a sculpting phase.

Those chisels and Xacto knives were sharp.

Unable to coax Onyx out of his hiding spot, Knox and I made our way back to the living room to find everyone awake.

Celeste was staring at Chase, her eyes the size of saucers while he grinned at her happily. I couldn't help but notice the way Evan had her pulled tightly against him, or the glare he was shooting at my friend. *Jesus fucking Christ, what did he do now?*

"What's got you so happy? Did you forget our girl is missing?" Knox asked grumpily, flopping down in one of the empty armchairs. He raked his fingers through his dark hair, the strands sticking up every which way.

"Well, I needed a little break from staring at the maps, so I decided to enroll Celeste here at SLA." He bounced excitedly, like a damn kid on Christmas. I narrowed my eyes at him in disbelief.

"Chase, you can't just *enroll* someone. There's a whole process." I pinched the bridge of my nose, a dull throb forming just behind my eyes from lack of sleep.

I loved my best friend, but sometimes Chase's perception of how the world worked was pretty fucking skewed. I guess growing up rich would do that to you.

"Well, she's not technically enrolled *yet,*" Chase shrugged, still smiling. "But my dad is currently sending an email to the admissions office and Headmaster Charles is guaranteeing her a full ride scholarship, including room and board. I figured it would be a nice surprise for when we get Everly back." The hopeful look on his face nearly broke me, his grin reminding me that he needed her just as much as I did.

"So what, she's just supposed to stay here, Stone? All her stuff is back at her house in Staunton." Evan huffed, poking any holes in Chase's plan that he could. It was a losing battle though. When Chase Stone set his mind to something, there was no stopping him.

He flashed his phone screen in Evan and Celeste's direction, his smile broadening even more. "Already taken care of. My dad is arranging to have movers pack up your stuff and drop it off here later today. He'll contact your parents to ensure everything you need gets packed. He also said he set up an account for you at the bookstore to get all your materials."

Celeste was stunned into silence, something I knew to be rare, even in the short amount of time we'd spent together. After several long minutes, she finally spoke, her voice thick with emotion.

"Chase, why would your dad do this for me? He doesn't even know me."

My friend leaned forward from his seat, his eyes softening as his smile turned sad.

"Because, Tinkerbell, I explained how important you are to my girl, and my dad knows how important she is to me. It was pretty easy to convince him from there."

Celeste drew in a ragged breath, tears brimming in her eyes. "Thank you," she said quietly, and I watched as Evan laced his fingers through hers, pulling her hand into his lap.

Chase swung his gaze over his shoulder to where I was standing. "I also explained our fear that Austin took Everly. Dad agreed, not involving the cops right now is our best bet. He's gonna use his connections and see if he can get us any other information about where he might be keeping her. Properties we might not know about, that sort of thing."

I nodded my head in approval. Out of the corner of my eye, I saw Onyx slowly creeping out from Knox's doorway, careful to avoid the angry painter. Once he'd cleared Knox, he scampered quickly across the room, hopping straight into Celeste's lap.

"Well, hi, Onyx," she crooned, giving him gentle scratches along his back. He nuzzled into her touch, a soft purring sound coming from deep in his chest. After reveling in her attention for a few minutes, he hopped onto the coffee table, sniffing the large map Knox and Chase had stolen from the archives in the admin building last night.

The quiet of the room was interrupted by a loud growling. Chase howled in laughter as we all turned to stare at Celeste, whose face was turning an incredibly bright shade of red. She shoved at Evan's chest when he failed to suppress his own laugh. "Shut up, Blackwell! I forgot to eat last night. I was getting ready to head to a late dinner when..."

And just like that, all the joy from the last thirty seconds vanished, bringing us all crashing back to reality.

"I'm gonna grab a shower," Chase mumbled before disappearing down the hall.

"I'll fix us some eggs. That way we can just eat here while we work." I trudged to the kitchen, pulling out the ingredients I'd need to cook breakfast.

As I whisked the eggs, I watched Evan and Celeste, their heads close together as they spoke in hushed tones on the sofa. Knox had disappeared into his bedroom again, most likely to keep painting, and I could hear the shower running from Chase's bathroom, telling me he'd left his door slightly ajar.

I was alone with my thoughts. And I didn't like them.

Onyx was still perched on the coffee table, prancing around one particular corner of the map we'd laid out last night. Every few seconds, he would chitter at Celeste, hopping around in front of her before going back to the corner.

I cocked my head, studying his odd behavior. It was as if he was trying to get her to look at the map. Like he was trying to show her...

"Familiars can sense their magical counterparts, even hundreds of miles apart. They are able to tell when their caster is hurt or in danger. Familiars may become agitated, even aggressive when separated from their caster or if they believe their caster to be in danger. Familiars are able to locate their casters on a deep magical level that is still a mystery to top researchers in the field."

The words from the book flooded my mind like a photograph. I dropped my whisk, the metal clanging against the glass bowl.

"Onyx knows where she is!"

"What?" Evan jumped from the sofa, his gaze swinging wildly between Onyx and me. Chase chose that moment to rejoin us, strolling into the living room with a towel slung over his bare shoulders, his black joggers hanging off his hips. Water droplets shook from his hair as he looked between the three of us, clearly feeling the tension in the room.

"Get Knox. NOW!" I barked. Something on my face must have said I wasn't fucking around because he spun quickly, shooting off down the hall toward Knox's room. Seconds later they were both in front of me.

"Onyx knows where she is. He's her familiar. He can sense where she is, if she's in danger. It's why he attacked you last night, Knox. He was trying to tell you." I recited the information from my book to them, watching hope bloom in each of their eyes.

"He could have told me with a little less teeth, little bastard," Knox grumbled under his breath. "So, where the hell is she?"

We surrounded the coffee table, each of us eyeing the spot Onyx was currently sitting on.

"Tenebris Forest."

"Let's fucking go!" Chase hollered, grabbing a sweatshirt laying on the arm of the sofa. He ran to the door, flinging it open.

"Uh, hi." A tall woman with hot pink hair stood just outside, her hand raised as if knocking on the door. "Is Everly here?"

Knox stalked up behind Chase, his eyes blazing with distrust.

"Who the fuck are you?"

twenty-six · Everly

A noise at the door woke me, my fight or flight mode kicking in as I readied myself for more abuse. I whimpered, pain shooting through every inch of my battered body. I squeezed my eyes shut as a wave of nausea washed over me.

"It's time to wake up, pet," Austin ordered, pushing the door open with one hand, holding a plastic tray in the other. Despite how shitty I felt, my stomach growled, and my mouth watered at the thought of food.

"I can't have you wasting away on me." He set the tray on the nightstand, and I eyed it cautiously. I wouldn't put it past him to poison me at this point. A simple piece of toast with a sliced apple sat on a small plate, a cup of water, and a napkin completing the meal. "Now, eat."

It wasn't a request.

For a fraction of a second, my thoughts drifted to another man that liked to order me around before quickly shaking them away.

He wasn't coming for me.

None of them were.

Might as well eat the goddamn food. If it's poisoned at least this will all be over.

I sat up slowly, trying not to show him how much pain I was in. Once I was upright, I reached tentatively for the toast, taking a small bite. It tasted like regular toast, and deciding it was safe, I scarfed down the single slice before moving to the apples. When the plate was empty, I guzzled down the glass of water, my stomach slightly happier now that it had some food in it.

Austin picked up the dishes, exiting the room momentarily, most likely to deposit them in the sink. He was back a few seconds later, taking a spot next to me on the bed. I leaned away on instinct, not wanting to be anywhere near him.

"Oh pet, don't be like that." He scooted closer, so close that our thighs were touching. I swallowed down the toast threatening to come up, pulling my injured wrist closer to my chest. "Would you like some ice for your wrist?"

Not thinking, I whipped my head to see if it was still Austin sitting next to me and not some weird pod person with actual feelings. Unfortunately, the sudden movement had my head spinning, a fun side effect from the concussion.

Seeing my shocked expression, Austin chuckled. Not saying another word, he took my uninjured wrist in his hand, pulling me gently to my feet. The tender way he held me was unnerving, the sudden change in behavior giving me whiplash. He led me out to the living room, not rushing me as I moved at a snail's pace, my ribs screaming in pain with each step.

What in the actual fuck was going on?

He helped me sit on one of the leather sofas before striding to the fireplace, and I took the opportunity to study my captor.

He was wearing a slate gray polo—complete with a popped collar—and black jeans, a pair of gray boat shoes completing his douchey frat boy look. He screamed entitlement, with high-end logos on his clothes and hair with too much product. Peeking out from the collar of his shirt was a single black cord, a dark crystal dangling from it. I watched as he expertly stacked several pieces of wood in the hearth. He stepped back and opened his hand, a flame bursting to life from his palm.

So he's a fire elemental. Good to know.

Noticing a vase of flowers on the coffee table, I called on my own elemental power, trying to make the water do *something*. But just like with my telekinesis, nothing. Austin had to be using something to block my magic. And without it, I was good and fucked.

He sent the flame into the stacked wood, and within seconds the fire sprang to life. He stared at it, almost lovingly for a moment before poking at the logs, moving them here and there. I looked around the main space of the cabin. There were large windows on one wall, giving me a beautiful view of a dense forest. Late morning sun streamed through a canopy of green, the light telling me I'd been here overnight and well into the next day.

Seemingly pleased with his fire, Austin took a spot on the couch opposite me, sitting in the middle and stretching his long arms along the back. He crossed one leg over his knee, looking completely at ease instead of the psycho I knew him to be. I eyed him warily as he smiled.

"Pet, seeing how last night didn't exactly go how I'd planned, I thought maybe we could try again today. If you can behave, we can stream some movies, play some board games, and I'll even make you some popcorn." He grinned at me from the couch, the smile showing too many teeth, leaving an uneasy feeling in my gut.

I didn't answer, just nodded my head in agreement. Whatever it took to keep him from beating me again.

With the maniacal smile still on his face, he continued.

"If you can't behave, well..." His voice trailed off, but the threat was clear. If I didn't do as he said, I feared broken ribs would be the least of my worries. And the violent gleam in his eyes made me wonder if he hoped I wouldn't listen.

Glancing at the grandfather clock tucked into the corner, I saw we were closing in on early evening, the small hand inching closer to the six with each passing minute.

Austin had moved the sofas for our 'day date' as he'd called it, pushing one to the far side of the room and turning the other to face the flat screen tv hanging above the fireplace.

We watched a bunch of movies, Austin letting me pick one before choosing the rest. I'd dozed off and on, my head still pounding from the night before, making it impossible to keep my eyes open at times.

I was just finishing off the last few kernels of popcorn in my bowl as the last movie ended when he rose from his spot. He'd been fairly quiet throughout the day, making small comments here and there, mostly about how he'd have to improve my taste in movies once I moved to his father's estate and what our plans for the upcoming holidays would look like. I cringed, panicking internally at the thought of being his prisoner for that long.

As inconspicuous as possible, I slid further down the couch. Austin progressively moved closer to me throughout the day as each movie played until his thigh was pressed firmly against my own, his arm sprawled along the back cushions, as if we were actually spending a cozy Saturday in. It took everything in my body to not curl away from him, but I knew that would be considered *misbehaving*, and I wasn't prepared to take another beating when the bruises littering my body were still so fresh and my ribs throbbed.

Shifting around, I let out a whimper when I bumped my hurt wrist against the arm of the sofa. Austin looked down at me, his brows pinched. His eyes focused on my injury before coming back to my battered face. "Well, Pet, I think you've behaved well enough to earn some relief from your discomfort."

He disappeared into the kitchen, and I rolled my eyes at his back. He returned a few minutes later with an ice pack, a glass of water, and three painkillers. I eyed the pills suspiciously.

"They're just ibuprofen, pet. Honestly, you think I would drug you?" He rolled his eyes as he held out the medicine. Unable to bite my tongue, I quipped back.

"You did drug me, remember? That's how I got here."

His face hardened, and I immediately regretted opening my mouth.

Fuck.

"*I* didn't drug you, Everly," he said, his voice clipped with annoyance. My curiosity getting the better of me, I pressed him cautiously.

"So if it wasn't you who did it," I paused, swallowing down the fear in my throat. Austin's entire demeanor had flipped on a dime with my comment, and I was afraid of what the repercussions for questioning him might be. "Then who took me?"

He stared blankly at me for a moment before throwing his head back, laughing loudly. The sound startled me, not because of the volume, but because I knew it wasn't a happy laugh. It was filled with evil and malice, and I shrunk back on instinct, ignoring the sting in my side.

"Pet, you're not really that stupid, are you?" The sickening smile that played on his lips made my insides knot, an unspoken threat of violence hanging in the air between us.

I didn't know how to respond, so I just sat quietly, praying he would forget I asked. Several long moments passed, his muddy-brown eyes studying me intently, as if I were a riddle he was trying to solve. I could feel the tension building between us, and my mind scrambled to think of a way to defend myself when, not if, he pounced.

In my peripheral, I could see the flower vase sitting on the coffee table. *Maybe I can hit him with that and make a run for it.* But fuck, how far could I make it with the amount of pain I was in? And I had no fucking clue where I was.

Just when I thought he was going to attack, the door of the cabin began to open, drawing my attention and breaking the unnerving staring contest I'd found myself in. Seeing my one opportunity for escape, I jumped from the couch, adrenaline masking the screaming pain in my ribs. I raced to the door as fast as I could, convinced that if I could just get outside I might stand a chance.

I could feel him at my back, his long legs giving him an advantage. He was on me within seconds, and a scream tore from my throat when his hands landed on my body. He wrapped an arm around me, pinning my arms down while the other grabbed a fistful of my hair, anchoring my head back. Guess he'd learned from me breaking his nose the other night.

I looked helplessly as the door opened wider, shadows dancing in the doorway. Night had fallen, and it wasn't until the flames from the fire behind me lit up the space that I was able to see the figure outside.

Bile filled my throat when I caught sight of her bleach blonde hair. That goddamn saccharine smile cut across her face, her joy at seeing me bruised and broken obvious.

"You fucking bitch!" I screamed, spitting at her.

"Hi, Everly. I told you Austin said hi." In the next second her fist collided with my gut, pushing the air out of my lungs. Austin released me as I fell to my knees, doubling over as I tried to breathe. I drew my eyes up slowly, but just as I reached her face, another punch landed to the left side of my head, and the world went dark once more.

As I slowly came to, my head throbbed, and I felt as if I'd gone ten rounds with Conor McGregor. I tried to open my eyes, but my left was refusing to cooperate. What the hell was going on? Muffled voices filtered into my ears.

"We need to go; they know you have her. Evan broke up with me last night."

"Where are your crystals?"

"I accidentally broke them when I was lugging her ass to the car last night!"

"I'll have to leave to get things set up before I can move her. We'll keep her here until then. They won't find us here."

Memories of Morgan punching me came flooding back. Panicking, I managed to open one eye, and I realized the other was swollen shut.

I tried to move, but found myself tied to one of the dining room chairs, smack dab in the middle of the cabin's living room. The heavy metal chain from the bedroom was wrapped around my legs, securing them to the wooden legs of the seat while my arms were handcuffed behind my back, uncomfortably stretched around the chair. The pain in my broken wrist brought tears to my eyes when I tried to wiggle it free.

"Oh, you're awake, goody," Morgan sneered from her spot directly in front of me. She was seated on one of the leather couches, her arms crossed over her chest. She gave an annoyed huff, as if I was inconveniencing her by being tied up. They'd moved the furniture back, but instead of the coffee table, I was now the centerpiece between the leather couches. I gave her the best glare I could muster with only one working eye, my lip curling back in anger.

She grinned, looking like the fucking cat that got the canary. Remembering what she said right before she sucker punched me, the lightbulb in my brain clicked on, and hot rage roared through my veins.

"You goddamn cunt! You fucking drugged me!"

Her grin widened as I screamed, thrashing wildly in the chair, my brain ignoring the immense pain each movement brought on.

"Oh, Everly," Her condescending voice was like nails on a chalkboard as she leaned forward, patting me on the cheek. "I told you Griffin was mine." Sitting back, she began inspecting her nails, like she was already bored with our conversation.

"Just going to kick my brother to the curb, then, you lying whore?" It probably wasn't smart to bait her, but I couldn't help myself.

She laughed, but it wasn't one of joy. No, this was cold and hollow, spite coating the sound.

"Did you honestly think I *liked* your brother? Are you really that stupid, *Emberly?*" She cut her eyes to mine, evil swimming in them. "He was just a way to fuck with you. Although, he was a fun distraction." She laughed mockingly while I considered the many ways I was going to murder her if I ever got out of here.

I felt him at my back before the sharp prick of the needle. Austin's venomous voice whispered in my ear just as my vision grew dark.

"And now, you. Are. Mine."

twenty-seven Knox

I eyed Everly's supposed new friend from my place on the couch.

She'd quickly explained the breakfast plans she and Everly had made for this morning. Muffins and coffee down by the lake. When my girl failed to show, Stella came by the dorm, first checking Everly and Evan's place, then moving down to ours.

Chase vouched for her, saying Everly had mentioned Stella several times.

I was still skeptical.

She was like some punked-out version of a Disney princess, her bright pink hair shaved close to her head on one side, long wavy curls on the other. She was wearing a black and white plaid skirt over ripped tights, the color matching

211

her bright hair. She'd paired them with an old Chevelle t-shirt, layered over a white long-sleeve tee.

At least she has decent taste in music.

A sad smile broke out on my face when I landed on her Converse, my mind drifting to the sneakers in a rainbow of colors that lived in Everly's closet.

Fuck. I'd screwed up so badly with her. We needed to find her. I had to make it right.

We'd given Stella a brief rundown of the situation, and she'd immediately jumped in, looking over the information Griff had gathered about Austin's caster ability. She sat in the living room with Evan and Celeste as they studied the area where Griffin was convinced Austin was holding our girl.

The problem?

Tenebris Forest was fucking huge, and we didn't have the slightest clue where to start.

I glanced out our large living room windows, the sun sinking low behind the trees. Bright oranges and yellows melded with the vibrant purples of dusk creating a stunning palette of colors in the evening sky.

My heart ached as I wondered if my little Monet was seeing the same sunset.

A call on Chase's phone cut through my thoughts, his phone vibrating loudly on the counter beside me.

"Chase," I called, tossing it to him as he walked over. He swiped at the screen, answering.

"Dad, any news?" He stopped moving, the phone pressed to his ear. His eyes narrowed as he listened to his father, nodding his head at whatever the elder man was saying.

"Put him on speaker phone, asshole," I ordered gruffly. He shot me a glare before placing the phone on the counter, Mr. Stone's voice filling the suite.

"Dad," Chase interrupted. "You're on speaker phone. Repeat what you just told me."

"Oh, okay. So, my investigators found a receipt of purchase for a cabin. Alaric purchased a small log cabin about a month ago. Looks like right after the ball."

I glanced around, noticing everyone was crowded around the countertop now. Evan had his arms wrapped around Celeste from behind while Griff and Stella stood on either side.

"Where the fuck is it?" My impatience and the lack of sleep were making me even more of an asshole than usual.

"Hello to you too, Knox," Mr. Stone snarked back at me. Chase glared at me as Griff whacked the back of my head.

"Oww!" I rubbed the spot, before apologizing. "Sorry, Mr. Stone. Do you know where the cabin is?" I knew I needed to rein in my surly attitude, but fuck was it difficult when I knew my girl was out there and in danger.

"I have the GPS coordinates," he explained, and a sliver of hope burrowed into my chest for the first time since Everly had gone missing. *"I'm sending them to Chase's phone now. It looks like it's about a two hour hike from campus."* The phone chimed as the information came through, Chase picking it up to open the attachment.

"Thanks, Dad, I got 'em. I'll call you when we've got her."

"Please be careful, Chase. From what the PIs told me, Austin is unhinged and dangerous. Will you wait and let me get some help out there for you?" I could hear the worry in Mr. Stone's voice, fear for his son obvious.

Griff spoke up from his spot next to me. "With all due respect, Mr. Stone, we can't wait. If we're right, then Austin has had her for almost twenty-four hours. Who knows what the fuck he's done to her."

A deep growl vibrated from my chest before I could stop it. Stella's eyes widened at the sound, but she kept her mouth clamped tightly shut.

Smart girl.

Mr. Stone let out a deep sigh. *"Alright then, since it seems I can't convince you to wait, please be careful. And call me the moment you get her back. I love you, Chase."*

"Love you too, Dad." Chase ended the call, silence blanketing the room. I looked around at my friends, both old and new, before Griff spoke.

"Everyone get packed up. We leave in ten minutes. Evan, take Celeste back to your place and, get a backpack with clothes for Everly." He issued the commands with swift efficiency, his tone leaving no room for argument. "Celeste, you're probably going to want to borrow some of Everly's clothes. It's going to be cold out in those woods this late at night. Stella, you too, if you're coming with us."

"Hell yes, I'm coming with you! Let's go get our girl!"

Stella's look of determination had the corner of my mouth drawing up into an almost-there smile. I didn't know Stella well, but it was obvious she was a good friend to Everly. She left a few moments later with Celeste and Evan with promises to meet us downstairs in ten minutes.

I turned to Griff. "What do you need me to do, man?" I was fighting the urge to pace the room like a caged animal.

The thought that we would soon have Everly back gave me hope, but I worried about what sort of state she'd be in when we found her. My stomach turned as my brain nose dived into all the terrible things Austin could be doing to her right fucking now.

"You and Chase go get changed. I'm gonna 'port to the janitor's closet and grab some flashlights. I'll meet you back here in a few minutes." With a snap of his fingers he was gone, leaving Chase and I staring at the empty space where he'd been standing only moments before.

Springing into action, we both raced to our rooms. Quickly, I tossed on a long-sleeve henley, followed by the hoodie painted with Everly's name, and a pair of fleece joggers. Snagging a pair of socks and my sneakers, I met Chase in the hallway, his outfit mirroring my own.

We strode into the kitchen together just as Griff appeared, juggling an armful of flashlights, five in total. "Let's get moving," he ordered, and we headed out the door.

Celeste, Evan, and Stella were waiting for us at the main doors, a small bookbag strapped to Celeste's back. Chase pulled out his phone, showing us each the map indicating the route we needed to take to reach the cabin.

We're coming, baby. Just hold on.

We trudged through Tenebris Forest in a single-file line, with the exception of Celeste and Evan, who walked holding hands.

Our flashlights illuminated the dark woods as Chase led the way. The nighttime sounds of the forest surrounded us as our footfalls filled the darkness. I could hear crickets chirping in the distance and the rustling of the small woodland creatures that roamed between the trees after the sun went down.

Stella and Celeste had been chatting softly, each girl trying to get to know the other. They seemed to have a lot in common, and my eavesdropping had told me that Stella was a bard, able to create magic with her flute, and an earth elemental, like Chase.

After walking for nearly two hours, Chase's steps slowed. "There should be a small clearing just down the other side of this hill; that's where the cabin should be." He spoke over his shoulder, his eyes studying the map on his phone. I'd never been so grateful for all the time he spent out in nature as I was tonight.

Picking up our pace, we crested the hill a few minutes later. Just at the bottom I could see several soft lights coming from inside a small log cabin, smoke rising from the stone chimney.

"There it is!" Celeste cheered. She started to pull away from Evan, preparing to race down the hill, but he pulled her back.

"Hey!" she started to protest, but Griff cut her off before she could argue more.

"We need to be smart about this. We don't know what we're walking into." We moved to form a circle on the path. "We'll all go down, but Evan, I think it's best if you stay outside with the girls. Chase, Knox, and I will go inside and get Everly. Between the three of us, I think we should be able to handle it if Austin is in there."

"Umm, excuse me?" Celeste glared at Griff, a challenge in her eyes. "She's *my* fucking best friend and I—"

But this time it was Evan that interrupted her.

"And she's my fucking sister. You need to be safe, so you can help her," He tugged her close, cupping her cheek before bending to whisper something in her ear. Her eyes welled with tears, but she nodded up at him. He looked back to us, a fierce determination blazing in his eyes.

"You guys go get my sister. Bring her back to me."

Without another word, we descended the hill, turning off our flashlights and silently moving toward the house. There was a small porch out front, and Evan huddled the girls to one end as Chase, Griff, and I moved to the door.

Griff tried the knob but it was locked. Glancing at Chase, he stepped aside. Chase gripped the handle, snapping it off with ease, the door swinging open. Soft light poured out onto the porch, and I couldn't wait another second.

Shoving by my friends, I rushed inside, my eyes scanning the space quickly before finding my girl tied to a fucking chair in the middle of the room.

"Everly." My voice cracked as her name escaped on a whisper.

Jesus fucking Christ, my poor Monet.

I ran to her still form, panic rising when she didn't so much as flinch at the noise I made. I could feel Griff and Chase behind me, curse words falling freely from each of their mouths.

Her head was slumped forward, her chin resting on her chest. I gently cupped her cheeks, lifting her head, so I could see her beautiful face. My eyes cataloged the swollen black eye, her split lip, and the bruises that covered her cheeks, each one adding fuel to the raging inferno sweeping through my body.

I would kill that cocksucker.

I would make him scream in agony for every mark on her perfect body.

Chase made quick work of the handcuffs around her wrists, her arms falling slack once he'd snapped the flimsy metal, before moving on to the chain around her legs.

Once she was free, she slumped forward into my waiting arms, still unconscious. I scooped her up, standing with her tucked against my body.

"Her wrist looks broken," Griff said through gritted teeth. He placed a hand over her heart for a moment. "But her heartbeat is strong. Let's get her back before Austin realizes she's gone."

"Fuck that," Chase growled, prowling through the cabin. "I'm gonna fucking rip that asshole apart. Limb by fucking limb." He was over turning furniture, smashing anything in his path as Griff tried to reason with him.

"Get her outside," Griff barked at me, wrestling a glass bowl from Chase before it dropped, shattering on the hardwood floor. Not needing any further directions, I huddled Everly close to my chest, cutting through the room quickly and out the door.

Celeste, Stella, and Evan ran over when I emerged. Both girls released heartbreaking sobs while Evan gasped, his eyes taking in his sister's broken body. "Is she..." Tears welled in his eyes, the words getting stuck in his throat.

"She's alive," I reassured them. "But she's pretty badly injured. We need to get her home." I ground my molars together so hard my teeth ached. Chase needed to get it the fuck together, so we could get out of here.

I squeezed her tighter, and she let out a soft whimper, so I loosened my hold a bit. I didn't know what sort of injuries she might have, but judging by what I could see, Austin used her as a fucking punching bag.

Celeste quickly pulled a small blanket from her backpack, draping it over Everly, tucking it tightly around her body.

Just as she finished, Griff and Chase emerged, Chase's chest heaving as he struggled to calm down. His knuckles were split open, blood smeared on the dark fabric of his sweatshirt. Griff followed him outside, a scowl on his face as he threw a cutting look at our friend.

Quickly turning his attention to me, he rushed over, brushing a gentle hand across our girl's forehead. Anger burned in his hazel eyes, the promise of vengeance and retribution shining bright.

"Let's get the fuck out of here." We all nodded quietly in agreement

He placed one hand on my bicep, the other on Everly's shoulder, and in the next instant we were transported back to our suite, the bright overhead lights making me squint when we landed.

Griff was gone a second later, heading back to get everyone else. But I wasn't fucking waiting around.

I went straight to my bedroom, Everly still cradled in my arms. Lifting a foot to the edge of the bed, I released her lower body, balancing it on my knee. Leaning down awkwardly with my free hand, I fumbled for a moment before I yanked the covers back, exposing the cool sheet below. Repositioning her in my arms, I gently laid her on her side near the edge of my bed.

Staring at her still form, I choked down a sob in the quiet room.

What if she didn't wake up?

What if he'd hurt her so badly she wouldn't come back?

Needing to hold her, I pulled my hoodie over my head as I toed off my shoes. Climbing in behind her, I looped an arm around her waist, pulling her into my chest. I curled around her protectively, my body shielding hers. Guilt tore through me.

Couldn't protect her before, asshole.

Holding her tight, I made a silent promise that I would never let Austin Thorpe or anyone else harm her ever again.

Even if it killed me.

twenty eight   Everly

I awoke too warm, my body covered in a sheen of sweat, my clothes sticking to my damp skin. I tried to throw the covers off, but I was pinned in place, something heavy pressing painfully on my ribs. Cracking open my good eye, I took in the dimly lit room.

Half painted canvases littered the floor, a broken easel tossed haphazardly in the corner.

Hanging off the back of a desk chair was a black hoodie. I'd painted my name on it one afternoon in October to mark it as mine.

To mark *him* as mine.

This wasn't the room in the cabin.

Terror gripped me, my blood running cold as the realization of where I was slammed into me. The arm around my middle suddenly felt like it weighed a thousand pounds, his hot breath tickling the back of my neck.

My stomach roiled, and a scream broke free, piercing the silence of the room. I scrambled forward, falling off the side of the bed and landing on my broken wrist as I tried to catch myself. The overhead lights flicked on as I did my best to crawl away from him, my body crying out in protest.

Knox.

He was sitting up in the middle of his bed, his dark brown eyes looking at me in bewilderment. His hair was sticking up every which way, his t-shirt wrinkled from sleep.

I spotted Onyx as he jumped to the floor, hopping quickly to where I landed. He scurried close to my body, his fluffy tail twitching as his obsidian eyes studied me.

I saw movement to my left and swung my gaze, only to be met with yet another man who had betrayed me.

Chase.

"Larkspur, you're okay, baby. You're safe." He held his hands in front of him, his voice calm as he slowly inched toward me. I moved away until my back hit the dresser, a picture frame crashing to the floor beside me.

"Blue girl, it's us. It's Griff, Chase, and Knox. It's us, baby," a deep voice said from my other side, drawing my attention in the opposite direction.

Griff.

My eyes darted wildly between them. I was fucking trapped. My fingers brushed a shard of broken glass by my side, and I snatched it up, holding it tightly in my hand.

"Everly." Knox's voice was soft and belied the violence I knew was hiding beneath the surface. He began climbing off the bed, crawling toward me on his hands and knees.

When he was a few feet away, I brandished the glass, swiping it in his direction. I felt as its sharpness sliced into my palm, the bite of pain nothing compared to the terror gripping my chest.

"Whoa! Easy, Everly." He backed off, his brows pinched, like he couldn't understand why the fuck I wouldn't want him anywhere near me. "I'm not going to hurt you, baby."

"Liar!"

I swung the glass again when he tried to move closer, nicking the fabric of his shirt.

"Get the fuck away from me!" I barely registered the blood running down my arm in rivulets, dripping off my elbow and staining the gray carpet. "Help! Someone! Please, help!"

Chase's eyes went wide at my cries, his mouth opening and closing like a fish. He looked at Griff, but he seemed just as confused by my reaction. Maybe Knox hadn't told them about what he'd done to me.

Fucking coward.

Just as I sucked in a painful breath, readying myself to continue yelling for help, the bedroom door swung open, Celeste, my brother, and Stella all rushing inside.

"Everly!" Celeste cried, sprinting across the room and dropping to her knees next to me.

My makeshift weapon clattered to the floor as her arms encircled me. A second later I felt another set of arms, Stella having joined us in our embrace.

I sobbed, my heart thundering as I did my best to hug them back.

I finally felt something that resembled safety in my best friends' arms. We held each other like that for a long time, and I was momentarily able to forget the monsters in the room with me, until a throat cleared nearby.

Pulling slowly away, I saw my brother hovering nervously near the door.

"Everly?" The pain in his voice brought tears to my eyes, but I couldn't stand to look at him, at any of them. They'd all betrayed me. "Are you... are you okay?" he whispered, sounding almost afraid of what my answer may be.

"Make them leave, C, please?" I begged, ignoring his question. Gripping the sleeve of Stella's long-sleeve shirt tightly, fear slithered up my spine once more.

While the comfort of my friends' touch had been nice, I knew realistically that if these men wanted to hurt me, they would.

Celeste stood, walking to where Chase stood near the windows. "You guys should go," she said to him quietly. His face fell, a sadness in his eyes I hadn't anticipated seeing, considering he'd been fucking Heather now for weeks. "I'll explain everything to her. But she's not going to listen with you all here."

Why *was* he here? Why were any of them here, after they'd handed me over to Austin?

Chase nodded his head in defeat, shooting me one last pleading look, his eyes wet with tears. Not understanding why he was so upset, I chose to focus on my friends, leaning into Stella's body as she held me tightly.

Griff and Knox followed Chase to the bedroom door, Evan moving further inside to allow them past. He took another step closer, but Celeste held up her hand.

"You too, Blackwell," she ordered, crossing her arms over her chest in a move I'd seen her use a thousand and one times before with my brother. They glared at one another for a minute before my brother finally relented, throwing his arms up in irritation.

"You better explain everything, Celly. Fucking everything." He gritted his teeth, his eyes softening when he looked at me. Without another word, all four men left, Evan closing the door behind him.

When it was shut, I snapped my fingers, engaging the lock.

At least my powers were working again.

"Celeste, you have to get me out of here," I pleaded, my voice low in case they were still outside the door. "They let Austin hurt me. Knox—Knox hurt me." Saying the words out loud was more painful than the actual abuse.

I sobbed, remembering the brutal way Knox eviscerated our relationship, the crack of his hand across my face shattering us into a million tiny pieces. His crass words echoed in my mind, setting off a fresh wave of tears.

I was struggling to stand, pain setting in as the adrenaline from our encounter wore off.

"Whoa there, girl." Stella placed a tentative hand on my back, her touch gentle enough that it didn't hurt my broken ribs. "Take it slow."

She guided me back to the bed, helping me sit on the plush mattress where I'd spent so many nights wrapped up between my men.

But they weren't my men any more.

Suddenly the idea of sitting here, being in their space made me sick.

"Can we go back to my place?" I asked quietly. "I—I can't be near them. Not after what they did."

I stared blankly at a paint stain on the floor, wondering how long it had been there. Did it happen when Knox was painting one of the pictures he'd gifted me for my birthday?

My heart seized in my chest, breaking all over again.

"Oh Eves," Celeste sat next to me, wrapping an arm around my shoulders. I leaned my head to her shoulder, my tears finally breaking free. She held me as

I cried, my tears soaking her shirt, as Stella laced her fingers with mine. "Everly, I promise, they didn't betray you."

I jerked backward, sucking in air as my ribs protested.

"C, I was there. I know what I saw. I know what I *felt*. Austin showed me the video of Chase and Heather fucking in the stairwell. He told me about Griff getting back together with Morgan. I saw Knox. He—" I couldn't finish the sentence, not ready to tell them the terrible things he'd done.

"Eves," Celeste said gently, taking my face delicately in her hands. "I swear to you. Those men have been going out of their minds for the last twenty-four hours. I was with them the whole time. It was all Austin. He tricked you."

"What? What are you talking about?" I stood again, moving a few feet away before I started pacing. I smeared blood across my dirty shirt as I wrapped my arms around my middle. Like if I held on tight enough, maybe I could hold myself together through this whole fucked up mess.

It was Stella who answered this time. "It was Austin, Everly. He's a mimic. He pretended to be your guys." The earnest look on her face made me believe she was telling the truth, and honestly, why would she lie? But I also knew what I'd seen...

Right?

"What about the greenhouse? I saw Chase and Heather with my own eyes!" I was so confused and frustrated, but Celeste shook her head before patiently explaining. I raked my fingers through my tangled hair in frustration, trying to wrap my head around what she was saying.

"You saw Austin mimicking Chase. Your boy was at the dining hall with Griffin and some guy named Preston for a late dinner."

I couldn't help but notice the reaction Stella had to hearing Preston's name, her eyes darting to Celeste for a second, a barely audible breath escaping her lips.

"I just..." I sank back onto the bed next to C, Stella plopping down on my other side. Tears blurred my vision, but the images were still as sharp in my mind as the glass in my hand earlier.

Chase's dick in Heather's mouth.

Griffin lying to me about Morgan.

Knox...

Jesus, I couldn't even think about what he'd done to me without wanting to vomit all over his navy blue bedspread.

But was it really Knox?

Or any of them for that matter?

If what Stella said was true, then my men never betrayed me. A glimmer of hope unfurled in my chest, shining on the shattered pieces of my heart.

It had initially broken into three separate chunks, each equal in size and depth, the first one snapping off the day I heard Griffin in the library.

The second?

The night in the greenhouse.

Number three was with Knox in the cabin.

But the more despondent I became, the longer I was with Austin, the more each piece fractured, all the cracks finally resting in a pile of sharp edges and jagged points.

But those shards remained inside, just like these men, stitched into the very fabric of my soul. Deep down, I knew what the girls were saying was true. But my head was still having a hard time accepting that what I'd seen hadn't been reality.

Drawing in as deep of a breath as my ribs would allow, I straightened my spine. Pushing my shoulders back, I grimaced at the pain radiating through my body. But I needed to do this. Rip the Band-Aid off and figure out what the hell was going on.

I looked between my friends, their expressions of concern mirroring each other.

"Bring them in. We need to talk."

twenty-
nine

Chase

I paced around the living room, practically wearing holes in the floor-
boards, my heart thundering in my chest.

What the fuck happened in there?

We'd all crashed just a few hours ago, once Griff got everyone back to the
suite. Evan and Celeste cuddled up on one sofa, while Stella had sprawled out
on a second we'd borrowed from the Blackwells' suite. Sometimes it paid to
be super strong and have a teleporter for a best friend, especially when you
needed to move furniture at a moment's notice.

By the time Griff and I reached Knox's room, he was already wrapped
around her like an octopus, his surly ass in the middle of the bed. Giving him
a knowing look, I climbed up next to him, folding my arms behind my head

and drifting off to sleep almost as soon as my head hit the pillow. Couldn't even tell you where Griff ended up.

Then her screams shattered the peacefulness my heart had found by having her home. Her cries for help... not for us, but *from* us. The thought that she believed we would hurt her made me physically ill. What the fuck did Austin do to her?

Just as the rage began to simmer while I contemplated all the ways I was going to murder that little cocksucker, Celeste emerged from the bedroom. I raced over, Griff and Knox on my heels. She held up her hands to fend us off, throwing a look over her shoulder at the closed door.

She shooed us wordlessly back to the living room where I took up a spot on the sofa. Evan was on his feet, trying to catch a glimpse of Everly. A frown pulled at his lips when he realized his sister wasn't with his girl. He flopped back down into the armchair he'd been occupying earlier, waiting until Celeste was near before snagging her hand and pulling her into his lap.

The corner of my lip tipped up. Everly told me about her best friend's feelings for her twin. I was glad to see he'd finally figured it out for himself. And knowing Morgan was using some sort of enhanced pathokinesis to control his emotions made me want to kick his ass a little less.

"She wants to talk to you. All of you."

I rose instantly, ready to storm into that room and do whatever it took to prove to Everly that I loved her. That she was it for me. Celeste held up her hand once again, stopping me before I could take off.

She continued once I sat back down, running my fingers through my dirty blonde hair and pushing it away from my face in an effort to stem some of the anxiety rippling through my veins.

"I told her I think she needs to see a healer first, but she said this can't wait." Her eyes narrowed as she looked between the three of us. "I explained everything about Austin, but you guys... he hurt her." She swallowed roughly, her eyes filling with tears for her friend as she focused on Knox. Her voice trembled as she spoke.

"He made her think it was you." She paused, the weight of her words sinking into the silence of the room. Just as I opened my mouth to ask what she meant, she spoke again. "Knox, he assaulted her *as you*." She choked on the words, her hand covering her mouth to muffle the sob. Utter devastation was written on Knox's face, his eyes wide with a fear I'd never seen before.

Well, that explained the visceral reaction she had to waking up next to him.

Evan held Celeste tightly as her eyes closed momentarily. When she opened them, she found mine next. I sucked in a breath, terrified of what she was about to say.

"You already know he pretended to be you at the greenhouse," she said softly. But I could tell by the hitch at the end of her sentence there was more.

"What else?" I gritted my teeth. I didn't even need to finish the question. She knew what I was asking.

I was already going to kill him for laying his hands on my Larkspur. On what was *mine*. But I would fucking skin him alive if he pretended to be me while he did it.

Celeste hefted out a deep, sad sigh. "He made a tape of him fucking some bitch named Heather in a stairwell. Made her watch it while he pretended to be Knox." She shuddered in Evan's hold, the memory of what my Larkspur told her drawing a haggard sound from her throat. "Then he—he grabbed her *there*"—she winced as she gestured between her legs—"and smacked her hard across the face."

Blood rushed in my ears. If I had thought I wanted to kill him before, it was nothing on how I felt now. He was a deadman walking. My vision darkened at the edges, a blind fury racing through my body. It was like a live wire was connected to my fingertips, the raw energy ready to burst through in an epic display of violent vengeance.

"As me?" Knox's pained voice was barely above a whisper. His usually tanned face was ashen, the look of a man so desperate for an answer it made my own heart ache for him. Celeste nodded sadly, a soft, "I'm so sorry, Knox," falling from her lips.

Lastly, Celeste looked at Griff. He'd dragged a barstool over and was perched just behind the sofa, his muscular arms crossed over his chest, pulling the black fabric of his t-shirt over the broad expanse. "What about me? What did Austin make her believe I did?"

"She didn't say much about you, Griff. Just that he told her you'd gone back to Morgan. That she was just using Evan to fuck with her, but you were her ultimate goal."

Griff's shoulders sagged in defeat. He scrubbed his hands over his stubble covered face, closing his eyes as a deep sigh reverberated in his chest. I heard Evan mutter under his breath, his features a mix of rage and sadness. I couldn't imagine how much this was fucking with his head.

An overwhelming despair hung heavily in the room, slowly suffocating us all. My skin felt tight, like it was too small for my body, an electric undercurrent thrumming through my veins. I needed to put eyes on my Larkspur. It was the only way to quell the riptide of emotions churning in my gut.

I jumped from the sofa, my legs carrying me down the hall and straight to Knox's door. Without even knocking, I pushed the door open. My Larkspur was sitting wrapped in a blanket, cuddled next to Stella at the foot of the bed. A gasp fell from her mouth at my brusque entrance, and I couldn't help but notice the visible way she tucked her legs closer to her body, making herself even smaller.

It was like a pickaxe to my already bleeding heart.

Rushing across the space, I dropped to my knees at her feet. Before she could react, I pulled her small hands into mine, needing to touch her, to feel her body against my own.

She hissed in pain, pulling her left hand back. It was swollen, black and blue bruises creating an ugly pattern across her beautiful skin. I made a mental note to make sure the same pattern crisscrossed Austin's entire body once I got a hold of him.

"Shit," I apologized, "I'm sorry, Larkspur." Securing her uninjured hand in both of mine, I finally looked up into those cerulean depths. So much hurt and distrust swam in them, but I could also see a flicker of hope, and I clung to it like a liferaft during a hurricane.

"Chase." Her voice was hoarse, rough, like she'd been screaming or yelling. *She probably was, dipshit.*

For a brief moment, I could see her in my mind, screaming, crying out for help, much like she'd done when she woke up. I would never forgive myself for all the ways Austin hurt her, ways that I still didn't even know.

She heaved a deep breath, her body shuddering under the weight of what that fuckwad had done, her muscles not quite relaxing even though she was safe at home with us.

"I——I know what I saw. My brain knows it. But my heart... my heart knows what I feel for you and what I thought you felt for me, too." Her voice cracked at the end, and it split my heart in two. Before she could say another word, I released her hand, cupping her jaw with both of mine, gently bringing my forehead to rest against hers. I felt her stiffen under my touch, but I kept the contact between our bodies, needing the warmth of her skin to remind me she was here.

"Everly Blackwell," I said with a quiet determination, my eyes closing as I spoke. "I love you more than I ever thought possible. I love you more than there are wildflowers in the forest, Larkspur. I always thought that nature, the trees, the lake, were the most beautiful, perfect things in the world.... Until I met you."

We stayed like that for several long minutes, just the two of us existing in this vacuum where everything was right again. I could feel the tears streaming down her cheeks, the salty wetness soaking into my calloused hands. She could drown me in her tears as long as I still owned a piece of her heart, her love the only thing I needed to keep me afloat.

I pulled back slightly to place a gentle kiss to her forehead, relishing in the feel of her soft skin under my lips.

"Baby, I know what you think you saw," I said, tipping her face up to meet my eyes. "But hear me when I say this: It. Wasn't. Me. It wasn't us." I nodded my head back in Griff and Knox's direction. "Austin used that mimic bullshit to trick you, to twist up your head. I would never, I mean *never*, betray you like that."

She was silent, and panic began to creep into my chest. I slipped one hand from her face, lacing my fingers with hers. I brought them to my mouth, kissing each fingertip, the pads pressed gently to my lips.

"Please say you believe me, Larkspur." My plea hung in the air like a thousand pound weight around my neck. I was struggling to tread water, and her answer determined if I would sink or swim.

She'd closed her eyes, her cheeks damp and ruddy from crying. I felt Griff at my back, his dominating presence pressing into the space. He reached in, stroking the backs of his fingers down her bruised cheek.

"Let us show you, Blue girl," he whispered, his other hand landing on my shoulder, gripping it tightly. Like I was the only thing tethering him to this moment with her.

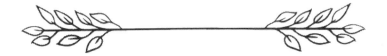

Griff texted Preston while we were waiting for Celeste earlier, asking if he could come by to 'help us out a bit'. Watching his eyes grow to the size of fucking frisbees was almost laughable as he took in the bruises and broken bones, except that it was my Larkspur who was injured, and that shit wasn't fucking funny at all.

He'd had her lay flat on the bed as he worked, pulsing his blue healing light over her cracked ribs first. I watched with rapt attention as the bruises disappeared slowly from her skin, her chest expanding a little bit more with each passing second until she was finally able to take in a full breath.

Each lungful lifted Onyx, having taken a spot directly between her breasts, his beady little black eyes scrutinizing every person in the room. He hadn't once left her side since we'd brought her home. Her tiny protector. I wasn't sure we would have found her if it hadn't been for him.

Once her ribs were healed, he moved to her broken wrist and the cuts on her hands, sweat beading on his brow as he hunched over her prone form. The blues and purples faded into greens and yellows before blending back into her natural sun-kissed tone, the swelling diminishing right before our eyes. The skin of her palms knitted itself back together, leaving a thin, pink scar.

Her eyes scrunched shut a few times, and I knew from experience that caster healing wasn't always the most pleasant experience. The pinch of bone and tissue reforming could be extremely uncomfortable, but my girl, my fucking warrior woman, never once complained. Finally, Preston let out an exhausted huff, flopping back in Knox's desk chair when he'd finished.

He looked drained, which told us that she'd had more significant injuries than we'd been able to see, and the stifling rage simmering in my veins climbed. Deciding I needed to rein in my fury for a more appropriate setting, I tossed Preston a sports drink, knowing he'd need the electrolytes after expending so much energy healing our girl. Twisting off the cap, he downed half of it in one go.

While he worked, I couldn't help but notice the way Stella's eyes were laser focused during the whole process... and not on what Preston was doing but rather on Preston himself. I chuckled when I noticed them alternating stares at one another from across the room. First him, then her, while a red flush that I was ninety-nine percent sure wasn't from the healing crept onto his cheeks.

Get it Preston.

I clapped a hand on his shoulder, and he turned his face up to look at me.

"Thank you, man," I said. "Seriously. It means a lot that you're helping us out like this. We couldn't take her to the health center, not with..." My voice trailed off as my mind ran through the list of injuries she'd suffered. We'd never be able to explain what happened, let alone get anyone to believe us.

No, this was the safest option.

Preston's face brightened at my praise and, Jesus fucking Christ, he was like a goddamn puppy looking to please its owner. "I'm sorry I couldn't do more, Chase, but she had like five broken ribs and a ton of internal contusions. Plus her wrist. It drained me pretty quick." He sat back defeatedly, clearly disappointed in his performance.

Not wanting him to sulk, I *gently* punched his shoulder—I didn't need to break the guy—grinning like we were old friends. "You did great, man. Thank you again." Thinking I might as well help the guy out, I looked across the room.

"Yo, Stella, would you mind walking Preston here out? That way we can get Everly situated?" I felt Preston tense under my hand, his face turning a hilarious shade of white then red at the mention of her name. And if Stella's shocked face was anything to go by, maybe I'd just played matchmaker for these two weirdos.

thirty

Everly

Once Preston finished healing my ribs, and I was finally able to take a much needed breath, I looked around the crowded bedroom. Chase was talking with Preston, who I was fairly certain had a crush on my boyfriend, and Celeste was huddled up with Evan, his arm around her waist—

Wait, what?

Catching her eye, I subtly jutted my chin to where their bodies met. She blushed, glancing up at my twin quickly before smiling at me. I grinned back, the first real smile I'd had in days, maybe even weeks. *Guess that means Morgan's out of the picture. Stupid twatwaffle.*

I absentmindedly stroked my fingers over Onyx's silky fur, watching everyone file out once Stella led Preston to the door. Evan shot me a wistful look before disappearing into the hallway. I knew I needed to talk to him, work through our bullshit, but right now? At this moment?

I needed a fucking shower.

My body still ached, even with all the healing Preston did, reminding me that getting the shit kicked out of me was on my list of things I never wanted to do again. I rolled my shoulders, the joints still stiff from being handcuffed to the fucking chair by Austin and Morgan.

Fucking cunts.

Standing slowly, I began making my way to Knox's bathroom, the lure of a long, hot shower drawing me in.

I didn't make it two steps before Chase swooped in, one arm going under my knees, the other around my waist, hoisting me against his hard chest. I tensed momentarily, my eyes squeezing shut at his touch.

We both froze, neither breathing. There had never been a time in our relationship where I didn't welcome Chase's hands on my body. But now, any touch felt like too much. I closed my eyes, trying to remind myself that this was my Chase not some psycho out to hurt me.

"I've got you, Larkspur. Always."

That was it. Nothing else. No explanation. I was too tired, too mentally exhausted to argue, so I simply wrapped my arms around his neck, leaning my head against his shoulder as he carried me to his room.

He strode through the space, and I quickly inhaled the earthy scent of his room. Chase always smelled like nature—the outdoors, fresh and clean. Like rain from a summer storm.

When we reached the bathroom, I was startled to find Griff and Knox both already inside, Chase's large bathtub filled with steaming water and a mountain of bubbles.

I recalled him saying once that his parents had installed it to help with his sore muscles after rowing. My collection of bath products was lined up on the vanity, along with a pile of fluffy white towels.

Tears sprung to my eyes, but I quickly wiped them away.

Chase slid me to the floor, my feet meeting the beautiful marble tiles as he stepped behind me. Griff reached out to steady me, his large hands resting tentatively on my hips. He looked at me, and I saw the question in his hazel eyes, the greens and golds shimmering in the bright light of the bathroom.

Was this okay?

I wordlessly nodded. I still wasn't over the lies he'd told me, his deception. But right now, I needed him. Needed them.

Using a feather light touch, Griff pulled my shirt over my head, tossing it toward the laundry hamper. Chase worked my jeans over my hips, both men making sure not to come in direct contact with my skin anymore than necessary, understanding without a word that at this point, any physical touch was going to be difficult.

I glanced across the room to where Knox was propped against the wall. His hands were shoved into his pockets, the sleeves of his paint-stained, gray henley pushed up to reveal his inked forearms, his tattoos rippling with each flex of his muscles.

He'd been painfully silent since we entered. Hell, he'd been quiet since I finally came to and freaked out in his bedroom, nearly slicing him open. And a small part of me wondered...

Was it real?

Or was Celeste right and that monster in the cabin had been Austin all along?

The longer Knox went without speaking, the more unease bubbled under my skin. What if it really had been him that hurt me, that grabbed, hit me? What if—

"Everly!" Griff's voice startled me, the sharp snap of his fingers bringing me out of the painful memory. "Fuck, Blue, you're shaking baby. Where'd you go? What's going on in that pretty head of yours?" He smoothed his palms down my biceps, the feeling grounding me in the moment. The heat of Chase at my back warmed my skin.

In the next instant, I became all too aware that I was standing in nothing but my bra and panties, a flush running through my body as three sets of eyes blazed across my skin. My gaze met Knox's as Griff straightened out, Knox's deep brown eyes flashing with hunger as he took in my nearly naked body.

A knot formed in my stomach as the memory of those brown eyes boring into mine while he grabbed my pussy, slapped me, told me I was nothing raced through my mind. A rapid thudding in my chest began, and my breaths started to come in short bursts.

No, that wasn't my Knoxy.

Closing my eyes, I repeated those five words over and over in my head until my heart rate slowed, and my breathing calmed. I stepped away from Chase and Griff, putting a few feet of distance between us.

"I—I'm not ready to—to be touched, yet." My voice trembled as I pushed the words out.

A piece of me wanted nothing more than to have their hands on my body, soothing the pain of the last twenty-four hours. Their flesh pressing into mine, melting away the memories.

But that same touch made me quiver in fearful anticipation, my stomach twisting at the mere thought. Casting my eyes downward, I unclasped my bra, sliding it down my arms as I turned my back to them.

I heard a sharp intake of breath accompanied by a low growl, making the hairs on my neck stand on end. Chase's bathroom was large enough that he had a mirror behind his vanity, plus a full length one on the opposite wall. Standing up straight, I caught a glimpse of the bruises littering my back.

Judging by the murderous looks on their faces, apparently Preston's healing abilities didn't quite reach that far.

Ignoring the mounting tension, I tried to inconspicuously cover my chest with my forearm as I shimmied my panties down my legs. Once they hit the floor, I quickly kicked them away, shuffling to the edge of the tub.

All three took an unconscious step forward, my body freezing with the movement. We stood, suspended in time for what felt like an eternity before Griff took the reins once more.

"Do you need us to help you in?" He approached slowly, the palms of his hands up, like he was showing me he was unarmed.

I knew now, though, you didn't need a weapon to do maximum damage.

"No, I'm okay," I answered softly, stopping his forward ascent. I braced my hands on the edge of the white porcelain, stepping into the warm bubbles with one foot then the other, slowly sinking beneath the water until it reached my chin. Drawing my knees to my chest, I let the heat seep into my muscles, my bones, warming me with each passing minute.

As I settled into the bath, the jasmine and peony scent of my body wash filled the quiet space, a tense silence fell over us. Chase and Griff each sat on either side of the tub, while Knox slowly crept over. He sat just on the edge, his proximity sending a tidal wave of emotions crashing through my body.

I loved Knox. I loved each of them. But where I could kind of, maybe, sort of wrap my head around knowing that it wasn't really Chase on that tape, I was still struggling with the idea that it wasn't my Knox whose hands had brought so much hurt and pain to not only my body but my heart as well.

There was also the giant issue of Griffin straight up lying to my face. I'd already been freezing him out when Austin and Morgan kidnapped me—I know, super mature—but he still hadn't explained why he was fucking tutoring her to begin with.

Deciding this was as good a time as any, I cleared my throat, my voice coming out rough and scratchy. "I think we need to talk." As softly as I spoke the words, they might as well have been blasted through a megaphone, bouncing off through the quiet of the bathroom.

Steam from the bath rose around my body, droplets forming on my forehead while the humidity curled my hair into small tendrils around my face. My shoulders broke through to the surface as I sat up straighter, bubbles sliding down my collarbones.

I watched Chase track the motion with his eyes, his tongue darting out to wet his bottom lip. A heat coiled in my lower belly, an instinctual, primal feeling. My brain, however, quickly shut that shit down, the idea sending me into a confused panic.

I wanted their touch, craved it. I knew deep in my soul the feel of their hands would help heal my fractured heart.

But it also scared the fuck out of me.

How could I reconcile what I'd seen, what I'd felt, with what I knew to be true?

"What do you want to know, Blue girl?" Griff leaned forward, resting his elbows on his bent knees. His gaze was laser focused on my face, those hazel eyes studying me, looking for any signs of distress.

"Why did you lie to me, Griff?" I whispered the question, my breath casting ripples across the warm water.

I thought asking him, out loud, would hurt, would shatter me. Instead it was like a weight lifting off my chest, the oppressive feeling slipping away, finally allowing me to breathe. I didn't look away, holding his gaze, as I waited for an answer.

Griff rubbed a hand over his stubbly jaw before raking his fingers through his short hair. He opened and closed his mouth several times before he finally heaved out a defeated sigh.

"I'm so sorry, Everly."

They were just four simple words. Nouns and verbs. But hearing Griffin say them, hearing the anguish behind them? It was almost too much to bear in my fragile state.

His hazel eyes grew glassy, tears threatening to spill over as he explained.

"A couple weeks ago, I received a letter... from Austin. He threatened you." His eyes bounced to Chase, then to Knox before coming to rest on me once more. "He threatened all of you. I—I couldn't let him hurt you. So I kept the letter a secret, hoping I could find a way out of it. Find a way to save you."

I wrapped my arms around myself beneath the water, considering his explanation for a minute, letting it roll around in my mind.

Did I believe he did what he thought was best?

The best I could do was give a shaky yes.

But that still didn't explain Morgan.

"Okay," I finally responded. "But, why did you lie about Morgan? What in the hell were you doing tutoring her?" I let the hurt of his betrayal bleed into my voice, sniffling a bit as more tears threatened to spill over.

I thought back to the day of my mom's funeral, how I was convinced I'd cried myself out, used up all my tears, and that I couldn't possibly have any more. Guess I was wrong.

I looked at Griff, truly looked at the broken man sitting on the hard tile only feet away from me. He was holding his head in his hands, an aura of defeat emanating from him. "Griff, please just tell me." I stopped breathing when the next question passed my lips.

"Are you back with Morgan?"

"No."

Zero hesitation. One hundred percent conviction.

"Everly." He quickly flipped to his knees, hoisting himself up to lean on the edge of the tub, so close to Knox they were practically touching. His proximity startled me, and I jumped back, the water sloshing around me.

"If I never see that fucking lying cunt again, it'll be too soon." A fierce fire danced in his eyes, his anger stoking the golden flames. "I took her on because I didn't have a choice. My professor asked, and with Austin's letter..." He paused, looking away. His jaw was tense, and I could sense the war raging inside him. "Since tutoring was a condition of my scholarship, I didn't want to give anyone a reason to take it away."

Griff's eyes found mine once again, honesty finally shining through all the bullshit and half truths. "I didn't want to leave you unprotected."

thirty-one

Griffin

My chest expanded, the weight of all the lies I'd been carrying finally falling away. I watched her face carefully, cataloging each subtle move, steeling myself for her response.

"You should have trusted me with the truth, Griffin."

Griffin.

She never called me Griffin. It was always Griff. Or Sir, when we played in the bedroom. My cock jumped in my sweats at the thought, and I berated myself for getting even a fraction of a hard on under the current circumstances.

Unable to meet her eyes, to see the mounting disappointment from my behavior, I looked across the sterile white bathroom to Chase, his brows furrowed as he met my gaze. Irritation drew his lips into a scowl. I saw the anger building behind his eyes, his large hands balling into fists. The skin across his knuckles grew tight with each flex.

Great, he's fucking pissed at me, too.

"Man, you know my dad would pay for you to go to school; he's fucking offered before!" It was a barely restrained shout, and I saw Everly flinch from the corner of my eye. *Christ, that motherfucker really did a number on our girl.*

Chase noticed her reaction, too, quickly apologizing. "Shit, sorry Larkspur. I just—" He focused back on me, directing all that frustration my way. "Fuck, Griff," he mumbled, a resigned sigh escaping his mouth as he tipped his head back to look at the ceiling.

The bathroom was warm from the steam of the large bath tub clinging to the mirrored surfaces. It shimmered on the porcelain tiles inside the shower. "You can't lie, Griff. You gotta tell us things like that when they fucking happen."

I could feel my cheeks heating with guilt. "I know, Cha—" but before I could try to justify my epic fuck up, my friend cut me off.

"No, man, you don't know. If you had just fucking told us about the goddamn letter and tutoring Morgan, then she wouldn't have been in the goddamn greenhouse alone!" By the time he finished, his voice was at a near shout, red coloring his face as he heaved deep breaths. "Fuck, Griff!"

Shoving his fingers through his waves, he pushed the blond locks away from his face. He huffed, his green eyes focused back on Everly. She was curled in on herself, the tip of her chin skimming the water as she rested it on her knees.

I took the opportunity and studied her bruised face, the jarring blues and violent purples littering her exquisite skin. She had a fairly large knot at her hairline, her pillowy bottom lip was split down the middle, and her left cheek was swollen and split as well.

Murderous intent simmered in my veins as my brain committed to memory each mark on her, like snapshots in a fucked up photo album. I gripped the side of Chase's big-ass clawfoot tub, my knuckles turning white from the force.

Chase was right.

I fucked up. Jesus, did I fuck up. If Everly hadn't been avoiding me, if I hadn't fucking *lied*, Austin and Morgan never would have been able to take her. I squeezed the lip of the tub tighter in an attempt to stem an outburst that could send Everly over the edge.

Knox shifted his weight from his spot next to me, twisting himself so he could see our girl better. Her eyes darted between the three of us, softening some on me, more on Chase, not at all on Knox.

"I'm so sorry, baby." My voice drew her gaze back to me. The electric blue of her eyes was dull, dark half-moons ringing the delicate skin just underneath, a visual reminder of how exhausted she was. I reached out, planning to stroke a finger down her damp shoulder but drew my hand back before making contact.

I didn't deserve to touch her, so I wouldn't. Not until she could trust me again.

Knox, however, decided at that moment that he did have to. Touch her, that is.

Everything happened in slow motion.

Knox's arm extended toward Everly's face.

Her eyes went wide with panic when she spotted his open palm.

The next thing I knew, water was flying every which way as Everly flung herself from the tub, landing unceremoniously in my lap. The wetness of her body soaked through my simple black tee and gray joggers almost instantly.

Instinctively, I wrapped her in my arms. I tucked her tightly against my chest, her body quaking as she breathed in rapid bursts.

Limp pieces of her drenched hair clung to her face as she curled her hands into the fabric of my shirt. I pushed them back, gently stroking my hand over her hair. Everly clung to me, and while I was scared for my girl, there was a significant part of me that was reveling in the feel of her body against my own.

It had been too long since I'd had my hands on her, felt her flesh beneath my fingertips.

Chase was already on his feet, grabbing one of the fluffy, white towels off the vanity. He carefully wrapped it around her body, rubbing the soft material against her skin, absorbing the water droplets.

Looking over her head, I caught sight of Knox's face.

I don't think I'd ever seen a man look so broken. As my Blue girl trembled against me, I watched as his world crumbled under his feet. His mouth was slightly open, in what I was guessing was an unfulfilled attempt at speaking.

Knox's dark brown eyes glistened in the bright light of the bathroom, unshed tears full of despair at her rejection. No, not rejection. Her *reaction*.

She was pissed at Chase, pissed at me.

But she was fucking terrified of Knox.

Snapping into action, I stroked my hand gently down her back, while I spoke to the guys.

"Knox, why don't you wait for us in the living room." It wasn't a request, and he knew it by the firm tone in my voice and hard set of my eyes. He stared at her longingly, a million emotions flashing across his scruff-covered face, before he shuffled wordlessly from the bathroom.

Shifting my head to see Chase, I issued my next order. "Chase, go grab Everly some clothes. She's got a couple pairs of underwear in my top drawer. Grab one of your sweatshirts." He jumped into action, disappearing quickly into his bedroom.

Knowing I only had about thirty seconds alone with her, I drew back to see her face.

"Blue?" As gently as I could, I turned her face, forcing her sapphire eyes to meet mine. "Baby, what just happened? You know Knox wouldn't hurt you." If we had any hope of repairing all the damage done—by me, by Austin—then I needed to know exactly what the fuck happened.

She was quiet for a long moment, those deep pools of blue filled with so much pain that I feared she might not answer at all. The shaking had stopped, but every once in a while her body would jolt with a shudder, and I wondered if it was from being wet or from the trauma of what had happened.

Her voice cracked when she finally spoke, the sound shattering a piece inside of me.

"When Knox..." She trailed off, choking down a sob before it broke free. Everly looked away, her cheeks flushing crimson beneath the bruising. She swallowed roughly, her fingers gripping the white towel.

She leaned away from me, sitting up a bit straighter, and a small sense of pride flooded me at seeing a glimpse of *my* Blue. The fighter. The girl who didn't take shit from anyone.

"When Austin was pretending to be Knox," she tried again, her voice soft but strong. "He hurt me. Bad." She was picking at a string hanging from the edge of the towel, her fingers twisting it tightly around her index finger.

I saw Chase out of the corner of my eye, hovering in the doorframe, not wanting to interrupt her confession. He gave a subtle chin raise, so as not to draw her attention, telling me to keep her talking.

"Is that why you freaked out in the tub?" If I could figure out the trigger, maybe we could work out a way to move past it. She nodded soundlessly, eyes fixated on the tiny piece of thread. It was wrapped so tightly, the tip of her finger was morphing from a bright red to an angry purple, the circulation being completely cut off.

In an effort to distract her, I snapped my fingers, transporting us to my room. I was sure our sudden departure gave Chase a scare, his muffled curse from down the hall confirming my suspicion.

Regaining her bearings, Everly slid from my lap, standing next to my bed where we'd landed during the teleport. She tucked the towel around her curvy frame, the large swath of fabric enveloping her tiny body. Her hair was still dripping, dark spots appearing on my gray carpet.

"Let me help?" When she looked at me in confusion, I gestured to her wet head. Understanding flashed in her eyes, and she nodded, closing her eyes as I swirled my finger through the air, drawing a gentle vortex around her head. Within thirty seconds, her dark brown strands were nearly dry, and she ran her finger through the long tresses, combing out the knots I created.

Chase finally joined us inside, I'm sure pacing the hall before coming in, unable to bear another moment away from her. Onyx darted in around his feet, a little black blur against the hardwood floor. He scurried over, hopping onto the mattress, and taking up residence on my pillow, his fluffy tail twitching every few seconds.

Chase handed her the clothing he'd collected per my instructions, a lacy pair of sage green boyshorts and one of his rowing sweatshirts that she loved to steal. She slipped the panties up her legs, my eyes eating up the expanse of skin.

She was still covered in bruises, despite the immense amount of healing Preston had provided. I noticed an especially dark one around one of her ankles, the tell-tale markings of a restraint embedded into her skin.

I inhaled deeply through my nose, holding the air in my lungs for a long moment, willing myself not to lose control. But the anger, the fucking self-loathing I felt seeing her like that, was killing me.

She pulled the large sweatshirt over her head, the bottom grazing against the silky skin of her thighs. She fiddled with the cuffs, rolling and unrolling them, her anxiety apparent in every movement she made. But she still hadn't said exactly what set her off in the bathroom.

"Larkspur," Chase said quietly. He'd closed my bedroom door, his broad body leaning against it, large arms crossed over his chest. Chase's imposing, muscular frame, coupled with his immense caster strength were enough to scare anyone.

But for her?

For Everly, he was a man ready to lay the world at her feet, to give her the fucking stars from the sky if she'd let him. She was his everything. She was *our* everything. And we'd nearly lost her.

He walked further into the room, stopping only a few feet from her. "Baby, what happened with Knox in the bathroom?" The question was gentle, soft. There was no demand, only unspoken assurances.

"When he went to touch me, I—" Tears erupted from her eyes, her arms curling around her middle, like she was trying to hold herself together. Her tiny frame shook, and before I could get off the bed, I watched her knees buckle.

"Fuc—" I lunged forward, but Chase was there, catching her before she hit the ground. He scooped her into his lap, sitting them both on the comforter next to me.

She tucked herself tightly to him, her cheek pressed firmly to his chest. We sat quietly as she cried, her soft whimpers the only sound for several minutes. Her words came out wet and muffled against the fabric of Chase's t-shirt when she finally spoke.

"When he went to touch me," she repeated, her voice sounding a little stronger. "It was like I was back in that goddamn cabin, chained to the fucking bed. He grabbed me, hit me. Hard. That was all I could see. Knox hurting me"— She shuddered at the last word—"Again."

Fuck.

This was way worse than I'd thought.

She wasn't just scared of him.

She was fucking petrified.

thirty-two
Knox

The look on Everly's face gutted me, the air punched from my lungs at her fear-filled eyes.

Griff ordered me out, away from her, like an errant child being sent to their room. I was pacing, my animal instinct begging to be set free. The walls felt too close, making my skin itch, this god awful creeping sensation playing over my flesh.

I was existing in two halves. One was enraged, fucking seething with fury. Not at my Monet but at what happened to her.

The other half? It was in fucking pieces.

She looked so fucking broken, so small, in that bathtub. I'd only wanted to touch her, to let her know I was there, that I wasn't going anywhere.

Well, except to go fucking murder Thorpe.

I'd thought the way she'd looked at me that night on the beach, after I beat the shit out of Evan, was bad.

It didn't come fucking close to the terror in her blue eyes tonight. The panic as she'd heaved herself out from the tub and into Griff's lap, the uncontrollable shake of her body, all in fucking response to *me*.

A snarl ripped from my chest as I cleared the coffee table with a swipe of my arm, empty beer bottles and a few bags of chips flying across the room. "Fuck!"

My chest rose rapidly, anger bringing my breath in heavy, sharp inhales. I scrubbed my hands down my face, the scratch of my week-old beard brushing my palms. Just as I began reaching for the mess I'd made, a soft knock on the door drew my attention.

Striding over, ready to murder whoever was on the side just on principle, I flung it open only to be met with Tinkerbell herself.

"Chase called. Said she needed me." The corners of Celeste's eyes softened as she took in my haggard appearance. I could feel the flush in my cheeks from my outburst, and I knew I must look like shit. We'd only gotten a few hours of sleep after we rescued Everly, and I hadn't slept at all the night before. Plus sleeping in my studio was uncomfortable as fuck.

You deserve it, asshole.

"Well, she certainly doesn't want me." I grumbled the words, my pity party already in full swing. I turned away, ready to go sulk somewhere else, when her tiny hand grabbed my forearm with more force than I'd thought possible from someone her size.

"Listen," she said firmly, her steely gray eyes fixed on my face. "She does want you; I know she does. I just think her head and her heart are on different pages right now. She knows in her heart that you wouldn't hurt her, but her brain is taking some time to catch up." Her grip on my arm loosened.

"She just needs time, Knox. Time to remember that you're a guy who's so fucking in love with her that you'd do anything for her. Even if that means giving her some space."

Before I could respond, I heard a bedroom door open and close, Griff and Chase appearing a moment later. They strode into the living room, Griff raising an eyebrow when he saw the mess on the floor. Rolling my eyes, I quickly picked up the remnants of my outburst, leaving the empty bottles near the sink before I tucked the bags of chips back into the cupboard.

Chase flopped tiredly into an armchair while Griff took up a cushion on the sofa. He leaned forward, elbows braced on his knees, hands folded between them.

"She had a flashback," he explained, the exhaustion obvious in the dark circles that ringed his hazel eyes. "When you tried to touch her, she said she had a flashback to the cabin, when Austin hurt her as you."

"Motherfucker," I said, my voice low as I fought back the emotions raging inside of me. I ran a hand through my hair, frustration buzzing in my brain like a swarm of wasps, setting my fucking teeth on edge.

"Celeste, we got her settled down. She was dozing, but she asked for you. Go ahead in. We'll all crash in the other rooms. I think you're the only person she really wants around right now." Griffin gave her a tight smile, sadness bleeding through.

Nodding, Celeste walked away, disappearing down the hall and into Griff's room. As the door clicked quietly behind her, I turned to look at my two best friends.

"How bad is it?"

Griff closed his eyes, his head hanging so his chin grazed his chest. "It's fucking bad, man." He sighed deeply. Chase rubbed a hand over his mop of blond waves before chiming in.

"Her brain is all fucked up with what Austin did, Knoxy. In her head, she knows it wasn't you, but he hurt her badly enough when that asshole pretended to be you that in her heart, she doesn't know which way is up right now."

Austin fucking Thorpe was going to fucking die for what he'd done to her. I clenched my hands into fists, the scabs on my knuckles pulling tight as the tendons flexed. We stayed like that, a heavy, charged silence passing between us until Griff spoke.

"We all need sleep, so we can deal with this bullshit. We'll talk more in the morning." I shot a look at the microwave clock, realizing it was still the middle of the fucking night as we crawled closer to four AM.

Griff lay himself across our sofa, tucking a throw pillow under his head before closing his eyes. Within two minutes, his breathing steadied, but the crease in his forehead told me he was anything but relaxed.

"Night, man." Chase shuffled off to his room, leaving me alone with my thoughts. I hauled myself to my feet, making my way to my bedroom.

I stripped down to my black boxer briefs before I collapsed on the bed, darkness quickly pulling me under. Dreams of Everly going missing filled my sleep. Images of her tied to that chair, but with no heartbeat, no life left, when I found her fueled my nightmares.

But the worst part?

How my brain couldn't stop replaying the fear in her eyes inside that bathroom when she looked at me.

Bright sunlight stabbed at my eyes as the mid-morning rays filtered through my window. I squinted, growling as I stretched out, rubbing my hands over my face, and wiping away the sleep that still lingered. Swinging my feet over the edge of the bed, I glanced at the clock on my desk.

10:35 AM.

Fuck.

I jumped up, not meaning to have slept so late. Snagging some clothes—a pair of black joggers and the sweatshirt Everly had marked as her own—I rushed to my bathroom, flipping on the hot water as I stepped out of my boxers. Steam quickly filled the room as I hopped under the spray, lathering up my juniper and cedarwood body wash, the suds rushing down my chest.

My hand found my dick as the water pelted my shoulders. Thoughts of my Monet filtered through my brain, my cock thickening with each downstroke until I was harder than steel. My pace quickened, remembering the last time I was balls deep inside her. The night in our suite with Chase and Griffin. She'd taken us so well, been such a good girl for us. And the night at the beach, when she'd let Chase and I play with her pussy on the sand.

As my body climbed closer to a release I desperately needed, an image of her tear stained face begging me not to kill her brother flashed behind my eyes.

Fuck.

My dick instantly deflated as I remembered her, pleading and crying. *God fucking damnit.*

I angrily finished washing my overheated body and flipped the water off. I roughly dried off with a towel before throwing on my clothes.

I made my way from my room and down the hall. Griff's bedroom door was still shut, but I could hear voices coming from the living room.

Chase had his ass parked on the kitchen counter, a plate of eggs in his hands as he hungrily shoveled them into his mouth. His chest was bare, the tattoos I'd given him over the years standing out against his tanned skin.

Griff's back was to me as he worked at the stove. The smell of his southwestern omelets made my mouth water, and my stomach let out a low growl. Fuck, when was the last time I ate? Celeste's head swiveled my way from her spot at the dining room table. She laughed. "Hungry there, Knoxy?"

I groaned at the nickname. *Not her fucking too.* She was sitting with Evan, two empty plates in front of them. I scanned the rest of the room, my heart sinking when I realized my little Monet was nowhere to be seen. Before I could open my mouth to ask, Evan spoke.

"She's still sleeping," he said, taking a quick sip of coffee. I noticed the crème brûlée creamer sitting on the table, the same flavor Everly always drank. Had he brought it for her? Or did he drink it too? Should I fix her a cup...

"Celly said she had a rough night." He lowered his voice like he was telling a secret. "She was up a lot, really restless." He drummed his fingertips along the sides of the coffee cup, the pads following a rhythm I couldn't identify. Anxiety creased his forehead as he considered his next words.

I could see the explosion coming before it happened.

"What the fuck are we doing about Thorpe?"

The pan of eggs sizzling on the stove was the only sound filling the quiet room. Chase swallowed down his last bite of food as Griff turned off the flame and pulled the hot skillet from the burner before plating more eggs. He carried the dish to the table, sliding it in front of me, along with a fork. He returned the cookware to the stove and leaned back against the counter.

"Well?" Evan demanded angrily. "That asshole hurt my sister. He needs to fucking pay." Celeste's lips tipped down as Evan spoke, his face turning a light shade of red with his anger. Just as I was getting ready to voice my agreement, Chase spoke up.

"I think she needs a break from here, just for a few days. Give her some time away from SLA, time away from all the bad things that have happened here." He hopped off the counter with a practiced agility from his years spent rowing. "So we stick with the plan to take her to my family's cabin up near North Pointe Falls, like we'd talked about before she—" He cut himself off before admitting her kidnapping out loud.

It was Griff's turn to speak next, his logical brain already poking holes in Chase's idea. "I don't know, Chase. Do you really think she'll wanna go anywhere alone with us?" He frowned, no doubt running through her meltdown last night.

I wanted nothing more than to prove just how sorry I was to her. Grovel at her fucking feet. But I shared Griff's apprehension. She couldn't stand to be in the same room as me. How in the hell would we spend a week together at some secluded cabin?

Maybe I should let them take her while I hunted down Thorpe...

"Nope, not at all." Chase took a long drink of orange juice straight from an open carton sitting on the counter. Wiping his mouth with the back of his hand, he grinned at Celeste. "But if Tinkerbell here helps, we may just have a shot."

thirty-three · Everly

I slept most of the day, flitting in and out of consciousness while the sunlight shifted through the curtains in Griffin's room. I woke intermittently, watching as the shadows danced across the walls.

At some points, I could feel Celeste curled around my back, holding me as I cried, the memories from the cabin following me into wakefulness. Other times, I would crack my eyes open, spotting Chase or Griffin perched in a chair near the bed, carefully watching over me.

By late afternoon, I'd slept all I could, my limbs stiff from lying in bed all day. Everything still ached, but I stretched out under the blankets Celeste tucked around me the night before.

My eyes scanned the room, finding myself alone. Well, not completely alone. Onyx was curled in a tight ball directly between my breasts, the rise and fall of my breathing ruffling his fluffy tail. I reached up, gently stroking his soft fur. He nuzzled into my touch, a soft purr vibrating into my chest.

A loud growl from my stomach had his head whipping up, his shiny black eyes zeroing in on my face.

"Guess we should get up, huh, buddy?" Scooping him into the crook of my arm, I sat up before he hopped onto the comforter. He loped off the bed, beelining for a small bowl on the floor near Griffin's door. I could see the pile of strawberries and bananas, and I smiled as Onyx began working his way through the fruit. A small piece of my heart, a tiny broken shard, healed itself, knowing one of my guys was looking out for my familiar.

I stood, stretching my arms over my head. Thank God for Preston. There was still an ache in my ribs, but Jesus was it a relief to take a deep breath and not want to vomit from the pain. Flexing my formerly broken wrist, I bundled my hair on top of my hair, snagging a pen from Griff's nightstand to secure it.

I walked to the door, pausing as my hand gripped the knob. I drew in a deep breath, closing my eyes, willing my heart not to beat out of my chest.

Could I do this?

Could I face them, especially after last night?

Deciding it was now or never, I opened the door and shuffled down the hall, tugging the hem of Chase's sweatshirt down my legs. When I entered the living room, all conversation came to a screeching halt as five sets of eyes swung my way, each one sweeping over me with an intense scrutiny that made my skin flush.

"Larkspur."

"Eves."

"Blue."

They all spoke at once, the sounds of their voices like a sweet, comforting melody, a caress to my broken soul, and another tiny piece glued itself back together.

Celeste and Evan were sitting together on the sofa, his arm slung around her shoulders as she leaned into him. She'd explained a little last night, just before I'd fallen into one of my fitful bouts of sleep, but I knew there was more to that story. She grinned at me from her spot.

My brother's eyes roved over the myriad of bruises that colored my cheeks, the anger on his face barely masked by his tight smile.

Chase took up the other end of the sofa, his feet kicked up on the coffee table, while Knox and Griff each sat in an armchair. Chase's emerald eyes brightened when he saw me enter, a big smile erupting on his handsome face. He jumped up from his spot, and I could see him struggling not to scoop me up into his arms.

"Hi." My throat was still sore from all the screaming and crying, my voice coming out rough. "What's going on?"

Ignoring my question, Griff hustled to the kitchen, grabbing a plate from the microwave, as Chase ushered me to his open seat on the couch. I sat hesitantly, my eyes flicking to where Knox sat across from me.

It wasn't him, Everly.

I inhaled deeply through my nose and closed my eyes. I opened them when I felt Griff kneel in front of me, a ceramic plate in his hands with an omelet on top. My stomach let out another growl at the sight of the tantalizing dish, my mouth watering with hunger.

Taking the plate, I began to eat, looking up after a few bites to see everyone staring once again. "What?" I asked, my mouth full of food.

They all remained quiet for a moment before Griffin's voice broke through the silence. He placed a hand lightly on my knee, his hazel eyes boring into mine, asking the unspoken question.

Was this okay?

I stiffened, swallowing roughly, the eggs sliding down my throat. Green eyes with the most beautiful gold specks I'd ever seen met mine, like tiny rays of sunshine bouncing off a field of clovers, the two colors intermingling until they coexisted in a perfect balance.

It's not him, Everly.

I consciously relaxed each muscle in my body, giving him a subtle nod, permission to keep his hand on my knee. I saw his shoulders visibly relax, the tense set of his jaw releasing some.

Knox cleared his throat from across the room, drawing my attention. When my eyes met his, they were clouded with doubt, pain. There was no cocksure attitude, no malicious smile like the Knox in that room at the cabin.

That's because it wasn't your Knox.

The words rattled through my brain, but I still tensed when he moved, shifting in his seat to lean forward, incrementally placing his body closer to mine. I watched the hitch of his breath when he saw me flinch, something akin to grief flashing across his face.

"How are you feeling?" Knox asked, the words low and gravelly, coming from deep in his chest. It was a loaded question. How *was* I feeling?

Confused.

Scared.

Relieved.

Fucked up.

Those chocolate brown eyes bored into my own, and a memory from the cabin flashed through my mind. Knox, pressing a brutal kiss to my injured lips. His eyes...

His eyes were lighter for a moment, not their normal deep brown.

A muddy, umbra hue.

Not Knox's eyes.

Austin's.

After breakfast, the guys explained what had happened over the last twenty-four hours. Griffin and Chase having dinner with Preston. Celeste bursting in and breaking Chase's nose, followed by my brother giving him a black eye. The late night calls with Mr. Stone to locate where Austin was holding me.

Celeste and Evan confirmed the guys, Knox specifically, never left the school until they'd come to rescue me. My mind was a mess, trying to make sense of what I'd seen versus what my friend was telling me. That these men couldn't possibly have done what I'd convinced myself they had.

When my brain couldn't hold any more information, I'd asked Celeste to take me to my apartment. Griff had offered to teleport us there, but I needed to stretch my legs, and the short walk down the hall was the perfect distance. I scooped up Onyx in my sweatshirt—well, Chase's sweatshirt—standing from the sofa.

"Umm, I guess I'll talk with you guys later?" Fuck, I didn't know how to handle this. Part of me wanted nothing more than to curl up in Griff's arms or let Chase hold me. But the sharp pain in my chest each time Knox and I locked eyes was proving to be too much.

"Blue, before you go, there was something we wanted to run by you." Griff rose from his chair, stretching his arms over his head, the move showing off a sliver of his toned abs. My gaze hung on his tanned skin before I realized he was waiting for an answer.

"What?" A small smirk tugged at the corner of his mouth before he responded.

"Before... everything, well the guys and I, we were," Griffin stuttered over the words, a pink flush erupting on his cheeks and the tops of his ears. I saw Chase roll his eyes from his spot at the end of the sofa.

"We were planning to take you to my parents' cabin up at North Pointe Falls for a few days before Thanksgiving," he cut in, "as a surprise." He ran his fingers through his blond waves, pushing them off his forehead, the muscles in his arm flexing.

"Oh! Umm..." I stared at the floor, shuffling my feet nervously. Anything to avoid making eye contact with the three men in the room. A knot formed in my stomach as a cold sweat broke out all over my body.

A cabin.

Alone for days.

With the guys.

Celeste was next to me before I even realized she'd moved. "Come on, babes, let's get you back to your place. We can talk more about it there." She shot my men—were they still my men?—a glare before ushering me out the door.

I gave a halfhearted, "Bye," as the door closed behind me, taking a deep breath when it clicked shut. My best friend led me down the hall, my brother trailing quietly behind us. He pulled out his key fob, unlocking our door and we filed inside.

"Go on and get settled," Celeste ordered gently. "I'll be there in just a second. I need to talk to Evan real quick."

I nodded numbly, my thoughts swirling like a vortex as I considered Chase's words. Could I really spend days alone in a cabin with them? The idea alone set my heart racing, and not in a fun way.

Making my way into my room, I set Onyx on my comforter, the sun streaming in through my floor-to-ceiling windows. He immediately scampered down, hopping across the floor to his perch on my windowsill and digging into a leftover bowl of cashews.

I looked around my room, evidence of the guys everywhere I looked.

A sketchbook Knox liked to leave for when he stayed the night sat on my nightstand.

One of Griff's textbooks, *Advanced Caster History,* lying on my desk.

The navy blue SLA rowing sweatshirt I stole from Chase with his last name stitched along the back.

Angry tears formed in my eyes, and I sucked in a gasp. While Austin and Alaric Thorpe set into motion the horrific current state of my life, it wasn't entirely their fault.

Each of these men—Griffin, Chase, and Knox— were all responsible for their actions. Griff lying to me. Knox blowing up at the beach. Hell, even Chase to a certain degree, although he didn't actually lie or cheat, so that did grant my heart and head a modicum of solace.

Hearing the telltale sign of footsteps approaching, I wiped my eyes with the heels of my hands, hoping she would let the tears go.

Yeah, right.

"What happened?" She spun me into her arms, holding me tight. "I mean, besides the whole kidnapping bullshit. Did something else happen?" She pulled back, looking over my bruised face.

Sniffling, I stepped away, flopping down on my bed. "No, I just..." I paused, the words getting stuck in my throat. Words that fucking terrified me. I stared up at the beige ceiling, swallowing before forcing them through my lips.

"C, what if I can't forget? What if I can't forgive them because my brain is so fucked up?"

"Oh, Eves." She crawled up next to me, lying on her back and linking her fingers with mine. "I know you're hurting right now, and I completely understand that." She inhaled sharply, and I knew she wasn't finished.

"But..."

See? Told you.

"Those men?" She hiked a thumb over her shoulder, as if they were standing in the room with us. "They were going out of their fucking minds while you were missing, Everly." She leaned up on her elbow, fixing her gray eyes on me.

"Knox was ready to storm every damn building on this campus. Chase poured over map after map, nonstop, trying to figure out where Austin could have taken you. Griff read over every fucking book he could find about mimics, anything that might have given us an edge in finding you." Her eyes softened, her lips curving into a sad smile.

"They fucking love you, Everly, with every fiber of their beings. If I wasn't sure before, I am now. I saw the panic, the frantic desperation when you were gone. It was like they'd lost a piece of themselves. They are so goddamn in love with you."

My vision blurred as the tears returned. Celeste affirming that the guys never gave up, never turned their backs on me, it mended a small part of the damage... but it wasn't enough.

Not yet.

Every time I closed my eyes, I saw Chase with Heather. Felt Knox's hand striking my face and heard his cruelty when he told me Griff had chosen Morgan.

I wanted so badly to believe her.

"What if I'm too broken, Celeste?" I whispered, the fear that I was too damaged to find my way back to the person I was before nearly suffocating me. "I nearly had a fucking panic attack when Chase asked about going to his family's cabin."

Celeste was quiet, a very uncharacteristic thing for my friend to be. We lay there in silence for a few minutes, and just when I was about to check if she'd fallen asleep, she shot up off the bed, scaring the shit out of me.

"I'll go!" She jumped off the bed, running to the door, but turning around just as quickly, flinging herself to where I'd sat up on the comforter. She wrapped her arms around my neck, smacking a kiss to my cheek.

Before I could even respond, she was already back at the doorway, a hopeful grin on her beautiful, pixie face.

"You go"—she scanned my room, waving a very enthusiastic hand at my art area—"paint something, or play with Onyx. I'll be back in a little bit." And then she was gone, disappearing out the door, the solid wood closing behind her, leaving me alone once more.

thirty-four — Everly

The passing of time is an odd thing. One minute feels like an hour but days are gone in the blink of an eye. It had been a week since the guys rescued me from Austin's little hideaway from hell, and I was currently packing a small suitcase for our trip to Chase's cabin. Celeste came up with the idea and doubled down her efforts throughout the week, finally wearing me down until I said yes.

"I'm going to go with you guys. And Evan." She beamed, bouncing on the balls of her feet as though she'd just solved world hunger. She was unpacking her duffle bag of shoes inside Evan's closet—scratch that, her *closet—while she explained her plan.*

The admissions office had called my brother bright and early Monday morning to say they were moving him to a single room just down the hall, so a new female transfer student could move in.

Damn, Carrick Stone was good.

"What do you mean, you're going with me?" I eyed her skeptically, watching as she lined up each pair of Converse in color order, her favorite lime green pair already on her feet.

"Just what I said. Evan and I are going to go with you guys. That way you won't feel pressured by being alone with them." She shrugged her shoulders, as if I were silly for even asking, throwing me a sideways glance. "Besides, I'm dying to see what Carrick Stone considers a 'cabin'." She grinned, drawing a bubble of laughter from my chest.

"Well, from the one time I met him, I can tell you, it definitely won't be some rustic little fishing shack."

She erupted into a giggle fit as we both pictured Chase and his dad wearing matching fishing vests and bucket hats.

And now, here I was, throwing my toiletries into my makeup bag while Onyx prowled around on my bed, sniffing each item I packed. I snapped my fingers, bringing my hair brush from the vanity in the bathroom, and lifted a folded sweatshirt as it nestled into the open space.

As soon as I was away from the cabin and felt up to it, I'd tested out my powers, making sure everything was in working order. My telekinesis, my water power, and my new super-speed were all present and accounted for. Evan's shocked face when I'd beaten him in a race from the dining hall was an image that would live rent free in my brain forever.

"Better be careful, bud." I booped Onyx on the nose when he tried to climb into my suitcase. "I may just pack you up in there if you're not careful." Not that he wouldn't be coming along.

I'd learned over the last few days that Onyx had a powerful calming effect on me, his presence soothing some of my anxiety since being rescued. I'd even gone so far as to take him to classes with me, tucked away in my hoodie pockets or in the top of my backpack. When I'd mentioned it to Griff, he said it was most likely our bond as familiar and caster.

Attending classes again had been fucking weird. While my entire life had been turned upside down and shaken like a goddamn snow globe, the rest of the student body just continued on with their day-to-day lives. The only thing different was Morgan was lying low, only moving about campus when necessary.

I always had an escort, no matter where I traveled on campus. Either one of the guys or Celeste was with me at all times. Chase was even able to get Celeste into several of my classes; luckily, or perhaps with some Stone money greasing the palms in the admissions department, all of her credits transferred seamlessly from Staunton to SLA.

When Professor Moore questioned Heather about Morgan's absence, she'd simply shook her head, saying she didn't know where her cunt of a friend was.

Well, she didn't call her a cunt.

I added that part.

Seemed fitting since she drugged, kidnapped, and beat me.

Fucking bitch.

Fortunately, the guys—Chase, in particular—were able to convince Preston to come over again for another round of healing Sunday night, so my face wouldn't be covered in bruises for classes Monday morning. This time had been a bit easier, the only injuries remaining were the contusions on my cheek and lip, although he was able to help ease some of the pain in the back of my skull from where I'd hit my head.

I zipped up my luggage just as a knock sounded from behind me. Twirling around, I was met with eyes the color of fresh-cut grass, the afternoon sun making them sparkle like emeralds.

"Hi, Larkspur." Chase smiled softly. He'd been quiet and gentle the last few days, always ready to carry my backpack, get my food at the dining hall, or simply sit silently while I studied. We were taking baby steps, especially since he'd put Heather in her place outside the Potions lab the other day, explaining in very simple words that Austin had been the one fucking her, not him.

The tears in her eyes *almost* made me feel bad for her.

Then I remembered she tried to fuck my boyfriend.

So, yeah, fuck her.

"You need help with that?" He strode across the room, his long legs eating up the space in just a few steps. He scratched Onyx on the head before lifting the suitcase with ease.

"You don't have to carry that, Chase." I reached for the luggage, but he held it above his head, grinning. I cocked an eyebrow at him.

"I know I don't have to, Larkspur." He stroked my cheek tenderly with his knuckle. "But I want to." Chase had been giving me small touches all week. Brushing my hair behind my ear, guiding me with a hand on the small of my back. Gentle reminders that he was there, willing to wait for me.

Griff was trying, too. Telling me exactly where he was going, who he was going with. I knew he wasn't tutoring Morgan anymore. That shit ended the moment I went missing. He'd scheduled a meeting with his professor to drop her from his roster, explaining that she was harassing him and his friends. It didn't take much convincing, given Griff's impeccable record and the fact Knox and Chase had backed up his claim. But he was making an effort to be completely transparent, and I appreciated the gesture.

Knox was another story. We'd been spending time together, but only as part of a group. He'd invited me to come to his studio to paint, but when I declined, I could see the hurt in his deep brown eyes. My heart yearned to be with him, but my memories from the cabin held me back.

He never pushed, respecting my need for space. Instead, I found a blueberry muffin, my favorite, on my desk in our Water Elementals' class. A new set of paintbrushes, a big red bow attached, on my art easel. Hell, I'd even found a plush animal bed after returning from classes the day before, Onyx already curled up inside, snoozing in the afternoon light.

This morning, I woke to find a painting in the living room, wrapped in lavender paper, a large white bow tied around it. Blues and purples filled the canvas surrounding an anatomical heart, a bouquet of wildflowers erupting around it in a spray of vibrant colors. Near the top was the profile of a beautiful woman drawn in black ink. Her eyes were closed, as if she were reveling in the stunning display surrounding her. Tears welled in my eyes as I took in each intricate detail, so much care and thought in every brushstroke.

At the bottom he'd painted in beautiful, swirling letters.

It will always be yours.

Knox couldn't tell me with words, but he was showing me.

He was still there.

Still fighting for me.

For us.

North Pointe Falls was about a two hour drive from campus. We all piled into a large SUV, generously provided by Chase's dad, hitting the road around two on Saturday afternoon to accommodate a few tutoring clients Griff had, most students having already left campus for the upcoming holiday break.

The interior of the SUV was spacious, with two seats up front, two in the middle, and a large third row in the back. Chase drove, playing what he called his 'Row Row Road Tunes' playlist. By the third Olivia Rodrigo song, I thought Knox's head was going to explode in the seat beside him.

Griff was seated next to me, a large duffle on the floor between us where Onyx had taken up residence, while Celeste and Evan were cuddled up in the back.

As happy as I was that my brother had *finally* pulled his head out of his ass, it was still a bit strange to see them so openly affectionate with one another. We had a discussion about it one night as we walked across campus from the library.

Evan tugged his backpack up on his shoulder, pushing the heavy door open for me. The cold night air stung my cheeks, and I pulled my jacket tighter around my body. Puffs of air blew in front of our faces as we walked silently along the concrete path.

"So"—I peeked up at him—"you and Celeste, huh? I take it you figured out Morgan was a raging cunt?" I saw him wince at my words, but he didn't deny them.

"Yeah, it happened while you were..." He gestured toward the woods with his free hand, his lips clamping shut. An embarrassed flush erupted on his cheeks as he stumbled over his next words. "We, well, the guys and Celeste, figured out that she was using her pathokinesis to control my emotions for her. Griff still

isn't sure how she was able to do it so well, though. He said she usually has trouble maintaining that level of control."

A memory from my time at the cabin or, well, a fragment of a memory crossed my mind.

"Where are your crystals?"

"I accidentally broke them when I was lugging her ass to the car last night!"

Morgan and Austin's voices filtered through my head, as a shudder ran up my spine. I stopped Evan's steps, grabbing his forearm. "I think she was using that bracelet she gave you. I think it enhanced her powers." I remembered my brother wearing the purple stones on his wrist, the jewelry similar to one I'd seen Morgan wearing.

"She broke it when she kidnapped me. It's why she couldn't control you anymore. It broke your connection to her," I reasoned, explaining my theory to Evan. "Thank fuck."

"That makes sense," he replied. "The night they took you, I was studying in the library, waiting for her. She was supposed to meet me but didn't show. I was sitting there, thinking about the next time I was going to see her, when all of a sudden, I felt this weird sensation in my chest. It was like someone flipped a switch, and I didn't really care if I saw her at all. I was so fucking confused."

"That must be when the bracelet broke. It severed her hold over you." Jesus, it made such perfect fucking sense. A flood of relief crashed through my body. My brother didn't betray me. That fucking bitch manipulated him, violating his emotions in an unforgivable way.

I took a deep breath, so I wouldn't rage out and circled back to my original question. "So, you're with C now?"

He rubbed a hand along the back of his neck. Oh my God, was my brother... blushing?!

"I panicked when she called to tell me you were missing. Griff called Knox at the same time, and we rushed to the suite. When I walked in and saw her, it was like something in my chest clicked into place. I just... I don't know how to explain it, Eves. It was like I was seeing her for the first time."

I hummed in reply, wrapping my fingers around my twin's arm. I leaned against him as we walked, a comfortable silence settling between us. I felt the most at peace with my brother than I had in weeks, maybe even months. As if we were finally finding our way back to one another. I smiled, grateful to have the other half of my soul back.

"Blue?" Griff's voice startled me from the memory. I turned to face him, realizing the car had stopped. "We're here." Unbuckling his seatbelt, he gently moved Onyx from the duffle bag before picking it up and slipping from the car.

I followed suit, scooping up my furry familiar and climbing out.

My breath caught in my lungs as I looked up at Chase's family cabin. Although, 'cabin' didn't fit the grand structure before me.

The house was three large levels, built into a hill, the yard sloping behind it down to a small lake. Exquisite golden oak logs made up the bones, large beams framing out the front entrance. Giant windows that had to be nearly twenty feet lined the front, and as we approached the door, I was able to see straight through to the backyard.

Flagstone pavers led the way to the door, two stunning gas lanterns hanging on either side, flames flickering within the glass. Chase pulled out a key, quickly unlocking the home, and we filed in one by one. The interior was light and airy, a large chef's kitchen with gray oak cabinets and white marble countertops off to the right, opening into a huge great room. A stone fireplace extended to the ceiling with a mounted flatscreen, and as I spun in a circle, I was able to spot a loft area overlooking the great room.

A large gray sectional took up most of the space, easily seating at least eight people while a massive dining table sat opposite it, overlooking the biggest deck I'd ever seen. Before I could make my way out—I could already see myself setting up an easel with my morning coffee—Chase placed a gentle hand on my hip, drawing my attention.

"There are six bedrooms, so enough for everyone to have their own." He shot my brother a wink. "But if you wanna share, by all means." Celeste's face turned a deep shade of pink as she ducked her head into my brother's side. Chase let out a small 'oooph' as Griff elbowed him in the ribs, a playful warning.

"You guys can take the rooms on the east side of the house,; we'll take the west." Chase scooped up his duffle and my suitcase, making his way to one side of the double staircase that framed the entryway, leading to the second floor. "Choose any room you like. Just take those stairs." He gestured across the way.

"The kitchen's fully stocked. My dad had supplies brought in last night. There's a theater and game room in the basement, along with a hot tub out back. We also have a fire pit down by the water." My brother's mouth hung open as he gawked at the splendor surrounding us. It wasn't like we'd grown up poor. Our parents had successful careers, and we'd lived comfortably, but this was some next-level luxury living.

Chase smiled broadly from halfway up the staircase.

"Welcome to Casa de Stone!"

thirty-five

Chase

I fucking loved coming to the cabin. Besides being out on the lake or between Everly's thighs, this was my favorite place in the world. Nature surrounded us on all sides, our private drive nearly half a mile from the main road, giving us just enough privacy. My parents purchased it when I was a kid, and we'd been coming here multiple times a year ever since. It had enough modern conveniences to keep my dad happy while still being secluded enough that we weren't bothered by neighbors.

When I asked Dad if we could use the cabin, he'd been more than willing, understanding our need to get Everly away from SLA for a while. He was still working with his PIs, trying to unearth any evidence that could lock Alaric Thorpe up for good. No one had spoken about Mr. Blackwell's contract since rescuing Everly, but it still hung heavy around our necks like a fucking albatross.

I got my Larkspur settled into the master bedroom, the large California king bed nearly swallowing her tiny body when she'd jumped on it earlier. It was a nice change of pace to see her smiling and happy, but the dark ghosts from her time with Austin still haunted her blue eyes.

We were planning to stay until Wednesday, then heading to my parents' house in Emporia for the holiday. I didn't say it out loud, but I was dying to introduce Everly to my mom. My dad had already filled her in on the... unique dynamic of our relationship.

"My love," she'd said when I called to ask about the cabin, "if she makes you happy, and she treats you well, then I don't care who is involved."

My mom was seriously the best.

We were all settled in the great room, sprawled across the sectional, a few beer bottles scattered on the end tables. Griff cooked chicken on the large outdoor grill while the girls fixed a fucking delicious pasta salad—sans artichoke hearts, because gross—and we'd eaten at the long black walnut table my dad had custom made for his and mom's twentieth wedding anniversary.

Feeling brave, I nudged Everly's foot with my elbow. She was lying on her belly, legs kicked up behind her in the air, a sketchbook open in front of her on the gray cushions. I was glad to see her drawing again, the piece a realistic charcoal sketch of Onyx. She turned her head, looking over her shoulder to meet my eyes.

"What do you say to a movie date, Larkspur? Just you and me?" I knew it was a ballsy request, but I also knew Celeste had been working with her all week, reminding her that what she'd seen in that fucking cabin of horrors hadn't been real.

She rolled onto her side, her bottom lip caught between her teeth. She gnawed on it for a moment, shooting Celeste a furtive glance. I held myself back from looking at her friend and trying to decode the unspoken looks they were giving, my eyes fixated on the freckles I loved so much that adorned the bridge of her nose instead. She inhaled softly, swinging her gaze back to me. Her shoulders rolled back, and it was like an air of confidence swept over her.

She flipped the sketchbook closed, moving it to the end of the sofa, before sitting up, her bare thigh brushing mine. She'd changed into a pair of black sleep shorts and a long-sleeved white crop, the taut skin of her midsection teasing me until my balls ached. It'd been too long since I'd been inside my Larkspur but, fuck, I'd wait forever if that was what she needed.

"Yes, Chase, I'd love to have a movie date with you." She stood, boldly holding out her hand for mine. Not one to look a gift horse in the mouth, I grabbed her hand, and quickly dragged her toward the basement stairs.

Tucked in the back of the lower level was a large rectangular room, about twenty feet long with ten foot ceilings. My parents had installed plush reclining loveseats, complete with cupholders. An old school popcorn machine and a stocked fridge were nestled into a small kitchenette off to one side, while a large screen hung on the far wall.

"Whatcha wanna watch?" I flopped onto one of the loveseats, flipping on the projector and linking it to my phone via the house's sick WiFi. Pulling up a streaming service, I began scrolling, hoping something would catch her eye.

"Umm, something funny?" She hovered near the door, her hands twisting nervously in front of her. Gone was the confident woman from upstairs, and in her place stood a scared girl unsure if she should trust me.

Well, challenge fucking accepted.

Using a soft, gentle voice, I coaxed her to the sofa. "Baby, you can sit at the other end if you want. Or hell, you don't even have to sit on the same couch

as me at all. I want to be near you, but I also want you to be comfortable."
I pulled myself up, making sure to occupy only my cushion, leaving the opposite end free for her.

She hesitated for a moment before finally sitting down, her feet tucked under her small frame, and I couldn't help but notice the quiet exhale that escaped her lips. She was studying the screen, watching as I scrolled through the selections. Spotting one she liked, she pointed. "That one. I heard it was really funny."

I hit play, settling back in the cushion and pressing the recline button. Everly watched before following suit, the bottom half of her seat rising. I cautiously slung an arm over the back of the loveseat, but my eyes never once moved from her angelic profile.

After about ten minutes, she finally called me out.

"Are you going to actually watch the movie? Or are you going to stare at me like a creeper all night?" The twinge of a grin lifted the corners of her mouth, and I barked out a laugh.

"Oh Larkspur, there's not a thing in the world I would rather watch than your beautiful face." I gave her a wolfish grin. "Especially when your mouth makes that perfect little 'o' when you..." I didn't get to finish as a playful slap landed on my arm.

"Chase Stone!" Her cheeks flamed red, but the smile on her face let me know she wasn't really offended. I snagged her hand before she could pull away, lacing my fingers with hers, resting them on my thigh. I wasn't trying to force her into anything, but I wanted to show her I still wanted her.

She glanced nervously at our hands before relaxing into the cushions, each muscle unfurling with every passing minute. As the movie played, I felt her sink further and further into my side, snuggling herself against the hard length of my torso. I unlinked our hands, curling my arm around her shoulders, tucking her in even further.

It felt like fucking heaven to have her beneath my fingers again. Even before she'd been kidnapped, things were strained between Everly and me, but now that we knew the truth, and the fucked up lengths Austin and Morgan were willing to go, it was like we were starting anew.

Darting my eyes down, I caught her staring up at me, and I smiled smugly. Deciding it was now or never, I snatched my phone out of the cupholder and paused the movie.

"Hey," she said, her voice betraying the fact I'd startled her. She sat up, leaning away slightly, and my body instantly missed the feel of hers curved to the shape of mine. "You okay? Why'd you stop the movie?" A divot appeared between her eyebrows as she scrunched them in confusion.

"Can I kiss you?" The words were out of my mouth before I could think, reminding me of the first time I'd told her I loved her.

She stared at me dumbfounded, her sapphire eyes going wide in surprise. She opened her mouth but no words came out, her cheeks flushing pink.

Fuck. Fuck. Fuck.

I fucked this up. I pushed her to fa—

"Yes."

One word. One goddamn word and my entire body lit up like the Fourth of July. One word that held so much promise.

Using as much self-restraint as I could muster, I slowly leaned forward, gently cradling her jaw with both of my hands. I brought my mouth to hers until only a breath existed between our lips. My eyes searched hers for any hesitation, and I asked, praying she wouldn't say no.

"Are you sure?"

Those deep cerulean pools darkened when she answered, her voice coming out in that fucking sexy, husky way that made all the blood rush to my dick.

"Kiss me, Chase. Remind me that I'm yours."

I crashed my lips to hers, my tongue licking at the seam of her mouth, begging for entry. She parted them, our tongues dancing a sensual tango. The kiss was slow, deliberate, neither of us rushing to the finish line. I tilted her head to the side, moving one hand to cup the back of her head, my fingers weaving through her long locks.

Everly melted into my touch, her small hands resting on my chest, and I could feel the pull of the fabric as she gripped it tightly.

I nipped her bottom lip gently between my teeth, soothing the sting with a lap of my tongue. She whimpered, shifting her body to rub her thighs together.

Reluctantly, I broke the kiss, pulling back so I could see her face.

"Baby." My voice was gravelly with need. It'd been a hot fucking minute since I'd had a good release, but I wanted to make this all about my girl. I needed to make her see that her body was the only one that brought me any pleasure. "Let me make you feel good, Larkspur. Let me take care of you."

I kissed along her jaw to the sensitive spot just below her ear I knew drove her crazy, working my way down her neck. She groaned, her skin heating beneath my touch. I trailed one hand lower, teasing the tips of my fingers over her collarbone, down the valley between her breasts. When I heard her breath hitch, I paused.

"Is this okay?" She needed only to say the word, and I'd back off. I wanted this to be good for her, but only if she was comfortable. My hand settled on her hip, giving it a gentle squeeze as I continued lavishing her neck with gentle nips and sucks, being careful not to leave any marks.

Her answer came on a breathless moan.

"*Yes.*"

Taking that as the only confirmation I needed, I slowly worked my hand below the waistband of her soft, cotton shorts, little sparks erupting everywhere my fingers touched her skin. There was an electric energy buzzing in the air, and I finally felt whole again as my hands claimed her body.

My dick was rock hard in my sweatpants, but I tried desperately to ignore the throbbing need. I could also jerk off later in the shower.

This was all about my Larkspur.

I found her sweet pussy, wet with her arousal, and ran my fingers through her slickness. Everly keened as I dragged them through her folds, my middle finger sliding over her clit, sending her back arching.

I pushed forward, pressing her backward onto the loveseat until she was tucked under me, my right leg between her sweet thighs, nudging them wider. Bringing my other hand from the back of her head, I pushed it under the hem of her cropped shirt, palming her perfect tit. Jesus, it was a perfect goddamn fit.

My balls were heavy with the need to fuck her, but goddamn, watching her come undone from my touch had me nearly erupting in my pants.

I slid one long finger inside her, the hot walls of her pussy immediately clamping down on me.

"Oooh." She gave what was probably the most erotic whimper I'd ever heard, her hips bucking up into my hand. I plucked at her nipple through the sheer bra she was wearing, coaxing it to a hardened peak before moving to the other, giving it the same attention.

Everly thrust her hips up to meet my hand each time I plunged my finger inside her. I added a second, stretching her walls as I rubbed tight circles around her swollen clit.

I could feel the pressure building beneath her skin, just waiting to burst through. I drove my fingers in one last time, curling them to rub that sweet spot deep inside her pussy, my thumb pressing down firmly on her clit.

She detonated like a fucking bomb, her walls clamping down so hard on my fingers, I could barely move them. I watched as her eyes rolled back in her head, her mouth opening in that perfect fucking 'o' while the most beautiful shade of pink flushed along her cheeks and chest.

I continued to thrust inside her, stroking her through her release until she was left panting beneath me, her body going slack under my hands. I pressed a soft kiss to her forehead before pulling my hand from her panties, making a show of bringing my fingers to my mouth as I licked off her arousal.

"Mmmm." I sucked on them obscenely. "You taste so fucking good."

thirty
six
Everly

I padded downstairs the next morning, my body still riding the high of my orgasm from the night before. By the time Chase and I emerged from the theater room, Celeste and Evan had disappeared to bed, Griff was passed out on one end of the sectional—a book lying open on his chest—and Knox was quietly sketching at the dining room table.

He'd glanced up briefly when we'd entered, not saying a word. Judging by the pained look on his face, however, he'd no doubt noticed the flush of my cheeks and rumpled clothing.

Guilt ate at me. I wanted to let Knox back in. I missed being wrapped in his arms, the way he always smelled vaguely like cedar and acrylics. I just needed to get my head and heart on the same page, but the painful memories of what I thought he did were still so fresh in my mind.

It'd felt good to let go the night before, to let Chase own my body, reminding me that his touch was safe. He'd been incredibly sweet afterward, quickly washing his hands in the small kitchenette before snuggling in behind me on the loveseat, curving his large body around mine. We probably looked ridiculous squished on the small sofa, but I didn't care.

Something in my chest unlocked when he wrapped me in his arms, cocooning me into his broad chest. I knew, on some level I couldn't begin to explain, that Chase loved me beyond reproach. Maybe it was the way he made my body come alive with his touch. Or the tender way he checked in, asking if I was comfortable. The sweet but dirty words he whispered in my ear.

I knew, deep down, Chase Stone loved me and only me.

And fuck Austin Thorpe for making me doubt that for even one second.

Now, we were hanging out in the backyard, enjoying an unseasonably warm day for late November while my brother attempted to grill hamburgers for lunch. Celeste let out a loud laugh as she watched him unsuccessfully try to flip a burger in the air. I let out a chuckle before I focused back on the sketch I started this morning, my fingers stained black from the charcoal.

The snow leopard's coat was a blend of whites and storm cloud grays, each mixed to the perfect shade throughout its silky fur while his spots stood out in dark contrast. His intense gaze was head on, but instead of the typical blue eyes, this majestic beast stared out with eyes the color of dark chocolate. They pulled you in, mesmerizing pools of darkness able to see into the very depths of your soul.

My eyes wandered across the patio, finding my shifter working intensely on his own art project. Deciding I needed some exposure therapy, I pulled up my big girl panties—figuratively speaking, of course—and bundled my sketchbook and charcoal in my arms. I had parked myself on one of the lounge chairs scattered across the large deck while Knox worked at a table on the opposite side. I rose from my spot, taking a fortifying breath before moving across the wide wooden planks.

I came up behind him quietly, trying to get a glimpse of what he was drawing. My shadow danced over his sketchbook, the sun warming my skin beneath my lavender tee. Knox threw an arm over the paper, effectively cutting off my view before twisting around to see me.

Swallowing down my nerves, I squeaked out, "Mind if I join you?"

His jaw hung slack, eyes going wide in surprise. "Uh, yeah, I mean, yes, of–of course." He gestured to the open seats surrounding the table, jumping up to pull one out. His eyes, the color of rich brownie batter in the afternoon light, were lit with a nervous excitement.

I looked at the chairs, noting I had a choice. I could sit next to him, in the seat he'd offered. Or I could sit across from him, putting distance between us. A *safe* distance.

Something Celeste said to me about Knox earlier in the week ran through my mind.

"You've gotta let him in, Eves. You have to give him the chance to prove that he's the guy you know he is deep down."

"Thanks." I slid into the open seat at his side, my heart fluttering when I saw his shoulders relax. I placed my book and charcoal on the table, opening to the sketch of the snow leopard. Knox's breath hitched when his eyes hit my sketch, a strangled sound vibrating from deep in his throat.

"Is that—" His voice was so full of emotion. I peeked up at him through my eyelashes, the butterflies in my stomach keeping me from making full eye contact. His proximity was crossing the wires in my brain, making my insides feel like a raging storm over the ocean, my emotions a tiny row boat being tossed wildly in the waves. I, as inconspicuously as possible, took a deep breath to steady my nerves.

This is your Knoxy. He's not going to hurt you.

"Uh, yeah," I answered, chewing on my bottom lip. I lifted my chin to see him better, and the look of absolute wonder on his face as he studied my drawing had my heart stuttering in my chest.

"Little Monet, it's…" His voice was quiet, reverent, his dark eyes drinking in the image. "It's amazing."

I felt my cheeks flush at his praise, but the feeling quickly waned when I saw his brows scrunched together, his gaze scrutinizing the page. "May I?" He gestured to my sketchbook. I nodded, my nerves flaring to life once more.

He spun the book to face him, studying my drawing intensely. With each passing second, nausea built in my gut. Just as I was about to ask him for the book back, he spoke, the words soft and cautious.

"Baby, he's perfect. But why are his eyes brown? Aren't my eyes blue when I shift?"

My heart clenched, and my eyes blurred with tears. There were no cruel words, no snide comments. He didn't raise his hand to strike me. Sitting there, I could see the man who created art for me, pouring every ounce of his love onto those canvases. I released a shuddering breath, another broken piece of my heart slotting back into place.

"Those are your eyes, Knoxy. Those are the eyes I fell in love with."

After lunch, which was delayed by nearly forty-five minutes because my brother burned the first round of hamburgers, I helped Celeste clean up the kitchen. Chase let it slip that there was a massive gaming console in the theater room downstairs, so all the guys were currently trying to beat each other in Mario Kart. We could hear the occasional 'whoo!' and some shit talking, mostly from Chase and Evan, as we finished up.

Tossing the dish towel on the counter, I turned to find Celeste with two stemless wine glasses and a bottle of rosé in her hands. She shook the bottle at me, grinning, as she skipped over to the large sectional. I rolled my eyes and chuckled, following her.

She poured us each a glass, and we sat in silence for a few minutes. I sipped the pink liquid, enjoying the fruity flavors as they danced across my tongue. I chuckled to myself when I glanced at Celeste, watching her stare longingly at the basement stairs. *Oh my God, she had it bad.*

"So," I said over the rim of my glass. "I've counted, I think, four times this week that Evan snuck into the suite after I'd gone to bed?"

I asked the question just as Celeste took a drink, the wine sputtering from her mouth in shock. Her eyes went wide as her cheeks turned a bright red.

"I—we—we thought," she stuttered, and I abandoned my wine on the table, her rambling making me nearly double over in laughter. The giggles erupted from deep in my chest, wrapped in a lightheartedness that I hadn't felt in weeks. I swiped at my eyes, fat tears rolling down my face as I howled. I watched as her face transformed, the embarrassment staining her cheeks lifting as the corners of her mouth curved upward.

"Har, har." She rolled her eyes, the hint of a guilty smile tugging at her lips. "I mean, if you really wanna know, your brother can do this thing with his tong—" she taunted playfully. But I shoved my fingers in my ears, singing loudly and off key until she tossed a throw pillow in my direction.

Grabbing my wine glass from the coffee table, I tucked my feet under myself. "Seriously though, things are good with you guys?" I asked her in a more serious tone. I knew she'd been crushing on my brother for years, and this sudden change in relationship status made me nervous for her. I loved my brother, but I would feed him his balls if he hurt my bestie.

She looked back at the doorway leading to the basement once more, a soft expression crossing her face. "Yeah," she acknowledged. "It all kind of happened fast."

"Listen, I'm the queen of jumping into a relationship headfirst," I reminded her. "Or, well, *relationships*." I fixed her with a serious look before continuing. "I just want to make sure you're not going to get hurt, C. I'd hate to have to kill my brother." I laughed as I said the last part, only a little serious. Okay, maybe half serious.

She waved me off, taking a quick sip of her wine. "Seriously, Eves, Evan and I are good. I think this was a long time coming and, as selfish as it is to say, you getting kidnapped kind of forced everything into motion. So, umm, thanks for that?"

I gawked at her for a moment before we both erupted into a fit of laughter.

Once she'd composed herself, Celeste pinned me with a look I knew meant trouble. "Soooo…" she started, stretching the word. "What about you? How are things going with your guys?"

My cheeks heated as memories of the night before flashed through my mind, the magical way Chase brought my body back to life with his sinful fingers and tongue making my lower belly clench with need. I flicked my wrist toward the coffee table, the bottle of wine lifting into the air. Tipping my index finger, I refilled my wine glass before setting the bottle back on the wooden table top, allowing myself a moment to collect my thoughts.

"Things are... getting there," I replied hesitantly. "I'm working on reminding myself that it wasn't them in the cabin, that it wasn't really Chase I saw with Heather. I know it deep down, but sometimes, when I get lost in the memories of what happened, I forget."

Celeste stayed quiet, a thoughtful look on her face as she processed what I said. Chase's loud voice echoed from the basement, breaking the silence in the room, and I laughed when I heard him whine about Knox beating him again.

"I sat with Knox today," I shared, proud that I'd taken the first step in healing our fractured relationship. Celeste's face lit up at the admission.

"That's great! How'd it go?" She sat forward from her spot, eager to hear my answer.

I glanced out the large windows to the spot where I'd joined Knox earlier in the day. The deck was drenched in the late afternoon sun, and I could see Knox's sketchbook still on the glass-top table.

"It was... good. A little scary at first, but he..." I thought about my next words carefully. "It was like sitting with *my* Knox again."

"That's because he *is* your Knox, idiot." She tossed another pillow at me, but I stopped it in mid air before reversing it back at her with a twirl of my finger.

I'd been unsure what to expect when I sat down next to him, but it was like settling in to watch your favorite movie. The ease of just sitting there, working on our art together like we'd done a million times before was such a relief. Hope swelled in my chest.

Maybe we'd be alright after all.

thirty-seven · Griffin

I loaded the coffee maker, popping a fresh filter in before filling it with a crème brûlée roast the girls seemed to really love. Setting it to brew, I wandered over to the folding glass doors that led to the deck out back. The weather had been so nice the last few days, we'd been able to leave them open while the sun was up, fresh air flooding the main area of the house.

Knowing it was still a little too cold to open them just yet, I admired the sky in the early morning light. Deep oranges crested the horizon, melting into a mesmerizing mix of purples and blues left over from the night before. There was a particular spot in the heavens where the blue perfectly matched my girl's eyes, the light of a fading star illuminating the area.

The smell of the coffee drew me back to the kitchen, but when I turned around, the sight of Everly in one of my old tour guide t-shirts, stretching on her tiptoes to reach a mug from a high shelf was not something I was prepared to see. My dick instantly thickened in my flannel sleep pants at seeing *Cardarette* plastered across her back, the shirt riding up her thighs and exposing the bottom of her ass cheeks.

Jesus, she fucking better be wearing underwear.

Adjusting my growing hard on, I made my way around the large kitchen island, placing a gentle hand on her hip as I reached over her head. She shrieked and jumped in surprise, the top of her head knocking into my chin, rattling my teeth.

"Jesus Christ, Griff! You scared the shit out of me!" She swatted my chest before snatching the coffee mug I'd grabbed.

"Sorry, Blue girl." I rubbed the sore spot on my stubbly chin. "My fault. Probably should have warned you I was there. I was just trying to help."

She shot me a glare before turning toward the coffee pot. "Seems to be your MO." She pulled the carafe and slowly filled her cup. "Trying to help but fucking it up instead."

Ouch.

I winced at her harsh words. They sounded foreign coming from my girl's mouth. I watched as her shoulders fell with a heavy sigh.

"I'm sorry," she said quietly, her back still to me. "I didn't mean that."

"Everly." I gripped her elbow gently, turning her to face me. She chewed on her bottom lip as she held tightly to the mug, her eyes downcast, but I could still see the tears tracking down her cheeks. "Baby, you don't have to be sorry. I fucking deserved that. I deserve a lot more than that for fucking this all up."

I tilted her face as I cupped her cheek, thumbing away the tears. Her blue eyes were glassy, and she sniffled, turning away, my hand falling to her upper arm. "I shouldn't have been rude." She twisted to set her coffee down on the white marble counter behind her. She wiped at her eyes, swiping the back of her hand where her cheeks were damp from her sadness.

We stood in silence for a beat before she spoke again, her words an angry whisper. "I'm really fucking mad at you, Griff." Those blue eyes I loved so much flicked up to look at me, shiny with tears, but lacking the stunning vibrancy I'd grown accustomed to. They were dull, lifeless, and it broke my fucking heart every time I looked into them knowing I'd had a hand in extinguishing that light.

I hung my head, the shame of hurting her sitting like a boulder in my gut. "I know, Blue girl. I'm so fucking sorry. I really did think I was doing the right thing." On instinct, I pulled her in close, circling my arms around her petite frame. She stiffened for a fraction of a second before she softened into me, causing a wave of relief to flood my body.

This was exactly where she was supposed to be: wrapped in my arms, safe from the dangers of the world. Everly wound her small arms around my middle, laying her cheek against my bare chest. The warmth of her breath skated across my skin, and I rested my chin on top of her messy bun, inhaling deeply.

Her familiar scent of peonies and jasmine calmed the restless part of my soul that had been adrift since that day in the library. Now, with her pressed against my flesh, that feeling dissipated, a sense of home settling deep inside my chest.

I stroked her hair, some of the strands loosening from her bun, tumbling down her back. We stayed like that, two souls suspended in time, fitting back together the jagged pieces that I broke with my lies and omissions. I knew by the gentle shake of her shoulders that she was crying, expelling all the damage her heart had suffered over the last two months.

Selfish as it sounds, I was happy to hold her as she cried. The feel of her skin beneath my hands was something I'd been missing, and not only in the physical sense. Everly completed a hollow spot inside me, filling in the empty cracks and crevices left behind by years spent alone in the system after I ran away.

After a few quiet minutes, she pulled away, wiping at her cheeks. I dropped my hands to the flare of her hips, the cotton of my old shirt soft against my fingers.

"Blue?"

She looked up at me, and finally, *finally*, her eyes held that spark that told me there just might be hope for us after all.

"Are we going to be okay?" I held my breath once the question left my lips, and I was fairly certain at least eight thousand minutes passed before she answered.

Leaning up on her tiptoes, she braced a hand delicately on my chest, the heat from her palm warming my skin like a brand. She stretched, her lips coming within millimeters of my own, her words ghosting over my skin in a gentle caress.

"Yeah, Griff, I think we're going to be okay." She pressed a painfully soft kiss to my mouth, her lips lingering for only a moment before they were gone. "I never stopped loving you."

My heart stuttered in my chest at the words I didn't know I needed to hear simultaneously shattering and mending my soul.

I leaned my forehead to hers.

"Same, Blue girl."

Everly and I took our coffee out onto the deck, snuggling in one of the large lounge chairs to enjoy the last remnants of the sunrise before everyone started filtering into the kitchen for breakfast. Having that quiet time together, before the world woke up, was exactly what we'd needed. Time to heal together, and just *be*.

I cooked pancakes, stacking them on a serving platter while Everly and Celeste chopped up some fruit as a side dish.

I flipped a pancake high into the air, winking at my girl before catching it back in the pan. She rolled her eyes, giggling as she mouthed '*show-off*' from across the counter. We stuffed ourselves full of delicious, syrupy goodness, talking about our plans for the day.

"I'm kidnapping Everly," Celeste said around a mouthful of pancakes. We all swung our gaze to where she sat at the end of the table, Everly's mouth dropping open in shock. My girl's best friend nearly choked on her food, the realization of what she'd said finally dawning on her.

"Shit! Not like that!" She coughed as she tried to explain. When she finally got herself under control, she sheepishly looked around the table.

"Too soon?"

The room went so deathly quiet, you could have heard a pin drop. I darted my eyes to Everly, noting the intense looks both Chase and Knox were wearing.

Then, I heard the most beautiful sound.

Everly laughing.

And I don't mean a few little chuckles. She was full on, gasping for breath, tears streaming down her cheeks, belly laughing.

Knox looked between her and me, his dark eyes wide in confusion. Judging by the expression on his face, I think he was trying to decide if our girl had finally cracked under all the stress.

After another beat, Chase let out a loud laugh as well, and before we knew it, the entire table joined in, making me feel the lightest I had in a long time. Seeing my girl laugh, seeing that radiant smile again, was like a balm to my damaged heart.

Once we'd all calmed down, Celeste explained that she and Everly were going to spend the day down at the water. While the guys and I cleaned up from breakfast, my Blue girl packed up a tote bag full of art supplies while Celeste grabbed a folding lounge chair and blanket.

I carefully observed Knox as he watched Everly, noting the hesitancy each time he thought she might need help with something. I knew for a fact that she and Chase were well on their way to mending any unresolved issues between them, and my time with her this morning told me I was headed down the right path as well.

But my quiet and surly friend?

He looked like he didn't have a fucking clue.

He didn't tell us about the gifts he'd left for her. We heard from Celeste, who'd heard from Everly. I knew Knox was trying his best. He was the first to admit he wasn't great with words, instead using his art to convey his feelings.

Our buddy needed our help.

Catching Chase's eye, I tipped my head toward the deck. Nodding, he finished loading the dishwasher, following me out into the late morning sun. Once we were both outside, I closed the doors so no one but the squirrels could hear us.

"Knox needs our help."

Chase turned to look at Knox still puttering around in the kitchen. He hiked a thumb over his shoulder. "What'd you mean? He looks fine. And besides, *I'm* the one who loaded the damn dishwasher, even though it was his turn." He pouted, huffing out a breath.

"No, you idiot," I said, smacking him on the back of the head. "Knox needs our help with Everly. He's too scared to make the first move with her."

Realization showed on his face. "Aahhh, I've gotcha." He rubbed his hands together in a way that told me he was on board. "So, what's the plan?"

"We've gotta get them together, alone. But it has to be done in a way that isn't going to scare her…" I pondered options, rubbing a hand over my chin as I ran through a variety of scenarios. Then the fucking light bulb went off.

"Remember that spot out by the ridge, where he went to paint a few times when we were here last summer?" Knox had disappeared for hours during that trip, saying he'd found an ideal location to work on some sunset pieces.

It was perfect.

But how did we get them there?

Chase and I brainstormed for the rest of the afternoon, our plan taking shape over several beers and a few slices of reheated pizza from the night before when we'd made personal pies in the outdoor wood-fired oven.

We'd ironed out all the details, bringing Evan and Celeste in on our romantic machinations once we were set with the plan.

Now all we needed to do was set it in motion.

thirty-eight — Knox

"Knooxyyy."

Someone wanted to die today.

"Knnnooooxxyyy."

Correction.

Chase wanted to die today.

"The fuck do you want, Stone?" I growled into my pillow. I was facedown in the plush, king-size bed, the blankets rucked around my hips. I cracked an eye to glance at the clock.

Seven fucking AM.

I was going to kill him.

Despite the bed being insanely comfortable, I'd slept like shit... again.

My brain decided to torture me nightly with terrifying dreams of Everly's kidnapping. Sometimes she was lifeless by the time we reached the cabin. Others, we arrived and she was gone, not a trace of her to be found.

And my personal favorite? Watching helplessly as Austin beat her.

"It's time to get up, Knoxy! It's our last day, so Griff and I thought it would be fun to hike to the ridge!" He yanked the blanket back, exposing my naked ass to the cool air of the room.

I jerked, scrambling to grab the comforter. A loud slap rang through the room as Chase's hand made contact with my ass, the sharp sting waking my nerves. I yelped, finally snagging the blanket, and yanked it over my body.

Motherfucker just slapped my ass!

"Rise and shine, shifter boy!" He sprinted from the room before I could even sit up, disappearing down the hall in a fit of laughter. I grumbled the entire way to the shower, letting the warm water wash away the sleep still clinging to my brain.

Twenty minutes later, I was dressed in light gray joggers, a black t-shirt, and black zip-up hoodie, waiting by the front door as the girls threw a couple sandwiches, some cut up fruit, and crackers into a backpack-style cooler. When they finished, Chase slung it over his shoulder, a stupid ass grin plastered on his face.

He was nearly vibrating, he was so excited. I knew the guy loved nature but, Jesus, this was a bit much.

I'd packed a small bag as well, with two sketchbooks, some charcoals, and a couple of graphite pencils, just in case the urge to draw struck Everly while we were on the ridge.

It was a beautiful location, the slate cliff providing a spectacular view of North Pointe Lake and the waterfalls that fed into it. I'd sat out there for hours last summer, hauling my easel and paints, so I could capture the amazing sunsets that bathed the trees and water in a multitude of golds and pinks.

The ridge was only about an hour walk from the house, so we all grabbed protein bars and hit the trail. The hike was quiet, Chase leading the way, followed closely by Griff and my little Monet. I watched her ass in her black leggings, the cropped sweatshirt she was wearing riding up every so often to show a sliver of her tanned middle. It was goddamn torture walking behind her, every step making those perfect globes sway from side to side.

Everyone was acting squirrelly, and not in an Onyx type way. Everly had left his fluffy ass back at the house, giving him a large bowl of sliced strawberries and bananas before we'd left. He still skirted around me most of the time, giving me a wide berth. A part of me wondered if it was because he could sense the animal inside me.

I noticed they'd all been throwing glances back and forth, Chase barely able to keep a straight face for most of the morning. I didn't know what the fuck was going on, but it was starting to piss me off. By the fifteenth time Chase looked back, his eyes darting quickly between Everly and me, I was ready to lay his ass out, but Griff's commanding voice stopped me.

"We're here."

We broke through the tree line, leaving behind the dense pines and overgrown brush bordering the trail head. A clearing lay before us, grass growing between the cracks of uneven slate. The rough rock created a natural decking that overlooked the lake, the rush of the waterfall at the north end crashing in the distance.

Chase tossed the cooler to the ground as Everly pulled a blanket from her backpack, working with Celeste to spread it across the ground. I meandered closer to the cliff's edge, admiring the rich autumn colors sweeping the small valley. A wash of orange, red, and yellow foliage shone in the mid-morning sun, like jewels in a treasure chest.

Tearing my eyes away from the stunning landscape, I turned, to ask what our plan was, but all the air got stuck in my lungs at the breathtaking sight before me. The sun was shining behind Everly, the rays filtering through her chestnut locks, lighting her up like an angel.

She caught me staring—okay, gawking was probably the more accurate term—a pink staining her cheeks. She tucked away the hair that escaped her messy bun, a shy smile playing on her lips.

As I tried to decide if I should approach her, Chase bounded across the clearing to where I now realized Celeste, Evan, and Griffin were all standing.

"Eves," Celeste called, a nervous lilt in her voice. "Please promise you won't be mad."

I looked to where Everly was standing, opposite me and the others, all of us making a weird triangle over the rock. She looked at her friend in confusion, hands resting on her hips. "What do you mean? I'm not mad about anything."

I caught Griff wince, alarm bells ringing in my head at their cagey behavior. "Blue girl, please understand..." Her eyes went wide with fear. I didn't know what the fuck they were up to, but I swore to god, if Griff betrayed her trust again, I was going to kill him.

Chase spoke up next, a stupid grin on his face, completely at odds with the worried looks Griff and Celeste wore.

"Larkspur," he called out. "You and Knox need to fix your shit. And the only way you're gonna do that is if you spend some time together. That's where we come in." He threw his arms wide, gesturing to their little party. "Or rather, where we *go*."

"Blue, I'm sorry," Griff apologized. He took one of Celeste's hands in his own, Chase gripping him on the shoulder. In the next second they were gone, fucking disappearing into the ether.

Evan took off a half second later, his super speed carrying him away in a blur.

I muttered under my breath, "God fucking damnit." I was beyond irritated, running a hand through my hair in frustration. What the fuck were they thinking, leaving us here? Everly was still fucking terrified of me. I mean, yeah, she'd come to sit with me the other day on the deck, and I'd caught her staring at me here and there, but Jesus Christ! How could they think she'd be ready for this?

She was standing across the way, wringing her hands nervously and shuffling her feet to kick at a loose stone.

Fuck. This was a goddamn disaster.

I was pacing now, running through a plan to get her safely back to the house without having a complete meltdown when I noticed her rummaging through her backpack. She pulled out a sketchpad and a satchel of oil pastels, her blue eyes shimmering in the sunlight when she stole a quick glance my way.

I stopped pacing, watching as she took her supplies closer to the edge of the ridge. She looked around for a moment before settling on a flatter piece of granite, bending to sit on the warm stone. She opened the book to a fresh page and began sketching out the valley's mid-morning beauty, her shoulders relaxing with each stroke.

I watched her intently, too scared to disrupt the peaceful way she worked. After a few minutes, when I knew she was completely engrossed in her art, I pulled out my own sketchbook. But instead of the scenic horizon, I focused on the woman before me. The way she bit her lip, looking between the burnt orange leaves and her drawing, smudging the chalk to blend the colors.

I drew her exactly as she sat, her back curved as she hunched over her sketch, fingers flying over the paper. She was stunning, lost in her work. Her tongue poked out between her plush lips, her eyebrows pulling together as she studied the image.

I worked on my own drawing, my eyes flicking up to soak in each of her soft curves and the way the loose strands of her hair grazed her delicate cheekbone.

I was so lost in watching her, I almost missed the musky scent that blew through the clearing, a hint of ammonia tingeing the air.

A bonus of being a shifter? The heightened sense of smell that came from my animal side.

The fine hairs on the back of my neck stood on end, my body immediately going on alert. I sensed the predator before I saw it, the lethal hunter stalking silently through the trees. As quietly as possible, I placed my sketchpad down, ever so slowly craning my neck in an attempt to locate the animal.

A movement so small it barely caught my eye flicked between two trees. The tail of a mountain lion.

Fuck.

I watched in terror as it prowled from the tree line, its lean muscles shifting with an inaudible grace under sandy colored fur. Everly continued to work on her sketch, none the wiser to the danger lurking fifty feet behind her. Like a lamb to the fucking slaughter.

Knowing I didn't have enough time to warn her, I toed off my sneakers and unzipped my sweatshirt, sliding it down my arms. The movement caught Everly's attention, and she turned to face me.

"Knox, what are yo—"

The lion crouched low to the ground, its long tail swishing back and forth, coiled like a goddamn spring, ready to pounce at any moment. I knew I had only seconds.

"I love you, Everly. And I'm so fucking sorry."

thirty-nine Everly

One second, Knox was standing before me, tense, like he was about to murder someone. And truthfully, I worried for a split second that that someone would be me.

The next?

His clothes were ripping from his body as he shifted into a goddamn mountain lion.

What in the ever loving fuck was happening?

He flew through the air, and if I hadn't been so stunned, I probably would have admired the graceful way his sinewy body moved. Following the arc of his leap, I was shocked to see another fucking hell-cat racing across the clearing, headed straight for us.

The two lions clashed, Knox's body colliding with the other beast in a brutal hit that punched the air from my lungs. The wild lion threw Knox off, and they circled each other so rapidly, I lost track of which was which.

A large paw flew through the air, long claws extended from the pads of its toes. A feline cry broke the silence as a large gash appeared on the chest of one of the lions. Blood stained its sandstone fur a bright red, a rivulet running down and dripping on the stone below.

They attacked again, long tails flicking wildly as snarls ripped from each of their chests. Teeth gnashed, snapping and biting as they rolled across the hard earth. Without knowing which animal was Knox, I couldn't risk using my powers to pull them apart, not wanting to free the feral lion and have it attack me.

They were inching closer to the cliff's edge as I moved in the opposite direction toward the tree line, making sure the lions' attention was drawn away from me. Knox gave me an opening to run, to use my new super speed and escape. But there was no way I could make it back to the house in time to get help.

And there was no fucking way I was leaving him behind.

They tussled on the ground, one of the lion's feet skidding over the loose stones. Jesus, they were less than a foot from the edge, dirt flying through the air as they grappled for dominance.

Blood and bites covered both their bodies, and I had no fucking clue which was Knox. Wild cries filled the air as one of the animals gained the upper hand, pinning the other down and sinking its teeth into the meaty flesh. The lion on the ground roared in pain, bucking wildly, razor sharp claws slashing out until it finally dislodged its opponent.

Being thrown off balance, the cat stumbled, its hind legs slipping on the loose stones near the cliff's drop off. Almost in slow motion, I watched as the lion flailed, the rocks giving way and breaking. The ass end of its body disappeared over the edge a split second before the entire animal was gone, lost to the forest below.

The harsh inhale of my breathing broke the silence as I tried to figure out what had just happened.

Holy fucking shit.

My heart was racing, but I stayed frozen to my spot, blood rushing in my ears. The remaining lion swung its dark eyes in my direction, meeting my gaze before letting out a gut-wrenching whine.

Knox.

He took one step before pitching forward, crumpling into an unmoving heap on the ground.

NO!

I sprinted, my super speed putting him at my feet in the blink of an eye. He was covered in blood, puncture wounds, and cuts all over his body. I went to reach for him but pulled back when he began to shift back to his human form. I watched in horrified wonder as the fur disappeared, leaving in its wake his damaged skin, slashes marring the beautiful ink tattooed across his flesh.

I rolled Knox to his back, my hands slick with his blood, tracking the slight movement of his chest as he dragged in a ragged breath.

He was still alive.

"Knox," I sobbed, my voice breaking on his name. I ran my hands over his body, trying to find the deepest wounds, so I could apply pressure, but there were too many. Coming up with an idea, I ran to where his clothes lay in tatters, scooping them up and rushing back to his side.

I ripped the fabric further, making long strands that I bound around his wounds, stemming the blood flow some. I even pulled off my own cropped sweatshirt, securing it around a large gash near his shoulder.

"Knoxy," I cried, tears running down my cheeks. "Please don't leave me, please!" I stroked his cheek, blood smearing across his stubbly cheek. His normally olive skin was a nauseating shade of white, the bandages already soaked with blood from his injuries.

Fuck.

Fuck.

Fuck!

Knox's eyelids fluttered, slowly opening to reveal those deep, dark eyes I loved so much.

"Knox!" It took all my self-restraint not to fling my body on top of his, the relief of seeing his eyes open crashing over me. "You're gonna be okay, baby. I've got you." I choked down the emotion in my voice, knowing I needed to be strong to get us both home safely.

"Monet..." he croaked, a thin line of blood leaking from the corner of his mouth. Fuck, I needed to get him out of here. Now.

How the fuck was I gonna do this? Why the fuck couldn't I have developed super strength instead of speed.

Speed.

Yes!

I could use my super speed to get us back! But how the hell was I going to carry Knox? He outweighed me by at least eighty pounds, if not more. My shoulders sagged in defeat. Knox's breathing was growing more shallow with each passing minute, and I was running out of both time and ideas.

Maybe if I could get him to shift into something smaller, like a rabbit, then I could easily lift him.

His eyes had closed once more, his lips a sickly pale color that made my stomach clench in fear. "Knoxy." I shook him gently. His eyelids fluttered open once more. "Knoxy, I need you to—"

He cut me off, his chocolate eyes finding mine. The lines on his face were creased in pain, and he winced as he tried to move. "Everly," he breathed out, the act of speaking clearly taking a great deal of effort. "Baby, I'm sorry." He coughed, flecks of blood appearing on his lips. I glanced at his abdomen to see one of the deepest wounds still oozing blood around the bandage.

"Knoxy, there's nothing to be sorry for, baby. Now come on, can you shift into a smaller animal? Something I can carry? I need to get you back to the house." I was on the verge of breaking, the deathly pale color of his skin making my stomach knot painfully.

I can't fucking lose him.

"No can do, Monet"—the words coming out in halted bursts—"I'm having a hard time breathing right now, baby." His eyes fluttered closed, his chest relaxing on an exhale.

"Knox!" I screamed his name, startling him, so his eyes opened once more. "Knoxy please, please, come on baby, help me out here." I frantically ran through any conceivable way I could move him.

The idea hit me like a fuck ton of bricks.

Standing quickly, I took a deep breath.

Fuck, this had to work.

Relaxing my shoulders, I bowed my head and closed my eyes. Drawing my hands up, I focused every ounce of energy I had out through my palms, picturing his body lifting from the ground, floating through the air.

"Come on, Larkspur, I bet you can do it." Chase's words of encouragement from the day I'd levitated myself across the suite rang through my mind, and a flood of telekinetic energy flowed through my body. The magic danced across my skin, the hair on my arms standing on end from the increased power.

I felt a blast of warmth crash over me, pulling a gasp from my lips, and I couldn't believe what I saw when I opened my eyes.

311

Bright purple and blue light was erupting from my hands, washing over Knox as he lifted from the stone. He rose til he was nearly three feet in the air, his body cocooned in the safety of my magic.

I watched his chest, making sure I could still see the steady but slow rise before I started to move us to the tree line. I walked slowly at first, testing how difficult he would be to maneuver along the trail.

By the time we reached the trail head, I had a good grasp on how to steer his prone form.

It's now or never.

"I love you, Knoxy. Hold on," I said, determined to save the man that I loved. It was the only motivation I needed to take off at a dead sprint, pushing him forward at a breakneck pace down the dirt-packed trail. We zipped around trees and over roots, my feet flying across the ground in a flurry of movement. The lavender and blue light from my hands kept him from being jostled, acting almost like a pillow, cradling his battered and bleeding body.

After close to five minutes of winding bends and a never-ending blur of autumn colors, I spotted the top of the house, sunlight glinting off the windows of the second floor. Pushing myself even harder, I doubled down, my feet barely touching the ground as we neared the backyard.

I flew across the lawn and up the backstairs, flinging one of the sliding-glass doors open with a nod of my head. I hovered Knox just inside, using my magic to lay him gently on the hardwood floor. As I drew the light back into my body, I suddenly felt bone tired, as if someone had sucked out every ounce of energy from my atoms. My knees buckled, and I landed hard on the cedar decking. Just before I lost consciousness, I cried out, hoping someone would hear.

"Help!"

Knox's bloodied face was the last thing I was before the darkness swallowed me.

forty

Chase

"**S**uck it!" I pumped my fist in the air, basking in the glow of yet another victory. I'd been crushing Evan all morning in a variety of video games, Celeste having left him in my capable and competitive hands, so she could get caught up on some reading for school.

"Motherfucker!" he shouted, tossing his controller on the large ottoman in front of us. "Man, how the fuck are you so good at all these games?"

"It's raw, natural talent, buddy." I smiled smugly before Griff swooped in, stealing all my thunder.

"It's more that he practices non-stop because Knox always whoops his ass whenever they play." Asshole was lounged at the end of the sofa, his reading glasses perched on his nose as he read a text about magical law.

Boring.

"Hey, Griff, how 'bout you shut the fuck up?" I beaned him with a throw pillow to the side, a loud grunt coming from his chest. Maybe I threw that a *wee* bit harder than I'd meant to.

I did say I was competitive.

Just as he was getting ready to lay into me, a scream sounded from upstairs, piercing the air like a goddamn gunshot. "Help!"

Everly.

We all moved at once, Evan and I jumping over the back of the sofa and racing to the stairs, Griff hot on our heels. We flew up the steps, crashing into the great room. I scanned the area, not seeing a soul.

What the fuck?

Griffin looked at me, confused, as Evan stalked slowly through the room. We'd definitely heard Everly scream. I'd heard that horrible sound enough times after we found her, it was burned into my memory.

A low groan came from the far side of the room, just as Evan rounded the sectional.

"Fuck, Knox!" He darted over, bending out of sight behind the large gray cushions. Griffin and I ran to where he was crouching over Knox's naked body.

He was covered in blood, pieces of ripped fabric crisscrossing his damaged body. I couldn't tell if he was breathing, if he was even fucking alive.

What the fuck happened?

"Knox!" Griff pressed two fingers to his neck, checking for a pulse. I held my breath, waiting to see if one of my best friends was lying dead at my feet. Griff let out a loud exhale, pulling his hand away. "He's alive, but his pulse is weak." He stood quickly, assessing the wounds on Knox's body.

"Evan, go grab some towels, and get Celeste. We need to put pressure on these wounds to stop the blood loss." Evan was gone in a flash, the sound of banging cupboards coming from the main level bathroom.

"Chase, call Preston, find out where he is *exactly*. I'll teleport and bring him back." I was lost, staring at the ashen color of Knox's skin... well, the spots that weren't smeared with blood. How the hell had this happened? And where—

"Chase!" Griff barked, tossing me his phone. I barely caught it, fumbling to punch in his code. I pulled up Preston's contact information and hit dial. As it rang, I asked Griff, "Man, why don't you just port him to a hospital?"

Griff ran a hand over his short hair, making several pieces stick up, Knox's blood smearing on his forehead. Evan was already back with Celeste, the two working silently to stop any further blood loss but holy shit. Our boy was in rough shape.

"I'm afraid the teleportation will be too much on his body. Without knowing what happened, I can't guarantee he'd make the jump."

"Hello?" Preston's voice came over the line, bringing my attention back to the call.

"Preston! Where the fuck are you?" I snapped. I was panicking, worried my best friend was dying at my feet. Fucking formalities would have to wait.

"What? I'm in my room on campus. I couldn't go home for the holiday. Why?" He was clearly confused by my call, but I didn't have time to explain. Looking up at Griff, I shouted. "His room at school. Go!"

Griff vanished half a second later. I took a deep breath, trying to wrap my head around how our perfect plan from just a few hours ago had gone so wrong. And where the fuck wa—

Preston appeared before me, glasses sitting askew on his face, his hair a disheveled mess. He looked like he was ready to puke, a sure sign it was his first time teleporting. His eyes quickly found Knox, assessing the situation.

"Preston, help him," I pleaded. "Please." He dropped down next to me, a mask of determination slipping over his face. He adjusted his glasses before hovering his hands over Knox's abdomen. The soft blue light I'd seen when he healed Everly began to pulse from his palms, seeping into the ugly wounds.

I watched as the deep gashes slowly knitted themselves back together, drawing low groans of pain from Knox. Thank fuck he was still unconscious, or else I could see him knocking poor Preston out cold.

Griff checked Knox's pulse again. "It's getting stronger. Keep going, Preston. It's working." Celeste was kneeling on his opposite side, a bowl of water and a pile of washcloths next to her as she worked to clean some of the more shallow cuts. Evan and I moved back, letting the three of them work to bring our friend back to life.

We were watching them work, Knox's color improving with each wound that was healed, when I felt a sharp sting on my bare foot. I yelped, looking down to find Onyx sinking his sharp little fangs into my skin.

"The fuck, Onyx!" I reached down to bat him away, but he was already darting out of my reach. He beelined toward the open deck doors, chittering as he ran. Little fucker thought just because Everly loved him...

Fuck, Everly!

In all the commotion with Knox, no one had even noticed that our girl was nowhere to be seen. Remembering everything Griff had told us about the bond between casters and their familiars, I pushed by Evan, following Onyx.

As I came to the open deck door, my heart stopped.

Everly's body was sprawled across the deck, the late morning sun highlighting the chestnut strands that fanned out around her head. Blood was smeared on her hands and body, her shirt was missing, leaving her in just her leggings and a pink sports bra.

She wasn't fucking moving. I couldn't even see a rise in her chest.

"GRIFF!" I yelled.

I rushed to her, dropping to my knees, much like I had the night of the ball in the hotel lobby. Except then I could see the life in her eyes, the blue pulling me in, letting me see a piece of her soul with each glance.

Now, they were closed, unopening even as I screamed her name over and over, cradling her to me. One of her hands dangled to the side, brushing the wooden deck. Onyx wiggled himself underneath it, nuzzling her palm as he softly began to purr.

Griff, Evan, and Celeste came flying out the door at my cries.

"Fuck!"

"Eves!"

"Blue!"

They all yelled at the same time, dropping to the deck next to me. Celeste was crying, and Evan was on the edge, tears welling in his eyes. Griff's face went white when he saw her wrapped in my arms, her head hanging backward over the crook of my elbow. She was warm in my arms, her body hot against my skin.

If she was still warm, that meant she couldn't be...

"Griff, check her neck." He hesitated for a moment, and I could see the absolute terror in his eyes. If he couldn't find a pulse, if she was gone... it would kill us. I could see Evan holding Celeste out of the corner of my eye, stroking her hair as he tried to soothe her.

Griff touched his fingers to the pulse point on her slender throat, his eyes boring into her flesh, holding them there for what felt like an eternity.

His gaze shot up to meet mine, his hazel eyes wide.

"She's alive!" The air whooshed from my lungs as relief crashed over me. I sucked in a breath, fighting back the tears that threatened to spill over.

I stood, making sure she was nestled safely in my arms, moving swiftly into the house. I glanced down to see Preston still hard at work healing Knox from his spot on the floor. His color had vastly improved, and nearly all of the larger wounds were closed, light pink scars the only evidence they'd been there in the first place.

Laying Everly on the couch, I grabbed a pillow to tuck under her head. Onyx bounded over, hopping right up onto the sofa with her. He nestled into the crook of her neck, his fluffy tail tickling her collarbone. When I had her settled, I hollered for Preston.

"Pres, is Knox out of danger?" I yelled over my shoulder, unable to take my eyes off of my Larkspur. I hadn't noticed it outside, but she had a red blush on her cheeks, the color nearly eclipsing the light freckles that decorated her face.

"Yeah, yeah, he's okay. I'm just finishing up with the last of the big wounds." His voice held a confidence I hadn't heard from him previously, and despite the circumstances, the corners of my mouth tugged up into a small smile.

Maybe Preston wasn't such a nerd after all.

"I need you to come check out Everly. She's unconscious, but I can't see any injuries." I stroked the backs of my fingers down her cheek as Celeste came over with a wet rag. She began cleaning what I assumed was Knox's blood from my Larkspur's hands and face, gently wiping the skin until all evidence of whatever the fuck had happened out on that ridge was gone.

Preston appeared just as Celeste finished and moved back to the safety of Evan's arms. I took a step back, watching as our resident healer hovered his hands over my girl's body, slowly moving from her head all the way down to her sneaker covered feet.

If I were a jealous man, I might take issue with his hands being mere inches from Everly's taut stomach, the breasts that were nearly spilling out of her sports bra. But I could see the intense concentration Preston used as he checked her over. I had nothing to worry about.

After a minute, his shoulders sagged. He turned to me, both relief and frustration etched on his face. "She doesn't have any injuries," he explained. "She just seems to be asleep."

"Oookay, so how long will she be asleep for?" Evan chimed in from a few feet away. Griff was knelt down near Knox, monitoring his pulse and checking the wounds Preston healed.

Preston shoved his glasses up his nose, a crease of worry lining his forehead. "I honestly don't know, guys." He stood, straightening his long-sleeve shirt. He was in flannel pajama pants, fuzzy moccasin slippers on his feet. I looked up at him, finally taking in the fact that we essentially kidnapped this poor guy, abducting him from his dorm room with zero explanation.

And he just fucking helped us, no questions asked.

"You're a good guy, Preston." I clapped him on the back. "Thank you."

"Yeah, yeah, Chase, it's no problem. Sorry I can't help more with..." He gestured to Everly's sleeping form. Worry still swirled in my gut, but I felt a bit more at ease knowing she didn't have any injuries.

Griff walked over, stepping right up to where our girl lay. He tucked a loose strand of hair behind her ear, pressing a soft kiss to her forehead before standing to his full height. "Chase, can you carry Knox to his room? He's gonna need to rest, and I'm pretty sure he'll be pissed if we leave him on the floor."

"On it, boss." I gave Griff a two finger salute before I went to move Knox's grumpy ass. "Pres, is he good to be moved? Can I throw his heavy ass over my shoulder?" He was prone on the hardwood, already looking a million times better than when we'd found him.

"Yeah, he should be good. All the big wounds are closed. He's gonna be sore, but I can heal the smaller ones a little later. I need to rest for a bit." He flopped on the sectional across from Everly, his eyes heavy with exhaustion. We'd been running the poor guy ragged the past week.

"Dude, I know it's early, but go grab a beer and relax. Griff can take you back in just a little bit once we get these two situated." I hefted Knox up to a semi-standing position, my arms supporting his full body weight. With a quick toss, I flung him over my shoulder, his slack body hanging down my back, hands bumping the backs of my thighs.

Preston shoved his glasses up his nose again—they seemed to slide down a lot— squinting at me through the lenses. "I don't mind staying for as long as you need me," he responded, his cheeks reddening with each word. "I-I don't really have anyone to hang out with back at the dorms, since most people are gone. And then I can heal the rest of Knox's injuries."

I shot him a wide smile. This poor guy. "Well, sounds like you're spending the rest of break with us. Welcome to the team." I lumbered toward the stairs that led to our bedrooms, pausing at the bottom step. I glanced back at him over my shoulder that wasn't carrying my friend's heavy ass.

"But don't get any ideas about Everly, Preston. She's *ours*." While I was half joking, the threat was still clear in my words. Preston was welcome as a friend, but that was fucking it.

I watched as his face turned an even brighter shade of red, stumbling over his words. "Yeah, no, I mean, I don't, that's not to say…"

"Don't worry, Preston, Chase is just fucking with you." Griff patted the healer on the back reassuringly.

I grinned at him, my smile purposefully not quite meeting my eyes.

forty-one
Knox

I groaned, slowly coming back to the land of the living. My body felt like it'd been run through a meat grinder, then spat out and run over by a truck. Rolling to my back, I tested my limbs, stretching carefully as I made sure everything was still in working order.

As my brain came back online, I pieced together the events of what happened up on the ridge, my memories coming back in bursts.

Griff, Chase, Celeste, and Evan leaving Everly and me up on the cliff.

Watching my gorgeous girl sketch out the morning sun as it kissed the valley below.

The mountain lion.

My breath caught in my lungs as the flashback crashed into me.

"I love you, Knoxy. Hold on."

I bolted upright, the scabs on my cuts pulling tightly at the abrupt movement. I winced but kept moving, swinging my stiff legs over the side of the bed. I hoisted myself to a standing position, my head swimming. Closing my eyes, I braced a hand on the nightstand next to the bed until the spinning stopped. Once I could see straight, I shuffled slowly to the door, curling my hand around the knob to pull it open.

I stepped out, silence and darkness greeting me. It was night, the hour late, judging by the moonlight streaming in through the window at the end of the hall. Meaning I'd been asleep for more than twelve hours.

I rounded a corner and saw light spilling from the master bedroom, soft voices coming from within. I pushed myself, finally making it to the slightly open door, giving it a hard shove. Beads of sweat dotted my forehead, the effort of moving like running a goddamn marathon.

Note to self: don't get into any more wrestling matches with a mountain lion.

But who was I kidding? I'd wrestle thirty lions if it meant keeping Everly safe.

My friends were spread throughout the room. Chase was curled into Everly's side, a large arm slung possessively over her waist, while Griff lay on her opposite side, propped up against the plush, upholstered headboard. He had an open book in his lap, but behind his glasses, I could see that his eyes were closed.

Across the room, on a small sofa, Celeste was curled up on Evan's chest, his long legs hanging over the end, both lanky arms wrapped tightly around her. A shift in the far corner caught my eye, and I turned just in time to see Preston stand from an overstuffed armchair.

"Hey, Knox," he called out quietly, quickly closing the distance between us. "How are you feeling?" He pushed his glasses up his nose, eyes roaming over my bare upper body. I'd somehow ended up in a pair of black sweats, probably courtesy of Griff, since I was pretty sure they were his.

"Like hammered shit, if I'm honest." My eyes immediately went back to the bed, watching the steady rise and fall of Everly's chest. "Is she okay?"

I glanced at him briefly, but long enough that I caught the wince on his face at my question. He rubbed a hand over the back of his neck nervously. "Well, see—"

I lunged forward, my injuries screaming in protest, grabbing him by his long-sleeved shirt. "What the fuck is wrong with her, Preston?" My voice was rough, somewhere between a growl and a snarl. I felt strong hands on my shoulders a second later, stopping me from shaking the shit out of the nerd.

"She's okay, man. Chill the fuck out." Griff's commanding voice was quiet in my ear, pulling me away. I twisted out of his grip, damn near knocking him over on my way to the bed.

She had a soft, serene look on her face, peaceful as she slept next to Chase. But I needed to see her eyes, to know for myself that she was alright.

I gently shook her shoulder. "Everly." She didn't move a muscle. "Everly, baby, wake up." Still nothing. Panic built in my chest. Why the fuck wasn't she waking up?

"Knox." Griff's deep voice was next to me again, his hand on my bicep. I jerked away, gripping her shoulders with both hands this time, giving her a forceful shake.

"Everly." My voice cracked as I said her name. "Please, baby, wake up." Tears were tracking down my cheeks now. She'd been safe when I lost consciousness. The lion was gone.

What the fuck happened?

I'd woken Chase, who was now sitting up next to our girl, watching me carefully, leaned over her ever so slightly. A protective guard standing sentry over his queen. He looked between me and Griff as I cupped my Monet's jaw, tenderly stroking the soft skin. "Griff, what's wrong with her?" I turned to face him, never breaking contact with her body. "Why won't she wake up?"

He sat next to me on the bed where he'd been sleeping just a few minutes ago. "Knox, what do you remember?"

I closed my eyes, replaying the morning's events. The ridge. The lion attacking and going over the cliff. Collapsing. Everly crying. A loud gasp ripped from my throat.

"I was floating. She told me to hold on and then I was floating." It was like watching a blurred movie reel, the images moving at a breakneck speed through my mind. The fall colors of the forest flew by as I drifted in and out of consciousness. "I think she carried me down the trail, or well, floated me."

"She must have used her super speed." Evan's voice broke through my thoughts. "She told us about it the other day, how she'd developed a new power because of Onyx. It's the only way she could have gotten you back here so fast." I threw a glance over my shoulder to see him standing with Celeste, everyone awake and gathered around the bed in a morbid vigil.

"Knox?" Chase prodded, and I realized I hadn't actually told them what happened. Anger swelled in my chest.

"After you fuckers deserted us, we got attacked by a fucking mountain lion," I spit at them. I was so goddamn pissed, the pain in my body forgotten. "You guys fucking left us up there alone, and we almost died!" I was yelling now, so fucking pissed that I was literally vibrating with anger.

Celeste looked down at the floor, cheeks red as she cried quietly. Evan pulled her in closer, while Chase and Griff just looked at our girl, guilt written across their faces. Not waiting for an explanation, I continued, "I shifted, to protect us. I fucking fought with that demon cat until I finally threw it off the cliff. But not before it fucked me up." I could still feel the pain of each bite, each time the beast's claws connected with my flesh hurt like hell.

"We're so sorry, Knoxy," Chase apologized. He was shirtless, just a pair of red basketball shorts on his muscular frame. He ran a hand over his head, pushing back his sleep mussed hair. "There was no way we could have known, man." He hesitated, shame drawing his lips down into a deep frown. "We were just trying to help."

"Help?" The word came out sharp, and I narrowed my eyes at him. "Yeah you fucking helped alright." His green eyes were glassy as he looked at Everly's sleeping body. It was obvious he felt like shit for what happened, they all did. I exhaled a deep breath, tipping my head back to stare at the ceiling.

"Look, I know you guys were doing what you thought was best. And on some fucked up level, it worked." I chuckled darkly to myself. "She told me she loved me. Just took a goddamn mountain lion to get her to say it."

We all took turns sleeping next to Everly over the next few days, even her brother taking a spot on the bed, laying between her and Celeste, who I'd noticed he always kept within arm's reach.

Chase called his parents, letting them know we wouldn't be making it to the house for Thanksgiving, explaining what happened on the ridge. They immediately made plans to come out on Saturday, promising to bring an entire feast. And they certainly didn't disappoint.

"Knox, come sit." Mrs. Stone patted the barstool next to her. We'd finished eating a bit ago, Chase and his dad loading the dishwasher before taking a bottle of bourbon out to the deck. Celeste and Evan were down in the theater room while Griff and Preston kept watch over Everly. We never left her alone, not for a second.

I slid onto the stool, Chase's mom pushing a slice of apple pie in front of me. Not wanting to be rude, and because it looked fucking delicious, I picked up my fork and shoved a bite into my mouth.

"Knox, she's going to be okay." Mrs. Stone's voice was soft, comforting in a way only a mother's can be.

Well, not my mother.

But from someone who actually gave a shit about their kid, I imagined.

I took another bite, chewing slowly before I spoke. "How can you know that? How can you be sure?" I swallowed, turning to look at her. She was dressed in a cream-colored blouse that seemed to wrap around her midsection and a pair of dark blue slacks, her honey blonde hair cut so it hugged her jaw.

Chase was a carbon copy of his dad. The blonde waves, broad chest, and shit eating grin all came from Mr. Stone. But Chase's eyes were all his mom. Her emerald greens crinkled at the corners when she smiled at me.

"Carrick did some research on our way here." She shifted in her seat, sipping her after dinner coffee. "He thinks she drained her magic when she saved you. Using the amount of energy necessary to levitate you, plus the super speed down the mountain? She depleted every ounce of power she had. Her body is just recharging right now."

I swallowed, a lump of emotion stuck in my throat. "I really hope you're right, Mrs. Stone." I laid my fork down, the pie suddenly tasting like ash in my mouth. "If she doesn't... if she can't and it's because of me..." My voice cracked on the last word, the thought that she might never wake up slamming into me with the force of a fucking hurricane.

"Knox Montgomery," she scolded, her voice strong for such a small woman. "You get that idea out of your head right now. That girl upstairs is going to be just fine." She laughed before adding, "And she's got three men who obviously love her more than life itself, seeing how you tangled with a mountain lion for her."

I laughed with her, the feeling almost foreign after how the last few weeks had gone. "Yeah, remind me not to do that again. Shit hurt like a bitch."

"Knox!" She swatted my arm. "You know I don't like hearing my boys curse." My face heated at her calling us her boys. Mrs. Stone had always been kind to me, showing me more affection in the few years I'd known her than I'd ever received from my own mother.

"Sorry, Mrs. Stone." I gave her a small smile, still not as convinced as she was that Everly would be okay.

She tutted at me, shaking her head, the gold hoops in her ears swinging. "How many times have I told you, Knox? Please call me Janine. Mrs. Stone is Carrick's mother." She laughed, patting me on the cheek lovingly.

Jesus, was this what it was like to have a parent who cared? I was going to kick Chase's ass if he ever bad-mouthed his mom in front of me.

Chase and his dad strolled into the kitchen with empty glass tumblers, having made a good dent in the bottle of bourbon. Mr. Stone plunked it on the counter, a happy smile on his face. I knew he was hard on Chase, but it was obvious his parents loved him so much.

I was about to excuse myself to relieve Griff when an earth-shattering scream erupted from the upstairs.

"Everly," I whispered her name, dread seizing through my insides.

I jumped from the barstool, my feet racing across the room and up the steps leading to the second floor. Luckily, Preston had done another round of healing on me, and most of my injuries were nothing more than a shitty memory.

I heard her shriek again, only this time, it was a distinct word and not just the terrifying sound of her pained voice.

"Knox!"

Again.

"KNOX!"

forty two *Everly*

The lion circled Knox, an apex predator stalking its prey with a lethal precision.

I screamed for him, shouting as the cat drew closer.

"Shift, Knox! Run!" But he just stood there, his deep brown eyes watching me, as if there were no threat at all. "KNOX!"

A somber smile broke across his face. "I love you, Everly. I'm so sorry." Just as the last word left his lips, the mountain lion pounced, knocking him off his feet. They rolled away, a tangle of flesh and fur and blood.

So much blood.

A strangled cry ripped from my chest as I watched the lion tear into him.

"Knox!"

"KNOX!"

"EVERLY!"

I was shaken awake, strong hands gripping my shoulders with a bruising force. My eyes flew open, and looking back at me were those espresso colored orbs from my dream. Only instead of a resigned defeat, they shined with a mix of fear and absolute devotion.

I sucked in a gasp.

Knox.

He was here.

He was okay.

I pushed myself up to a sitting position, my hands finding their way to his face, touching every inch of skin, running my fingertips over what we could officially call a beard at this point.

He was alive.

"Knoxy." I exhaled his name before I flung myself at him, wrapping my arms tightly around his neck as I tucked my knees underneath me. "Is it really you? Are you okay?" I buried my face in the crook of his neck, letting his familiar cedar scent wash over me.

I was trembling, shaking so badly, I could feel myself vibrating against his chest. He stroked a hand soothingly down my back, the other cupping the back of my head.

"Sshhh, little Monet. It's alright. I'm okay," he murmured against my hair. "We're both okay."

We held each other like that until I heard a throat clear deeply from beside the bed. Pulling back, I was met with the relieved, smiling faces of Griff and Chase. Onyx was hopping around at their feet, but the second our eyes locked, he launched himself onto the bed. He nuzzled into my lap, his soft purrs making me smile.

"Welcome back, Blue girl." Griff grinned like I'd just given him every item off his Christmas list, his hazel eyes shining with a happiness I hadn't seen in weeks. He was dressed in an SLA hoodie and a pair of loose-fitting jeans slung low on his hips. I didn't get long to appreciate how good he looked, however.

Chase lunged forward, shoving Knox back before yanking me straight out of the bed, my poor little fluffy familiar leaping off of me and onto the safety of the comforter. He chittered angrily in Chase's direction.

"Ohh!" I yelped as he engulfed my upper body with his strong arms at the same time Knox yelled, "What the fuck, Stone?"

"Larkspur, oh thank fucking God." He squeezed me so tightly I worried I might pop. I hugged him back, patting him on the shoulder.

"I'm okay, Chase. But I may suffocate if you don't let me go." I forced out a wheezing laugh against his steely grip.

He released me immediately, lowering me until my feet reached the floor. "Shit, sorry, Larkspur. But fuck, am I glad to see you awake." He crushed me against his chest again, dropping a kiss to the top of my head.

A warm hand found mine, gently tugging me away from Chase's hard body. "Come here, Blue girl." I went willingly, Chase mumbling about having just gotten me back, and I couldn't help but smile at his grumpy words.

Looking up at Griff, I saw his green-gold eyes glitter with joy, a broad grin on his perfect face. He laced our fingers together, his other hand curling around the side of my neck, drawing my forehead to his lips. He pressed softly, making me melt into his touch.

It was as if the universe had finally righted itself, a feeling of peace washing over me as the three men I loved more than life watched me with adoring eyes.

Once Griff, Chase, and Knox were convinced I was truly okay, they released me to Celeste and my brother, who'd been hovering near the door. Preston shot me a quick wave as he leaned against the wooden frame.

"Eves," Celeste whispered in my ear as she and Evan wrapped their arms around me in a makeshift group hug. Her voice shook with tears as I held them both tightly.

"Don't ever fucking do something like that again, sis, you hear me?" Evan pressed a kiss to the top of my head, the words taut with emotion. I squeezed him around his waist, Celeste curled around my back.

"Sorry, Ev. I'll try to be more careful the next time we're attacked by a wild animal." He chuckled, the sound vibrating against my cheek.

"Smart ass," he grumbled.

When they finally released me, which was really more me extricating myself from their hold than them really letting me go, I turned to find Chase standing with an older couple, and I immediately recognized Carrick Stone.

The woman he was with closed the distance between us quickly. She was the picture of poise and sophistication, not a hair out of place, but with a warmth only a mother could possess. Without waiting for permission, she wrapped her arms around me, the gentle embrace reminding me of my own mom's hugs. Tears burned in my eyes at the unexpected memory, and I hugged her back tightly.

"Mom." I could hear Chase's voice from behind me, playfully teasing. "Jesus, you just met her for Christ's sake." She pulled back, laughing. Her green eyes were the same shade as Chase's, a cross between emeralds and fresh cut grass. They crinkled at the corners in the exact way her son's did, and I could see the deep love she held for him swimming in their depths.

"I'm sorry, my dear. I'm Chase's mom, Janine." She smiled at her son. "Better?" The sass in her voice had a loud laugh pulling from my chest. Mr. Stone walked over then, draping an arm around her thin shoulders.

"Everly, it's good to see you again. I'm glad to see you're doing better." He smiled, the warmth tugging at my heart. I couldn't help but think of my own dad, wondering where he was and if he had any idea of all the horrible shit that had happened since that fateful night of the ball.

We all trekked down to the living room, Onyx catching a ride on my shoulder. Janine bustled off to the kitchen for a few minutes before reappearing with a tray of hot chocolates for each of us. The guys took turns filling me in on the last few days, explaining their theory about me draining my magic when I rescued Knox.

"Dad, did Lou find out anything else that may help us?" Chase asked once I was caught up on everything.

I was snuggled into Chase's side, stealing all of his body heat. The tank top and sweats Celeste put me in while I was unconscious just weren't enough to cut it now that the temperature had finally dropped back down to the seasonal norm. His warmth had me feeling all fuzzy inside.

We'd taken over part of the sectional, Chase on one side of me, his fingers skating over my shoulder, Knox on the other, a hand planted firmly on my thigh. Griff was on the floor at my feet, his hand up my pant leg, fingers wrapped around my calf, slowly massaging the muscle. The feel of their hands on me offered a grounding sense of security that my heart had been aching for. I sipped on the decadent chocolate drink, listening intently to Mr. Stone.

A look of disappointment washed across his face. "Not much. We were able to learn he made recurring monthly payments to a company called Mendacium Investments over the last ten years. We haven't found out much, other than it's listed as a venture capitalist firm." He hefted out a deep sigh, his frustration with the situation obvious.

Mrs. Stone—*Janine*—patted his leg from their spot across the sofa. "You'll find something, my love." Carrick reached forward, trying to snag a cookie off the tray Janine had brought in with the hot cocoa. She swatted his hand, tutting him in a sweet way.

We spent the rest of the evening talking until my eyes grew heavy, a yawn breaking free.

"Come on, Larkspur, let's get you to bed. We'll pack up tomorrow afternoon and head back to campus." He leaned down and pulled me up, tucking me into his side. I twined my arms around his middle, sinking into the heat of his body.

"We're going to head out. I texted the driver about an hour ago to come pick us up." Chase started to protest, but Janine cut him off. "Chase Thomas, we're not about to cramp your style. No one wants their mom crashing their slumber party." She winked at me, a knowing smile on her face.

My cheeks heated as my eyes went round in surprise. Janine laughed before guiding Carrick to the front door. We followed, giving hugs and kisses good-bye, with the promise that we would come by their house next weekend to work on finding some answers about the Thorpes.

As soon as the door swung closed, Knox was on me, scooping me into his arms, the air catching in my lungs. I twined my arms around his neck on instinct, snuggling in close. He marched us to the stairs that led to our wing of the house. Evan and Celeste, along with Preston had all tapped out about an hour earlier, heading off to their respective bedrooms.

"Uh, dude, wait up!" Chase called out, laughing as he jogged our way. "Where do you think—" He was caught off guard as Knox turned abruptly, leaving my head spinning.

"Everly is mine tonight." Knox's voice left no room for argument. But Chase, being Chase, decided to press his luck anyway.

"Now, hold on a minute..." He started, reaching out a hand, no doubt to pull me from Knox's arms. But before he could take another step, an animalistic growl vibrated through Knox's chest. The deep sound climbed up his throat, goosebumps erupting on my flesh at the possessive sound.

"I said she's mine tonight, Stone." His voice was low, deadly. He narrowed his eyes at Chase in challenge. "Fucking try me."

Griff gave a deep chuckle from behind Chase, rubbing a hand over his stubbly jaw to hide his smirk. "Taking a page out of my book, eh Knoxy?"

Knox didn't bother to respond, instead taking off up the stairs, my body bouncing in his arms. I let out a laugh when I saw Chase running after us down the hall. I winked at him, letting him know I was okay. He grinned, keeping up the farce of chasing us down.

Knox jogged into my bedroom, kicking the door shut behind him. He launched me onto the bed, something between a yelp and a laugh breaking free from my chest. He sprinted to the door and flicked the lock just as Chase slammed into the wood, laughing as he shouted, "This isn't over, Montgomery!"

I watched the muscles in his back ripple under his black t-shirt, desire curling in my core. Knox turned to me, his dark eyes smoldering with heat.

He slowly stalked across the room, shedding his shirt as he walked, gripping the back of his collar with one hand before smoothly pulling it over his head, all evidence of the lion attack gone, leaving only his smooth, ink covered skin on display.

I scooched back toward the middle of the bed as Knox knelt on the mattress, his arms bracketing my waist as I leaned up on my elbows.

I studied his face, a face I'd been so terrified of only a week ago.

But I knew, deep in my heart, even then, that Knox, *my* Knox would never hurt me. Knox saving me on the ridge, putting his life on the line for mine as he put himself between me and that lion, repaired the part of my soul that Austin had so badly damaged. It was amazing how seeing a man willing to die for you could change everything in the blink of an eye.

As I looked in his eyes, I saw the deep cosmic connection that tied our hearts together in an inexplicable way, reminding me, assuring me, this man loved me.

He surged forward, and where I thought he would have slammed his mouth to mine, he stopped just short, and instead, pressed our lips together in a worshipful, reverent way that had my heart trying to escape my chest.

His tongue licked at the seam of my lips, begging for entry. I immediately complied, opening for him, our mouths melding together in a beautiful, sensual dance. I reached a hand up, my fingers running through the dark curls at the nape of his neck.

I arched up into him, lifting my hips and grinding my core against his thigh. My hip brushed his dick, a deep feral sound coming from him that had my pussy wet with need.

It had been weeks since my body felt the searing touch of Knox's fingertips. The night at the beach was the last time his mouth was on me. Now, each loving caress was stitching our souls back together, bringing us closer than we'd been before.

I pulled back for a second, just long enough to pull the tank top over my head. Knox's hot mouth immediately found my nipple, sucking and biting at the sensitive flesh. His breath ghosted across my skin as he moaned my name.

My hunger flared, the need to feel him inside me, to cement the bond that tied us to one another, roaring to life. Using my feet, I pushed on the waistband of his sweats, shoving them down past his hips. His hard cock sprang free, the silver of his piercings catching the light.

Thank fuck for no underwear.

"I thought I was the only one who didn't like to wear underwear." I smiled at him teasingly, recalling all the times he'd yelled at me for going commando. He grabbed the sides of my leggings, pulling them down.

Well, he was in for quite the surprise in about three, two, one…

forty-three Knox

"Goddamn it, Everly. You've been unconscious for fucking two days! Where the hell are your underwear?" A devilish grin spread over her plush pink lips, making my dick leak precum from the engorged head.

She wiggled her hips, working the leggings down to her knees. "I took them off earlier when I ran to the bathroom. You know I don't like wearing them." I peeled them the rest of the way off her legs, not giving a fuck that they were inside out by the time I finished.

Everly was spread before me, her tanned skin flushed red, the perfect palette brushed over the flawless canvas of her body. My eyes dragged over every inch of exposed flesh, drinking in each and every detail. The freckle next to her belly button. The dusky pink of her nipples.

I stood from the foot of the bed, shoving my sweatpants the rest of the way off, leaving me naked before her. Wrapping a hand around my dick, I gave it a firm stroke, the pressure doing nothing to alleviate the ache in my balls. Jesus, the things this woman did to my body.

Climbing back on the bed, I knelt between her legs, running my palms up them. I started at her ankles, not breaking contact until I reached the apex of her thighs, pushing them as far apart as they would go, her shiny, wet pussy inviting me in for a taste.

Don't mind if I do.

But before I could dive in for my meal, Everly shot up to a sitting position, leaning forward enough that her warm breath seared over my cock. She planted a soft kiss on my hip bone, her finger tips grazing over the sensitive skin. A shudder ran through my body at her delicate touch.

She opened her mouth, her tongue peeking out, to lick a hot line up the underside of my shaft.

"Uhhh, Everly," I could barely form words, the wires in my brain short circuiting as she took me deep in her mouth. She felt so fucking good, so unbelievably right. Like she was fucking made just for me.

I ran my fingers through her dark chestnut hair, gripping a handful at the crown of her head. I halted her movements, so I could thrust in fully, nudging the back of her throat. She let me fuck her mouth, tears running from the corners of her sapphire eyes with each stroke inside. Her velvety tongue swept along my barbells sending a jolt of pleasure up my spine.

I stared into those cerulean depths, seeing the absolute trust she had in me, the heavy feeling that had lived in my chest the last few weeks finally lifting.

"Goddamn, Monet, your mouth feels so fucking good." I groaned, my hips stuttering as she drew me closer to the precipice. "You're so goddamn beautiful with my dick between those pretty lips."

I pulled out of her mouth before I blew, pushing her back by the shoulders until she was flat on the bed.

"My turn, baby."

I dove in, my tongue lapping at her soaked slit. Flicking my tongue against her swollen clit, I traced my fingers along her entrance, slowly inserting one up to the knuckle. I withdrew it, adding a second as I drove them back inside, making sure to keep a steady rhythm with my tongue that I knew would drive her wild.

Her hips bucked up into my face, her wetness coating my lips and beard. Good. I wanted to taste her, fucking smell her on me forever. The animal part of me needed to lay claim to her.

But not before she came.

I continued to fuck her with my fingers, licking and nipping at her clit until she grinding against my face with abandon. With my free hand, I pressed on her hip, holding her down as I drove her higher.

"Fuck! Knox!" She screamed my name, and I grinned wickedly.

No way Chase and Griff hadn't heard that.

Everly's body went slack, and she came down from her orgasm, my fingers still buried deep inside her needy cunt. I gave her one last, long lick from entrance to clit before pulling out, sitting back on my heels.

Her face was soft, her hair spread out around her head like a halo. A small smile danced on her lips, and she sighed in contentment.

"Good, little Monet?" I grinned at her smugly and ran my tongue across my bottom lip before popping my fingers in my mouth, savoring the taste of her.

Those blue eyes I saw every night in my dreams were nearly black, the pupils blown wide. Her breasts heaved as she drew in a ragged breaths, her gaze skating down my body, zeroing in on my hard-as-fucking-steel dick.

I gave it a long, slow stroke, squeezing the base enough to push more precum from the tip.

"Knox," she said, her husky voice making the last bit of blood flowing through my veins rush to my cock. "You better fuck me in the next three seconds, or so help me—Aahh!" As much as I loved her voice, the sound of her crying out as my dick stretched her tight pussy was even better.

I fell forward, my forearms taking most of my weight as I railed into her. Weeks worth of pent up sexual tension, anger, hurt—all of it releasing from my body with each powerful thrust. Bracing myself on one arm, I palmed her breast, my index finger and thumb plucking at her nipple, tweaking it until it was hard enough to cut glass.

I was so fucking close, but I needed to feel her come around me before I could let go. Abandoning her tit, I sat up so I could see myself sinking into her, my barbells rubbing along her inner walls.

I reached between us, my fingers running over her slick folds, feeling the taut skin as she took every single fucking inch of me. Everly locked her petite legs around my waist, angling her hips, so I hit that sweet spot on every stroke.

"Jesus, Knox," she breathed out, panting. Her body rocked with every thrust, and I pressed a finger to her clit.

She went off like a fucking rocket, her pussy clamping down around me like a goddamn vise. Her orgasm triggered my own, the rush of release barreling through me like a goddamn freight train. I pumped into her a few more times, making sure each and every drop was painting her insides.

I collapsed on top of her, pressing my chest to hers, the sheen of sweat coating our bodies mingling to create a mixture that was solely made up of just *us*. I had this strange, overwhelming desire to combine it with my paints, to spread it on a canvas, so I could hold onto it forever.

Rolling to my back, I pulled her with me, my dick slipping from her pussy as I moved us. She sprawled across my upper body, her fingers dancing lightly across the intricate lines of my tattoos.

Holding her in my arms again, the *rightness* of it... it was like when I had a painting in my mind, and it translated perfectly onto a canvas, the image and the colors marrying together seamlessly.

"I love you, Knox," she whispered against my chest, the words so soft I almost missed them. "I never stopped. Even when I thought it was you who hurt me." I felt the first tear fall against my skin. "I still loved you."

I held her tightly, pressing a kiss to her hair. "I love you, baby. It broke me that you thought it was me, but I understand." I would never forgive myself for the part I played in her kidnapping. "If I hadn't fucked up on that beach, then maybe—maybe you wouldn't have been alone that night."

She sat up, leaning her forearm across my chest, so she could see me. Her eyes were wet with tears, but the furious look on her face took me by surprise. "Knox." Her tone was sharp but strong. "You didn't force Austin or Morgan to take me. If they hadn't done it that night, they would have found a different time or place."

She twisted around, sitting at my side, legs tucked underneath her. I sat up, putting us face to face. This close, I could see each individual freckle dusting her cheeks, the bridge of her nose. She was so beautiful, and it made my heart ache, thinking about the time we'd spent apart.

I lovingly stroked my knuckles down her damp cheek.

"Baby, I will spend every fucking day reminding you just how much I love you."

forty-four

Griffin

I tossed my duffle bag into the cargo area of the SUV, shutting the trunk before climbing into the driver's side. I'd offered to teleport us all back to campus, but Everly insisted we drive, saying she didn't want to miss the beautiful fall colors. And fuck if I could tell her no.

Everyone loaded in, Everly up front with me, Chase and Knox in the middle seats, while Evan, Celeste, and Preston took up the third row. Onyx had plopped himself down in my Blue girl's lap, already asleep before we'd even pulled out of the driveway.

The drive back to campus went by in a blur, Everly's Foo Fighters playlist belting through the speakers. Chase whined intermittently, begging for some 'old school Miley' but my girl put her foot down, refusing to give up control of the music. At one point he even attempted to sing "Wrecking Ball" as "Everlong" played, but Knox shut him up with a quick jab to the ribs.

As we pulled up to the parking lot next to our dorm, I could see other students unpacking from their week away. I pulled into a spot near the front, next to a red BMW 1 series, the back driver's side door open.

Throwing the car in park, I cut the engine and unbuckled, quickly making my way to the back. Everyone else followed, taking their bags as I pulled them from the trunk. We were nearly finished unloading when I heard the distinct sound of a pissed off Everly.

"Get fucked, Heather."

Rounding the SUV, I was met with Everly gripping Heather by the collar of her pink peacoat. My girl had murder in her eyes as Chase tried to pull her off.

"Your boyfriend already did that, *Emberly*," Heather snarked, clearly not understanding the danger she was in. She blew a bubble with her gum, the sticky substance cracking directly in Everly's face. "More than once."

"Yeah, Everly, besides"—the voice of my ex ripped through the space, anger flooding my veins—"I heard you're with Austin Thorpe now. It'd be a shame if he found out you're whoring around behind his back." Morgan strutted out from between two cars toward us, stopping just a few feet from where Everly stood.

Her blonde hair was pulled back from her face in a tight ponytail. She was wearing one of my old tour guide sweatshirts, one I knew for a fact had my last name across the back. Goddamn fucking psycho.

Everly blanched for a fraction of a second, the trauma of what happened at that cabin haunting her blue eyes. I watched, however, as she transformed, like a phoenix rising from the fucking ashes. Rage consumed her. She shoved Heather away, sending the stupid girl sprawling on her ass. She cried out, but my attention was on Everly and keeping her from committing a felony in the parking lot.

"You fucking bitch."

Where I would have expected yelling, screaming, or something to indicate the level of pure hatred Everly held for Morgan, her voice came out in a deadly calm.

And it was fucking terrifying.

In one swift move, Everly drew back her arm, launching her fist directly into Morgan's face. It was like poetry in motion, the perfect line between her elbow and knuckles, the sound as flesh and bone met. I'd taught her well.

"Goddamn cunt!" Morgan screamed, holding her now bleeding nose. The tissue was already swelling, but Everly wasn't done. She pushed closer, boxing Morgan in against the red car.

"You listen to me, you fucking twat." Everly hissed the words loudly, a crowd of students forming behind us. "I will fucking end you." Everly gripped her chin tightly, twisting her face until she had nowhere to look but into the eyes of my girl. "Not so tough when you can't drug me, huh? You fucking coward."

She released Morgan with a rough shove, turning away. Snatching her suitcase off the ground, she strode over to where Chase stood, his mouth open in shock. In a move that had my dick hard in a second, Everly grabbed him by the front of his shirt, yanking his face to hers. She kissed him possessively, *owning* him, showing the entire world he belonged to her and only her.

Everly glanced over her shoulder at Morgan and Heather, the two girls huddled together.

"Stay away from my men. That's your only fucking warning." She glared, her eyes narrowed with the promise of violence. "And stay the fuck away from my brother."

"Evan!" Morgan screeched, although the look he shot her way had her clamping her mouth shut.

Evan strode toward her, each step purposeful and full of malice. He stopped only a few feet away, his hands balled into fists at his sides. Celeste was right behind him, unfurling one of his hands, lacing their fingers together. His voice was calm, belying the lethality of his words.

"Leave us alone you fucking delusional fake-ass bitch. I will fucking burn you to ashes until there's nothing left if you come near us again."

Morgan gasped, shocked at the change in his demeanor. She risked a glance in my direction, but I just shrugged a shoulder, grinning widely as all her plans crumbled around her. She screeched again, stomping her foot like a goddamn toddler before whirling around, her hands still pressed to her broken nose.

They hurried into Heather's car, Morgan clamoring into the passenger seat a half second before Heather peeled out of the spot, the tires riding up on the curb as she pulled out of the lot.

We all stood frozen for a few seconds, murmurs going through the crowd as the scene ended, until Everly marched toward Bliss Hall, Celeste and Evan right behind her. Preston trotted off after them, stopping short for a moment when he spotted Stella across the lot. The rest of the crowd quickly dispersed, everyone filing into their dorms now that the entertainment had ended.

Evan was noticeably quiet as the entire situation unfolded, an array of emotions flying across his face. I could only imagine the complete mind fuck he was currently experiencing, knowing what Morgan had done to his sister and how much she'd fucked with his emotions.

Chase slung an arm around my shoulders, grinning like an idiot.

"Our girl's a fucking badass," he bragged, but he wasn't wrong. "Jesus, that was hot. I'm so goddamn hard right now."

Knox rolled his eyes, picking up his duffle. "Chase, you're a fucking idiot." I couldn't help but notice when he subtly adjusted himself through his sweats, though.

By the time we reached the top floor of the dorm, my dick was ready to burst through my jeans. We said a quick goodbye to Celeste and Evan before hustling into our suite, Everly following Knox and Chase inside.

I kicked the door shut, startling the three of them as they dumped their bags by the kitchen counter, all three turning to face me. Something on my face must have told them what I was thinking because I watched as heat flared to life in Everly's eyes.

"You." I pointed at her as I unbuckled my belt, leaving it hanging open at my waist. "Naked. Now."

The deep tenor of my voice made it clear I wasn't fucking around.

She bit her lip, contemplating her decision before sashaying over to the sofa, stripping her long-sleeve black henley off as she went. Her dark blue skinny jeans rested just above the delicious curve of her ass. She was all soft curves and tanned skin, and she was so goddamn sexy, it had my dick weeping at the thought of being inside her.

"All of it," I barked, ripping my own shirt over my head. "You two gonna join us?" I glanced to where Chase and Knox were staring, the outlines of both their hard ons evident in their pants. They both unfroze and sprang into action, a flurry of cotton and denim flying around the room as they shed their clothes.

Everly stood in front of the couch, a lazy smile on her lips, and she trailed a finger down her chest, through the valley of her breasts, tracing the lacy cups of her dark purple bra. Her skin flushed hot, and her breathing kicked up a notch as her finger moved south, tickling the skin of her abdomen until she reached the button of her jeans.

She was taking her sweet fucking time following my instructions.

Guess we'd have to do something about that.

"Don't make me ask twice, Everly," I warned, heat searing through my veins. That heat turned to a burning inferno as she lifted her chin, throwing me a defiant grin. She dragged her jeans down her thighs, her panties going with them. Inch by torturous inch, her perfect skin was exposed.

"Oh shit, Larkspur. You're gonna make Daddy Griff mad." Chase was standing off to my right, stroking his dick with long languid tugs, Knox on my other side doing the same thing. I chuckled, the deep sound making her shudder in anticipation.

"Last chance, Everly." She smiled wickedly, pushing her long hair over her bare shoulder.

Well, alright.

I advanced before she could respond, gripping her arm and spinning her so her back was pressed to my front. I snaked my hand between her breasts, my fingertips brushing over her delicate skin before wrapping around the base of her throat.

I felt her breath hitch in her chest. "Baby, if this is too much, you say 'red' understand? You say 'red' and we stop." I whispered the words in her ear, not moving a muscle until she nodded her head. "This only goes as far as you want it to, Everly."

"Chase," I snapped, my restraint teetering on a razor's edge. "Go get supplies."

"On it!" He bounded out of the room and down the hall. I turned Everly and I to face Knox, his hand working his dick in slow strokes. The muscles of his forearm flexed with each downstroke, and I heard the almost inaudible gasp Everly made as she watched.

"You like watching him like that, knowing he's that hard for you?" I added a bit more pressure to her throat, feeling the thundering of her heartbeat against my arm, the flutter of her pulse strong under my fingers.

Knox's eyes were dark with lust, a feral groan breaking free from his chest, sounding through the room as he took in the masterpiece before him. "Knox, come hold our girl while I make sure she understands what happens when she doesn't follow directions."

He stepped closer, taking her thin wrists in his large hands, pulling her so they were chest to chest. She looked so fucking good, compliant and wanting, a crimson flush creeping up her neck.

I yanked my belt from my pants in one pull, her eyes widening at the swift motion. Gently twisting one arm behind her back, then the other, pressing her wrists together, I wrapped my belt around them, securing the buckle tightly. My eyes met Knox's over her shoulder, a hint of worry buried beneath the desire I could see burning in there.

"Everly, what do you say if you want to stop?" I purred in her ear, nipping the lobe. I kept my eyes trained on Knox as she answered.

"Red."

"Good girl." I stepped back, lowering the zipper on my jeans, pushing them and my black boxer briefs to the ground. I stepped out of them and moved over to the sofa, sitting in the middle, my arms stretched along the back cushions. Chase had come back into the room while I was securing Everly, the lube and jeweled plug now on the coffee table.

"Bring her over here." I leaned back into the cushions. "I want to taste that pussy before I fill it with my cock." Knox walked her over, helping her step up on the couch, a foot on either side of my thighs. Chase rushed to help steady her as she wobbled, her feet sinking into the plush fabric. She tipped forward, her knees resting next to my ears, bringing her mouthwatering pussy right to my face.

And I was fucking hungry.

Reaching up both hands to cup her ass, I gave her a long, wet lick, the taste of her arousal bursting on my tongue. And she tasted fucking divine.

I lapped at her, twirling my tongue around her clit before spearing it inside her entrance. Her back arched as she ground herself down against my face, soaking me in her juices. She moaned loudly, the sound rushing to my dick and making it impossibly harder. I pulled back just enough to speak, my lips moving against her wet flesh.

"Knoxy, why don't you fill our pussy while Chase makes sure her ass is ready to take him." I went back to eating her, enjoying every inch of my meal.

Knox's fingers brushed my chin as he inserted them into her slit. She groaned in pleasure, her hips gyrating with each stroke of his thick digits.

I knew the exact moment Chase breached her ass, her whole body going stiff for a moment. "Let him in, baby," I murmured against her, kissing her clit before flicking it with the tip of my tongue. She relaxed as I pulled her ass cheeks apart, giving Chase better access to her back hole.

We worked that way for about five minutes, Knox and I building her up until she was on the brink of detonating before backing off, keeping her dangling on the cliff. Chase was busy working the plug into her, stretching her out.

She was nearly sobbing by this point, begging us for release. "Please, sir, please!" I could hear the desperation in her cries, her body trembling beneath our practiced hands. We knew this every inch, every curve, every possible way to make her scream.

She belonged to us.

"You want to come, baby?" I asked. She whimpered in response, the quaking of her thighs giving away just how fucking close she was. I thrust a finger into her cunt alongside the ones Knox was fucking her with, filling her to the brim.

"Then fucking come, Everly. Come for us." Her back arched so far I thought she would snap in half, her release flooding my mouth, running down my chin. She finally went slack against me and, Jesus, if I died like this, with her legs wrapped around my head, face buried in her pussy, I'd die a happy man.

Knox helped lower her until she was straddling my lap, her eyes glassy from her orgasm. My cock nudged at her entrance, throbbing with the need to be inside her.

"Oh, Blue," I cupped a hand around her jaw, angling her face to mine. "We're not finished with you yet."

forty-five

Everly

C hase worked the plug in and out of my ass, swirling it in slow, wicked circles. The rush of my orgasm was still racing through my body, my nerves on overload from the intensity of their touches.

I felt Griff's dick at my pussy. "We're not finished with you yet." Not a second later he was pushing inside, surging into me, filling me so full I cried out. The hand on my jaw slid down to my neck, pulling me so our foreheads touched, the other gripping the fleshy part where my hip and ass met with a bruising force.

"More," I whispered against his lips. I needed them, all of them, inside me. Owning me. Possessing me. Reminding me that I was theirs, and they were mine.

Griff's hands settled on my hips, lifting so he could bounce me on his dick. I heard the telltale sound of the lube cap being popped open before I felt a hand wind through my hair, pulling it tight, making my back bend.

"As you wish, little Larkspur." The cold liquid drizzled down my ass crack. Chase pulled the plug out, only to replace it with his fingers, massaging the lube into the tight ring of muscle. He slid two easily inside, my flesh already stretched from his earlier work. He notched himself against me before pressing slowly inside.

Each inch burned in the most delicious way. Griff had paused his thrusts, letting me feel the incredible pressure of both of their dicks inside my body. After what seemed like an eternity, I felt the press of Chase's hips against my ass, telling me he was fully seated.

My nerves were on fire, heat blazing across my body in waves. I was so goddamn full.

"Move," I rushed out breathlessly. "Please." I was going to die if they didn't fucking move in the next three seconds.

Like a switch being flipped, they began to thrust, first in unison, then alternating, one filling me as the other pulled out, just to repeat the pattern over and over. My eyes fluttered closed, relishing in the way they worshiped my body. Griff moved his hands to the tops of my thighs, Chase taking over at my hips, his fingers digging into the soft flesh.

Fingers brushed down my cheek, a thumb pulling my lip from between my teeth.

"Open." The word was more a growl, and I opened my eyes to see Knox behind the sofa, his dick standing hard from his body. Without a thought, I complied, opening wide as he slipped between my lips. Chase used his grip on my hair, guiding my head up and down Knox's cock, and I savored the taste of his precum as it coated my tongue.

They used me, battering into my body, branding me with their hands, their cocks. I welcomed it, the way they owned me, each whispering sweet and dirty words of devotion.

I was their religion, my body the altar at which they worshiped. And fuck if they weren't praying for a miracle.

Grunts filled the room as each man neared his release, my own building again in my lower belly, desire curling through my insides as Griff and Chase worked to rearrange them. Griff shifted a hand between my legs, his skilled fingers immediately finding my clit, aching with need. He rubbed tight circles, building me up to the peak faster than I knew possible.

"Give me one more, Everly," he growled through gritted teeth. "Come for us one more time before we fill you so full of our cum it will be leaking out of you for days."

His words pulled the trigger on my orgasm, the climax rocketing through me like a goddamn shotgun blast. White bursts exploded behind my eyelids, and words I'm not even sure were English fell from my mouth in a loud cry, Knox's dick making them come out in muffled gasps.

I clenched around Chase and Griff, setting them off, one after the other. Chase roared from behind me, pulling my hair so hard it brought tears to my eyes as he filled my ass. Griff came a second later, painting the inside of my pussy.

Knox followed, spurting ropes of hot cum down my throat. I swallowed around him greedily, not wanting to lose one single drop. He pulled himself from my mouth, bending to kiss me, not giving a shit that he was tasting himself on my tongue.

I slumped against Griff's chest, my arms and fingers tingling from being bound for so long. Chase undid the belt, rubbing my wrists gently to get the blood flowing again, his half-hard dick still buried in my ass. He pulled out, and I winced at the loss. He scooped me up, pulling me off of Griff's dick, before bundling me against his chest.

I nuzzled against him, my eyes heavy with exhaustion. Who knew getting railed by three guys would be so tiring?

Chase carried me to his room, settling us in the middle of the bed. Griff and Knox joined us a minute later, Chase allowing Griff to slide in between us while Knox curled himself around me. He looped an arm over my waist, pressing his chest against my back, his body touching me from head to toe.

Griff lay facing me, Chase propped on an elbow, looking at the three of us.

"Thank you, Larkspur," he whispered, leaning over Griff to brush a stray strand of hair from my face.

I closed my eyes, yawning sleepily. "For what? Cause I'm pretty sure I'm the one who had multiple orgasms."

There was no response, not even a chuckle. I opened my eyes to find myself the center of Griff and Chase's intense stares, while Knox nuzzled the back of my neck.

"For trusting us, Everly."

Soft sunlight streamed through Chase's bedroom windows the next morning, our bodies a mess of limbs under the soft duvet. Even Onyx had found his way into the pile at some point, curled on the pillow above my head.

I'd woken during the night several times, once with Chase's face between my thighs and another as Knox thrust into me from behind. My body ached in the best way, and for the first time in nearly two months, I felt completely happy.

My stomach gave a loud rumble, reminding me that we'd skipped dinner the night before in favor of fucking.

"You hungry, Blue girl?" Griff chuckled, his eyes still closed. He looked like a dark angel, the sun casting a golden halo around his dark hair.

I stretched, pressing my ass against Knox's morning wood. He groaned in my ear, a hand gripping my hip tightly. "Little Monet..." he warned. I giggled until my stomach rumbled again.

"Well, three men decided not to feed me last night." I pouted, throwing Chase a quick wink as he sat and stretched his arms over his head.

"Come on then, let's get you some food." They each rolled away and off the bed. I took advantage of the empty space, stretching my limbs like a starfish under the covers. Suddenly, the blankets were ripped away, leaving my naked body exposed to the cool air. I shrieked, making all three guys erupt in laughter.

"Haha, very funny," I muttered, snatching one of Chase's t-shirts off the floor and tugging it over my head. They had all already pulled on sweats—bastards—and I followed them into the kitchen. Griff was busy brewing a fresh pot of coffee, so I meandered over to the sofa, images of the previous night running wildly through my head. I felt my cheeks heat, Knox catching my eye. He smirked, running a finger over his bottom lip.

I flopped down, dragging a blanket over my bare legs while the three of them fixed us cups of magical bean juice.

They settled into the living room with me a few minutes later, Knox and Griff each taking an armchair while Chase snuggled up right next to me, putting my mug on the coffee table. I was about to open my mouth to ask what our plan was for the day when a knock sounded harshly against the door.

"Everly!" Stella's voice called from the hall. "Everly, open up!"

Griff jogged to the door, opening it as Stella bolted inside. "Oh my God!" She was breathless, like she'd run up the four flights of stairs to reach our floor.

"Stella, come sit." I sat up straighter, patting the sofa cushion next to me. "What's going on? Are you okay?" Her pink hair was braided back away from her face, her dark blue eyes wide and wild. Her cheeks were tinged red with exertion, but the rest of her skin was pale, making the midnight blue of her eyes stand out in stark contrast.

Instead of sitting, she paced across the room. "Did you guys hear?"

"Hear what, Princess Punk? We just got up," Knox groused from his seat. He took a long sip of his coffee, his brows furrowed in annoyance.

"Oh my God, you haven't heard yet," Stella whispered, her face paling to a disturbing shade of white.

"Heard what, Stella?" I coaxed, trying to get her to answer. She was obviously upset about something.

"Morgan's dead. They found her body this morning down by the lake."

The room fell into silence as we processed Stella's revelation.

Did it make me a bad person that I felt... relieved? There was a small sliver of sadness that a life was lost, but given the company Morgan kept, I couldn't say I was surprised.

"What the fuck happened?" Griff asked, his voice gruff, a confusing array of emotions clouding his hazel eyes.

I snapped my fingers to bring my coffee mug to my hands.

Instead, a fucking spark erupted from my palm.

I screamed, flinging the flame at the coffee table where it ignited one of Chase's business textbooks. Griff quickly dumped his mug on the fire, extinguishing it before it could do further damage.

"What the fuck was that, Everly?" Chase's voice was quiet, shocked. He stared between the coffee table and my hand, the flame now gone.

"I–I don't know. I've never—I don't—how?" I stammered, desperately trying to come up with an answer that made any type of sense.

What the fuck just happened?

"Fire."

Stella's voice was so soft, I almost didn't hear her the first time, but she repeated the word again, louder this time.

"Fire."

Knox rolled his eyes, huffing out an exasperated breath. "Yeah, we know, princess, that was fire. You wanna see me make water next?"

"No, you asshole." She whirled to face him, real fear on her face. "Morgan. They found her down by the lake." Her gaze shifted to me. "She was burned alive." Every eye in the room swung to me.

Oh fuck.

Acknowledgments

I know, I know... Another cliffy! But hey, at least Morgan got what was coming to her! Ever Bound will be coming out this fall, the final installment in the Solis Lake Academy series!

Ever Dark was most definitely a challenging book. It took me to a much darker place as I wrote Everly's story and I'm so incredibly grateful to the amazing people who helped me along the way.

To my husband, who keeps me in rock candy while I hunker down in my writing cave; thank you baby. I've been living a half life, my whole life, til I loved you (X Ambassadors).

To my incredible Alpha Team: This book would not have happened without all of you. Thank you for loving these characters (okay mostly the guys) and for talking me off of more than one ledge. I will forever be in your debt.

Lauren, you'll always be my ride or die. Thank you for taking a chance on a first time alpha reader and for giving me the push I needed to start writing. Never, ever stop being the amazing person you are and promise to never leave me.

Amanda, I'm so incredibly grateful the universe brought you into my life. You've saved my ass more times than I can count and I feel so lucky to know you. I feel incredibly blessed to call you my friend.

Nicole, so much of this story wouldn't exist if it wasn't for you and your willingness to listen to me ramble in voice messages. Everly might be his girlfriend, but you'll always be Knoxy's #1 girl.

And Sadie... girl, the next year is gonna be a wild one for us. Thank you for staying up until all hours, sending plot ideas and stupid gifs, and fangirling with me. I can't wait to see where Ace and Caz take us!

To my Smutty Buddies: Y'all are dirty af! I love it and all of you!

Lastly, to my readers: Thank you for sticking with Everly and her guys, and for sharing in their story. I hope you've found a piece of yourself in these characters and that you come back for the conclusion of the Solis Lake Academy series. I love each and every one of you!

K.D. is a country girl, born and raised in the backwoods of western New York. She has two kids and is married to her college sweetheart. She is a former teacher and now spends her time writing and organizing the lives of others. K.D. is a die-hard Buffalo Bills fan and may or may not have named one of her characters after a certain tight end. She loves rock candy (a necessary staple while in the writing cave) and espresso martinis. The X Ambassadors are always on her play list, as well as a healthy dose of early 2000's rock.

Made in the USA
Columbia, SC
16 September 2024

41879029R00202